The Walls of Westernfort

What Reviewers Say About BOLD STROKES' Authors

❧

KIM BALDWIN

"Her...crisply written action scenes, juxtaposition of plotlines, and smart dialogue make this a story the reader will absolutely enjoy and long remember." – **Arlene Germain**, book reviewer for the *Lambda Book Report* and the *Midwest Book Review*

❧

ROSE BEECHAM

"...a mystery writer with a delightful sense of humor, as well as an eye for an interesting array of characters..." – *MegaScene*

"...her characters seem fully capable of walking away from the particulars of whodunit and engaging the reader in other aspects of their lives." – *Lambda Book Report*

"...creates believable characters in compelling situations, with enough humor to provide effective counterpoint to the work of detecting." – *Bay Area Reporter*

❧

JANE FLETCHER

"...a natural gift for rich storytelling and world-building...one of the best fantasy writers at work today." – **Jean Stewart**, author of the *Isis* series

❧

RADCLYfFE

"Powerful characters, engrossing plot, and intelligent writing..." – **Cameron Abbott**, author of *To the Edge* and *An Inexpressible State of Grace*

"...well-honed storytelling skills...solid prose and sure-handedness of the narrative..." – **Elizabeth Flynn**, *Lambda Book Report*

"...well-plotted...lovely romance...I couldn't turn the pages fast enough!" – **Ann Bannon**, author of *The Beebo Brinker Chronicles.*

"...a consummate artist in crafting classic romance fiction...her numerous best selling works exemplify the splendor and power of Sapphic passion..." – **Yvette Murray, PhD**, *Reader's Raves*

The Walls of Westernfort

by

Jane Fletcher

2005

THE WALLS OF WESTERNFORT

ISBN 1-933110-24-4
This Trade Paperback Original Is Published By
Bold Strokes Books, Inc.,
Philadelphia, Pa, USA

First Edition: March, 2005 Bold Strokes Books, Inc.

Credits
Editor: Cindy Cresap
Executive Editor: Stacia Seaman
Production Design: J. Barre Greystone
Cover Image: Tobias Brenner (http://www.tobiasbrenner.de/)
Cover Design: Judith Curcio

Thanks to:

Cath, Ginger and Barbara for reading the manuscript and giving constructive suggestions

Rad and Lee for welcoming me to a new home

Cindy for sorting out my dangling modifiers and obscure British terminology

My friends and family for helping me through the last two years

And, most of all, Lizzy, for reading each chapter hot off the printer and encouraging me to keep on writing. The memory of you is what sustains me now—nothing but death could have parted us.

PART ONE

Walking In A
Dead Woman's Shoes

24 August 553

CHAPTER ONE—A MEETING IN THE TEMPLE

The skies over the city of Landfall had been clear sapphire blue all day, but as the sun started to drop, the color became tinged with a hint of turquoise, and wisps of high cirrus drifted over from the east. Shadows softened in the bustling streets and passageways, and though the breeze now held the first chill edge, the reds and browns of the bricks were richer and warmer.

The light was less glaring, but still it flashed off the polished helmets of the two Guards on sentry duty at the main gates of their headquarters and ran like liquid fire down the edges of their drawn swords. The two women were motionless except for the hems of their long red cloaks stirring in the breeze. Their eyes were glazed, seemingly oblivious to the traffic on the road before them. And for their part, the passersby spared no more than cursory glances for the sentries. Only one dawdling child stopped to stare open-mouthed at the brilliant uniforms and the long, sharp swords until an impatient shout from her mother called the girl away.

The city bells were chiming the hour when a captain appeared in the gateway, her uniform even more lavishly embellished in gold braid than the sentries'. Another Guard marched at her heels. The captain stamped to a halt beside the sentry on the right and then rotated sharply through 90 degrees to stare directly at her.

"Guardswoman Ionadis." The officer's voice gave the impression of shouting without being exceptionally loud.

"Yes, ma'am." The sentry's eyes did not flicker as she acknowledged her name.

"You are relieved of duty and may stand down."

"Yes, ma'am."

In a display of rigid, martial choreography, the sentry sheathed her sword and swapped places with the replacement Guard.

"Come with me." The captain snapped out the order.

The road into the headquarters ran between stables and barracks until it reached the central parade ground. On three sides, the open space was bordered by administration offices; on the fourth, it abutted the temple grounds. Few people were about, mainly orderlies running their errands. The captain stopped and, for several seconds, stared at the younger woman as if she had noticed something unusual about her. The subject of her regard stood stiffly at attention.

"I have instructions for you." The captain spoke in an assertive undertone.

"Yes, ma'am."

"You are summoned to a meeting in the temple. Present yourself at the entrance to the sanctum in one hour."

"Yes, ma'am." This time, the Guard's voice was not so crisp. She was clearly confused, and as the captain turned to go, she spoke again. "Ma'am?"

The captain looked back. "Yes?"

"Is there anything else?"

"You will learn all you need to know at the proper time." The captain's face gave nothing away.

"Yes, ma'am."

Guardswoman Natasha Ionadis watched the officer disappear around the corner of a building before letting her forehead crumple in a frown. "Sanctum?" she repeated, confusion giving way to anxiety. The summons was definitely not the one she had expected, and it would have been nice to have a few hints on how best to spend the intervening hour.

Natasha's shoulders sagged. Her eyes drifted over her surroundings in bemusement, finishing by looking down at herself. Her uniform had been immaculate at the start of sentry duty, but she could imagine that it now had the faintest coating of dust. She pursed her lips in a wry pout, thinking of the unofficial maxim of the Guards: *When in doubt, polish it.* A wash and general spruce-up were as good a use of the time as any other, but wandering toward the bathhouse, Natasha shook her head slowly and again whispered, "Sanctum?"

❖

A fair part of the allotted hour still remained when Natasha left the barracks. She paused in the doorway and tried to evaluate her appearance, using the back of her helmet as a mirror—a pointless exercise. She was of medium height and athletic build, but in the helmet, she looked like a potbellied giant. Her softly formed, square-cut face was contorted like a pig's snout, with her lips smeared across. The only thing she could tell for certain was bad news; her hair was far longer than the specified soldiers' close crop. Natasha grimaced. She had put off the visit to the Guards' haircutter for far too long, and there was no time now to rectify it. *Oh, well. Perhaps I'll be able to keep my helmet on*, she told herself optimistically, stepping into the sunshine.

The sight of her uniform cleared the way as she walked up the steps and into the great hall of the temple. Groups of worshippers faded from her path. Natasha was hardly aware of them or of the anxious looks they shot in her direction. She stood just inside the entrance while her eyes adjusted to the scented gloom and felt the familiar waves of peace and reverence wash over her. Directly ahead was the main altar, where Himoti's eternal fire burned. Natasha felt as if the light were flowing through her, filling her with the blessing of the Goddess. She took a deep breath and exhaled slowly; then she took her eyes from the flames and began to walk slowly around the perimeter of the hall.

A painting of the first landfall dominated the bay on her right. It showed the blessed Himoti about to alight from Celaeno's sacred shuttle, her foot descending on the grass of the new world—the world Celaeno had chosen for her daughters. Natasha knew that the shuttle symbolized the loom of fate, with all of creation woven in its great design, but there was also something in the twisting strand of wool reaching up into the heavens that suggested an umbilical cord, connecting the world to the mother Goddess.

A group of the Elder-Ones stood behind Himoti on the enormous shuttle. Studying them, Natasha whispered the words from the *Book of the Elder-Ones*, "Their skins were diverse in tone, and their hair was yellow and red and black, and all the shades between." Her gaze left the painting and flitted over a huddle of fellow worshippers. Like all women, they had light brown skin and dark brown hair. Natasha tried to imagine meeting one of the multicolored Elder-Ones, such as the figure depicted at the blessed Himoti's shoulder, with the improbable mane of golden hair and the sky blue face. Natasha shook her head in entranced awe and continued her slow march.

Along all the walls and surrounding every column were shrines where the pious might pay their homage to the appropriate Elder-One, the patron of their trade or calling. The size of the shrine was a fair guide to the status of the occupation. Natasha's destination was one of the more impressive, although none could match the grandeur of the monument to Himoti, patron of Imprinters, the greatest of Celaeno's disciples. Natasha's footsteps halted at the military shrine, set into a deep alcove in the wall. She wished to take time to pray. It was why she had rushed her grooming slightly. She had the feeling that prayers might be necessary.

When the captain had taken her away from sentry duty, she had assumed that it was to learn the result of her application for promotion to corporal, but that would be purely a military matter. She would not be notified at the temple and certainly not in the sanctum. Something else was at issue—something serious. Again, Natasha searched her memory for some clue about the summons but found nothing, either in the barrack-room gossip or the official dispatches.

She tried to push the anxiety from her thoughts and stepped into the alcove. The statues of three of the Elder-Ones looked down at her: the patrons of the Guards, the Rangers, and the Militia. She bowed her head to her namesake, Natasha Krowe of the Rangers, and then knelt before Su Li Hoy, the Guards' patron. The figure's bright yellow skin and flame-red hair mirrored the uniform of the Guards. Natasha's eyes fixed on the comforting statue, and she began to pray:

> Please, my patron; guide me in the ways of honor
> and courage
> That I might find favor with Celaeno, who is Goddess
> over all...

❖

By the time the bell rang out the hour, Natasha felt far happier. The calm of the temple had soaked into her, and she had reached the reasonable conclusion that she was unlikely to be in trouble. Not only was her conscience clear, but also, if she were accused of a crime serious enough to warrant the Sisters' attention, the authorities would have dragged her to trial in chains.

The entrance to the sanctum was set to one side of the main altar, the secret world within hidden behind hanging drapes. Six Guards from Natasha's company were on duty. Their eyes showed the barest flicker of recognition when she came to a halt, slightly unsure what to do next. Within seconds, the curtain was pulled aside, and a white-robed Sister appeared.

"You are Guardswoman Ionadis?"

"Yes, ma'am."

"Follow me."

Stepping into the sanctum, Natasha felt a confusing tangle of emotions. Curiosity and reverence were at the forefront, with apprehension and a degree of smugness playing a part. Many Guards would pass their entire careers without ever setting foot inside the sanctum where the Sisters and Imprinters lived out their daily lives. This was the heart of the greatest temple in the world. Nowhere else could a woman get closer to Celaeno. As she followed her guide, Natasha felt her soul swelling with love of the Goddess—a sensation hindered only by the urge to peer around like an inquisitive child, drinking in every detail of her surroundings.

The route took them through a series of courtyards and corridors. Eventually, Natasha was ushered into a small room on an upper floor, clearly someone's office, with shelves containing books and a large desk covered in piles of paper. A window at one side led to a balcony overlooking the Guards' parade ground. Two women were waiting for her in the room, and at the sight of them, Natasha's feeling of happiness vanished.

The one standing at the side was familiar from dawn parade each morning. Natasha did not need to count the gold stars on the epaulette to identify Commandant Jacobs of the Guards. The face of the other was hidden behind the gauze mask of a Sister, which would have made her impossible to name with certainty, except that this Sister wore Himoti's pendant hanging on a thin gold chain at her throat. With a jolt, Natasha realized that the woman seated at the desk was Chief Consultant Pereira, the leader of the Sisterhood, and the thirty-second to have held the title since the blessed Himoti, the first Chief Consultant.

Natasha felt her stomach turn to ice. She could not begin to guess what reason the most important person in the world had to speak with her. Fortunately, her trained reflexes took over, and without conscious thought, she snapped stiffly to attention.

"Guardswoman Ionadis reporting, ma'am." Natasha was surprised to hear her own voice.

The Commandant acknowledged her and said, "You may stand at ease, Guardswoman, and remove your helmet."

Oh, no, my hair, Natasha thought in anguish, even as she moved to obey. She prayed that no tufts were sticking out and fought the temptation to try frantically to smooth them down. It would only draw attention to her lapse. Natasha's mouth was dry as both women continued to study her, but after several nerve-wracking seconds, she realized that neither appeared to be hostile.

At last, the senior Guard spoke again. "I guess you're wondering why we've called you here."

"Yes, ma'am." Natasha was not sure if she should admit to curiosity, but to deny it would have been blatant lying.

"That is understandable." Commandant Jacobs' lips compressed in the tight line that was the nearest her habitually stern face ever came to smiling. Jacobs was well below average height and was rumored to cultivate a stern demeanor deliberately to counteract any perceived deficiency, although other schools of thought claimed that she was just naturally humorless. She exchanged a look with the seated woman, as if asking permission to continue. The Chief Consultant indicated her consent.

Jacobs relaxed her stance slightly and drew a deep breath. "We're planning a very important mission, and we're looking for volunteers. For several reasons, your name has been put forward as a candidate, but before I say more, I must warn you that the chances of our agents returning is low—not impossible, with the grace of the Goddess, but very unlikely. Which is why we want volunteers."

"I'll do it," Natasha said instantly, almost before the Commandant had finished speaking. It was the sort of opportunity she had not dared dream of. Then she remembered the status of her audience and tried to restrain her childish overeagerness. "I...I would count it an honor, ma'am."

Commandant Jacobs' face showed approval. "Which is the response I'd been led to expect from you. However, before I accept your offer, you must learn more of what the mission involves, and this is what the Chief Consultant wishes to talk to you about."

Natasha turned her attention to the woman behind the desk. For a few seconds, the eyes above the gauze mask continued to regard Natasha in silence. The skin around them was deeply lined; the Chief Consultant was not young. Her body was completely concealed by her white robes, but from the way the folds lay, the form underneath was approaching skeletal thinness. When she spoke, her voice held a trace of a waver.

"Guardswoman, what I am about to relate is not in complete agreement with what we are obliged to tell the general population. If you're accepted for this mission, you may discuss what I say with the other members of the team, but you must give your oath never to repeat it to anyone else."

"Yes, ma'am. I swear by Hoy's sword." Natasha gave the traditional Guards' oath.

The Chief Consultant pressed her fingers to her pendant in recognition of the vow. "Then first, I would like to know what you have heard about the heretics who follow the accursed Gina Renamed."

Natasha drew a deep breath, torn between pride and nervousness, dreading that she would say something wrong and disqualify herself from the mission, but it was not a difficult question. "The heretics set themselves against the divinity of Celaeno. They renounce the teachings of Himoti and the Elder-Ones, and they use their perverted creed to justify the hideous crimes they commit. Most have been brought to account for their sins, but a few have escaped and are hiding in the wildlands." From the nod of agreement, Natasha knew that she had given the right answer.

"Have you also heard of the place known as Westernfort?"

This was a slightly more awkward topic. Natasha hesitated for a moment before restating the official account. "It's the name given to a fictitious town the heretics are supposed to have in the mountains."

"And what have you heard via the barrack-room gossip?" The eyes above the mask narrowed shrewdly.

"Er..." Natasha swallowed, but she could not refuse to answer, and lying was unthinkable. "Some Guards...claim there really once was a strong, defended base, and we took heavy casualties before finally conquering it."

"I suppose it was only to be expected that the survivors would talk." The Chief Consultant's voice was quietly rueful. She tapped her fingertips together and then looked up sharply. "And lastly, do you recognize the name of Kimberly Ramon?"

It's a trap. The thought shot through Natasha's head. Everyone must have heard the banned songs, but only a fool would admit it. Natasha's eyes fixed on the paneled wall as her stomach contracted, but before she could formulate an answer, the elderly Sister spoke again.

"It's obvious from your face that you do. Don't worry. We didn't bring you here to accuse you of spreading sedition. I'm afraid there are very few who haven't been exposed to the doggerel."

Natasha found her voice. "I've paid no attention to it. The few bits I've heard have been idiotic fantasy. It couldn't—"

The Chief Consultant interrupted her with a quote from a song:

> *For all the Sisters' traps and plots,*
> *Ramon cannot be caught.*
> *She lives safe with her love behind*
> *The walls of Westernfort.*

Silence filled the room until the Chief Consultant sighed and continued. "Yes, it is fantasy, but unfortunately, there's a basis of truth in it." She pushed back her chair and walked to the window.

Natasha glanced at the other woman in the room, hoping for some hint of what was meant, but Commandant Jacobs' expression was as stony as ever. Eventually, the senior Sister left her contemplation of the scene outside and turned around.

"Kimberly Ramon was a Ranger." A bitter tone had entered the Chief Consultant's voice. "She even reached the rank of lieutenant before her true nature was discovered and she was court-martialed. Then she deserted, taking the rest of her squadron with her. They joined with Gina Renamed and her heretics, hiding in the western mountains, and together, they founded a settlement, which they called Westernfort."

Natasha stared in wide-eyed astonishment. The Guards held an ingrained contempt of the Rangers, seeing them as irreverent rabble, but for a whole squadron to desert was unbelievable, and the Chief Consultant had not yet finished.

"That was sixteen years ago. If we could have located the settlement immediately, we might have been able to do something about it. Alas, by the time we found them, they'd dug themselves in. We sent every Guard we could muster to capture the site, but I'm afraid both the official and unofficial reports fall short of the truth. We were unable to overcome the defenses and lost nearly two hundred Guards in the attempt."

A faint sound from the Commandant as she shifted her feet was a momentary distraction, but Natasha could not take her eyes from the woman in white.

"For the last five years, we've been forced to leave the heretics in control of the western mountains. The 23rd was a top-notch squadron. Guards are no match for them on their home ground, and the Rangers we send have a tendency to go over to their side. Ramon may lack any sort of morals, but she doesn't lack powers of persuasion."

The Chief Consultant walked forward until she stood scant centimeters from Natasha. Her eyes were as hard as her voice. "Their lives are an insult to the Goddess, and a day does not pass without my praying to be forgiven for allowing them to continue in their foul depravity. But at last, Celaeno has given us the chance to strike a blow in her name.

"Yesterday, we captured a group of three heretics who were fleeing to join their confederates. From them, we've been able to learn their planned route to Westernfort. It's our intention to send three disguised Guards in their place. Once our agents are inside the defenses, they'll carry out the death sentences that have been passed on the leaders. It's too much to hope that resistance will crumble, but it will be weakened, and the Goddess will know that we do not ignore insults to her divinity."

The elderly Sister returned to her desk and sat down. She gestured to the Commandant, passing control of the briefing to her. Jacobs cleared her throat.

"Guardswoman Ionadis, your name has been put forward for three reasons. First, we believe you possess the quick wits necessary to carry off the impersonation. Second, you bear a passing physical resemblance to one of the heretics. Third, the strength of your devotion is beyond question, and this last point is the most crucial. It is not an easy mission. You must be ready to kill to order, not in the heat of battle.

"And as I started by saying, there is little hope of your returning to Landfall. The season is against you. By the time you reach Westernfort, it will be winter. Even if you escape after fulfilling your mission, the weather in the mountains will make the return journey impossible. It will not be counted against your record if you decline this mission."

Natasha's head went up. "It would be an honor to destroy the enemies of the Goddess, and I am not frightened to die in her name."

"Then all that remains is for the Chief Consultant to tell you of the three leaders who will be your targets. All three have been duly tried and sentenced in their absence, and in executing them, by whatever means, you will not be committing murder. You will be carrying out the sanctified orders of the Goddess' earthly representative."

The Commandant bowed respectfully to the leader of the Sisterhood. The Chief Consultant acknowledged the action and turned to Natasha.

"Indeed. The first is Gina Renamed, the leader of the heretics, who first began spreading the blasphemous lies. To our shame, I must confess that she was once a Sister in this temple. She did suffer a severe brain injury, which might explain—although not excuse—her actions. She is the source and root cause of all that has happened and deserves to die a hundred times over.

"Your second target is Kimberly Ramon, and she will probably present the greatest challenge. She's an experienced and capable soldier. Do not underestimate her. The Goddess has blessed her with many admirable qualities: courage, leadership, even personal charm. But she has chosen to use her talents only to defy her creator. The deaths of the Guards who attacked Westernfort were her work."

The Chief Consultant paused. "Your third target is in many ways the most serious. She's called Lynn. She has no last name, since she is an Imprinter."

Natasha felt as if a whirlwind had blown through her head, scrambling her thoughts. The most impossible part, in all the preposterous songs, was the claim that Kimberly Ramon had won the heart of an Imprinter, inducing her to forsake Himoti and the temple, and that they were now lovers. The very suggestion was outrageous. Imprinters were the chosen of the Goddess—the ones so gifted with the healer sense that they could not merely induce pregnancy in a woman, but also imprint new patterns on the embryo's DNA. The Imprinters alone could create new, unique human beings. Surely the Goddess would not bestow this divine power on anyone susceptible to heresy.

The Chief Consultant clearly noticed Natasha's response. "I know. It is...unbelievable. Of all the heretics' crimes, the corruption of one of Celaeno's chosen is surely the worst, and even more harmful than we at first realized, since initially, we were sure that the Goddess would withdraw her gift. But I'm afraid we have gathered evidence that Lynn is, rather than was, an Imprinter."

"But ma'am"—Natasha could not help speaking—"don't Imprinters have to be celibate in order to do their work?"

"Yes, they do, and I know what parts of the songs you're referring to." The Chief Consultant's voice held a shadow of humor. "It's a good lesson in not believing anything they say. It's too easy for the faithful to get caught in the web of lies spread by the heretics. Believe me, I would be much happier if she and Ramon were lovers, for then we would not be faced with the problem of a second generation of heretics to defy the Goddess. This is why Lynn, more than anyone else, must be eliminated if we're to see the end to this heresy.

"The execution of the leaders at Westernfort is not just punishment for their past crimes. It's to protect the future from the spread of their blasphemy. This is the sacred charge laid on you, for the glory of the Goddess." The Chief Consultant placed her hands face down on the desk and looked toward the Commandant. "And I think that concludes all that must be said, unless you have anything to add."

Commandant Jacobs stepped forward. "Only to say that I have been very pleased by your response, Guardswoman. However, I feel it would be wise for you to spend a little more time thinking things over. This will be our one chance to destroy the enemies of the Goddess. If you have the slightest doubt about your ability to carry out the mission, it would be far better to let someone else go in your place. Sleep on it, and come to see me first thing tomorrow morning."

Natasha was about to reaffirm her willingness but settled for saying only, "Yes, ma'am."

The Commandant nodded. "You are dismissed."

Natasha brought herself to attention and then turned to the door, but as she opened it, the Commandant spoke again. "Guardswoman Ionadis."

"Yes, ma'am."

"You will be passing yourself off as a civilian. Don't bother getting your hair cut."

❖

A Sister was waiting outside the room when Natasha left, possibly the same one who had guided her to the meeting, although the mask made it impossible to be sure. Again, Natasha was led through the sanctum. Unlike she had been upon her arrival, she was now so preoccupied that she was unaware of her surroundings until she returned to the great hall.

The light from the windows high in the dome was muted. The day was almost over, and the temple was closing for the night. Few people were in sight, just a gaggle of late worshippers being herded toward the doors and a pair of Sisters in white, tending the shrines. Natasha's gaze slipped over the scene; it felt unreal, dreamlike.

Her eyes fixed on the sacred fire burning on the main altar. The sight drew Natasha, half stumbling, to the steps. The dancing flame seemed to replicate the rapturous emotions swirling inside her.

Natasha knelt. She could not remember ever feeling quite so happy or so proud. She had joined the Guards to devote her life to Celaeno, but sometimes, over the previous three years, she had been tempted to question her decision. There was the jeering taunt thrown at anyone joining the Guards: *Not so much a soldier, more a laundress.* Frequently, it had seemed quite justified. But now, she had a chance to fight for her faith, to give her life to overthrow those who rejected the Goddess. She would truly be a soldier for Celaeno.

An inappropriate urge to giggle welled up inside her. Natasha clasped her hands together and closed her eyes. Then she bent her head in prayer:

> *I promise, Celaeno, I will destroy your enemies. My life is yours to do with as you will. Make me strong in your love that I may triumph for your sake, and if I turn aside from this task, may I be damned forever.*

CHAPTER TWO—THE STREETS OF LANDFALL

Dusk was not far off when Natasha left the temple grounds. Soon, the huge iron gateway would be closed and barred, releasing her comrades of the 3rd Company from sentry duty. Several stood at attention by the exit. Natasha looked at them briefly and considered returning to the barracks to await their arrival, but she felt in need of space to think. So instead, she turned and strolled slowly up the road, in the direction heading away from the Guards' headquarters.

The familiar, hectic street life of Landfall swept by around her, the daily activity of the busy city. It had been home for all of her twenty-one years. Its thoroughfares and alleyways had been her playground as a child and her workplace during her two years in the Militia. At different times in her life, she had found the city exciting in its energy and depressing in its vulgarity. Now she felt a gentle affection for its unchanging cheerful audacity.

At the end of the road, closely packed houses on either side gave way to the broad, cobbled square of the marketplace. Trading was still brisk despite the onset of night. The cries of peddlers and store holders battled in a riot of sound. The pathways between the stalls were crammed with prospective customers.

Natasha stood to one side and surveyed the scene. Her eyes fixed on a group of girls in one corner, playing football with a discarded cabbage. Eight years ago, she would have been one of them. It seemed to symbolize a part of her life that was over. There was not the slightest doubt in her mind that the next morning, she would restate her willingness to undertake the mission and would soon be leaving the city, never to return.

I suppose I should go and see Mother one last time. Natasha considered the idea with mixed feelings and sighed. It would not be pleasant. It never was. But it was best to get it over with. Her jaw hardened. There was also something she had to ask, although she did not know how likely it was she would get an answer. Things might be eased if she took a gift, and only one thing would be acceptable. She moved away, walking purposefully toward the nearest wine merchant.

The shopkeeper hesitated at the sight of the uniform, obviously taken aback to have a Guard as a customer. Natasha did not bother to explain that the merchandise was not for herself; it should have gone without saying. She paid the money after only the most token effort at bartering and walked out with a bottle of sweet brandy in her hand.

As she headed away from the market, the streets became narrower and shabbier, although Natasha was still some way from the slums when she reached her destination: a thin, terraced house squeezed between two larger neighbors. The door was unbarred and swung open when she knocked. Natasha stepped through to the dimly lit room inside.

"Is that you, Louise?" her mother's voice called out.

Louise? Natasha thought. The name was not one she recognized, but even when she had lived in the house, she'd had difficulty keeping track of her mother's lovers. Cilla Ionadis clambered to her feet and stood, swaying slightly in the firelight that flickered over the squalid clutter covering every horizontal surface in the room. Natasha fought to keep the contempt from her face. The house was a shambles, as usual, and her mother was drunk, as usual.

"Oh, it's you." Her mother's voice was hardly welcoming.

"Hello, Mom. I'd thought I'd come and see you. I've brought you a present." Natasha held out the brandy.

Cilla looked as if she was about to tell her daughter to go, but the sight of the bottle deflected her. She pointed Natasha toward a chair and then stumbled to an overflowing dresser, returning with two chipped mugs. She slumped back in her seat, put the mugs on the floor by her feet, and held out her hand for the brandy. The quantity of the strong spirit slopped into one mug would have been more appropriate for wine. Or water. Before she moved on to the other, Natasha forestalled her.

"It's okay. I won't have any."

Cilla's mouth twisted into a sneer. "Of course. You don't drink, do you? My pious little soldier. And you don't swear, or dance, or gamble. I'm amazed you ever got around to sex." She laughed without humor. "I bet you were lousy at it. No wonder Beatrice chucked you."

Natasha made no reply. There was no point. The spiteful words were offered as much out of habit as anything, and getting into an argument was not a good way to proceed. Instead, Natasha settled back in her chair and studied her mother's face in the firelight. Despite age and drink, Cilla Ionadis was still a very beautiful woman. Her lifestyle had not yet spoiled the chiseled perfection of her profile, but surely her looks could not last much longer. *And what will she do then?* Natasha wondered. The string of besotted lovers had provided her mother's main income for as long as Natasha could remember.

When she saw that her taunts had produced no response, Cilla took a deep mouthful of brandy and then asked sarcastically, "And why have I been privileged with your exalted company tonight?"

"I wanted to see you before I left," Natasha replied evenly.

"Where are you going?" Her mother sat up slightly, the derision in her voice curbed.

"I'm being posted out of town for a while."

"What will happen while you're gone?"

It might have been a cryptic question, had Natasha been less familiar with her mother's thinking. "I'll arrange to have my pay sent directly here. You can take your share and look after the rest until I get back."

It was an amusing piece of fiction. They both knew that all the money would be spent, and they both knew that the other knew. Cilla's eyes narrowed as she looked at her daughter, suspecting some trick, but Natasha was not about to offer enlightenment by explaining that there was no chance of her returning to claim the money.

For a while, the only sound in the room was the crackling of the fire. Then the older woman snorted, drained her mug, and poured herself another shot. Natasha watched pensively, trying to judge her mother's mood and level of intoxication. The drinking had definitely gotten worse over the past few years, while its effects had become less dramatic. *Mellow* was not the right word; it was more as if Cilla's ability to react to the external world was fading, as if she no longer cared about it. Maybe her indifference would be enough for her to answer Natasha's question, or maybe she would lapse into surly silence. There was only one way to find out.

"Mom, there was something I wanted to ask you."

"What?"

"My other mother...my gene mother."

"What about her?"

"I just wondered, who was she? What happened to her?"

Cilla gave a loud bark of laughter. "She's been gone for twenty years. You certainly took your time asking."

The assertion was not quite true, but the last time Natasha had asked, she was still young enough to receive a clip around the ear by way of an answer. "I know that you don't like to talk about her."

"True. So why are you asking?"

Natasha hesitated. Maybe there was genuine grief behind her mother's evasiveness, but it was far more likely just another childish game. Cilla enjoyed feeling that she had a hold over everyone, and little else was left in her power to grant or deny. In fact, now that Natasha was an independent adult, the information was the only thing her mother had that she wanted. Direct threats did not work well when Cilla was drunk; they only provoked a hysterical outburst. But it might help to remind her that Natasha also had something to withhold.

"I assume she's dead, since she never visits or writes, and there seemed no point stirring things up. But now that I'm leaving town, I thought I should visit her grave and maybe have a statue or something put there. It would only be right, as I'm her daughter. I could have my pay sent to a stonemason instead of here."

"You can save your money. She isn't dead."

"So who is she?"

Cilla scowled into the fire. Initially, it looked as if she were not going to reply. Then she shifted her gaze and stared blearily at Natasha. "Who is she?" Cilla repeated the question and then answered it. "She was once a lover of mine. And she left, like they all do."

The response was not very informative, but at least she was talking. Natasha leaned forward and said, "But she must have meant more than all the rest. You must have had to save the imprinting fees for the temple. And..." Natasha halted. What she wanted to say was, *I can guess why she left you, but why did she leave me?* The approach was not a good one to take. "Separating can't have been quite so easy."

"The imprinting fees were nothing to her. She was rich, really rich. One of the Tang family. She wanted a child, and I thought she'd look after me. I thought..." Cilla's words faded, and her face crumpled. Tears formed in her eyes.

There was no need to say more. *You thought you'd be living in luxury for the rest of your life.* Natasha mentally finished the sentence. She slipped back in her chair and looked at her mother cynically, watching the first of the tears trickle down Cilla's face. The loss of the money, rather than the lover, would be the cause of her distress. Lovers had never been in short supply. Natasha closed her eyes, thinking bitterly of the small fantasy she had once concocted for herself: that her mothers had adored each other; that some awful tragedy had overtaken her gene mother; and that her birth mother had treated sex as a job thereafter, because she had lost her only true love. It had been a childish daydream; she should have known better. Mention of the Tang family was the only truly surprising bit.

Cilla was rapidly sinking into a maudlin state. "You were just a little baby. You'd think she'd have wanted to keep her daughter."

"She can't have just abandoned you," Natasha pointed out, although actually, the Tangs could do whatever they wanted. They had enough money to bribe a magistrate. They probably could afford to buy off even the Sisterhood.

"She bought me this house," Cilla mumbled. "Sent money until you were sixteen, but she never came to see you...never came to see me. They leave me; they always do. Why don't they stay?"

Tears were now flowing in earnest as Cilla wallowed in self-pity. Natasha could almost bring herself to pity her mother too. It was rarely more than a few months before a new lover would see through the beautiful exterior to the petty, insincere, self-centered woman beneath. The lover would leave and would be instantly replaced. Cilla had been spoiled, quite literally, by her good looks. With a never-ending stream of women to tell her how wonderful she was, she had never needed to listen to criticism. Perhaps if she had been ugly, she might have been a nicer person.

The door to the room opened, and another woman entered. Cilla wiped the tears and sprang up, her face transformed into a smile of delight. *This must be Louise*, Natasha thought, but it would not matter if it was not. It was someone to reassure her mother that she was the center of the universe, which was the only thing Cilla wanted.

Natasha's words of farewell were answered with the barest effort at courtesy, and she let herself out of the house. As she walked along the road, she wondered how long it would take her mother to drink her way through the death-in-action payment.

❖

True night had fallen while Natasha had been inside. The streets of Landfall had become much quieter. The only people visible were two members of the Militia, strolling with the unhurried tread of a patrol. As she overtook them, Natasha thought about her time policing the city. The only way to enter the military was via the Militia. Then, after a two-year probation, and if she could pass the entrance tests, a soldier could transfer into either of the elite services: the Rangers or the Temple Guard.

The Rangers dealt with any physical threats too difficult for the Militia to handle. In the main, they guarded the borders against the wild animals and occasional gangs of bandits that lived outside the domesticated Homelands. The Guards' responsibilities covered not just this world, but also the next. In accordance with the Chief Consultant's orders, they protected the spiritual integrity of Celaeno's daughters. They were holy warriors of the Goddess, the martial counterpart of the Sisterhood.

Becoming a Guard had been Natasha's only ambition. At the time of enlisting, she had viewed the subsequent probation period as an upcoming ordeal. Her only intention had been to get through it with as little fuss as possible and apply for transfer to the Guards on the very first day she was eligible. She was certain that her record and knowledge of theology would get her through the entrance tests without difficulty. But she had not disliked being in the Militia as much as she had expected. Many of the Militiawomen paid no more than lip service to religion. Some were little better than the criminals they pursued. But the difficult task of enforcing the law in the swarming city engendered a real camaraderie. It had been an exciting time—and, of course, there had been Beatrice.

They had met while Natasha was engaged in identifying the rightful owners of a recovered haul of stolen property. Beatrice was a clerk in the jewelers' guild who had helped in the search. She was a few years older than Natasha, with casual grace and a wry sense of humor. On the last day of the investigation, Natasha had surprised herself by inviting the clerk out for a drink on impulse, and Beatrice had surprised her even more by accepting.

For a while, Natasha's intention of joining the Guards had faltered. Celibacy was essential for Imprinters and compulsory for Sisters. For the Guards, it was officially no more than a desirable trait, but it was taken as a good marker of a woman's devotion. Before long, Natasha would have been obliged to choose between Beatrice and her career.

As her probation period had drawn to a close, the arguments had begun. Natasha had retreated into an obstinate determination to apply for transfer, refusing to show any emotion, including anger. They had tried to part in a civilized fashion, and failed. Beatrice had felt rejected, which was not unreasonable. She had been. But had love of the Goddess triumphed, or had the relationship simply run its course?

Natasha remembered the last time they had spoken. Two years ago, Beatrice had made the gesture of inviting her over on Natasha's nineteenth birthday, an attempt to relinquish the past and rebuild their friendship: a meal, a drink, and a chat. And Natasha had awakened the next morning in Beatrice's bed, which had led to the worst argument of all. In hindsight, Natasha knew that she had been totally in the wrong. Beatrice had not seduced her. If anything, it had been the other way around.

Natasha's footsteps halted. The house where Beatrice now lived was only a few streets away. She could go apologize and make a decent finish to the whole affair. Natasha bit her lip; then she turned and continued walking. It was doubtful that Beatrice would be pleased to see her, and the new lover certainly would not.

Natasha passed through the market square and entered the road leading to the Guards' headquarters. Ahead of her, the imposing bulk of the temple was a hole in the field of stars. A jumble of associated buildings lay to one side. Among them was the school where the daughters of the well-off were tutored by the Sisters, receiving a more comprehensive education than that available in the public institutions. Natasha had been a pupil there. She smiled grimly. The anomaly had never occurred to her before, but it must have been her wealthy gene mother's doing. Cilla would never have wasted good beer money on her daughter's education.

Natasha remembered the day she had decided to become a Guard, sitting in class, listening to Sister Kapoor read from *The Book of the Elder-Ones*. The Sister had described the purity of devoting one's life to the glory of the Goddess and the honor of being ready to fight and die in her name. Natasha's smile softened at the thought of Sister Kapoor, the short, round Sister with kind eyes who had played mother hen to all the youngest children. Sister Kapoor never hit her, never got drunk, and never had trouble remembering the name of the woman she was eating breakfast with.

The gateway to the headquarters was getting closer with each step. Soon, Natasha was inside and threading her way through the rows of stables, stores, and barracks. When she entered her dormitory, a group of comrades from her company were sitting on the bunks, talking. They looked up, their faces revealing a fair degree of speculative interest. The news that she had been summoned to the sanctum must have made the rounds.

"Hi, Tash. How's it going?" one asked with poorly disguised curiosity.

"Not bad." Natasha sat down on the end of one bunk. She was going to have to say something without compromising her oath of secrecy. "I've...er...been given an assignment that will take me out of town for a bit."

"Anything interesting?"

Natasha shrugged. "Well, hopefully, a bit more interesting than sentry duty."

Several laughed. "That's not saying much."

Another asked pointedly, "Have you been offered promotion?"

Natasha hesitated and then said slowly, "Nothing was promised, but…um…it's definitely the way I want my career to go."

The sergeant smiled and said, "Then we should offer prayers for a successful conclusion and your speedy return."

Without need of more inducement, the Guards slipped to their knees and began an impromptu rite of worship. The thought drifted through Natasha's mind that in similar circumstances, the Militia would have headed to the nearest tavern.

It was getting late. One small lamp burned in Commandant Jacobs' office. The day's business had not been easy—too many critical decisions to make and not much time to make them in—but the end was getting close. Jacobs stifled a yawn and watched the woman sitting on the other side of the desk, whose attention was in turn focused on the piece of paper in her hand. The woman had been announced with the rank of major, but her manner did not show the crisp formality of military protocol. Neither was there anything military about her appearance. In fact, there was nothing noteworthy at all about her. It occurred to Jacobs that the woman could have walked through any street, shop, or tavern in the Homelands without getting a second glance from anyone.

As the Intelligence Corps major read, she spoke aloud, voicing her thoughts. "Just under 170 centimeters. That's good…Broad shoulders…solid build, but not overweight…quite attractive?" Her tone made the last two words a question as she looked up.

Commandant Jacobs shrugged. "That has to be a matter of opinion."

"But do you think most people would describe this candidate of yours as quite attractive?"

"I think most people would use the word *very,* rather than *quite.*"

The major laughed. "And as you say, it is a matter of opinion." Her eyes returned to the sheet, scanning for the information. "I though I saw her age here somewhere."

"Twenty-one."

"A touch on the old side. Could she pass for eighteen?"

Jacobs was thoughtful for a moment. "It shouldn't strain people's credulity too much."

"Good." The major put down the paper. "Now, that's the surface description, but if I'm going to be working with her, I need a bit more. Tell me what she's like—your evaluation of her character."

"She's a good soldier."

"And that can mean virtually anything."

"Can you be a bit more specific about what you want to know?" Jacobs hedged.

"Is she intelligent?"

"Yes."

"Able to use her own initiative?"

"Yes."

"Enough to cause trouble?"

"No...no, I don't think so." Commandant Jacobs relaxed slightly, sinking in her chair. "She was a student at the public school in the temple. She learned her doctrine directly from the Sisters. Her devotion to her duty and her faith is beyond question. She can think for herself, but she has no problem obeying orders. Her record has been perfect. In fact, she was in line for promotion to corporal very soon, and she would go a lot higher. She—"

The other woman cut her off. "But sometimes, our brightest and best go off the rails unexpectedly."

"There has not been the slightest indication of it yet."

"Which is all that can really be claimed for anyone," the major said, nodding. "So do you have any misgivings about recommending her for this mission?"

"I'm not happy about losing one of our most promising candidates for officer."

"It is for the greater glory of the Goddess."

"I know." Jacobs tried to express both her regret and her piety by her tone.

"Any other misgivings?"

Commandant Jacobs thought for a moment. She had a whole range of misgivings, but it was not prudent to express them, and it was bitter knowledge that her command of the Guards became so shaky at the first mention of heresy.

The furrows on Jacobs' forehead deepened. Although nominally part of the Guards, the Intelligence Corps tended to act as a law unto itself, and that was all right by her. Jacobs had found that the less she knew about the Corps' activities, the more easily she slept at night. Everyone would be much happier once the Intelligence Corps reported directly to the Sisterhood, and that situation could not be far away. For the meantime, Jacobs tried to focus solely on the candidate and the mission in question.

"I would not have said she was a natural candidate for undercover work. I don't think she'll be happy playing a part. It will be a bit too much like lying for her comfort."

"But you think she'll be capable of it?"

"Oh, yes. As I said before, she's bright. And she'll willingly do anything necessary to fulfill the mission...for the glory of the Goddess."

"Any doubts about her courage?"

"None whatsoever," the Commandant said firmly.

For the first time, the other woman smiled. "Then I think she'll do very well."

Chapter Three—Jess Korski

Natasha was shown in immediately when she reported to the Commandant's office the next morning. The senior Guard looked up from the papers on her desk.

"Guardswoman Ionadis. Have you thought things over?"

"Yes, ma'am."

"And are you still willing to undertake the mission?"

"Yes, ma'am."

Commandant Jacobs nodded and then picked up one sheet that had been lying slightly apart from the rest. "I have here a recommendation for your promotion." She took a pen and quickly signed the bottom. "I'm approving it. Congratulations, Corporal."

"Thank you, ma'am."

"If, by the grace of the Goddess, you return successfully, you will have more than deserved it."

And if I don't, the death-in-action payment will be bigger, Natasha added to herself.

"You need to meet with the other agents on the mission and receive a detailed briefing. Go straight to the intelligence block and ask for..." The Commandant paused and consulted another paper. "Rohanna Korski. She's the commanding officer of your group. And Corporal..." Commandant Jacobs looked directly into Natasha's eyes. "Remember how important this mission is. It's for the glory of the Goddess and the honor of the Guards. I'm sure you'll prove worthy of the trust laid on you."

"Thank you, ma'am."

"You are dismissed."

Walking through the sunshine, Natasha felt herself swelling with pride, and the bitter taste left by the meeting with her mother washed away. Only as she drew near to the unremarkable brick building did her feeling of elation fade. The intelligence block, and the women who worked there, had an uncomfortable relationship with the rest of the Guards. Rumor claimed that there were underground prisons, and far more people went in than came out. It was also known that the intelligence agents traveled the country in disguise, trying to unmask the spies sent by the heretics. Of course, that was necessary; they could hardly do their job in uniform. But somehow, it seemed dishonorable to act a part rather than unequivocally affirm one's faith. Natasha's lips pulled down at the corners. It was the very role she was about to adopt herself.

Natasha gave the name of her contact to a Guard stationed at the doorway. She was escorted under the archway to a central courtyard and then up a narrow flight of stairs to the second floor. To her surprise, the room she was finally shown into was a small, unoccupied sleeping chamber, empty apart from a narrow bunk lining one wall. One small window was directly opposite, with a view of the temple. The sentry pointed to a set of civilian clothes lying across the foot of the bed.

"Get changed into those. Once you're ready, report to the second room on the left."

Natasha nodded to show that she understood and was left alone.

❖

She reemerged a few minutes later, transformed. Her boots were badly scuffed and liberally splattered with dried-on mud, as were the knee-high woolen socks. The pants tucked into them had once been blue but were now mostly faded to gray. The drawstring at the waist was frayed; mismatched patches covered both knees. The shirtsleeves were too long, requiring folding back at the wrist. A heavy, rain-resistant jacket had also been laid out on the bed, but Natasha had decided against wearing it; the weather was too warm for it to be comfortable. All the clothes held a musty, unwashed odor.

Natasha knew that her appearance would not attract the slightest attention on any street in the Homelands, yet she felt strange and awkward as she knocked on the door. *When in doubt, polish it* was certainly not relevant to the situation. A voice called out immediately, bidding her enter.

Natasha found herself in another bedroom, considerably larger than the one she had just left. A square table stood in the middle, with two women seated at it. Both were dressed in civilian attire similar to her own, although judging by her close-cut hair, the smaller of the two was clearly a soldier. She was of middling height and had a thin, wiry build. There were etched creases around her eyes and mouth, though she was probably no more than in her mid-thirties. The other woman was larger, big-boned rather than fat, and she looked to be the older by a good few years. Her hair was liberally sprinkled with gray and far longer even than Natasha's untrimmed crop, sufficient to cover her ears and reach almost to her shoulders.

"Is Rohanna Korski here?" Natasha asked cautiously.

"That's me." The larger woman spoke.

Natasha drew herself up. "Ma'am, Corporal Na—" She was cut off abruptly.

"No. You are my daughter, Jess Korski, and you should call me Mom. Always." The woman smiled at Natasha's startled look. "If we don't know each other's real names, there's no risk of using them by accident." She pointed to a chair. "Bring it over and sit down. We've got a lot to discuss and not much time to do it in."

When Natasha was settled, she went on. "I'll start by introducing my lover, and your gene mother, Calinda Rowse."

The wiry woman grinned and said, "But I believe I answer to Cal."

Rohanna nodded and continued. "As you must have realized, we're a family, and we must act like one whenever there's the faintest chance we might be overheard—which, once we leave this building, will be pretty much always. We must immerse ourselves in the parts we're playing so we don't have to think about them, almost so that they cease to be an act. But for this time only, we'll say a little about our real backgrounds, so we'll understand what skills we can contribute to the mission. And I'll start with myself."

Rohanna shifted back in her chair. "I'm a member of the Intelligence Corps, and have been for the last fifteen years. I'm better acquainted with the heretics' lies than any daughter of the Goddess would want to be, and I've considerable practice at working undercover. I'll try to share my experience with you, but it's not possible to pass on all you need to know in the time we've got. If you're ever in doubt about how to respond to a situation, try to follow my lead. And for my part, I'll be looking out for you and trying to anticipate any pitfalls." She turned to the woman on her right. "Cal, if you'd like to say something?"

Cal pursed her lips for a moment. "I've been told one of the main reasons I've been selected for this mission is that I used to be a Ranger before I joined the Guards. The heretics will provide us with a guide, but it was thought that it might not be a bad idea to have someone who understands the wildlands. Although Westernfort is referred to as a town, the conditions aren't what we'd expect from the term. My skills might come in handy if we have to start improvising."

Natasha looked at the woman with surprise. There was nothing in the rule book to stop someone transferring from the Rangers to the Guards, but she had never heard of its being done. "A Ranger!" she could not help blurting out.

Cal nodded, clearly amused. "Oh, yes. An impious, immoral Ranger. And you know what is said about them. The only time I ever prayed was when I called on the Goddess to cure my hangover." Cal drew a breath. "Yet even though I was unworthy, Celaeno had her own plans for me. One winter, my squadron was up north, chasing snow lions, and I got separated in a blizzard. I managed to dig myself a hole in the snow, but I knew I was going to die when..." Cal's face twisted as she tried to find the words she wanted. "For the first time in my life, I felt wrapped in the love of the Goddess. I knew she cared for me, that she had a job for me, and if I just put my trust in her, I'd be okay. I was warmed by her glory."

Cal smiled and spread her hands. "As you can see, I survived. I couldn't go back to my old ways, so I transferred to the Guards. And as I said, I knew the Goddess had a job she wanted me to do. Now I know what it is."

There was a second or two of silence before both of the older women turned to Natasha. Her feeling of awkwardness returned in a surge. She did not see that she had any skills to match those of the others; neither could she claim to have been hand-picked for the mission by Celaeno. She looked at Cal with something approaching envy and mumbled, "I think I was chosen just because I look like one of the heretics."

Rohanna smiled supportively. "Yes, and it's not as trivial a qualification as it might seem. Yours was the hardest place to fill. The daughter of the family had just turned eighteen." Natasha opened her mouth to speak, but Rohanna held up a finger. "I know you're a couple of years older, but you shouldn't have any problem carrying it off. However, there was no one in the Intelligence Corps who could even begin to fit the part. We tend to be a bit on the mature side. It wasn't easy finding someone young enough with the necessary qualities. You come highly recommended by your captain."

Natasha's eyes dropped to the table as she tried not to look conceited. She was caught by surprise when Rohanna deliberately reached over to rub her head; a casual gesture—a maternal gesture. Rohanna continued speaking, "And we've been even luckier with your appearance than I dared hope. I was expecting hair to be a problem. There's only a month until we have to meet our heretic guide, but by then, your hair should be nicely inconspicuous."

Natasha felt her cheeks go red. "I was going to get it cut, but it—"

Rohanna interrupted her. "Obviously, the Goddess intervened. She knew you'd be playing the part of a civilian."

"Is this a way of telling me I'm going to have to wear a wig?" Cal asked dryly.

Rohanna threw back her head and gave a yelp of laughter. "No. The risk of having it spotted would be much too high. And we should be okay. It would have been awkward if all of us had turned up with crewcuts, but one out of three shouldn't raise suspicions."

Her face became more serious, and she leaned forward. "Now, let's move on. I'm afraid you've got me to thank for all of this, as it was my idea. When the three heretics were brought here for interrogation, it occurred to me that I matched the general physical description of one, and from a little questioning, I realized that it wouldn't be hard to pass myself off as her. The family was from Clemswood, well to the east. They were newly inducted into the heresy, and to date, their contact has been solely with one of the heretics' spies. As far as we can tell, no one we're likely to meet in Westernfort has seen them, but reports describing them will have been sent back."

Rohanna's eyes became harder. "These three heretics were helpful—far more so than usual. They needed very little inducement to tell us everything: where they were going, when they were due to get there, even the code words to identify themselves. Normally, we'd have sent Guards to capture the people waiting for them, but I've managed to get permission to try this instead.

"The prize is high, and the Goddess has given us a great opportunity, but she isn't doing everything for us. We're going to have to work to prove ourselves worthy. We've got a tight schedule, and we have to leave Landfall tomorrow. It doesn't give us long to learn our roles. So a few words about us—and remember that from now on, the word is *us*, not *them*."

Rohanna got to her feet and began to pace around the table. "I regret I must inform you that we're degenerates, even by the standards of the heretics. Petty criminals; horse thieves." Her hands fell on Natasha's shoulders. "Despite her youth, our fine daughter here has already got a couple of convictions. Over the years, we've had to skip from town to town, keeping ahead of the Militia. Of course, we'll be vague about it, since we don't want to worry our new friends, but with any luck, they'll already know a bit about our background. So the good thing is that even if we make up things and contradict each other, it won't be out of character."

She moved on to Cal. "We are lovers." Rohanna bent down, planted a quick kiss on her lips and then stood up. Cal's face went through a range of expressions, starting with astonishment and ending in amusement. Rohanna patted her shoulder. "Don't worry. We've been together for twenty-three years, so no one will expect us to be too...enthusiastic."

Rohanna crossed to a small locker and pulled out a sheaf of papers. She returned to the table and sat down. "This is a copy of all the information we have about us. We'll spend some time going through it. But don't make the mistake of thinking that memorizing the facts is the difficult bit. The difficult bit is what I just demonstrated. We're a family. We have to be happy joking with each other, arguing with each other, touching each other, and not looking self-conscious when we do it."

She spread the papers across the table. "Obviously, we won't be able to take these with us when we leave, so let's start reading..."

❖

Night had fallen by the time Rohanna dismissed them. Natasha returned to the small bedroom. She had been told that she was now part of the Intelligence Corps and would sleep in the block. Her possessions had already been removed from the dormitory of the 3rd Company, although they had not been brought over. Nothing to link her with her old life could be taken with them on the mission. All she would have were things belonging to the young heretic she was impersonating—no more than the clothes she was wearing and the one large rucksack standing in a corner of the room.

It was late, but Natasha did not feel ready to sleep. She stood by the window and stared out at the night sky. Both moons were visible, hanging low over the rooftops of Landfall—small, shining Laurel and the larger crescent of Hardie. The things she had learned that day kept running around her head. Rohanna's instruction had covered more than just details of the family's background; she had also instructed them in the heretics' beliefs. Obviously, they could not be ignorant of the very teachings that had made them fugitives. Yet hearing the sacrilegious nonsense had made Natasha feel soiled. The claims were so absurd that she could have taken them as a tasteless joke, if it were not true that some people actually believed them.

Natasha wished she had a copy of *The Book of the Elder-Ones* to read. It would have been comforting, but it was hardly likely that there would be one in the rucksack of the young heretic. Natasha closed her eyes and began to quote softly from the first chapter, reciting the words from memory:

> *At the start of time, there was only Unsa, the spirit of life, who called the stars into being and cast them into the dark void and named them. Then, so she might*

better know her creation, Unsa took form and made
of herself Celaeno, the mother, that Unsa might have
material presence in her universe. For ten thousand
years, Celaeno searched the depths of space, seeking
a home for her children, and in her belly slept the
Elder-Ones, who were not born of this world, who
would arrange all things according to her design.

The heretics did not believe that Celaeno was the physical manifestation of the Goddess and the holy mother of all the women on earth. They did not believe that the Elder-Ones were semidivine creatures with knowledge and abilities far exceeding those of ordinary women, who, now that their mortal toil was done, existed as spirits, watching over the children of the Goddess. They did not believe that Himoti was the greatest of the Elder-Ones, who had created the Imprinters and cloners with the power and sanctity of her prayers.

Natasha shook her head in horrified bewilderment as she reflected on what the heretics actually did believe. They held that humans were native to another planet, somewhere else far across the galaxy. On this world, the people had practiced a miraculous science that had enabled them to make ships that could fly between the stars, and Celaeno was merely one of these ships. The ship had been made to take a colony team to a new planet, but it had malfunctioned and stranded the crew far from the world that had been their goal. In the teachings of the heretics, the Elder-Ones were no more than these lost crew members.

The teachings became ever more bizarre. They claimed that like wild animals, humans originally had two sexes, but the males had been unable to function in the new, alien environment, so Himoti had engineered the healer sense, using no more than the preposterous science of the mythical home planet.

Natasha's face grew pensive as she thought of the healer sense—the extrasensory ability that allowed women to manipulate the bodies of others. Natasha herself was totally devoid of the gift, but many were able to use it to good effect, curing illness and repairing injury. Those who had the gift to a greater degree could induce domestic animals to clone themselves, and a few—

Celaeno's chosen—could mentally step inside a cloned cell and imprint new patterns on the DNA within, so that the child would also carry the genetic code of the birth mother's partner. The healer sense was the sacred proof of Celaeno's love for her children, and the heretics reduced it to a mechanical contrivance made by human tinkering rather than divine grace.

The teachings of the heretics came from Gina Renamed, who alleged that she had discovered these *truths* while working in the temple library. The woman was clearly mad or evil, and probably both. The same could be assumed for her followers. However, Rohanna had said that the three Guards needed to immerse themselves in the roles they would be playing.

Natasha left the window and sat down on the bed. How could she even pretend to believe such foul lunacy?

She pulled the rucksack over and began to empty the contents, hoping for an insight into Jess Korski, the woman she would be impersonating. There was nothing—just the pathetic, cheap belongings of a small-time thief on the run. Natasha looked at the boots she was wearing. The hard brown leather was creased and cracked. Remnants of the lining stuck out in tufts around her ankles. The soles had been worn down and patched repeatedly. She tried to imagine the roads the woman had walked along—the journey, both physical and spiritual, that had brought her to Landfall and to her death. Natasha's frown deepened. Rohanna had not given any details but had spoken of the young heretic in the past tense.

Natasha began to repack the rucksack, trying to silence the sudden doubts assailing her. Executing the heretic was the only sane and proper action that the Sisterhood could have taken. The blasphemy could not be allowed to spread, corrupting still more of Celaeno's children. But Jess had been a young woman, younger even than Natasha herself. She should have had a full life ahead of her.

Natasha pulled the drawstring tight and tossed the rucksack aside, her face grim. Jess' life had been ruined and wasted, and it was the fault of the leaders of the heretics. They were the ones who were responsible for the death of the real Jess Korski—dispersing their lies and infecting others with their sickness. In executing them, she would be avenging the death of the young heretic and all the others who had fallen in the battle between good and evil.

Natasha pulled off her outer clothes and knelt beside the bed to pray before sleeping. Jess Korski had died a heretic, severed from the love of the Goddess. By the teaching of the Sisterhood, her soul would be lost forever, but it did not seem fair to be deprived of both this world and the next. Maybe even after death, her soul could re-enter a state of grace.

With a simple intensity, Natasha prayed to Celaeno to forgive the heretic and show her mercy, and to grant success to the mission so that no others might suffer Jess' fate.

❖

Natasha awoke before dawn the next day and joined Cal and Rohanna for a quick breakfast. The sky was just lightening to washed gray as they crossed the gravel paths of the Guards' headquarters and reached a little-used side entrance. They stepped into the narrow street beyond, where two sentries stood on duty. Civilians leaving in such a furtive manner should have been stopped and questioned, yet neither of the uniformed women moved a muscle. It seemed to Natasha that they were making a deliberate point of not seeing her.

The sounds of her footsteps echoed sharply from the blank brick walls of the alleyway until the side street joined a larger thoroughfare. The first carts of the day were rumbling over the cobbles, and the shutters above their heads were being flung open. Rohanna led the way toward the docks in search of passage downriver. Following her, Natasha thought about the inaction of the sentries. It was a small thing, but the memory left her feeling strangely uneasy, a feeling that intensified as the people on the street passed her by without a second glance.

To say that she felt invisible was too simplistic and not quite accurate. Natasha knew she would be playing a role and had expected to feel like an actress, but instead, she felt as if she were the only real thing, and the world around her was the part that was false. She viewed the familiar street like a detached observer. Nobody knew what or who she was, apart from Rohanna and Cal. They were her only link with the truth.

Rohanna looked back at her and smiled. Something in her eyes said she understood Natasha's sense of displacement, but all she said aloud was, "Come on, Jess. Don't dawdle. We've got a long way to go."

CHAPTER FOUR—THE VIGILANCE OF THE MILITIA

The town of Newsteading looked dreary in the light of a gray late-September afternoon. Natasha jumped off the back of the farm cart and turned up her jacket collar against the fine mist of drizzle. Rohanna handed the driver a few coins as a token of gratitude for the ride before joining the other two Guards on the cobbled main square. They huddled together as if for mutual protection from the rain.

"We're doing well. Only about fifty kilometers left before our rendezvous with the heretics." Rohanna spoke quietly, although nobody else was anywhere within earshot.

"What now?" Cal asked

Rohanna weighed up the purse in her hand. "Well, this is the last town we go through. From here on, there's only a scattering of hamlets, and we won't find much to spend our money on. How about we splurge on a night at an inn?"

"You could talk me into it." Cal grinned.

"Although we'll have to stay in character and pick the cheapest one in town."

"As long as it has a roof over it and serves hot meals, I won't complain."

Neither would Natasha. The long walk across the Homelands had been grueling. Hitched rides, like the last one, had been a rare break. Most nights, they had slept in the open or burrowed into haystacks. The weather had been kind for the first weeks of the journey, but with the start of autumn, rain had arrived. She still had not dried out properly after the last miserable night, with no more than a hedgerow for shelter.

Newsteading offered a choice of three inns. A quick appraisal of the frontages left no doubt which would meet Rohanna's role-playing requirement. Natasha looked around as they entered. The tavern was decidedly seedy, the furniture pitted and split with age, the flagstones sticky from spilled beer. Yet despite the shabby decor, the fire burning in the hearth was welcoming, and the warmth had attracted a fair crowd of locals. The most boisterous section was gathered around the fire, talking and jostling in a reasonably well-meaning way.

Once Rohanna had bargained with the innkeeper for a room and a meal, the three Guards occupied a small table in a dark corner, well toward the rear. To Natasha's surprise, Rohanna ordered them beer to drink with their food. Guards were supposed to renounce alcohol. Then Natasha smiled at her own inexperience. Of course—in such surroundings, abstinence would have made them very conspicuous.

The beer arrived shortly, and she took a sip. The bitter taste brought back thoughts of her time in the Militia, as did the sounds and smells of the tavern. She eased down in her chair, and her eyes drifted idly over the scene. It had a distinctly rural feel but was not so very different from many bars in Landfall—such as the one where she had first kissed Beatrice. The memory jarred uncomfortably. Natasha batted it away.

At the other side of the table, Rohanna and Cal were engaged in a conversation about the state of Cal's boots; a mundane topic pursued with the casual familiarity of long-standing partners. Natasha listened intermittently, paying attention more to the affectionate tones than to the actual words. Over the previous month, the pair had developed a way of talking and a set of gestures to create such a good pretence of being lovers that even Natasha was sometimes half convinced that they were. They both displayed more tenderness toward Natasha than her real mother had ever shown. Natasha did not think, and did not want to think, that this was also purely an act.

On the third day after leaving Landfall, when the blisters were at their most painful, the thought struck Natasha that they could have traveled most of the way openly as Guards, adopting their disguise only when the mountains were in sight. They could have ridden on horseback, changing mounts at military way stations, and completed the distance in less than half the time, allowing more opportunity for training. But Rohanna had been right; the most crucial thing was learning how to treat one another like family, and for this purpose, the journey had been ideal. They had been thrown into continuous close contact, working together for a common goal and isolated from all other support. It had fostered deep trust among them. Never had Natasha felt so close to her comrades as she did with Rohanna and Cal.

She settled back in the warmth of the tavern and watched their faces. Not for the first time, she wondered what her childhood would have been like if they really had been her parents. They were people it would be easy to love, respect, and trust. She would never have felt like an unwanted encumbrance, never felt frightened to go home, never felt ashamed to acknowledge them.

Natasha's brooding was interrupted by the experimental twangs of someone tuning a guitar. She sighed and dismissed the pointless game of "If Only." All around the tavern, people were looking expectantly at the woman with the guitar. Natasha hooked her arm over the back of her seat, twisting to get a better view of the musician. From the way the woman handled the instrument, she was clearly one of the locals, rather than a professional entertainer—a view confirmed when she began thumping out a simple set of chords. But her voice was passable.

> *The western mountains tower high,*
> *Their rivers deep and cold,*
> *And there dwells Kimberly Ramon,*
> *The Ranger captain bold.*
>
> *The Guards have tried to conquer her,*
> *But she had victory.*
> *Now Captain Ramon's Rangers ride*
> *The mountains, brave and free.*
>
> *For all the Sisters' traps and plots,*
> *Ramon cannot be caught.*
> *She lives safe with her love behind*
> *The walls of Westernfort.*

The smile froze on Natasha's face. The ban on the song was broken frequently. You would hear it sung in half the taverns in Landfall if you waited long enough, unless you were wearing a Guard's uniform. And the singer here could not be blamed for being unaware that she had three Guards in her audience. Even so, the brazen glorification of Kimberly Ramon made Natasha scowl.

Cal reached across the table and tapped her arm. Natasha leaned over to hear her whisper. "Smile. Remember, she's our hero."

Natasha cursed herself. After all her preparation, she had let her role slip at the first provocation. Fortunately, no one in the tavern was looking in her direction, and at that moment, one of the bar staff arrived with the food to provide further distraction. Natasha forced a smile onto her face as she attacked her meal. Before long, she would be meeting Kimberly Ramon in person. And killing her.

❖

The door was kicked in with a crash. Half-asleep, Natasha tried to struggle free of her bedding, but before she could rise, a harsh voice barked out, "Nobody move!" Someone was holding a lantern high. The swaying light filled the small inn room, little more than two meters square, with its tiny window set in the sloping roof. There were no furnishings apart from the two straw-stuffed pallets on the floor. There were also no weapons, no escape, and nowhere to hide.

Natasha could see Rohanna and Cal on the other mattress, sitting up, surprise on their faces. Her fists clenched in reflex, and she was about to leap up, but Rohanna slowly raised her hands in a gesture of surrender. The action was backed up by an expression of fear, yet Natasha was certain that the response was part of an act. After a month in their company, Natasha knew her companions better than to think that either would panic so easily, and the memory of the instruction given her in Landfall echoed in her head: *When in doubt, follow my lead.* Rohanna wanted to keep up the pretense of being ordinary citizens.

Natasha willed herself to remain lying on the mattress on the floor, with the blankets half thrown aside. She shielded her eyes from the light and peered up. In the doorway stood two members of the Militia in their black uniforms. One was a captain with a star and bar on her badge. Her fists rested arrogantly on her hips. The other was a private, holding the lantern, and clearly less confident; her free hand clutched the grip on her truncheon. In the dimness of the corridor beyond were at least three other Militiawomen.

Natasha rested back on her elbows and stared at them, her initial alarm fading to confusion. Rohanna was right not to make trouble and draw more attention to themselves. The raid by the Militia had to be a misunderstanding; maybe they had been mistaken for some others. All that was needed was to sort out the mistake, and the Militia would leave—probably looking rather sheepish for disturbing the sleep of honest citizens.

"Are we all awake now?" the captain jeered sarcastically.

"Wh...what's this?" Rohanna's tone was of bewildered innocence.

"What's this all about?" The captain finished the sentence. "Well, why don't you tell me?"

"I...what?"

The Militia captain glared at them each in turn and then snapped out the question, "What are your names?"

"I'm Rohanna Korski; this is my partner, Calinda Rowse; and that's our daughter, Jess." Rohanna spoke meekly.

"Where are you from?"

"Clemswood, east of Landfall."

"You're a long way from home." The captain's assertion was undeniable. "Why are you here?"

"We're on our way to Winterford. Cal's sister lives there. She's got us jobs in the town." Rohanna gave the prearranged story.

"Your sister lives in Winterford?" The captain snarled at Cal, who nodded in confirmation. "Well, call me a skeptic, but I don't believe you. I think you're a bunch of heretics hoping to scurry off into the wildlands."

Natasha could have laughed at the irony of it. She looked at Rohanna, wondering what the intelligence agent would do. Was there a code word by which she could identify herself? Rohanna did not slip from her role, however. "N...no, we are j...just—"

The captain cut off Rohanna's stuttering. "You're just innocent weary travelers on your way." She snorted. "Maybe you are. The good thing is that it won't be hard to check your story, and the even better thing is that it ain't my job to do it. There's a company of Guards stationed up the road at Longhill. Tomorrow, I'll send you to them. With a suitable escort. The Guards can try to find this sister of yours, and if they can't find her, I'm sure they'll be more than happy to deal with you...it's the sort of thing they enjoy. But for tonight, I will offer you the hospitality of our humble town jail." Her voice rose again to a shout. "Come on, now. On your feet, facing the wall, hands above your head."

Carefully, Rohanna moved to obey, avoiding any sudden action that might be misconstrued. Natasha and Cal exchanged an angry glance before following the lead of the intelligence agent. Neither was feeling kindly toward the aggressive woman in black. Once all three had complied with the order, the captain stepped aside and gestured her subordinates into the room. Natasha felt her hands dragged behind her back and bound; then she was roughly pushed out of the room while one of the Militiawomen collected their belongings.

As they were taken through the tavern, Natasha saw the innkeeper watching them with a smug expression and jangling some coins in her hand. Natasha told herself that she should be pleased by the vigilance of the Militia, even if they did it by paying bribes to informers, but it was hard to muster the enthusiasm for heartfelt congratulations.

From the position of the one visible moon, Natasha estimated that it was close to midnight. The streets of Newsteading were dark and deserted. The sound of the Militia boots on the cobbles echoed in the silence. The three prisoners were barefoot—something Natasha was painfully aware of on the cold, uneven surface. They wore only the light clothes they had been sleeping in. It was an extra disincentive to running away. Fortunately, it was only a two minute walk to the town jail.

The street door opened directly into a large, well-lit room, its layout instantly familiar to Natasha from her time in the Landfall Militia. Station briefing rooms were the same across the Homelands, right down to the unwashed tea mugs and half-eaten sandwiches by the stove in the corner. A long table stood at one side, surrounded by an assortment of haphazardly arranged chairs. A weapon rack was bolted to one wall; wooden lockers covered another. Natasha would have laid money that at least a third of them contained illicit alcohol.

A very solid door stood in one corner—presumably leading to the lockup. Natasha's guess was confirmed when they were herded through, but she discovered two marked differences from a similar facility in Landfall. For one thing, the cell itself was quite small, little bigger than the room they had left behind at the inn, and second, they were alone. The lockups she had known would have held at least a dozen occupants by this time of night.

Once they were in the cell, the Militiawomen removed the ropes from their wrists. The door was slammed shut, followed by the sound of the key turning in the lock. The captain muttered quietly for a while, obviously giving instructions that she did not want the prisoners to overhear. Then the street door opened and closed. It was a fair bet that the captain and some of the Militia had returned to their beds, but there were still at least two jailers left on duty, judging by the simultaneous screeching of chair legs on the tiled floor.

It was dark in the cell. The high, barred window let in only a hint of starlight. The main source of illumination was the ten-centimeter gap under the door. Natasha's eyes took a while to adjust, but even before she could see clearly, Rohanna put an arm around her shoulders and hugged her close. Cal was also drawn into the embrace. Natasha realized immediately that the gesture was not merely intended to offer comfort, although that was how it would look if they were interrupted.

With their heads close together, Rohanna started to whisper very softly. "Don't worry. I can get us out."

"You know a code word to prove to intelligence agents who we really are?" Natasha said.

"Well...I do, but I'm not going to tell it to anyone here. For one thing, they won't recognize it, and for another, we can't trust the local Militia. This close to the borders, it's not unlikely for some to be in league with the heretics. If we tell the truth, the captain still won't believe us, and spies might send word on ahead."

"So what do we do?" Cal whispered.

"We do it the hard way and escape." Rohanna grinned. "And as soon as possible. If we waste time going to Longhill, we'll miss the rendezvous with our guide."

"And you know how to escape." Cal's tone contained humor rather than skepticism.

"Of course." Rohanna started fumbling at the waist of her pants. After a few seconds of manipulating the thick hem, she extracted a thin piece of metal. She stood and held it out. "I present...one lock pick." Despite her triumphant tone, her voice stayed at a whisper.

Natasha stared at the lock pick in astonishment—and admiration. The Intelligence Corps sent its agents out well prepared.

Rohanna continued speaking. "We'll give them another twenty minutes to calm down. Then, Jess, I want you to look under the door and warn me if anyone comes near. And Cal, can you make noise to cover the sound of the pick? Give us a song."

"My singing is pretty dire," Cal warned. "Snoring would be better. And just as musical."

"That will be fine."

The twenty minutes passed painfully slowly, but eventually, Rohanna gave the signal to begin. The gap under the door was probably designed to allow food to be pushed in without unlocking the cell. It gave Natasha a good view of the briefing room when she lay down, pressing her cheek against the hard floor. There were three jailers, visible from the waist down. Judging by their conversation, the nearest two, sitting at the table, were playing cards. The third was next to the stove with her feet up on another chair.

Natasha stayed a little way back from the door, close enough to see all three Militiawomen, but not so that her face was in the light, where it would be obvious to anyone glancing over. Rohanna stood above her, working carefully at the lock. From the rear of the cell, Cal gave an unbroken succession of snores, sufficient to mask any clinks or scratching but not so extreme as to seem false.

Ten minutes passed before Rohanna tapped Natasha and indicated that she could leave her post as lookout. The older woman briefly took the vacated spot on the floor, studying the room outside. She stood up and said aloud, "Hey, Cal, you're snoring. Can't you give us some peace?"

"Huh...what?" Cal joined in the act, sounding like someone roused from sleep.

"You were snoring," Rohanna repeated.

"Oh. Sorry."

In the following quiet, Rohanna gathered them together for a last set of instructions. "Right. That's the first bit done. The door's unlocked, and there's three Militiawomen to deal with, so we get one each. Cal, if you take the one on the left of the table, I'll take the one on the right. Jess, you go for the one by the stove. She's the farthest away, but I'm sure she's asleep, so you should have no trouble in getting to her before she starts moving. Okay?"

Natasha nodded. Rohanna moved to the door. On the fingers of one hand, she silently beat out the count of three. Then she threw the door open. Natasha leapt through immediately after the others. In three steps, she had crossed the room.

As Rohanna had predicted, the sleeping jailer had barely opened her eyes by the time Natasha reached her. She was a big woman, her weight mainly muscle, although there was a touch too much fat as well. Her nose looked as if it had been broken more than once. There were healing scabs on her knuckles. Even before she was fully conscious, her face had twisted into a savage scowl, and her hands were clenched in fists. The station thug. Natasha recognized the type. The sort of Militiawoman who enjoyed a brawl and would deliberately start one when things got too quiet. She would be useful with her fists; otherwise, she would not have survived long in the job. Natasha smiled wryly; she was not without talent in such things herself. A childhood spent playing in the marketplace in Landfall was a good starting point, and the formal lessons in the Guards had sharpened her skills in unarmed combat.

The woman dropped her feet to the floor and began to stand. She swung her arm wildly—an action clearly intended to keep Natasha away and allow herself time to rise—but Natasha ducked around the careless punch and thumped her own fist into the woman's solar plexus. The jailer keeled over, bent almost double, wheezing. Natasha caught hold of her opponent's arm, twisted it up her back, and then wrapped her own free arm around the woman's throat, stifling any cry. Natasha felt very pleased with herself—until she smelled the alcohol and realized that the jailer was drunk, which took some of the satisfaction out of the easy victory.

Natasha looked to the other side of the room. Cal and Rohanna between them had one Militiawoman held down securely. The other was motionless, sprawled across the table. Rohanna glanced up at the same time as Natasha. Their eyes met, and Rohanna grinned. "That's part two gone to plan. Now let's get these locked up and reclaim our things."

Natasha's opponent still had not regained her breath by the time she was shoved into the cell. She made no resistance as she was tied and gagged. The other conscious Militiawoman was outnumbered and unable to cause problems as she was also bound. Rohanna felt for a pulse in the neck of the third woman.

"She's alive." Rohanna's voice made her relief plain.

With Cal's help, the woman was carried into the cell, and the door was locked. Meanwhile, Natasha searched the room. Their rucksacks, boots, and outdoor clothes were in a pile under the bench beside the lockers. In little more than a minute, they were all ready to go. Rohanna edged the street door ajar and peered through the crack; then she gestured to the others to follow and slipped out noiselessly into the night.

The town streets were as silent and empty as when they had been taken to the station. Rohanna led the way along alleyways and around the edges of darkened squares. At one point, they heard the sound of heavy Militia boots on cobbles, but it came from an adjoining street and was only the unhurried tread of a routine patrol. Rohanna and Cal moved without sound. Natasha tried to copy their stealthy progress, but she felt clumsy by comparison. It was a skill that the other two had learned in the course of their duty, Cal in the Rangers and Rohanna in the Intelligence Corps.

Newsteading was not large. Soon, the buildings became spread out. Terraced rows changed to detached houses surrounded by walled gardens and then open plots of vegetables. Without any marked transition, Natasha found that they were on a rough track through farmland. The route carried on across the fields for a couple of kilometers, but not too far ahead were tree-covered hills. The dark, rounded shapes were clearly visible in the light of the second rising moon. Cal led the way, wherever possible keeping to the shadows of the hedgerow.

Natasha started to feel less tense, but she was not really relaxed until they reached the trees and the town was hidden from sight. The road went straight through the forest, but before they had gone far, Cal called a halt.

"Do you think it might be an idea to leave the road? They'll overtake us quickly enough on horseback, but I'd challenge any Militiawoman to catch me in a forest."

"Yes. A very good idea," Rohanna agreed.

It was dark under the trees, but with Cal in the lead, they made better progress through the snarled undergrowth than Natasha would have thought possible. Still Cal moved without sound. In the dim light, Natasha could not understand how the ex-Ranger managed to avoid the twigs that snapped under her own feet, and she noted that Rohanna now did little better than herself.

After a couple of hours, they stopped for a rest. Everyone was in high spirits, and for once, even Rohanna did not try to keep in character. But then, the chances of being overheard in the middle of a forest were very slim. When she thought about their escape, Natasha felt a childish urge to giggle. She smiled at her two comrades. She had come to respect them as people, and now she could see that their skills were also something to be admired. Rohanna in turn was looking at her with approval.

"You did well with your opponent. You had her flattened without a squeak, and she wasn't a small challenge—a lot bigger and tougher than I expected. It was hard to judge from looking at her under the door. But like I said, you coped with her easily."

"I can't take too much credit. She was drunk," Natasha admitted honestly, though she felt herself blushing at the praise.

"Don't be so modest. Women like that are at their most dangerous with a bit inside them."

"And you didn't do badly yourself," Cal joined in, addressing Rohanna.

"A touch too well. I wanted to be sure I overpowered the woman, so I went in hard and overdid it. I was frightened I'd killed her. I wouldn't want to be responsible for the death of a faithful daughter of the Goddess."

"In the circumstances..." Cal began.

"For the glory of the Goddess, I'll do whatever I have to, but it would still have been a little too close to murder." Rohanna's voice held grim undertones that spoke of bad memories. "We had to escape, but if I'd been thinking properly, we wouldn't have been caught in the first place. I'm afraid the local Militia were a bit more effective than I expected. In most towns, they're no use for anything other than common criminals. This lot must have paid attention to the alert for a group matching our descriptions."

"Who'd have sent them our description?" Natasha was confused.

"Well, strictly speaking, it's the description of the three real heretics, but it fits us as well, of course. When the family first fled, the word went out. Which was how we caught them in Landfall. We couldn't then send another message telling everyone to stop looking for them. If the heretics heard, they'd know that the real family had been captured."

"People have been hunting us ever since we left Landfall?" Natasha said in surprise.

"Yes. Weren't you warned?"

"Sort of, but we haven't had any trouble so far. And I just assumed..." Natasha's voice faded, she was not too sure what she had assumed.

"Ah, but I know the net set to catch heretics, so I know the holes in it." Rohanna spoke with a faint tinge of irony. "That's why we haven't had any problems. But my information for this region was obviously out of date. There used to be an old captain who was utterly incompetent. It would seem that she's been replaced."

"Typical Militia. You can't even trust them to make a mess of things when you want them to," Cal joked.

"True. It's always awkward when you end up fighting people who are on your side when they don't know it. If things had turned nasty during our escape, I wouldn't have been the first intelligence agent to be killed by her allies," Rohanna concluded, and again, there were the echoes of old regrets.

"You did well with the lock pick," Natasha said, to change the subject.

Cal laughed. "What other surprises did the Intelligence Corps send you out with?"

"It wasn't from the Corps," Rohanna said. "Like you, I don't have a single thing that wasn't taken from the heretics when they were captured. I told you they were thieves. When we found the hidden lock pick, we weren't too sure whether I should keep it. It wouldn't make us popular with our new friends if they found it on me, but in the end, we decided it gave authenticity to my impersonation."

"Obviously, the Goddess guided your decision," Cal said piously.

"Obviously," Rohanna agreed.

"And you knew how to use the lock pick," Natasha added—something else that had impressed her.

Rohanna smiled at the tone of admiration. "Oh, yes. One picks up all sorts of useful skills in the Intelligence Corps."

Chapter Five—Rendezvous

Two days later, they stood atop an open ridge. The ground was covered in untidy tufts of rough grass, bent by the cold wind blowing from the north. A blanket of heavy cloud hung low overhead. The air felt damp. Behind them in the valley, a few squat huts and barns were strewn around a muddy farmyard. Natasha stood for a moment, looking back on the scene in the dismal light; then she adjusted the straps of her rucksack and turned to follow the other two over the brow of the hill and into the straggly brush land of the next valley. They had passed the boundary of the Homelands. Ahead was nothing but wilderness until they reached Westernfort.

They walked for another three hours, while the light faded to a premature dusk. It would rain before nightfall. In the middle of a broad expanse of grass, Rohanna called a halt. Nothing around them on the hillside grew more than knee high. The other two huddled close, trying to provide mutual shelter against the biting gusts of wind.

"Okay. I think there's no risk of being overheard." Despite the obvious truth of her words, Rohanna's voice was a whisper. "However, the site for the rendezvous is on the other side of this hill, an abandoned homestead, and we are most likely being watched right now. One reason people were happy to let me try this scheme is because even if we'd sent a company to arrest the heretic guide, it was by no means certain the attempt would have succeeded. Heretics can be very hard to sneak up on. Once they meet us, they may realize we aren't the people they were expecting, but this is still the best chance of getting close enough to capture or kill them. Of course, if they fall for the disguise, killing the sacrilegious Imprinter and the other leaders in Westernfort will be a far greater prize."

Natasha's stomach contracted. Suddenly, everything was very serious.

"If we're being watched, won't they wonder what we're talking about now?" Cal asked.

"They might. But I think even the real family might have stopped to discuss some of the things I intend to talk about." Rohanna gave a lopsided smile. "If the information I got from the prisoners was correct, we'll identify ourselves by giving the right answers to a set of three questions. The questions themselves are innocuous; it's the wording that's important."

"Does the blue pig sing at midnight?" Cal suggested with dry irony.

Natasha looked at her in amazement. She understood the reference to the antics of heretic spies, but she could not understand how Cal could joke so casually.

Rohanna was merely amused. "Nothing so melodramatic. In fact, the questions are structured to sound very ordinary in the circumstances, just in case an innocent traveler stumbles upon the homestead by mistake. The first question is 'Are you lost?' And the main thing I want to say is, leave it to me to answer. Neither of you say anything until I've completed the sequence and the heretic guide has indicated that we've been accepted.

"The next thing I want to say is that it may all go wrong, and it's hard to make plans. I don't know how many heretics will be there—maybe only the one. Hopefully we won't be outnumbered if it turns nasty. But if arrows start flying, try to do something sensible. I can't give any better advice than that. If I sense things are going awry, but we have a little time, I'll snap my fingers. Count to three in your head and then move. If it's my left hand, turn and run. If it's my right hand, draw your knife and leap on the nearest heretic."

Natasha's mouth was dry. She tried to match Cal's calm expression, but it was not easy with her jaw clenched. Rohanna looked at her and then wrapped an arm around her shoulders, reaching out with her other hand to include Cal in the hug—a nice family gesture for any observer. Whether it was part of an act or not, Natasha was grateful for the comfort.

"There's one more thing." Rohanna's voice dropped even lower. "This may be the last chance we ever have to speak without being overheard. During this past month, I've gotten to know you very well. No woman could ask for better comrades in arms. I want to say how much I respect you both, and how proud I am to fight and die by your sides, for the glory of Celaeno."

"The same goes for me," Cal added solemnly.

Natasha could do no more than nod, but the tension in her stomach melted a little. Instinctively, she put her own arms around the other two and squeezed them. Cal rubbed a hand over her head and smiled. Then Rohanna stepped back to break up the huddle and started on the way up the hillside.

A light drizzle was starting as they reached the top, and their destination came into view. The deserted longhouse lay on the slope below them, with drystone walls and a turf-covered roof. The building was the typical homestead of poor farmers. At one end was a cattle byre; at the other end were the domestic quarters, with a dairy and workshop in between. It was obvious that no one farmed there currently. The vegetable patch contained nothing aside from weeds, and there were several holes in the roof, but the basic structure looked sound. Natasha did not know why anyone had chosen to live out here or why they had abandoned the building, but the sight was immensely comforting. The information acquired from the family of heretics had been accurate, at least in describing the location of the rendezvous.

As they drew closer, it was also apparent that someone had arrived before them. A thin trail of smoke seeped from the chimney, and the faint sound of horses came from the byre. The women rounded the end of the building and paused at the door. Then Rohanna raised her hand and knocked. A voice called out in answer.

Natasha could feel her pulse racing, and she fought the urge to look to the others for reassurance. *But it's okay*, she told herself, *surely a certain amount of nervousness won't be out of character*. Rohanna pushed open the door and stepped inside. Cal and Natasha crowded into the entrance behind her.

The interior was dark and smelled of mildew and smoke. The earthen floor was uneven. A young woman was crouched by the hearth. She had obviously been tending the fire; one hand held a small branch, and the other was hidden behind a pile of kindling. The glowing embers in the grate did not cast enough light to show the details of the room.

The woman looked up and asked, "Are you lost?" The delivery could not have been less dramatic, but Natasha felt her heart thump against her ribs.

"Not anymore," Rohanna answered firmly.

"What brings you out here?"

"We're heading west."

"Do you know the way?"

"We'd heard you could take us."

That was three questions. In the following silence, Natasha began to relax. From what she could see over Rohanna's shoulder, the heretic appeared to be satisfied with the answers. The kneeling woman stared into the fire, her lips pursed. Then she turned back and said deliberately, "And when shall we set out?" She looked at them steadily, expectantly, awaiting the reply.

Rohanna floundered. "Er...she didn't say...I don't think..." Then Natasha noticed that Rohanna's right hand was raised, fingers ready to snap, miming the gesture of someone trying to summon a memory.

Natasha could not take her eyes off Rohanna's fingers. Then a curt voice behind them said, "Dani, you've got to stop winding people up. This isn't a game."

Natasha spun around, banging her shoulder against the door frame. In the open, a few meters away, stood a woman, dressed in clothes roughly approximating a Ranger uniform, a drawn bow in her hands. Natasha froze in shock. She had not heard this woman's footsteps. Had Rohanna or Cal known that a second heretic was standing behind them? And were there any more? But even as these thoughts raced by, she saw that the bow was being lowered, and laughter came from inside the house.

"Oh, come on, Ash. I've been really sensible all summer. You can't expect me to keep it up forever."

Natasha's head jerked back. The solemn expression of the woman by the hearth had dissolved in amusement, but it quickly shifted to something faintly apologetic as she considered the three in the doorway. "I'm sorry. I was joking. Come in, and close the door."

Natasha felt sick at the thought of how close she had been to getting an arrow in the back. Then the woman by the hearth rose, revealing that she also was armed. The pile of kindling had concealed a small loaded crossbow. Natasha stared at the weapon, trying to work out what the odds would have been had it come to a fight. Three against two, but the Guards would have been caught in crossfire. It was a pointless and unpleasant calculation.

The second heretic was standing by Natasha's shoulder and noticed the direction of her gaze. "I know; it's worrying. With Dani's aim, I was in just as much danger as you. I strongly suspect she'd be hard put to hit a barn from the inside," the woman teased her companion.

"Oh. Um..." Natasha's mouth was too dry for her to answer. She jumped when Rohanna put a hand on her arm and gently pulled her farther into the room, clearing the doorway so that the second heretic could enter.

People shuffled around to give one another space. The heretic by the hearth put aside her crossbow, picked up an unlit lantern, and then made a spill by twisting strands of straw together. The sudden flare when she lit the wick highlighted her cheekbones, her head bent over the lantern. Natasha's pulse slowed. They had passed the first real test. She fought to calm herself, trying to concentrate on the two strangers. She dared not make a mistake through inattention.

Natasha estimated that the woman referred to as Dani was in her early twenties, lightly built and maybe a centimeter shorter than Natasha herself. Her face held an impish quality that was not entirely due to her mischievous grin. She gave no sign of being in the least offended by the aspersions cast on her marksmanship. The other woman was far older, easily past fifty, her skin etched by the weather. Yet her body was still strong and agile. Something about her made Natasha think of granite. You did not need to see the sword at her side to know she was a warrior.

This woman was, in turn, subjecting them to a thoughtful examination. Then she addressed the Intelligence Corps agent. "You must be Rohanna Korski."

Rohanna nodded in reply.

Natasha felt her tension reduce still further. Rohanna had told them that the heretics would have the names and descriptions of the real family. If the guide could "identify" Rohanna from the information, they must be believable in their roles.

The situation was clearly one in which introductions were appropriate. Rohanna placed an arm around Cal's shoulder and said, "This is my partner, Cal." Then she indicated the corner where Natasha had wedged herself. "And our daughter, Jess."

The warrior spoke again. "I'm Sergeant Aisha O'Neil, or Ash, if you prefer—"

She got no further; the other woman interrupted. "I think 'Ash' suits you best. It nicely suggests both wooden and burned out."

Ash sighed in mock exasperation and pointed with her thumb. "And that's Danielle Diwan."

"Dani," the woman herself amended, grinning broadly.

Natasha looked between the two women, suddenly aware of feeling both fascinated and repelled. A thought shot through her head. *These are heretics. I'm standing in a room with people who don't worship Celaeno.*

❖

While the dusk thickened, the wind dropped, and the rain began in earnest. The sound of its drumming on the thatch rose and faded in waves. Fortunately, the roof at the domestic end of the longhouse was still intact. The hillside opposite was lost in poor light and low cloud. There was nothing else to see, yet still Natasha stood in the half-open doorway, staring out blindly and listening to the conversation behind her with half an ear.

It quickly became apparent that Ash was their guide. Dani's role in the party was not yet explained. Ash had wanted to check their rucksacks so she could assess the state of their supplies. Judging from what was being said, Rohanna was actively helping her, while Cal and Dani stood on the sidelines. Natasha knew she should join in, but her stomach was a knot, and she did not think she was up to playing the part—talking with the heretics in the shifting blend of politeness, curiosity, and good humor with which strangers sounded each other out.

Cal broke a spell of silence by asking, "You called yourself 'Sergeant.' Are you a Ranger of some sort?"

The same question had occurred to Natasha. Ash's uniform was not standard, and the woman was far too old to be on active service. She listened with more attention to Ash's answer. "Oh, yes...some sort. I was a member of the 23rd Squadron before we deserted. Now I belong to the Westernfort defense force."

"But—" Cal began.

Dani interrupted. "I know. You're wondering what a geriatric is doing out in the field."

"The word is *veteran*," Ash said in a dry voice.

"It's not the word most people use for you," Dani quipped back.

"Are you a Ranger as well?"

Rohanna had asked this question, presumably of Dani, but before she could reply, Ash gave a bark of laughter. "Oh, no. We may not be a regular squadron, but we do have some standards. Why do you think they had to send me to escort her home?"

Dani made a quick retort that Natasha did not catch, but everyone else laughed.

"While you finish the inventory, shall I start dinner?" Cal volunteered. She was easily the best cook among the Guards.

"Sure, but don't let Dani help you. We don't want to lose sleep with indigestion," Ash said.

"Right." Dani's tone was of mock indignation. "I'll go and see to the horses. They don't complain about the food I give them."

"Only because you don't have to cook their hay."

There was more laughter. Then Rohanna raised her voice. "Jess, make yourself useful and help Dani. And close the door. It's cold enough in here without the extra draft."

It was an order, even though it was delivered in the style of parental nagging. Natasha knew she could not duck out of her part in the charade any longer. She trailed Dani down the length of the building, through the derelict workrooms, until they arrived in the animal byre. Seven horses were tethered loosely to the wall. The nearest one nuzzled against Dani's shoulder. Natasha watched with a confused muddle of thoughts. Somehow, she had half expected the animals to shy away from the heretic instinctively.

Dani stroked the horse's nose and then looked toward Natasha. "I'm sorry."

"Pardon?" Natasha was startled. Had she missed something?

"Playing tricks with the questions. I shouldn't have." A suppressed grin teased at the corners of Dani's mouth. "But your face was...um...quite amusing."

You nearly got us all killed. Natasha held back the angry words, and then the absurdity of it hit her. In associating with heretics, Natasha had envisaged having to work at hiding her disgust of foul-mouthed blasphemies and coarse, uncivil behavior. Of all the unpleasant personal traits she had imagined, a dubious sense of humor was decidedly on the mild side.

Dani left the horse and patted Natasha's arm, her grin gone. "I really am sorry. I didn't mean to frighten you. But these last five months have been..." She sighed and moved away again. "It's been a strain...worse than I'd imagined. I let the euphoria of leaving the Homelands get to me. I'm sorry. It was childish."

"You've been in the Homelands?" Natasha asked in surprise. She had assumed that both Ash and Dani had come directly from Westernfort.

"Yes, all summer. Following people, codes, passwords, secret messages, that sort of stuff."

"Oh, you're a..." *Spy.* Natasha swallowed the word. "Er... undercover agent."

Dani laughed. "Just this once, and never again. I don't have the temperament for it."

"So what are you normally?" Natasha asked uncertainly.

"Would you believe a potter?" At Natasha's bewildered expression, Dani grinned and went on. "There were hints that one of our real agents was passing on information to the Guards. Someone had to check up on her, and it had to be someone she wouldn't recognize, so they asked me." Dani paused. "Actually, there were a lot of people she wouldn't have recognized—probably, most of Westernfort—but she was a potter, so I was able to find work at the same pottery as her and get close that way without attracting suspicion."

"And was she passing on information?"

"Yes. But she won't anymore." Dani's face was grave.

"You killed her?"

"Not me, but yes, she's dead." Dani shrugged uncomfortably. "When I agreed to the job, I'd expected to be scared, and I was sometimes, but that wasn't the worst part. What I really hated was not being myself...trying to get someone's trust when she shouldn't have trusted me at all. Acting like nothing was wrong when I saw a group of Guards. Having to think about everything I said." Her expression adopted a rueful pout. "Which is all a long way of explaining why I mucked about when you arrived."

"That's all right," Natasha said, and it was. In a strange way, it was reassuring to know that Dani had also been working as an impostor. They were all playing the same sort of game, and none of them were enjoying it. Somehow, it made Natasha feel as though she fit in.

Dani turned around, indicated the horses, and picked up a brush. "They don't need much. They've been out grazing all day. We just have to check that they're happy and have enough water."

Natasha considered the horses. They were sturdy and deep-chested, although shorter than the mounts normally used by Guards. She patted one. "Where did you get them from?"

"Ash brought them with her from Westernfort."

Natasha frowned, trying to sort out the timing. "How did she know to bring enough for us?"

"She didn't. When she left Westernfort, she was expecting to meet just me, but she had a string of horses with her to sell to the local hill farmers. Luckily, I'd gotten word you were coming. I was only a few days ahead of you, so we held onto enough horses for everyone."

"People in the Homelands buy horses from you?"

"Oh, the farmers won't ask directly where they're from, but they know. Surely you've heard about Westernfort horses." Dani looked up from the hoof she had been cleaning.

"Um..." Natasha hesitated. Rohanna had said nothing on the subject, and Natasha had no idea of what she ought to admit to knowing. "Well, yes, a bit."

It was not a good answer, but fortunately, Dani let the subject drop. Natasha grabbed a brush. While working, they kept up a stream of idle chatter about pretty much nothing. Natasha was surprised by how easy it was. She could almost forget that she was talking to a heretic. Dani's active sense of humor had its uses. As she relaxed, Natasha could even see the funny side of their arrival at the homestead.

By the time they finished with the horses, the rich scent of cooking was wafting through the air. They put away the tools and made to leave the byre, but Natasha paused at the doorway.

"Dani?"

"Yes?"

"When you played the trick with the question, did my face really look that funny?"

Dani smiled. "Yes."

❖

The pounding of the rain had eased by the time they finished eating and cleared everything away. Although it was time to sleep, Ash pulled on her cloak and hat and opened the door. Cold, wet air blew in. There was no light outside. Thick clouds obscured the moons and stars.

"Are you going to keep sentry watch?" Cal asked.

Ash shook her head. "Not all night. If the Guards know we're here, I think they'd have made their move a bit earlier." She smiled. "They don't like stumbling around in the dark and the wet. It makes a mess of their nice uniforms."

"And it takes hours of cleaning and polishing to get them looking pretty again," Dani added the derisive jeer.

"Despite that, I'd sleep better if I have a quick look around first and check that nothing's out there. I won't be long, but don't bother waiting up for me," Ash said, pulling the brim of her hat low over her eyes and stepping out into the night.

Once her vision had adjusted to the darkness, Ash set off through the knee-high grass of the hillside. The rain was now little more than drizzle. Clouds low on the horizon were torn with ragged slashes, allowing a hint of moonlight to show details. Her experienced eyes scoured the landscape, alert to signs of danger, but her attention was split as she reviewed the events and conversation of the evening, and her expression was concerned, even worried.

It was an hour later when she returned to the longhouse. Everyone inside was asleep. Ash knelt beside Dani and gently shook her awake. With a jerk of her head, Ash indicated that Dani should follow her down to the byre end of the building. Once they were there, Ash positioned herself so she could look back through the open doorway, ensuring that no eavesdropper crept within earshot.

"So that's them," Ash whispered grimly.

"What do you make of them?"

"They seem perfectly okay, which is what you would expect."

"I suppose so." Dani also looked back thoughtfully.

"It's a bad situation."

"Umm," Dani agreed.

Ash ran her hand through her graying hair. "Damn Jules. Why did she have to go and recruit a bunch of horse thieves?"

"Are you sure they're thieves?"

"Well..." Ash sighed. "There was nothing in their rucksacks, but when you add all the reports together..." Ash let the sentence hang. "Did you pick up on anything?"

"Jess seemed a bit"—Dani waved a hand vaguely—"about the horses. Like she didn't want to admit being interested in them. Do you think they'll nab them and leave us stranded?"

"They must be sincere about wanting to go to Westernfort. Otherwise, they've made a hell of a trek for the sake of stealing seven horses."

"So what do we do?"

"Act normal, but keep a close eye on them."

"Right. Well, you take the older two, and I'll watch Jess." Dani's face was solemn, but something in her tone made Ash look at her quizzically.

"This is serious."

"I know, and I'll watch her very closely." A corner of Dani's mouth twitched up, and she shot a sideways glance toward the door. "She's cute."

CHAPTER SIX—COMRADES-IN-ARMS

The rain stopped well before dawn, and they emerged from the longhouse to a bright, clear sky. The sun was just lifting clear of the horizon when they rode away from the abandoned farmstead. Ash was in front, leading two of the horses as pack animals on long reins. Dani maneuvered her horse to ride next to Natasha at the rear.

The heretic shivered despite her warm clothes. "It's cold." Dani stated the obvious.

"And it will be getting colder," Natasha agreed.

"We'd intended to set out a few days ago. But we've had to wait for you. I hope you appreciate it."

"Oh, we do," Natasha said smiling. She could not help it; Dani's grin was infectious. Her thoughts moved on. "How long will it take to get to Westernfort?"

"Ash reckons to get us there by early November, before it starts snowing in earnest."

Natasha considered the rear view of the elderly woman. "How good is her estimate likely to be?"

"Probably right on the mark," Dani said happily. "Don't worry. I was teasing about her age. She's one of the best guides we have. That's why the captain chose her for the job."

"The captain?" Natasha inquired. "That would be Kimberly Ramon."

"Not anymore."

"Has something happened to her?"

"No. At least, nothing disastrous. Gina used to be our leader, and Kim was in charge of the Rangers. But Gina's health has been..." Dani broke off and swallowed. "Well, she's getting old. She stepped down as leader, so we elected Kim in her place. Chip

Coppelli is captain of the Rangers now."

"Oh." Natasha was feeling confused, and not just because of the possible implications for their mission. She realized that she had been expecting the heretics to be repugnant and that she would have to make an effort to disguise her distaste for them, but both Ash and Dani seemed to be reasonably pleasant people. She stole a sideways glance at the woman riding beside her. In fact, she was not sure she needed to qualify the assessment with the word *reasonably*.

❖

That night, they made camp on the wooded lower slopes of a mountain. The bare crest of cracked rock hung over them. Ahead were more peaks, filling the skyline, but these were higher, and their tops were capped with snow. The trees around them were ancient, knurled and twisted by the weather, their leaves dull with the onset of autumn. No marked paths ran between the trunks that Natasha could detect, yet Ash had led the party without hesitation along a route that somehow avoided all the densest tracts of undergrowth.

As she looked around at the trees, Natasha was aware of a childish panic deep inside. The feeling was not going to take control of her, but it was there. She fixed her eyes on the fire and tried to ignore her nervousness. It was ridiculous. With the exception of a few nights, she had been sleeping outdoors ever since leaving Landfall. But these trees had an indefinable quality that marked them as the wildlands, beyond the boundaries of the civilized world. The streets of Landfall were undoubtedly more dangerous, especially after dark, but they were home, and their dangers were familiar and understood. Her unease was not helped when Ash announced that there was no need to post sentries that night.

Something of Natasha's mood must have shown on her face. Dani shuffled closer and asked, "Are you okay?"

"I...yes. I'm fine," Natasha mumbled.

"You're looking worried."

"It's just..." Natasha paused and raised her eyes to the black silhouettes of treetops against the darkening sky. "I've never been outside the Homelands before, and the wildlands are...wild. I trust

Ash if she says it's safe, but it doesn't feel that way to me."

Dani looked surprised. "I thought most people escaping from the Sisters were relieved to get beyond their reach."

Natasha cursed herself for her carelessness. She looked around the campfire, to judge the effect of her words on the rest of the party, but Rohanna and Cal were talking quietly to each other at the far side and not listening. Neither censure nor support was to be had from them. Ash was closer at hand. However, she was staring into the flames and also did not appear to be paying attention.

Natasha went for a shamefaced grin. "You have to allow for me being a city-bred wimp."

"Well, if you're feeling nervous and want someone's hand to hold, you only have to ask," Dani said, laughing.

Natasha glanced across, unsure how to interpret the suggestion, but Dani's smile held nothing apart from friendly teasing. "That's a very kind offer." Natasha matched the mischievous tone.

"I'm a very kind person."

Dani did not push the topic any further, and after a few seconds of silence, she asked, "Which town do you come from?"

Natasha's relief at escaping her previous blunder faded. Her only option was to tell a direct lie. She swallowed and said, "Clemswood." The word felt like sawdust in her mouth.

"And you lived there all your life?"

"No, we...moved from place to place quite a bit."

"Have you ever been to Eastford?"

"Um...I don't remember it. Maybe as a child. You'd have to ask my mothers." Natasha's head dropped, and she bit her lip. *Pretend you're an actor in a play*, she told herself. *Pretend it's not real*. The advice did not help.

"Bad memories?" Dani asked gently. She must have noticed Natasha's distress but misinterpreted it.

"I..." Natasha did not know what to say.

Dani reached out and squeezed her shoulder. "It's all right. I shouldn't have asked. Nobody flees the Homelands because they're having more fun than they can cope with. You don't have to say anything. But if you ever want to talk and need a sympathetic ear, that offer goes without saying as well."

"Thanks." Natasha looked up and smiled at Dani with true warmth. Sympathy was very welcome, even if it was misplaced.

They chatted for a while longer, until Ash announced that it was time to sleep. Dani shared a last friendly exchange and crawled over to where she had dropped her pile of blankets. Natasha was tempted to move her own bedding a little closer, but the action might easily be misconstrued, especially following the joke about holding her hand.

After Natasha was settled in her bed, she lay awake for some time, trying to resolve the confusing barrage of emotions. She was in the middle of the wilderness, in the company of her enemies. Any second could bring the slip that would lead not only to her death—that was an accepted part of the plan—but also to failing in her mission for the Goddess. It was not surprising that she felt a childish wish to be hugged by someone. Even the idea of holding Dani's hand was comforting, and that was the greatest source of confusion.

Despite her horror of heresy, Natasha could not help liking Dani. She wished it were possible to talk things over with Rohanna—someone who had experience of such things. Yet why had Rohanna not shared her experience more to start with? Why had she not warned that when one met them, the heretics might not be as repulsive as expected? At last, Natasha drifted off to sleep, thinking about Dani.

❖

The necessary jobs for breaking camp were divided among the party after breakfast the next morning. Ash and Dani had the task of saddling the horses. They worked together in silence for a while but once she was certain they would not be overheard, Ash said, "That was quite an impressive display of flirting last night."

"It...from whom?"

"You, of course."

"*Me?*" Dani's voice was all hurt innocence.

Ash paused in her work long enough to give Dani an accusatory stare that was not totally without humor. "Yes. You. If there hadn't been us three old 'uns as an audience, I think you'd have thrown yourself on her."

"No, I wouldn't." Then Dani's air of affronted dignity broke down in a broad grin. "But I might not have put up much resistance if she'd tried throwing herself on me."

"Quite. But be sensible. We have every reason to think they're a bunch of horse thieves."

"I'm not going to do anything stupid. And as you said, with you three as chaperones, I'm hardly likely to get the chance. But there's no harm in talking."

"You're not so young and naïve as to believe that," Ash said dryly. "Be careful. If you start trusting her, you're laying yourself open to get hurt...and not just emotionally."

"I'm not—" Dani broke off, considering Ash's words. She sighed. "Okay. I promise I'll be careful and not let anything slip that I shouldn't, either in word or action. But I can't stop myself from liking her. Hopefully, by the time we get to Westernfort, we'll know where they stand. And if they're okay, and the attraction hasn't worn thin, there'll be plenty of time then to..." Dani paused suggestively and then finished. "Become better acquainted with Jess."

"You're assuming she'll be interested in becoming better acquainted with you," Ash teased.

"Oh, she's interested already. Though I'm not sure if she knows it yet."

Ash laughed, but anything else she might have said was curtailed by the arrival of Natasha herself.

"Do you need any help with the saddles?" she asked, looking at Dani.

"An extra pair of hands would be useful. Here, take this." Dani dumped the harness in Natasha's hands and led her on to the next horse. When Natasha ducked down to grab the girth strap, Dani shot a broad grin back at Ash that said as clearly as words, "I told you so."

❖

On the evening of the eighth day after leaving the longhouse, they camped below the crest of a thickly wooded hill. They had passed through the first range of mountains and were about to descend onto a stretch of open moorland. From their viewpoint, they could see the rolling expanse of gray-brown bracken and beyond it, the next line of peaks. While the older ones made the camp ready, Natasha and Dani scrambled down through the trees to a river flowing at the bottom, in search of fresh water.

Natasha's confusion had grown. With each day, it had become harder to see the two heretics as enemies, particularly Dani, who had gone out of her way to be friendly. Dani's good humor was irrepressible. She was quick-witted and sociable, and showed no sign of being particularly immoral. The only problem with her was that she did not worship Celaeno, and the only way Natasha could reconcile things was by reaching the conclusion that Dani had been tricked into renouncing the Goddess. Natasha even wondered if it might be possible to entice the young heretic back into the ranks of the faithful. However, it was not a safe or easy thing to discuss.

While they negotiated the last of the heavy undergrowth, Natasha tried to approach the subject from a roundabout route. "Were you born at Westernfort?" she asked.

"No. I'm too old for that."

Natasha looked at her, unsure what relevance age had to do with it. "Too old?"

"There weren't any children born out here before Lynn arrived. Tanya Coppelli is the oldest, and she's only fifteen," Dani said, stepping out into the comparative open of the riverbank.

"So you were led into renouncing Celaeno by one of the agents in the Homelands?"

"No, by the Guards." Dani's tone suddenly grew uncharacteristically harsh.

"By the...what?" Natasha said in confusion.

"The fucking Temple Guards." Dani glared unseeing at the trees on the other side of the river, her expression sour. When she spoke again, her voice was quieter but no less intense. "I'd like to kill every last one. Or failing that, I'd like to kill three."

Natasha crouched down beside the water, averting her face. "Any particular reason for three?"

"Yes."

Dani did not offer any more explanation and Natasha concentrated on filling the leather flasks. The only sounds were the rustling of leaves in the breeze and the rippling of the river. The light was fading toward dusk.

Abruptly, Dani hissed, "Jess!"

"What?"

"In the bushes over there. I think I saw..." Dani drew a sharp breath. "Shit! Run!"

Natasha's head shot up. A glint of red flashed in the bushes about fifty meters upstream, and then a uniformed Guard stepped clear of the trees. The woman shouted and pointed, and another pair of soldiers appeared. These two began to ford the river while the first raised her bow.

It took Natasha a moment to realize the danger; then she leapt up and chased after Dani. An arrow whistled by and embedded itself in a trunk as Natasha darted past. She dived into the thick vegetation. Dani was heading downstream, away from the campsite on the hill. The shouts behind them were rising, including an optimistic cry of "Stop!"

Natasha did not hear the second arrow. There was a crack to her head, jarring her neck, and the forest slipped out of focus. Only a glancing blow, Natasha realized. The Guard had been shooting blind into the undergrowth. Two centimeters either way, and the arrow would have missed completely or killed her. For another five steps, Natasha continued to run; then her knees gave way, and she stumbled and crashed to the ground. Dani skidded to a halt and raced back.

Natasha tried to rise, but her legs felt like water. "Leave me. Run," she gasped.

Dani did not bother to answer. Judging from the sounds, the Guards had crossed the river. For a second, she looked around frantically. Then she rolled Natasha over and over until she was lying beneath the cover of a large, dense bush. Dani took another few precious seconds scuffing the fallen leaves to obscure their tracks; then she also threw herself under the thicket.

They lay side by side, listening to the sounds of the running Guards. The cracking of branches seemed like an excessive amount of noise for just three women. The voices were almost on top of them. Natasha turned her head and peered out through the curtain of leaves. Less than five meters away, she saw the undergrowth part as a Guard burst into view. A booted foot landed within arm's reach. And then the Guards were gone. The noises faded away.

The ground under Natasha's back felt as if it were rocking up and down. The pulse beat in her head like hammer blows, sending darts of pain through the nausea. Dani twisted around to look at her.

"Why didn't you leave me?" Natasha managed to whisper.

"Don't be stupid."

"I..." Natasha began. The dark shadows under the bush began to twist and flow. They expanded before her eyes, swallowing her vision. Natasha passed out.

❖

When Natasha came around, Dani was still lying beside her, raised on one elbow, with a hand pressed over Natasha's forehead. The pain had softened to a gentle ache, and the nausea was no more than the tiniest flutter in her stomach. Dani's face held an expression of intense concentration.

"You've got the healer sense?" Natasha asked in surprise.

Dani's lips turned down at the corners. "I've got a pathetically small talent with it." She removed her hand. "The next-best thing to useless. But can I take it that I've helped you a bit?"

"Yes. You've helped a lot." Natasha took a few deep breaths. "The Guards...won't they be coming back?"

"They already have. And gone again. They heard us moving off to the right."

"They?" Natasha grimaced as she tried to collect her scrambled thoughts. "What did they hear?"

"I couldn't say for certain, but my money would be on Ash," Dani said lightly.

"Is there any risk they'll catch her?"

"Not in the way they're hoping to. The risk is all theirs."

Natasha closed her eyes and tried to relax. She lifted her hand to the gash across her temple. The hair around it was sticky with blood. Dani's intervention had given the healing process a good start, and the wound was already closed, but it was not a complete cure.

"Should we get back to the others?" Natasha asked, although she was not sure of her ability to walk.

Dani pursed her lips. "Best to wait. We don't want to bang into the Guards again. Ash is on to them, so it won't be long before the world is improved by their departure. Then Ash will come and get us."

"How will she know where we are?"

"She'll know," Dani said confidently. She turned her head to look out into the darkening forest. Unexpectedly, her expression shifted to a bitter anger. "Three Guards, and all I could do was run. Ash was right about my marksmanship, and I'm completely hopeless with a sword. But one of these days, I'm going to get an opportunity. That's why I accepted the job in the Homelands, hoping something would crop up. I'm not bothered about giving the bitches a sporting chance. A knife in the back will do."

Natasha covered her face with her arm. It was the only way to hide her expression. She did not know what to feel. Three Guards were probably about to die. They were not from her company, but they were still comrades in arms. It was not their fault that they had tried to kill her. They were servants of Celaeno, and it was very, very wrong to feel relief that someone was about to murder them. Yet Natasha could not stop herself from wishing Ash success. And soon.

It was also impossible to resolve her feelings about Dani. The heretic was someone Natasha found it easy to like. Yet the woman was an enemy of the Goddess and, therefore, Natasha's enemy as well. Dani had just saved her life, but only because she was taken in by the deception. *She's not a friend*, Natasha told herself, *I can't trust her. If she knew what I am, she'd kill me. But I'm sure she's not an evil person.*

Nothing about the situation made sense, and the complications were getting worse. The effects of the head injury sapped Natasha's strength. She felt sick and feeble. But despite the weakness, or maybe because of it, Natasha was suddenly very aware of Dani's body lying close beside her—like a lover. Natasha had only to remove the arm over her face, and their lips would be very close.

She would only have to turn her head, and they could kiss. Until that moment, Natasha had not realized that she wanted to. A sound, half groan, half sob, formed at the back of her throat.

"Jess. Are you okay? You're shaking," Dani spoke anxiously.

"I'm freezing," Natasha said evasively—not that it was untrue. A chill was seeping into her bones.

"It's shock. You've lost a bit of blood. We need to get you back to the fire. But there's no point being warm if the Guards get you." Dani bit her lip, weighing up the risks. Then she said, "Roll onto your side." She stripped off her own fleece-lined jacket; laid it over them like a blanket; and molded herself against Natasha's back, wrapping her arm around Natasha and hugging her close.

"Now, I'm just doing this for warmth, you understand," Dani mumbled into the back of Natasha's neck in her usual bantering tone.

Natasha made no reply. She was very grateful that Dani could not see the warring emotions on her face.

❖

No more than ten minutes had passed when there was a soft stirring in the bushes and Ash's voice said with dry humor, "I trust I'm not disturbing anything."

Dani rolled out from under the bush. Natasha clumsily shuffled after. Dusk was thickening under the trees. Ash was a dark silhouette against a patch of light sky, her face invisible.

Dani got to her feet, grinning. "No. We were just having a bit of a sleep while waiting for you to deal with our visitors."

"Are you both okay?"

"I am. Jess got a nasty crack on the head, but she'll be fine once we get her back to the camp."

Natasha was gently assisted to her feet, and Dani reclaimed her jacket. Together, the two heretics helped her through the tangled undergrowth to the campsite. The fire had been doused to avoid attracting attention, but the covering of trees was less dense, and Laurel was rising full on the eastern horizon. Its light was sufficient to let them see more clearly. Rohanna and Cal rushed over, and both of them hugged Natasha in a display of motherly concern.

"Jess! Are you all right?"

"She got struck by an arrow, but nothing serious," Dani answered for her.

"An arrow?" Rohanna's voice held a slight quaver.

"She's got a hard head, and the arrow glanced off. She just needs to warm up." Dani's attempt at humor sounded supportive rather than dismissive.

Natasha could not remember ever being so cosseted. Rohanna held her hand while Cal carefully washed the matted blood from her hair. Ash was a solid, comforting presence in the background, seeing to both fire and food. Dani was also attentive, again using her healer sense to inspect and treat the wound, but her touch aroused an awkward awareness in Natasha—one that she felt too unsteady to confront. It could wait until she felt stronger.

Only when Natasha was clean and warm, with a bowl of food in her hands, did the conversation turn to the matter of the Guards.

"Were there just the three?" Dani asked.

"That's all that were in the forest. They were a scouting party. But there's more around. The rest of the company are camped on the plain," Ash replied.

"What are they doing out here at this time of year?"

"From the comments I heard before I finished them, they're after you three." Ash addressed her answer to Rohanna.

"You must have really annoyed the Chief Consultant. You weren't singing rude songs about her, were you?" Dani joked with Natasha.

"I don't know any."

"Would you like me to teach you some?"

"Dani. This isn't a game," Ash said sharply.

"Do you think the Guards have anything to do with our encounter in Newsteading?" Rohanna asked. They had already recounted a carefully amended version of the tale, omitting the lock pick.

"I fear so. There wouldn't be such a large force out here if they weren't certain you were around."

"Can we avoid them?"

"Well, yes, but..."

"But?"

"We can't keep to our original route. Even the Guards will have no trouble spotting us on the open moor."

"So what do we do?" Cal asked quietly.

Ash rubbed her head and sighed. "We can detour south, sticking to these foothills."

"There's a problem with that?"

"Yes. We'll have to take the high pass over the next range. It's not my preferred route to Westernfort, but it's probably the safest with Guards about. As far as we can tell, they don't know about the pass. But it's a bit too high to be fun at this time of year. We'll have to cross the snow line."

"You're worried about snow lions?" Rohanna said.

"More about bad weather and avalanches."

"Is there no other way?"

"Not without either exposing ourselves in the open or going way off track. And we can't risk hanging around here until they give up and go away. If we're delayed getting to Westernfort, we run a greater risk of trouble with the weather."

Rohanna leaned forward. "You're the guide. We'll follow your lead...whatever you think best."

Ash nodded and stood up. She turned to face west, staring out over the dark moors; then she looked back down at the others. "We'll take a few hours' rest and set off again after midnight. Hardie will have risen by then. We don't want to still be here in the morning, just in case they come searching for the scouts." She sighed. "And we'll take the high pass."

CHAPTER SEVEN—THE HIGH PASS

Ash led them confidently through the wilderness. She seemed to know every rock and tree, and there were plenty of them. The scale of the land was disconcerting for city-bred Natasha. She knew she could never have survived the journey on her own. Despite the Guards' traditional disdain for Rangers, Natasha felt a growing respect for the women who patrolled the borders of the Homelands against attack from outlaws or wild animals. Standing sentry duty outside a temple did not seem particularly demanding by comparison.

They kept to the wooded hills for five days, skirting the southern edge of the moor, while the next range of mountains grew closer. Once, they heard distant shouting, but they saw no further sign of the Guards. Initially, the hills were gently rolling contours, but they became steadily more rugged as the route started to climb into the mountains.

For another three days, they followed a winding route through the range, keeping to the path of a river valley. As they got higher, the temperature plummeted, and patches of snow appeared on north-facing slopes. The trees were hardy dark green firs. The bushes and shrubs were more stunted and sparse, making riding easier. The journey continued at a greater pace until finally, they seemed to reach a dead end. Ahead was an unbroken arc of rock, rising sheer.

"We're going to get over that?" Natasha voiced her doubts.

Ash overheard and twisted around in the saddle. "It's much easier than it looks from a distance. I've ridden over this pass a dozen times or more." She gave a grin worthy of Dani. "It's the other side you need to worry about."

That night, they camped in the shelter of an isolated clump of firs. The ground cover was more snow than grass, although it was clear under the trees. It was Cal's turn to cook the evening meal. Leaving the others chatting with her by the fire, Natasha went and stood at the edge of the trees. The spot provided a good view of the cliffs they would ascend the next day. The sun was lost behind the mountains, although the sky was still pale blue. The rock faces looked harsh and grim in the fading light. Dani came and stood by her shoulder.

"If Ash says we can get over, then we can get over," Dani said encouragingly.

"Oh, I trust her. She knows what she's doing."

"She ought to. She was an official Ranger for over twenty years, and she's done another sixteen since the 23rd Squadron deserted to Westernfort."

Natasha said nothing. She was not sure whether she was being too sensitive or whether Dani was standing too close. She knew she was hopelessly drawn to the young heretic. It was a huge ethical dilemma. Her commitment to celibacy had not been so severely tested for a long time. The circumstances enforced by the journey were a mixed blessing. There was no escape from Dani's daily company, but the continuous presence of the other three gave her no opportunity to yield to the temptation.

Natasha clenched her teeth. No. Even without the others, there was no way she would act on the attraction. When they got to Westernfort, she, Rohanna, and Cal would complete their mission, and almost certainly be killed themselves. When Dani found out that she had been deceived, she would hate the women who had lied and abused her trust. But, Natasha told herself bitterly, there would be a limit to the abuse. Dani would have enough cause to curse her memory as it was.

While these thoughts had been going through her mind, Natasha's eyes had dropped from the mountains to stare, unseeing, at the snow before her. Suddenly, she registered what it was she was looking at. She twisted around and shouted, "Ash!"

"What is it?" The veteran Ranger came running.

Natasha held out her arm, pointing to a double row of paw prints.

Ash stood over the tracks, her expression of concern turning to relief. "Mountain cats," she pronounced and then smiled at Natasha. "They're much too small to be snow lions, if that's what you were worried about."

Natasha felt foolish. Now that she looked more carefully, even to her untrained eye, the prints were not nearly big enough for the huge predators. Sheepishly, she mumbled, "Sorry to bother you."

Ash patted her shoulder. "No. You were right to bring them to my attention, rather than try to identify the marks yourself and risk making a mistake. And even mountain cats can be nasty, though not at this time of year. There's still plenty of their natural prey about." She turned to walk back to the camp, Natasha and Dani tagging along. Ash continued talking while they walked.

"You don't get snow lions this far south until late December at the very earliest, and like the cats, they won't attack people while there are fenbucks and spadehorns around. We're poisonous to them, and they can smell it. They have to be starving to try. Early spring is the dangerous time."

Rohanna and Cal were looking anxiously in their direction, wondering what had caused the excitement. "What's up?" Cal called.

"Nothing much. Some mountain cats have been around here."

"That's hardly a surprise." Cal turned back to the task of preparing dinner, although Rohanna continued to look apprehensive. Ash began to repeat what she had already told the two younger women.

Natasha flopped down in the warmth beside the fire. The smell of the cooking food was welcoming after the long day. She stretched out her hands toward the heat and tried to act at ease as Dani also sat down close by.

❖

Ash was quite correct about the climb; it was far less difficult than it looked. Once they got closer to the cliff, an oblique shadow at one side turned out to be a gully, a path eroded into the rock by the action of wind and frost. They were even able to ride for most of the ascent, needing to dismount only at the more awkward spots. In little over an hour, they had reached the top, where they found themselves on the brow of a snow-covered ridge, slung between two jagged peaks and barely more than a dozen meters wide. Ash led the way across and then stopped to let them take in the view.

The cliff they had climbed had been chiseled out of the side of a mountain by the elements. The summit was still high above them, to the south. The towering crest of rock blocked out half the sky. To the north, the line of mountains continued and was eventually lost in the distance. A steep slope of snow fell away at their feet until it reached a line of firs two or more kilometers below. Beyond the trees, they could see the terrain drop in a series of folded steps, eventually leveling out in a rolling, tree-covered plain. The lowland was still several days' travel away, but they had reached the top of the high pass.

Ash pointed out the route. "One good thing about coming this way is that once we get down there, we've finished with high mountains. It's a fairly straightforward run from here to Westernfort. The detour will only add four or five days onto the journey overall." She smiled and slipped from her saddle. "Now, this is the tricky part. The horses will need coaxing down. Hold the reins tightly, but if you think you're going to lose the fight, let them go. If you trip and start rolling, you won't stop until you hit the trees at the bottom."

The slope was nearly vertical in parts. Ash began to scramble sideways down it, kicking footholds into the hard-packed snow, while leading her horse and one of the pack animals. Rohanna and Cal followed, sharing the second spare horse. As usual, Dani was close by Natasha at the rear, but the need to watch their footing, and at the same time urge on the horses, prevented any conversation.

Despite the need to concentrate on the descent, Natasha's thoughts and eyes kept straying in Dani's direction. Of course, there was no telling whether the heretic was interested in anything more than friendship. She might well have a lover waiting for her in Westernfort. Or more than one. For a moment, Natasha considered the tales of wild heretic orgies. But now that she had met some real heretics, the claims seemed even less credible than they had in the taverns of Landfall.

Natasha's foot slipped, and she went down on one knee in the wet snow. *And if I don't pay attention to what I'm doing, I won't even get to see Westernfort,* she told herself firmly.

After several overcast days, the sun was dazzling off the snow. The wind felt warm on Natasha's face, as if the weather had switched from winter to summer in the space of a few hours. The party was wearing blankets as additional cloaks, and by the time they were halfway down the slope, Natasha found that she was sweating. She was trying to work out how to remove the blanket without losing control of her horse when a sudden eruption of noise broke out above, starting with a roar and ending as thunder.

Natasha looked back. Her immediate impression was that the mountain peak had come to life. One corner near the summit shuddered like a sleeper roused from a deep sleep and then detached itself from the rest of the mountain. It simultaneously crumpled and billowed out, and began to flow toward them.

"Avalanche!" Cal shouted.

The distance at first confused Natasha's assessment of speed; then she realized that the wall of snow was racing down the mountain toward them, getting swifter by the moment. She stared at it, stunned into inaction, until her horse tore the reins from her grasp and began to plunge down the hill, bolting away from the oncoming danger. Natasha was turning to follow when Ash's voice rang out.

"Let the horses go! Quick—follow me! Get to cover!"

Natasha saw where Ash was headed: a heavy shelf of rock, breaking through the snow and overhanging a deep hollow. The spot was a good twenty meters away and slightly above where they stood, but fortunately, the gradient of the slope had leveled out slightly. Rohanna and Cal were already chasing after Ash. Natasha took one step and then stopped, halted by the sound of scuffling.

Several meters downhill, Dani was engaged in a battle with her panicked horse. The animal was fighting to escape toward the firs. Dani was virtually lying in the snow to prevent herself from being dragged after it and fumbling at the knife on her belt. The pair clearly had no wish to stay together, but Dani's wrist was tangled in the reins. Without stopping to think, Natasha bounded toward them, drawing her own dagger. The tough leather of the reins put up a brief resistance before parting. The horse skidded backward, floundered, half fell, and then fled. Natasha hauled Dani to her feet, and they began to run.

Up ahead, Cal was already diving into the hollow. Rohanna and Ash were a few steps behind. The wall of snow had reached the ridge where they had stood and taken in the view. It was apparent that the main body of the avalanche would miss them, but even the fringes would be lethal to anyone caught in the open. The ground under Natasha's feet was shaking with the sound of rumbling.

To Natasha, the scene felt like running in a nightmare. Hands in the snow grabbed at her feet, and each step took her no nearer her goal. She tripped once, but Dani jerked her onward. The vibration of the ground was starting tiny snow slips all across the hillside. The roar of the avalanche drowned out all other sound.

Out of the corner of her eye, Natasha saw the first boulders of ice thunder by, crashing over the spot they had just left. The hillside was rearing up, blocking out the sky. And then, with one more stride, they reached the edge of the hollow and dived over. They found the rock face and pressed their backs against it as the towering wave of snow broke over them.

Everywhere was filled with whiteness and movement. Hard shards of ice pelted down on their heads and whipped around their faces. The snow pounded them like a waterfall, trying to suck them from their shelter. The rocks behind their back boomed like a drum from the pounding blows. Snow filled their mouths, noses, ears. Natasha was certain that they would be buried or swept away. Then the fury softened. The continuous thunder was split into bursts, interrupted by quiet moments when they could hear the creaking of the snow. The torrent slowed to a sluggish flow and finally stopped.

They were encased in snow. Natasha struck out with her arm and broke free into the open air. The white blanket was less than half a meter of loose powder. She was about to tunnel her way out, when she felt movement beside her. Natasha realized that she had been sitting with her arm around Dani, hugging her tightly, and that Dani in turn had an arm wrapped around her waist. Natasha could not remember taking hold of Dani—unsurprising, since her mind had been on other things at the time. Now that she was aware of it, the solid feel of Dani's body was immensely comforting. Natasha was tempted to steal a few seconds more, but Dani began to squirm toward freedom.

Natasha restrained a sigh and copied her actions. Within seconds, they emerged from the covering. The hollow was now two-thirds full of loose snow. A little way off, Ash was also scrambling clear, and two further moving humps revealed the positions of Cal and Rohanna.

"Looks like we're all safe, then," Natasha said to Dani.

"Thanks to you," Dani replied. Then her voice softened. "And I really mean thanks. Without you, I'd still have been caught in the reins when the avalanche hit me."

Again, Dani's arm slipped around Natasha's waist. Natasha turned her head. Their lips were scant centimeters apart. Dani's eyes looked into hers, steadily, intensely.

"I...it...er..." The words died in Natasha's mouth. She felt a blush flow over her cheeks.

Dani's serious expression changed to amusement. She squeezed Natasha, her eyes deliberately holding the lock, and then let her arm fall and moved away.

The other three were all clear and wading through the powdery snow. Rohanna and Cal both appeared to be slightly dazed. Natasha suspected that she looked the same herself, and for more reasons than just the avalanche. Every time she blinked, she saw the afterimage of Dani's eyes.

None of them was seriously hurt, merely a little bruised and cut from the battering by the ice. Natasha had barely recovered her wits enough to appreciate their good luck when the sight of Ash's expression warned her that the danger was not over. The guide looked worried, even frightened.

"What is it? Might it start up again?" Natasha asked.

"The horses."

At Ash's words, any feeling of relief disappeared. With the horses gone, they had lost not only their transport, but also their supplies.

"Do you think they'll have survived?" Rohanna asked.

"No," Ash said bluntly.

The party continued down the hillside—a slow, dangerous task in the aftermath of the avalanche. The ground was part compacted ice and part unstable debris, all hidden beneath a thick layer of loose snow. They could see at the bottom where rows of firs had been felled by the force of the avalanche, but there was no sign of the horses until, as they reached the last few meters before the flattened tree trunks, Ash spotted a hoof protruding from the snow. The horse was dead. A bit of digging revealed that it had been one of the pack animals, and the baggage was still in place.

"That's a stroke of luck," Cal said, in tones that showed she was clearly underwhelmed by their good fortune.

The whinny of a horse sounded faintly over the whisper of the trees. While the others removed the pack from the dead horse, Ash and Natasha set off to investigate. The animal was nearer at hand than they had expected, its cry weakened by pain. It was the horse Ash had been riding. It called desperately when it saw her and tried to lift its head, but its rear leg, and possibly its spine, were broken. There was nothing they could do except release the animal from its suffering. Ash used her knife with the skill of a professional, but she wept as she did so.

They returned to the others with the reclaimed saddlebag. After a search, they found another dead horse, but no trace of the rest. If the animals had escaped the avalanche, they might wander back of their own accord; otherwise, they were lost. Ash compiled an inventory and reached the quick conclusion that they had about half of what they would like, although wearing the blankets as cloaks was a stroke of luck, since none had been lost. With winter approaching, the blankets might save their lives. The greatest shortage was food.

"There wouldn't be a problem if it were summer," Ash said. "But at this time of year, not much is growing, and we don't have time to waste harvesting it anyway...not if we want to get to Westernfort before the weather turns really nasty."

"Aren't we going to run into trouble anyway?" Cal asked.

Ash scrunched her face as she calculated the journey. "With luck, we'll make Westernfort by the end of November. The weather might hold. But it will be a hard trek on foot."

"The..." Natasha bit off her words.

"What?" Dani asked.

Natasha had been about to say, *The Goddess will help us.* She improvised, "Then shouldn't we get started?"

Ash was looking pensively at the nearest horse. "Before we go, I think we should take as much of the horse meat as we can. I'm not keen on the idea, but I prefer it to the thought of starving."

"Have you never eaten horse meat before?" Cal asked in surprise.

"Oh, yes. But these animals were imprinted, not cloned."

Natasha fought to keep the expression of outrage off her face. She looked to Rohanna, hoping for a lead, but even the intelligence agent appeared to be stunned.

Dani noticed their expressions. "Didn't realize you were riding something with a soul?" Her voice held an unexpected bite of sarcasm. She drew her knife and went to kneel by the carcass. "And now's our chance to find out what a soul tastes like."

"Dani. It isn't funny." Even Ash sounded shocked.

"Oh, I know, and believe me, it isn't something I joke about." And for once, Dani's face did not hold a trace of humor. She started the butchery.

Natasha was appalled. Animals were never imprinted, because then they would be unique, which meant they would have souls. The principle was one of the foundations of the faith. Souls were unique and could not be split, so a cloned animal could not take a share of its mother's soul—even if it had one. The beast had life, but no immortal spirit; therefore, it was not a sin to kill and eat it. But to make a creature with a soul to be used as an object was an obscene sacrilege. Only cloning a human would be worse. And surely, even the heretics would not create such a soulless monster, bearing the form of one of Celaeno's daughters but without that divine spark from the Goddess.

Ash shuffled her feet. "At Westernfort...Lynn, our Imprinter, has spare time on her hands. The population isn't big. She's worked on improving the livestock. But we don't eat the imprinted animals—just their cloned descendants. Some of us still aren't very happy about it." From Ash's face and halting speech, it was obvious that she belonged in this group. "The horses, well...you tend to think of them as friends anyway. But..." Ash sighed. "If

Gina is right, then all the bit about souls is nonsense, and if she isn't, then the horse's souls are with Celaeno, and they don't need their bodies.

"But I understand if you find it a bit much to take. If you want, you three can go stand somewhere else. Dani and I will see to the carving. I've had longer to get used to the idea of imprinted horses than you. And Dani, um..." Ash shrugged awkwardly. "Anyway, we won't eat the horse meat until we get desperate. But the time will come."

Cal and Rohanna nodded and walked off into the trees. Natasha stood for a while, staring at Dani in horror. *She's a heretic.* The words had never struck Natasha so forcefully before. How could she be attracted to such a person? But she was. And maybe the feeling was returned. Natasha remembered Dani's eyes meeting hers and the arm around her waist. The situation was becoming a mess. Dying might prove to be an easy way out—before she fell hopelessly in love.

A touch on her arm made Natasha jump. Rohanna had returned and beckoned her away. When they had gone far enough to be out of earshot of the two heretics, Rohanna started speaking. "I know what you're feeling, and I understand, but you must remember our mission."

Natasha took a deep breath. She had not realized that she was being so obvious, but before she could talk, Rohanna continued. "It's something I've had to contend with in the past. You feel revolted by the heretics, but you have to keep up the pretence of being one of them. You were staring at the faithless slut as if you wanted to throw up. Your response does you credit, but you have to act as if you like her."

"I didn't...just now...with Dani..." Natasha's words died. Rohanna did not understand at all, and Natasha could not bring herself to explain.

The senior Guard continued to misconstrue Natasha's response. "I know. Now that you've got time to think, you must be hating yourself for saving her life back there. But you acted on impulse, and the Goddess will forgive you. You can be sure Celaeno will take her revenge on every last heretic when they come to her halls of judgment."

Rohanna slipped her arm through Natasha's and led her on, still talking. "And as for eating the horses, Ash was right. Their souls are with Celaeno. If we have to eat them to fulfill our mission for her glory, we will. The best that we can do is assassinate the corrupt Imprinter and prevent the creation of any more abominations."

CHAPTER EIGHT—A DANGEROUS GAME

The descent from the high pass was miserable. Natasha was permanently cold, and the weight of her backpack chafed sores on her shoulders. The glare off the snow gave her a headache. Traveling became a little easier once they reached the lowlands and left the snow behind, but it was only a temporary respite. With the year passing, it would not be long before winter crept down from the heights and even the plains were snowbound. Ash pushed the pace hard. The loss of the horses had slowed them, which could prove fatal if blizzards struck early that year.

The forest on this side of the mountains was noticeably different in character from the one they had left. The trees belonged to a type that even Cal did not recognize. Ash called them yellow cedar. The trunks of the largest were so broad that it would take eight women to link hands around them. The branches fanned out high overhead in layers, home to troops of long-tailed skirrales. The black-and-white-striped nut eaters were familiar to Natasha from the parks around Landfall, although somewhat bigger than their city-living cousins. The ground beneath the trees was thick with dead needles. Little grew apart from fungus and creeping bramble. Dozens of icy streams flowed down from the mountains, easily jumped as long as they found a spot where the banks were free of mud.

On the third day after leaving the mountains, they came to a far wider waterway, a good twenty-five meters across. The river was flowing briskly, its surface rippling with a dull metallic luster. Under the right conditions, it might have been pretty, but the day was cold, and it had been drizzling since dawn. The thick canopy had shielded them from the rain, but the forest floor was soggy. Natasha felt damp to the core, as if the moisture had seeped in through her pores.

Ash marched confidently up to the river. In the sullen gray light, the water looked as hard as the rounded rocks lining the bed. She slipped her pack off her back and turned to the others. "Well, girls, the good news is that the river isn't very deep here—less than knee high. We'll have no trouble fording it. The bad news is we'll have to do it barefoot. Our skin will dry a lot quicker than our boots."

Dani groaned dramatically and then said to Natasha, "I don't suppose I could talk you into giving me a piggyback ride across?"

"I was just about to ask you the same thing," Natasha joked in reply, although the image of Dani's arms wrapped around her neck was not without its appeal.

Ash had already rolled the legs of her pants above her knees and removed her boots and socks. She tied the laces together and slung them over her shoulder; then she reclaimed her backpack. The rest soon copied her lead, and they carefully trod over the pine needles to the riverside.

Dani put one experimental toe into the water and yelped. "Shit! It's cold enough to freeze Himoti's tits off."

"And any other part of her anatomy you'd care to name," Ash agreed dourly before stepping into the river.

"Why is the water so cold?" Dani asked.

"Melted snow from the mountains." Ash threw the answer back over her shoulder.

The shock of the icy temperature when she entered the water was enough to make Natasha agree with Dani's assessment, but then she noticed Cal's face out of the corner of her eye. The older woman's expression was guarded, yet Natasha could sense her outrage. Of course, the reference to Himoti had been blasphemous. Natasha wondered why she had not also been shocked by the vulgar profanity. *Maybe I've been out of the temple too long.* It was a disconcerting thought, but she could not devote much attention to resolving it. All her concentration was taken with the search for safe footing. The water was so cold that tingling darts of pain shot up her thighs, and the soles of her feet soon lost their feeling.

Ash led the way, with Natasha immediately behind. They were two-thirds across when Ash stumbled and lurched sideways.

Instinctively, Natasha put out a hand and grabbed her. For a second they swayed, both in danger of falling. Then Natasha managed to get her balance, and they steadied.

"Watch out for the hole here." Ash's voice was strained as she called back to those behind.

"Are you all right?" Natasha asked, still holding on to the guide.

"I banged my instep. I think I'm okay. My feet are too numb to feel anything."

The same could be said for them all. The only reason Natasha was certain that her own feet were still attached to her legs was because logic said she had to be standing on something. They no longer hurt, but it did not mean that they were uninjured. She hesitated a second before slipping Ash's arm over her shoulder and supporting the guide for the rest of the crossing. That Ash did not object to the assistance was worrying, and even before they had left the water, Natasha noted a ribbon of red swirling away.

Once they were on the bank, it became apparent that Ash had come down hard on something sharp, probably a broken splinter of rock. The elderly Ranger hopped to a dryish patch of ground, leaving a splattered trail of blood, and sat down heavily. Dani knelt to examine the injury, while the others dried their feet on leaves, replaced their socks and boots, and then stood around with grim expressions.

Dani sat back. "We aren't going any farther today."

"I..." Ash opened her mouth to protest.

"You can't walk on that foot, and at the moment, I'm too cold to concentrate enough to use the healer sense," Dani said firmly. "We need to make camp and get a fire going."

"I'll see to the fire," Cal volunteered and immediately trotted off into the trees.

Ash was moved a little farther into the shelter of the forest. From her expression, it was obvious that the guide was angry at the delay but far too experienced to indulge herself in ill-judged heroics. The wound was not merely a scratch. She winced as Dani pressed the heel of her hand hard over the cut to halt the flow of blood. Rohanna and Natasha went back for the packs.

"The blasphemer punished," Rohanna murmured under her breath after they had gone a few meters.

"We've certainly had our share of bad luck," Natasha said, loudly enough for the two heretics to hear.

Rohanna nodded faintly to show that she took Natasha's point, or what she thought was Natasha's point. It had been one of Rohanna's own injunctions to stay in character and not give way to the temptation to make unnecessary asides, regardless of whether they could be overheard.

Cal returned shortly, carrying some dead branches. All the available kindling was damp, but Cal did not appear to be concerned. After dropping the wood, she reached into a pocket and pulled out a large seed case and a few nuts. With deft movements, she slit the seed case in half and then cracked open the nuts, using the handle of her knife as a hammer. The inside of the seed case was packed with fibrous strands that she smeared with an oily residue from the nuts. At the first spark from the flint, the fibers burst into flames.

Ash was propped against a tree trunk. She watched the fire making with interest. "That's a classic Ranger trick," she said once the wood was alight.

"It certainly is," Cal agreed easily. "I learned it from my aunt."

"She was a Ranger?"

"She used to be."

Ash closed her eyes and settled back. "Which squadron?"

From her tone, it was impossible to tell whether Ash was expressing anything other than a mild professional interest to distract herself from her injury. Cal acted deliberately casual. She frowned thoughtfully for a moment and then said, "I'm not sure... the 14th, I think. Or maybe the 18th. It was a long time ago. I was just a young kid when she took me camping, but I remember a lot of the bits she taught me."

"And you were working as a fur trapper when I met you. I'm always amazed at the things you picked up there," Rohanna added affectionately.

Ash asked no more questions. Attention shifted to the fire and food. Dani had managed to stop the bleeding by the application of pressure, but she would not be able to use her talent with the healer sense until she was rested and warm. Even those who lacked the gift knew that it took immense concentration to step beyond the boundaries of the ordinary and use the healer sense. Mild discomfort was enough to block those who had the talent from using it. A sick healer could not heal herself.

As she helped around the campsite, Natasha was caught in an internal battle. The questions about Cal's fire-lighting skill had reminded her that she was not on the same side as Ash and Dani. *They're enemies. I've sworn to execute their leaders, and if they knew who I am, they'd kill me.* Natasha repeated the words over and over in her head. The only people she could trust were Rohanna and Cal. They were her true comrades and would stand by her. Rohanna's quick-witted invention about Cal's working as a fur trapper was an example. No mention of any such profession had existed in the notes about the real family, but the intelligence agent had clearly realized that Cal's knowledge of the wildlands needed more explanation and had stepped in to cover for her. She, Cal, and Rohanna were a team, working together against the heretics. But nothing seemed quite as simple here as it had in Landfall.

She could not even be sure of her reasons for making the remark about bad luck. She had felt an instant rejection of Rohanna's pious assertion. It had been Dani, not Ash, who had uttered the original blasphemy, and from her experience in the Militia, Natasha knew that the Goddess routinely ignored far greater sacrilege. However, Rohanna was her commanding officer. Natasha should not even think of offering implied criticism. *I* have *been out of the temple for too long.*

Natasha knew that she must tighten her mental discipline. She had been letting her emotions get out of control, and not just with regard to Dani. Before going to sleep that night, she would take extra time for silent prayer. If she could clear her mind of every feeling except love of the Goddess and obedience to her will, perhaps she would recover her certainties. Their mission was far too important to risk failure, and the chances of success would be better if she were not in the grip of doubt.

❖

The injury to Ash's foot cost them yet more time, but once she was halfway healed, Ash drove them on with even greater determination. Eventually, the forest of cedars gave way to open moorland, covered with coarse bracken and spindly, wind-torn bushes. The land was raw and broken. Sweeping hills were crowned with eroded buttresses of granite. The wind was colder, and now there was nothing to shield them from its force. November was drawing to a close. For several days, the clouds hung low, blanketing the hilltops. The rain fell as sleet. Twice, it snowed, but the white flurries did not settle.

At the end of another long, cold day, they climbed to the brow of a hill. The clouds had lifted slightly to unveil a range of mountains lining the western horizon. Judging their height or distance was impossible, but in the dull evening light, the mountains loomed gray and inhospitable.

"You aren't going to tell us we have to get over them?" Cal asked with a sigh.

"No." Ash smiled. "I'm going to tell you that, though they look solid from here, the mountains are split by a wide plain, like the range is being pulled in half. It runs up behind there." She held out a finger to point. "And Westernfort is in the middle, overlooking the plain."

"How far?" Natasha asked eagerly.

"Seven days."

"I hope they're cooking something nice when we arrive," Dani chipped in.

The wish was one they could all agree with. Despite careful rationing, the food had run very low, and everyone had been willing to eat the horse meat, imprinted or not. At most, the remaining supplies were enough for three more days. Thereafter, they would be walking on empty stomachs. So long as nothing else happened to delay them, they should make it, but the weather was a critical factor.

Dusk was falling, and it was time to select a campsite for the night. But instead of heading down to the shelter of the valley, Ash turned to walk up the hill toward the granite outcrop on their left. These rocks looked much like the other formations they had passed, although more extensive than most. The etched stone pillars huddled together like the towers of a town. Only when they got close did Natasha spot a natural passageway disappearing between two of the columns. The path twisted through the outcrop until, deep in the heart of the rocks, Ash led them to the door of a rough building of drystone walls, sandwiched between the faces of ancient granite. To her surprise, Natasha even spotted a pile of firewood, stacked to one side.

"A Ranger outpost?" Cal guessed.

"One of many," Ash agreed as she pushed open the door. "We have a ring of them around Westernfort."

Inside was an irregularly shaped room, more natural cave than man-made building. A fireplace was built under a fissure at one side. In another corner stood a wooden chest. Ash threw back the lid. "Could be worse," she said after rummaging through the contents. "Enough dried food for another two days, some waterproof canvas, a lantern, and a bottle of wine."

"A surprise birthday party for me! You shouldn't have." Dani mimicked delight.

"We couldn't forget your birthday." Natasha went along with the joke.

"But it's not my birthday. That's why I'm so surprised."

Ash laughed and said, "I didn't mention this outpost before, in case we were disappointed. With the way our luck's been running, the stores might have been empty. They're kept stocked for emergencies. I'm not sure what sort of emergency the bottle is intended for, but I'm going to open it anyway, birthday or not."

Before long, there was a blazing fire in the hearth, and food was cooking. Natasha felt warm for the first time in weeks. The spirits of the group rose, although they all knew that they were not yet safe. A blizzard could pin them down for days, and then starvation would be a real threat.

After the meal, Rohanna and Cal went to bed early. They took advantage of the warmth to move away from the fireside into the relative privacy of a dark alcove at the far end. Possibly they wanted to make plans for Westernfort, or they were reinforcing their pretence of being lovers. Or maybe they genuinely wanted to be together. Natasha could hardly go ask them.

Ash wrapped a blanket around her as a cloak and said, "I'm just going out to take a quick check on the weather." She slipped out into the dark.

Natasha and Dani sat in front of the fire and listened to the crackle of the wood and the wind whistling over the rocks.

"I don't know why Ash needs to go outside. I could tell her that it's cold and miserable," Natasha said.

Dani propped her chin on her knees. "She feels responsible because the journey has gone so badly."

"It's hardly her fault. And without her, there's no way we'd have gotten this far."

"I know...like I said, she's the best. And she's really pushed herself with the injury to her foot."

"I just hope I'm that tough when I reach fifty-five," Natasha said, and then bit her tongue. Little chance existed that she would live long enough even to make twenty-two.

The silence dragged out while both of them stared into the fire. Natasha reached for the empty bottle and held it up to the firelight. One tiny mouthful was left at the bottom. She was about to drain it when Dani spoke. "You can tell me to mind my own business, if you want, but you haven't said much about your life back in the Homelands."

Natasha lowered the bottle. Her pulse leapt. She was not in the mood for lying, but she managed to ask, "What do you want to know?"

Dani shrugged. "Oh, just general things. What your home was like; what you miss about it."

"That's hardly a cheerful subject for conversation." Natasha tossed back the last of the wine.

"True." Dani paused. "Well, how about something happier? When did you last get laid?"

Natasha nearly choked on the wine. When she had recovered her composure, she looked across at Dani. The expression on her companion's face assured Natasha that she had not misheard the question. Dani's eyes danced with amusement.

Natasha turned back to the fire and pulled the corners of her mouth down in a wry grimace. "And what makes you think *that* would be a happier subject?"

Dani laughed. "I see. It didn't go too well."

"I think a better description would be 'utter disaster.'"

"So it wouldn't be a hard act to follow?"

Despite herself, Natasha could not help grinning. Dani was cheerfully, and quite deliberately, flirting with her, and it was a dangerous game to play along with. She should try to distance herself, but she did not know what to say. Fortunately, the door opened, and Ash returned with a report on the weather. They continued to chat while the fire burned down and then went to bed, but Natasha lay awake a long time.

It was now impossible for her to see Dani and Ash as enemies. She could not understand how two such decent women had become ensnared in heresy, but she knew who was to blame. When she thought of the leaders of the heretics—the fiends whose lies had corrupted Dani's soul—Natasha felt seething anger. Losing her own life was a small price for the honor of executing them. Her only regret was that she would not get the chance to explain things to Dani.

Natasha stared at the red glow flickering over the ceiling. With the grace of the Goddess, all things were possible. Was it too much to hope that, with the leaders gone, the heretics would see that they had been deceived, and Dani might escape the fate of the wicked? The final triumph of the mission, one to outstrip all Natasha's hopes, would surely be if Dani would rejoin the faithful. And then maybe, after death, she might meet again with Dani in the light of Celaeno's love, when all would be understood and forgiven. It was something to pray for.

❖

Five days later, they reached the entrance to the wide canyon that split the mountain range. The flat bottom of the rift valley was easily five kilometers wide. On either side, the cliffs rose sheer. The vegetation had increased to a sparse woodland of evergreen shrubs, which had little effect in breaking the force of the elements. For the first time, it was snowing in earnest, and the wind was rising. It was not a night to spend in the open. Fortunately, Ash had spoken about another outpost close by.

The building was at the bottom of a gentle hollow and partially concealed by bushes. It was a timber construction, like a scaled-down version of the deserted longhouse where they had met. The smell when they entered confirmed that one end was normally used as stables. The main room was small but dry, and a pile of chopped wood was ready by the fireplace. When Ash checked the stores, however, the news was not so good. The chest contained only one small bag of oatmeal.

"A lot of people stop here," she explained. "We're one day's ride from Westernfort. Usually, this post is well stocked, but someone else must have been through recently."

"Any chance of getting to Westernfort tomorrow?" Rohanna asked.

Ash thought for a moment. "If we were all fresh, and the weather was mild, we'd make it. But we're going to have knee-high snow tomorrow, and none of us are in top form after the trek we've had. It will have to be the day after."

Cal made a watery gruel from the oats and the last of their food. Nobody spoke much as they sat in the firelight, sipping the thin, tasteless liquid and listening to the wind. There was no likelihood of having anything else to eat until they reached Westernfort, and the weather outside was turning into a blizzard. Natasha was worried by the thought of being snowbound. Yet Ash was confident that the storm would blow itself out by morning, and experience had shown that her judgment was dependable.

Natasha's thoughts skipped ahead to the next few days. They would soon get to Westernfort and complete their mission with as little delay as possible, although it would be nice if they could get at least one decent meal first. Rohanna had not spoken about her plans for the executions. Doubtless, the details would depend on the circumstances they found in Westernfort, but with three Guards and three targets, it would only be fair if they were allocated one each.

Natasha had played with this idea before, wondering which of the three leaders she would most like to execute personally. Not that it took much thinking about. It was Kimberly Ramon who had forced Ash to desert, contaminating a good woman with her own evil. Killing her would put an end to the songs about the bold

Ranger captain. Furthermore, Ramon was a soldier. The risk and the glory would be much greater in tackling her than in killing an old woman or an Imprinter, regardless of how much those two might deserve to die.

Natasha glanced toward Rohanna and sighed. Chances were that she would be assigned a supporting role while the two older Guards carried out the executions.

Dani misinterpreted the reason for the sigh. She grinned at Natasha and joked, "Finished already?"

Natasha remembered her surroundings. She stared down at the unappetizing dregs in her bowl. "I don't know whether to be relieved or disappointed that there's so little of it."

Dani laughed and was about to say something else when they heard the whinny of a horse over the wind, followed by clinks and a voice. The first thought to go through Natasha's mind was *Oh, no. After coming so far, we can't have been caught.* Yet Ash was clearly unbothered. She jumped up with a broad smile and raced toward the stables, pausing only to grab a lantern on the way. Her arrival at the far end of the building was followed by much excited shouting.

Dani had evidently seen Natasha's expression of dismay and guessed her fears. She reached out to grasp Natasha's shoulder. "You aren't going to meet any live Guards this close to Westernfort. Don't worry. They'll be friends."

Within seconds, Ash returned to the room, leading three strangers. All were dressed like her, in the modified Ranger's uniform. Their shoulders were dusted with melting snow.

"Do you mind sharing your fire?" one asked playfully.

"Only if you'll share your dinner," Dani answered.

The three were clearly very familiar to both Dani and Ash, and their greetings were the casual teasing of reunited friends. Even without understanding all the overtones, Natasha found a broad smile spreading across her face. And the thought of food made her more than well disposed toward the newcomers.

Before long, everyone was settled by the fire, and Ash was preparing a more substantial meal. The oldest of the newcomers looked to be in her early forties. She was the tallest by a good few centimeters, with a light, firm build. Despite her informal manner and the absence of a badge denoting rank, she was obviously an officer of some sort. While the others continued their joking, she considered Rohanna, Cal, and Natasha with shrewd eyes.

Rohanna had also noticed the attention they were receiving and ran through a quick introduction. "I am Rohanna Korski. This is my partner, Calinda Rowse. And that is our daughter, Jess."

The officer's astute gaze took in the three women. Then she smiled and said, "And I am Kimberly Ramon."

PART TWO

Keeping Faith

CHAPTER NINE—THE ENEMY STRONGHOLD

The battle to disguise her reaction to the name absorbed all of Natasha's self-control. She was so concerned with keeping her face impassive that she completely missed the introductions for the other two. The evil fiend she had come to kill sat less than two meters away, chatting amiably like a normal human being. *And what was I expecting?* Natasha derided herself. Cal's words in the tavern came back to her, *Smile. Remember, she's our hero.*

Rohanna and Cal also appeared to be taken aback by the newcomer's identity, and Ash was noticeably subdued. Fortunately, Dani was doing enough talking to make up for everyone. Most of the conversation passed by Natasha as noise, but she got back in touch in time to hear that some people called Jenny and Madra were doing well and had finally decided to have a child; Tanya was still determined to join the Rangers, and Shelly was keenly awaiting Dani's return. At that news, Dani groaned melodramatically before going on.

"And what are you doing back in uniform, Kim?"

"The uniform, yes." Kim adjusted to the change of topic. "We wondered where you were. Chip wanted to send out search parties. I wasn't busy and fancied some fresh air—or thought I did—before the snow started. This old uniform is the best clothing I have for tackling the wildlands."

"That's a weak excuse if ever I've heard one. We think she just wanted to play at being a Ranger again," another of the newcomers said, grinning.

Kim raised her eyebrows at the teasing but did not dispute the words. "So what happened to you? We were expecting you by mid-November."

Ash cleared her throat. "Er...I'm afraid to report, ma'am, we ran into problems, and I made some questionable decisions. It—"

Even before Natasha could step in to dispute Ash's self-criticism, Kim interrupted. "It's easy to question decisions with hindsight. But I'm not captain anymore. I wasn't expecting a formal report; you'll have to save it for Chip. But I can tell you straight off, both she and I know that if *you* had problems getting here, then with any other guide, there'd be five new little piles of bones out in the wilderness. So just give us the heroic version of the story, and we'll all applaud in the right places."

Ash's face showed a mixture of gratitude and relief. She ran a hand over her cropped hair. "Well, I guess the problems began when Jess and Dani were ambushed by Guards." She launched into the tale, aided by the others. Dinner was cooked and eaten by the time they had finished, and the fire was burning low. The group settled down for a last round of news before sleeping.

"So what else has happened in Westernfort while we've been away? How's Gina?" Dani asked.

The three new arrivals hesitated, their smiles gone. "Well..." Kim began reluctantly.

"Bad news?" Ash said.

Kim nodded. "I'm afraid Gina—"

"She's been ill?" Dani did not let her finish.

"She was," Kim said gently. "I'm sorry. Gina died three months ago. I should have said sooner."

Dani's lips twisted in pain, and she hid her face in her hands. After a moment of hesitation, Natasha put an arm around her shoulders, yet it felt wrong to be offering comfort for the death of someone she had been planning on killing.

"She'll be missed." Ash's eyes had also filled with tears.

"She is. Lynn took it hard. She feels that she failed, but even an Imprinter has limits to what she can heal." Kim shrugged with one shoulder. "Gina was seventy-eight. She didn't do too badly."

"Was it another stroke?" Ash asked.

Kim nodded in reply. She spoke a little more, describing the details of Gina's last days. In listening, Natasha was aware of her own contradictory impulses. It was impossible not to be moved by the anguish of the others, yet Gina had been the source of the heresy, the one who had incited hatred of the Goddess. Her death was long overdue, and any true daughter of Celaeno should have felt only joy in learning of it.

Kim finished talking.

"I'd have liked to say goodbye," Dani mumbled through her hands.

"It's hard. But I think Gina felt we were making more than enough fuss as it was."

"I can imagine." Dani sat up and wiped her eyes. For a few seconds, she fought for control of her lower lip. "Anyway, isn't it time for sleep?" It was obvious from her face that she would not fall asleep easily. Natasha guessed that Dani wanted the privacy of darkness to deal with her grief. She discreetly removed her arm from Dani's shoulder and was rewarded by a quick half smile of thanks.

Natasha's head was also in far too much turmoil for sleep. Once the lanterns were out, she lay wrapped in her blanket, staring at the dull red glow on the ceiling and trying to sort out her thoughts. Naively, she had expected Kim Ramon to be like the sinister villains of street theater. The Chief Consultant had conceded that the woman had many admirable qualities, yet Natasha had blithely assumed that she would easily see through the transparent mask to the evil within her soul. If it was a mask.

The memory of Ash's face when Kim had refused to let her blame herself for the problems on the trail came to mind. Kim might no longer have been the captain of the Westernfort Rangers, but from that one small exchange, and from her tone and expression as much as her words, Natasha knew that Kimberly Ramon would always command the loyalty of those who had served under her. Natasha thought of the popular officers in the Guards—the ones who had not relied on military discipline to cover for their own weaknesses, who had led by encouragement, and who were trusted because they in turn trusted their subordinates. At last, Natasha could begin to guess why somebody like Ash had willingly followed her captain and deserted.

The mission was unraveling in Natasha's head. She realized she was grateful that Gina was already dead, despite Dani's grief. Now the number of people to kill had been reduced by one. Even though striking down the founder of the heresy might have been to the glory of the Goddess, Natasha no longer wanted any part in it. Yet, two women were still left to kill, one lying just a few meters away—sleeping, breathing, warm blood pulsing through her heart. For the first time, Natasha desperately wished that she had never volunteered for the mission.

❖

The search party had a spare horse with them, a well-laden pack animal. The supplies were left in the outpost, allowing everyone to ride if they doubled up. However, the horses could not carry the extra load for the whole journey. The day was spent taking turns riding and walking. Natasha found it painfully arduous, even though preferential treatment was given to the women who were worn out from the trek across the wilderness. Night fell long before they reached Westernfort. The wind was freezing against her skin.

Natasha realized that they had made it to their destination only when they stopped. Thick clouds obscured the moons, and a black cliff reared up close by. Cascading water was the loudest sound, but rumbling beneath it were the soft grunts of many drowsy animals. Natasha slipped from the saddle and looked around. No one was in sight, apart from a few hostlers who took charge of the horses. No lanterns shone in the darkness. In the absence of light, she could just make out buildings looking like rough barns. Cal had said that Westernfort might not match their idea of a civilized town, but Natasha had not been expecting anything quite so basic.

"Where do we go?" she asked.

"Up," Ash replied cryptically and pointed to the cliff.

Natasha tilted her head and spotted a pair of lanterns. They appeared to be floating in midair. Then her eyes adjusted to the darkness. A hundred meters above them, the face of the cliff was broken by a broad chasm. A waterfall spouted at one side. The opening was undoubtedly natural, but the bottom was too regular, and now that Natasha looked more closely, she could see that a barricade had been built across the entrance. Its shape was outlined by lamplight glinting on a thin coating of snow. The two lanterns hung on either side of a gateway in this wall.

A pathway up had been carved into the vertical side of the cliff. The rest of the group was heading toward it. Natasha and Dani followed. The cutting was scarcely an armspan wide. As they got higher, Natasha was grateful for the darkness so she could not see the drop over the side; she was even more grateful that someone had taken the trouble to sweep the snow away from underfoot. She kept as far from the edge as she could, to the amusement of Dani, walking beside her.

"Don't you like heights?" Dani asked.

"Heights are okay. It's falling I'm not keen on."

"No one's been killed on this path yet." Dani paused before adding cheerfully, "Except for a couple of hundred Guards, of course."

Natasha clenched her teeth. The Chief Consultant had spoken of the losses received in the attack on Westernfort. *They were brave women who died heroically for their faith,* she wanted to say, but could not. *They deserve respect.* In a flare of anger, she fixed her eyes on the approaching gates—unguarded, as if the heretics were flaunting their invulnerability. But then a voice called out an irreverent welcome from above.

"Dani...back so soon?"

Dani laughed and shouted in reply, "Try saying that as if you're pleased to see me!"

Natasha looked up. The faces of several Westernfort Rangers were smiling down at them from the top of the wall. The Guards would have posted sentries outside the gate, with swords drawn. The heretics had posted theirs where they could have the greatest military, rather than visual, effect. *You can show respect by taking your enemy seriously.* Natasha's anger faded. She was about to enter into the heart of the enemy stronghold. She needed to show the same respect.

The party passed through the gateway. Natasha stopped in surprise. She had been expecting the sides of the cleft to draw in, with a few houses close by and maybe the opening to some caves. Instead, she found that she was standing at the mouth of another valley. In the darkness, it was impossible to tell its extent, but it was clearly far larger than anyone would have guessed from below. The lights of a fair-size town shone about a quarter of a kilometer away.

"As elected leader, may I welcome you to Westernfort." The tinge of self-parody marked Kim's voice. She continued talking to Rohanna and Cal. Natasha hurried to catch up so she could also hear what was being said. "It's rather late. We need to sort you out somewhere to sleep. The full introductions can wait. I'll get someone to show you around tomorrow. I'm afraid the accommodations won't be luxurious. We're getting a bit cramped here. The population is now over seven hundred. Which is why we've started a second settlement."

"Another town?" Rohanna asked sharply.

"It's under development. The site isn't as strong as here. So it will take a few years' work to make it fully defensible. Fortunately, the Guards have been leaving us alone. Some folks are living there already. We won't be moving anyone in midwinter, but come spring, more will go, and we'll probably ask you to join them. We've renamed the place Ginasberg."

"I'm sure Gina would have been pleased by the honor," Rohanna said.

"And I'm sure Gina would have said something rude." Kim laughed. "But she might have been secretly pleased as well."

After a few minutes, they reached the first of the buildings. The houses were solidly constructed, with proper doors and windows. The road was unpaved but level. From what Natasha could see, Westernfort was as substantial as many towns in the Homelands.

At an intersection, Ash stopped, searching awkwardly for words. "Um...this is where I say good night." She pointed with her thumb. "My home's down there. I'll be seeing you around. And I'm sorry it wasn't a more pleasant journey."

"Thank you for getting us here, and..." Rohanna's voice also trailed off.

There was not much else to say, certainly not while they were standing in the freezing cold. After two months in her company, watching Ash walk away was strange. Natasha felt still odder when Dani also made to head off. The young heretic plainly shared her unease and dithered, "I live behind my shop. If it was earlier, I'd invite you in, but...of course, if you'd like, you could—"

"Jess needs to get herself settled in with us," Rohanna interrupted on Natasha's behalf. "I'm sure she'd be happy to visit you tomorrow."

"Yes," Natasha quickly agreed.

"Right, then. I'll be off. And I'll come and find you tomorrow... after dinner."

"Fine." Natasha wanted to say more, but the words would not come. By tomorrow evening, the mission would probably be over, and she would be dead. Natasha watched Dani disappear around a corner. They had, most likely, just said their final good night.

Kim led the way to a large square in the center of town. She dispatched one Ranger on an errand and dismissed the other; then she pushed open the door of a substantial stone house. "I've just sent for Mirle to find out where you're being put. She deals with such things. We can wait in my house until she gets here. It will be warmer."

The room they entered was large. Several doors led to adjoining rooms. The furnishings were simply, but solidly, constructed with a table and benches in one corner and a couple of deep chests against a wall. The only light came from the dying fire in the hearth, but the room was not unoccupied. A woman had been dozing in a chair in front of the fire. The sound of the door roused her.

"You're back already? Did you find them?"

"As you can see." Kim lit a lantern and gestured to where Natasha stood with the others, just inside the doorway.

The woman slipped out of her chair and came forward. She was a good few centimeters shorter than Natasha and looked to be about forty. Her eyes were large, set in a delicately molded face. She and Kim exchanged a hug and a quick kiss of greeting; then Kim partially freed herself from the embrace and turned back. "This is my partner, Lynn. I'm sure you've heard of her. And these are Rohanna, Cal, and Jess." Kim pointed out the respective people as she made the informal introduction.

The Chief Consultant was wrong. They are lovers! The thought hit Natasha like a blow, immediately followed by, *We're alone with our remaining targets. Will it be over so soon?* She looked at the two women standing arm in arm. The knife in her belt felt alive, as if it were twitching of its own accord.

Natasha's eyes flicked toward Rohanna, dreading to see the signal to strike, yet the senior Guard was behaving as though nothing exceptional had happened or was likely to happen. She was going through a bland set of responses—how pleased they were to arrive, how nice it was to meet at last. Natasha had gotten used to feeling like an actress, but now, she did not seem to be in the same play as everyone else.

The door opened again, and a thin-faced woman entered. Her hair was streaked with gray, though she did not look much older than Kim or Lynn. A cloak was pulled tightly around her square shoulders. "I hear you found them," she mumbled through a yawn.

"They'd almost made it here on their own," Kim replied before launching again into rapid introductions. She finished by indicating the newcomer. "This is Mirle Lorenzo, deputy leader of Westernfort. She gets the job of sorting out all the administrative parts I can't be bothered with. I salve my conscience by telling myself she enjoys the challenge."

Mirle laughed. "Oh, but I do. And can I assume that the current challenge is finding a home for these three?"

"And reading my mind is another part of her job," Kim tacked on.

"And not grumbling when I get dragged out of bed."

"Were you in bed?"

"No. But I wouldn't have grumbled if I had been."

The leader and her deputy were clearly on friendly terms, but regardless of whether Mirle had been in bed, it was too late for anyone to want to linger with idle chatter. Polite words of good night were exchanged, and then Natasha was back in the open, trailing Mirle and the others across the darkened square. The lateness and cold meant that the streets were mainly empty, although there was still some activity around something that looked suspiciously like a tavern.

After a short walk, they arrived at another stone building and entered a large common room where several people were gossiping by the hearth. Natasha felt detached from her surroundings. She stood back while Mirle and another woman talked to Rohanna, explaining the living arrangements of the block and the locations of various amenities and giving the names of other residents. Then they were led along a corridor leading off the communal area.

Doors lined both sides. Mirle finally opened one halfway down the row, and they were ushered through.

The room they entered was small, three meters square, with plain, lime-washed walls. A shuttered window was opposite the door. The only furnishings were a box bed built into one wall and a chest under the window. A ladder led up to an opening for the loft space.

"There's a pallet and blanket up there for you," Mirle said.

Natasha realized that the comment was for her and nodded. After a last round of advice, Mirle bid them good night and closed the door behind her.

"It's a bit small, but better than camping in the snow," Rohanna said in a loud but ordinary voice. "Would you like something to eat before sleeping?"

Natasha stared at her. For a moment, she doubted her own sanity. Maybe she really was Rohanna's daughter, and the mission was a delusion. Then she saw that the senior Guard was checking the room while keeping up a string of idle chatter, inspecting both the loft and outside the window. At last, Rohanna beckoned the other two closer until their heads were touching.

"The new information means there has to be a change in plan," she whispered so quietly that even someone standing at the other side of the room would have been hard-pressed to hear.

"Which part of it?" Cal asked.

"The new town, Ginasberg. Do you realize what it means?" Not waiting for an answer, Rohanna went on, "If the heretics have two strong bases, we'll never manage to purge the planet of them. If we attack one town, we'd have another gang of heretics at our back, free to hit our supply lines. We failed to conquer Westernfort because we discovered it too late, but with the new site...even Ramon admitted that it's not yet secure. We must get word about it back to Landfall."

"How?" Again it was Cal who asked the question.

"We must wait until spring, when you, with your Ranger training, will have a chance of getting through." Rohanna paused. "And there will be another slight change in the plan since Gina is dead. The mission was to execute the heretics' leader, the captain of their Rangers, and their Imprinter. Gina has been called to account for her crimes, and Ramon is now the leader. The captain is Chip Coppelli, and executing her has therefore become our third objective."

"But..." Natasha began and then stopped. She wanted things over and done with. Though her enthusiasm for the mission had gone, delay would only make it worse. Neither did she want to add more names to their list. "The Chief Consultant gave our targets by name. She said it wouldn't be murder to kill those three, since they've already been tried and convicted."

"Every heretic is under sentence of death," Rohanna whispered. "The more we dispose of, the better. Those the Chief Consultant named were merely our top three." She paused. "We needed Ash O'Neil to get us here, but I'll admit I spent some time on the trail wondering if I could engineer an accident for the other one, especially once the food ran low."

Natasha spun to face the window, unable to control her expression. Rohanna put an arm about her shoulder and gently pulled her back into the huddle. "That shocks you?"

"It's just...Dani...after everything...I mean...I'm sure she could be..."

"Brought back into the faith?" Rohanna finished the sentence.

Natasha nodded.

"It's easy to forget how young you are. You don't have our experience of the world." Rohanna spoke gently, brushing the hair from Natasha's forehead. "It can be hard if you spend too much time with any heretic. You start to feel pity for her. You wonder if some awful tragedy turned her away from the Goddess and whether you can return her to a state of grace. But you can't. I've met dozens like Dani, and I've learned to see through the façade. It's not hard. Ask her what she'd do if she had a wounded Guard at her mercy. Her soul is polluted. The pity you should feel is for the innocent ones she'd corrupt if she had the chance. You must wear the love of the Goddess about your heart like a shield."

Natasha closed her eyes and breathed deeply. It was desire rather than pity that she felt, but the rest of Rohanna's words hit their mark. Dani was her enemy, yet it was hard to subdue her emotions. She felt in need of help. "I wish I had a copy of *The Book of the Elder-Ones* to read from."

"I'd also be grateful for the comfort. I don't think we'll find one here, but I could go and ask in the common room." Rohanna's voice held a dry irony. She kept her arm around Natasha and hugged her as she went on. "You're doing well. It's easy to pray in the temple—much harder when you're isolated and surrounded by nonbelievers. You were chosen for the strength of your faith. Don't let it slip."

Cal joined in. "It was a rough journey. The five of us had to work together. I had to force myself not to think of them as comrades."

"And I guess you're not happy about delaying the mission? You'd rather get it over with?" Rohanna suggested.

"Yes."

"That's understandable. I'd find it easier myself. But you must remain strong for another few months. I know you can do it. And if you ever need to talk to someone, you only have to ask. At least now, we have the privacy of our own room. I wouldn't leave you to battle alone through the web of the heretics' lies."

Natasha could only nod, but it was comforting to know that Rohanna understood her confusion and was neither critical nor angry. Rather, the older woman was willing to offer support. Rohanna was more truly her mother than Cilla Ionadis had ever been. And surely it would be easier, now that she could spend more time alone with the two Guards and less with Ash and Dani. This was her chance to rebuild the purity of her faith, before death took her to Celaeno's halls of judgment.

Rohanna continued. "The delay will be a mixed blessing. There will be extra risk and temptation. But it gives us time to plan for the successful conclusion of our mission and Cal's return." She smiled sadly at Natasha. "But it's only Cal's return that is certain. I'm afraid you and I might still be required to give our lives."

"I have never been frightened to die for the Goddess," Natasha said firmly. And it was the truth. Killing for the Goddess was the thing that was starting to hurt.

Rohanna's lips gently brushed Natasha's forehead in a mother's kiss. A lump rose in Natasha's throat as their eyes met. They were sworn comrades, united in the service of the Goddess. Unlike the treacherous attraction to Dani, the love and trust between them was genuine and sanctified. She was determined to be worthy of it.

CHAPTER TEN—AN AWKWARD SITUATION

Natasha rinsed out her porridge bowl and returned to the bench by the hearth. All around, the common room of the lodging block was emptying as women finished their breakfast and headed out to work. Before long, only Rohanna, Cal, and a couple of elderly residents remained. The older folk engaged in an unexciting conversation, mainly about the weather, that Natasha felt little desire to join. She was wondering how to excuse herself when the door opened and a young member of the Westernfort Rangers came in.

"Hi. Are you the new arrivals?" The woman must have known the answer and went on without pausing. "My name's Shelly, and I've been assigned to show you around."

"Right. We'll just get our coats." Rohanna spoke for the group.

Shelly was a solidly built young woman with a round face and a very earnest expression. It quickly became apparent that she was taking her responsibilities seriously and was determined to do a thorough job in pointing out absolutely everything. Rohanna and Cal clearly found it wearing and started to hang back, but Natasha was prepared to make a bit more effort for the company of someone her own age.

In daylight, Natasha was able to make a proper evaluation of Westernfort. The town was far more substantial than Natasha had expected, although a little rough by Homeland standards. None of the streets were paved, and the civic buildings lacked grandeur. On the other hand, there was nothing like the crumbling hovels that housed the poorest farm laborers in the Homelands. All the buildings were of solid stone construction, with slate-tiled roofs. The presence of flues showed that many had under-floor heating—

something Natasha had already noticed in their lodgings. The building had apparently been built as a barracks but was now used as temporary accommodation for new arrivals.

The bathhouse was well designed and more than adequate for the size of the population. A range of shops and businesses provided all the normal facilities. The shouts of street vendors were identical to those in the Homelands. *And what was I expecting?* Natasha asked herself ironically. *"Get your unholy potatoes here"?* The only discrepancy that struck her was the absence of a chapel, but of course, it was hardly likely that the heretics would have one of those.

Outside the town, the valley was shaped in an unequal V, with the entrance at the bend. The longer arm looked to be a few kilometers in length, with a small lake lying a short way along. The flat bottom of the valley was farmland, currently covered with snow. Virtually the entire population had homes in the town. Only the most remote farms had separate homesteads. Natasha spotted no more than half a dozen in the distance. Forests of dark green pines made a solid band on the higher slopes; above them, sheer-sided mountains formed an almost complete ring. The only place the mountains failed was at the mouth.

Shelly concluded her tour at the fortification built across the entrance. At its broadest, the valley was over a kilometer in width, but here, it narrowed to a bare fifty meters. The stone wall was about eight meters high and three meters deep. Steps on the inside gave access to the top, where a crenulated parapet provided further protection for defenders.

From this vantage point, Natasha looked down on the flat plain outside the walls. As she had seen on their arrival, the valley emerged halfway up a massive cliff face. Livestock was kept below. The lowland was dotted with assorted herds and their barns. The only way up to Westernfort was the path that had been hacked out of the cliff—a route so narrow that even in daylight, Natasha was not sure it was wise to walk two abreast. To her mind, the defensive wall across the valley mouth seemed unnecessary, and she said as much to Shelly.

"We needed it when the Guards attacked five years ago," Shelly said with feeling. "There must have been over a thousand of them camped down below."

In Natasha's opinion, this had to be an exaggeration. All the Guards in the Homelands numbered barely two thousand. *Yet even if they'd sent every last one, it would be a completely wasted effort against the wall.* The thought was uncomfortable.

"We knew they were coming, so we'd brought all the animals up here," Shelly continued.

"That must have been fun."

"Oh, it was. The sheep were okay on the path, but pigs can be awkward bastards. Anyway, the Guards couldn't starve us out. So they just kept trying to storm the gates."

Natasha leaned through one of the crenulations and looked down on the pathway. Anyone standing below would have been a sitting target for archers. "Isn't there another way into the valley?"

"There are two trails. We call one the back gate and one the side gate, but they're only suitable for small scouting parties, and we've got them well protected. Other than that, it depends on how good you are at mountain climbing. You could always try coming over the top." Shelly pointed to the nearest peak to illustrate her point.

Cal and Rohanna had already left the top of the wall and were huddled at the base, out of the wind. Natasha followed them down, but rather than join them, she wandered to the entrance, followed by Shelly. The gates were made of heavy timber, reinforced by iron bars, and even if enough Guards had made it that far, the space on the path outside was not sufficient to maneuver a battering ram large enough to have any effect.

"Couldn't they see it would be impossible to force a way through here?" Natasha voiced her thoughts aloud.

"I know what you mean. I thought they would give up after the first day, when they saw how many women they lost. But they kept on coming. I almost got bored with shooting them. I'd been in the Rangers for a couple of years. I'd just finished my probation. This was the first time I'd killed anyone. It wasn't like I thought it would be. The Guards were..." Shelly's sentence trailed away; her face held a deep frown. Then she shrugged. "Mind you, I don't know what I was expecting."

Which is not surprising, Natasha thought. Shelly struck her as someone who possessed limited imagination.

With Shelly beside her, Natasha stepped through the gateway. The wind was stronger and colder on the unprotected cliff face. She walked a few paces down the path and looked up at the outside of the wall, shielding her eyes from the small particles of ice whipped up by the gusts. Five years before, she had been a new recruit in the Militia, but if she had been two or three years older, she might easily have been in the force sent against Westernfort. She might have been killed on this very spot by the woman she was now talking to. She tried to nurse a desire for revenge, but it would not fix in her heart. Instead, she felt her anger grow at the officers who had ordered the attack. They might as well have commanded their women to dig a hole, stand in it, and slit their own throats. The outcome would have been the same, but there would have been less distance to carry the bodies for burial. *They died not only heroically, but also senselessly.*

"Did any Guards make it inside the wall?" Natasha asked, wondering if the sacrifice had been totally futile.

"No. Some got as far as the gate. If you look carefully, you can see one or two hack marks in the wood. But no Guard has ever gotten into Westernfort. They all died on the path."

"Did you feel sorry for them?"

"For Guards?" Shelly sputtered with laughter.

Silly question, Natasha thought.

"Shelly? Is there much more?" Cal called from the gateway.

"No. That's it. We've finished," Shelly replied

"Right. Well, we're going back. We're getting cold."

"We'll come too," Natasha said.

Natasha followed Shelly back through the gates and toward town. Rohanna and Cal were going briskly and already had quite a lead. The two younger women walked at a more leisurely pace.

"I hate Guards," Shelly said abruptly.

"Why?" It was probably another silly question, but Natasha got the feeling Shelly wanted her to ask.

"Because of what they did to my grandmother." From her tone of voice, it was obvious that Shelly had indeed wanted to be asked. She launched enthusiastically into the story. "I was only seven at the time. My family had to escape from Landfall. We got as far as the wildlands, but then we were caught by the Guards. They tortured my grandmother...burnt her with a red-hot iron bar. They were going to start on me, to make my parents say where Westernfort was. But Gina and Captain Ramon had only just started it, so we didn't know. The Guards wouldn't believe us. I was too young to understand what was going on, but I remember being terrified. Then Captain Ramon came and rescued us. And she killed the Guard major who'd been in charge, though that was a bit later..."

Shelly rattled on, losing Natasha. It was clear that she had a very severe case of hero worship for Kim Ramon. Natasha almost expected the story to end with an account of the dance Kim that performed on the surface of the lake. She also found some of the claims hard to believe. No Guard, in Natasha's experience, came anywhere close to being as evil as the major described by Shelly.

By the time the story was finished, they had reached the town, and Rohanna and Cal had disappeared, presumably back to their lodgings. Natasha was about to go after them when Shelly said, "It's nearly lunchtime. Do you feel like coming for a drink?"

Natasha hesitated before saying, "Yes. Sure." If she was going to stay in Westernfort until spring without being unmasked, it was important to act as ordinary as possible. Abstinence from alcohol was not a good idea.

Although the tavern was like the rest of Westernfort, with the emphasis on functionality, this didn't make it unwelcoming. Early in the day, few customers were gathered, but the fire was blazing in the hearth. Wooden tables and benches ran the length of the room. Flagstones covered the floor. Barrels and bottles stood in the corner behind the bar. Shelly paid for the beer and then led the way to a seat in a quiet corner, close by the fire.

"I hear you had a rough journey getting here." Shelly initiated the conversation.

"Yes. We'd have been dead without Ash."

"You had Danielle Diwan with you as well?" The question was stilted and unnecessary. Surely Shelly already knew the answer. She was trying to sound casual, and failing. Natasha realized that the young Ranger was after something. She hoped it was just general information.

"And my parents." Natasha played for safety.

"Did Dani talk about me at all?"

"Er...to be honest, we were pretty much taken up with day-to-day survival." It wasn't strictly true, but for the life of her, Natasha could not remember what they actually had talked about.

"She's really nice, isn't she?"

Natasha got the feeling that agreeing too enthusiastically would be unwise. "Um...I suppose so."

"Dani and me, we've...sort of...got this thing going," Shelly said indistinctly.

Is she warning me off? Natasha wondered. However, Shelly seemed to be too unfocused for such a definite plan, and there was a vacant smile on her face. *Or does she just want to talk?* Natasha was not certain if she wanted to hear, but she was not given the option. Shelly was on a roll.

"I've had a soft spot for Dani for years, ever since she came here, but it never seemed like she wanted to know. Then there was a party in the square, last spring, for Landfall, and we just clicked...became lovers. Then Dani took the job in the Homelands. I was dead against it. She could easily have been killed, but she was determined. We had a big quarrel, but we didn't actually finish with each other. And now she's back. I haven't seen her yet. But I thought if she'd been talking about me, perhaps I should stop by." Shelly stopped and looked at her expectantly.

If that was a question, do I want to answer it? Natasha wondered. Either way, something vague was best. "Um...maybe."

Shelly smiled and took a mouthful of her drink. "Yes. I'll go and see her this afternoon."

Natasha looked at the surface of her beer. All things considered, it would be much safer and easier if Dani did have a lover waiting for her. Natasha knew that she dared not risk the mission by getting further emotionally involved. It might be the Goddess' answer to the problem—removing temptation. She looked up again at Shelly's happy, good-natured face, and to her surprise, she felt a sudden, ridiculous, and unwarranted desire to murder the woman.

❖

They spent the afternoon meeting various people about the town. The three conspirators returned to their lodgings after dark and shared a meal of bread and stew in the common room. Most of the other residents were recent arrivals in Westernfort and of a similar age to Rohanna and Cal. Apart from one baby, Natasha was the youngest by a good few years. People were pleasant, but she felt that she was on the outskirts of the general conversation, which was fine by her. Rohanna and Cal could do all the lying about their supposed life history in the Homelands.

When the meal was over, she found a quiet corner to sit in. Rohanna had joined a card game on the other side of the room, and Cal was talking to a group by the hearth. Natasha considered going to the tavern. Surely that was what a young heretic in her position would do. But then she wondered whether there was something more useful she should occupy herself with—something that could advance their mission.

They would need to collect provisions for the return journey, weapons to supplement the small daggers they carried, and maps. In Cal's estimate, they had at least three months to complete their preparations before the weather would be safe for travel, which should be ample time. Possibly the trickiest part would be in finding somewhere safe to store the things they gathered. They would also need horses, although obviously, they could not take the animals before the executions had been carried out.

Natasha looked up, and all other thoughts flew out of her head. Dani had just entered the common room. It was sleeting outside. Dani's boots were splattered with mud, and her cloak was wet. She pushed back her hood and peered around. Uplighting from the oil lantern in her hand enhanced the impish quality of her face but did nothing to spoil the smile when she spotted Natasha.

"Hi. You said you'd come over and visit my place... remember?"

Natasha scrambled to her feet. "I wasn't sure if you'd be free."

"Why?"

"Something might have cropped up." Natasha did not want to mention Shelly by name.

"No. I'm all yours."

Natasha tried not to speculate on how literally she could take the phrase, but she could not help hoping that it meant Shelly was missing from the gathering at Dani's home. There were enough potential complications in meeting Dani's family without adding extra tensions.

On the short walk across town, Dani was mainly silent, apart from apologizing for not coming earlier and making a few vague comments about things she'd had to sort out. It gave Natasha time to prepare for the forthcoming introductions, although it was hard to know what to expect, since Dani had never spoken of her family.

They arrived at a shop situated on a corner just off the main square. Dani lifted the latch and led the way into a small oblong room. A window was at the front; another door was in the back. Apart from this, every square centimeter of the walls was taken up with deep shelves, although there was far more empty space on them than pots.

Dani indicated the gaps. "It seems while I've been away, people have been going in for plate-smashing in a big way. But at least it will keep me busy for a while." She put down the lantern by the rear door and bent to untie the laces on her muddy boots.

Natasha copied her actions in silence. She did not know a single thing about Dani's family, not even how many sisters she had. She prayed that there would not be a mass family gathering, complete with nosy grandmothers. She had lied in Dani's presence more than enough already.

Dani slipped out of her boots and opened the door. Natasha followed. The room they entered was larger than the shop, although still not huge. It appeared to be a combined workshop and living room. A bed stood in one corner and a potter's wheel in another. A large chimney took up most of one wall. Logs were burning in the grate, casting a cheerful glow over the well-ordered clutter. Nobody else was in the room.

Natasha looked about, confused. "Where are your mothers?"

"Dead," Dani said simply.

Natasha bit her tongue, but before she could draw breath to say, "Sorry," Dani appended, "And so is my sister." She hung the lantern from a hook on the ceiling and turned around. Her expression was hard to read, but when she spoke, her voice was quietly unemotional. "It's all right. It was years ago. I've mostly gotten over it."

"Oh. So you live here by yourself?" Natasha cursed to hear how weak her words sounded, but they clearly amused Dani. The smile returned to the heretic's face, and she nodded.

The thought occurred to Natasha that she had never been totally alone with Dani before—she did not count lying under a bush while they were being hunted by Guards. It was an awkward situation, but one that needed facing sooner or later. *Always assuming she is going to make a pass at me*, Natasha mocked herself. It would be desperately disappointing if Dani did not.

"Would you like some tea?" Dani's voice interrupted her thoughts.

"Er..." Suddenly, Natasha could not even think of an answer to so trivial a question. She opened and closed her mouth a few times, feeling like a complete idiot, while the smile on Dani's lips grew. At last, Natasha managed to nod before collapsing onto a bench in front of the fire, stretching her stockinged feet out to the heat. The wooden planks of the floor snagged gently on her heels.

"I'd have invited you over for dinner, but my cooking suffers from my trade. I tend to bake everything until it is white-hot and has a hard glaze finish. Did you notice how Ash never let me help with the food?" Dani spoke lightly as she filled a kettle from a large urn and hung it from a chain over the fire. Then she also sat down on the bench.

Natasha fought to regain her composure. If Dani did make overtures, it would be necessary to display a lot of tact. Natasha tried to prepare suitable phrases. Her gaze caught on the doorway. Of course, running away would be far easier, but very hard to do in a dignified fashion. Her eyes continued to travel around the walls; she tried not to make too big a point of not looking at the bed. There was not much space for all the things squeezed into the room, but the effect was cozy rather than cramped.

"What are your first thoughts of Westernfort?" Dani asked, reclaiming Natasha's attention.

"It's more civilized than I expected," Natasha managed to answer and then reconsidered her words. "I mean the amenities, not the people...not that the people aren't civilized. But I wasn't expecting...I mean, I was..." Natasha stopped. She could not believe the mess she was making.

Dani laughed, her eyes searching Natasha's face. "Oh, I don't know. There are some very dodgy folks around here."

Natasha tried to start again. "I hadn't been counting on a bathhouse and sewers. I didn't think you..."

Natasha felt that she was starting to dig herself another hole. Luckily, Dani took mercy on her and turned away to stare into the fire. "The town has advanced a lot recently. I've been here eight years, and I've seen the changes. Many of the houses have under-floor heating, but I like a real fire." Dani indicated vaguely in the direction of the hearth. When she lowered her arm, her hand, as if incidentally, ended up on Natasha's thigh.

Somehow, Natasha stopped herself from yelping at the shock that tore through her body. The tingling from Dani's hand exploded down her leg and up her spine. She felt the hairs on the back of her neck stand on end, while her stomach performed a complicated sequence of flip-flops. Dani continued looking into the fire and talking, but it might as well have been gibberish. Natasha heard the individual words but could not hold them in her head long enough to construct any meaning from them. Occasionally, Dani would pause, as though she were waiting for a response. Natasha could only reply with strained, noncommittal noises.

I've got to do something, Natasha thought. *I can't let this go on.* Her leg under Dani's hand was throbbing. It was the most wonderfully paralyzing sensation she had ever experienced. Her pulse was doing crazy things, and her stomach had taken on a life of its own. *Natasha, this is serious. Say something,* she pleaded with herself, but her willpower had evaporated in the heat building inside her.

Dani continued talking about something; possibly it was making sense. But at last, she stopped, bit her lower lip thoughtfully, and turned to look at Natasha with a soft smile on her face. "Tell me—how much encouragement can I take from the fact I've had my hand on your leg for the last five minutes without you complaining?"

The time for playing was over. Natasha fought to control herself—her face, her voice, her breathing. "Er...well, I'm sorry, but...I'm afraid I was trying to think of some tactful way to ask you to remove it. But I didn't want..."

Dani's expression slowly retreated to a forced blankness. "Ah...right. Sorry." She lifted her hand, interlaced its fingers with those of her other hand, and shoved them both between her knees. Her eyes fixed back on the fire.

"It's not that I don't like you a lot, but..." Natasha could not bring herself to continue.

"But you don't like me like that," Dani finished for her.

"I really want us to keep..." Natasha's voice died.

"Are you going to say we can still be friends?"

"I'd have hoped that went without saying." Natasha's voice regained some cohesion.

Dani nodded and tried to smile, but to Natasha's dismay, she could see tears forming.

"Do you want me to leave?" Natasha offered.

"No. You haven't had your tea yet. Mind you, the kettle has probably boiled dry."

Dani got up from the bench and attended to the kettle. Natasha saw her surreptitiously wipe her eyes. She felt on the verge of crying herself, but by the time Dani sat back down with two steaming mugs, they had both rebuilt a degree of self-control.

"We were talking about your impressions of Westernfort." Dani bravely restarted the conversation. "I take it you've been given a tour of the place."

"Yes. This morning. We were shown around by a Ranger called Shelly. She said..." Natasha hesitated, remembering the conversation in the tavern.

"She talked about me?" Dani suggested, a hint of amusement returning to her voice.

"Yes. I...er..." Natasha wanted to make excuses. "Coming here tonight...I didn't mean to lead you on, but I didn't expect to be alone with you, and Shelly implied you and she had a relationship going, so when..." Natasha swallowed. "You caught me by surprise."

Dani's lips formed a wry grimace. "My relationship with Shelly exists purely in her dreams. She's been chasing me for ages. I've tried dropping hints, but I'm afraid hints don't work with Shelly. She's ever so sweet and well meaning, and she's not actually stupid, but it can be very hard work getting through to her."

"She said you'd been lovers," Natasha said, probing.

This time, Dani groaned and buried her face in her hands. "Okay, I confess...once." Her hands dropped. "I'm afraid I was very seriously drunk at the time."

"That's not the way Shelly tells it."

"I can imagine," Dani said in ironic despair. "I'm going to have to say something to her. Being nasty to Shelly is like kicking a puppy dog, but this has been going on too long. I keep hoping she'll hit on someone else. I've been away eight months. That should have given her plenty of time."

"I'd have thought Westernfort was big enough to offer a range of candidates."

"But obviously, none of them are right for Shelly. We need somebody new...like you." Dani's eyes focused on Natasha for the first time since the rebuff. She playfully adopted a tone of serious intensity. "Right, okay, I'm not your type, but how do you feel about Shelly? I really would see it as the most enormous favor."

Natasha joined in the game. "Well..." She drew out the word, pursing her lips thoughtfully. "I don't know...how would you rate her technique? Points out of ten?"

"Can I use fractions?"

"Do you need to?"

Dani shrugged. "It'd give a spurious air of precision, because like I said, I was far too drunk to be making accurate observations. But I'm sure she did her best."

Both of them were laughing. An underlying rawness remained, but the first steps had been taken in rebuilding the easy friendship they had shared on the trail. The humor continued at the expense of the unfortunate Shelly before moving to a range of other subjects. But despite her effort at nonchalance, Natasha could still feel her leg tingling where Dani had touched her. She tried hard not to think of it, to work on the idle chatter, but there was an ache deep inside.

Eventually, Natasha put down her empty mug and rose to go. She stopped in the shop to reclaim her muddy boots while Dani went ahead to wait by the door, ready to bid her guest good night. Natasha tied her laces and crossed the room, about to offer some polite words of thanks. And then their eyes met.

Natasha's pulse leapt, and the tingling in her leg resurged. She knew she was standing too close and holding eye contact for too long, but there was nothing she could do. She was paralyzed in the battle to stop herself from wrapping her arms around Dani, pulling her close, and kissing her. The moment dragged on forever. In the end, it was Dani who moved away, backing off and dropping her eyes.

"Look, I'm a big, grown-up girl, and I can take no as an answer, but that isn't the message I'm getting from you." Dani's voice cracked in pain.

"It's..." Natasha squeezed her eyes shut. What could she say? "It's just that...I do like you. But back in the Homelands..."

"You've left someone there," Dani said quietly, clearly trying to make sense of Natasha's words.

Natasha opened her eyes, grasping at Dani's suggestion. "Er... yes."

"Will she be joining you here?"

"No."

Dani sagged against the door frame. "But?"

"But at the moment, I don't feel ready for...that it would be right..." Natasha's throat tightened. She could not make herself lie again.

Dani nodded slowly. In silence, she paced across the shop and then turned to look at Natasha. "So there might be a chance for me if I wait?" The softness of Dani's voice did nothing to hide her emotions.

Natasha's expression battled between a half smile and an agonized grimace. She all but fled from the shop.

Dani sighed, closed the door on the night, and wandered back to the fireside in the rear room. She surveyed the scene. While she had been away, the friend who had minded the shop had also kept the room clean and dusted but had done nothing to clear the piles of jumble scattered across the place. Finding homes for it all had been the job occupying Dani for most of that day. Her room had not been so tidy for years. She could see whole runs of floorboard.

"I must have it bad for her if I even tidied up before she came round." Dani spoke her thoughts aloud. Her face started to crumple, but she concentrated on breathing. Crying would not help. The situation was not hopeless, and even though it had not produced the desired result, the time spent clearing the room was not a complete waste. She had found several items she had thought to be lost.

❖

Three of the residents were huddled around the hearth in the common room as Natasha raced through. She kept her head down, anxious to avoid eye contact. Her mood was not up to exchanging pleasantries. Fortunately, Rohanna and Cal were not present. Neither were her comrades visible in their room, and no candles were burning. But at the sound of the door closing, Rohanna's voice called out from the box bed, "Is that you, Jess?"

"Yes."

"Where have you been?"

"At Dani's."

"Is everything okay?"

"Yes, sure." The lie was no more blatant than those she had told Dani. "Good night."

Natasha scrambled up the ladder to the loft. She could not bear to be pulled into a discussion. To her relief, no further questions followed from the room below.

Hurriedly, Natasha removed her outer clothing and crawled under her blankets. Then, despite all her effort, tears squeezed from beneath her eyelids—tears of shame at the lies she had spoken and despair that they had been necessary. Although maybe the impression she had given to Dani was not a complete lie. She had indeed left a woman behind in the Homelands—a truthful, honorable woman called Natasha Ionadis.

Chapter Eleven—The Blasphemous Imprinter

At the same time that Natasha was visiting Dani, another meeting was taking place in the center of town. Ash settled back in her seat and fixed her eyes on the red tiled floor. Gentle heat was radiating across the entire surface from the hot air circulating below. The fire in the hearth was purely for effect, making the domestic room look far more cheerful than Ash's mood. She lifted her head and considered the faces of the other women gathering in the main room of Kim's house. Nobody was smiling, but a few were casting hopeful glances in her direction. Ash again searched her memory for any clues she had missed, wishing that she had good news to pass on, or even definite bad news, so they could form a plan of action to counter it.

Once the last of the invited women were seated, Kim turned to Ash. "So. What do you make of them?"

Ash's face twisted in a frown. "I don't know. And that's the most worrying part. I don't know. After the journey we've been through, we should be closer than sisters...well, either that or ready to kill each other. But I'm left feeling I don't know them any better after two months than I did after two days."

"And what was your impression after two days?"

"They were far more intelligent and far more likeable than I'd expected. But you spoke to them at the outpost and rode back here with them. What did you think?"

"I didn't get past the stage of being pleasantly surprised. I'd been ready for another case like Jo Elson, but she was just a very stupid woman. She honestly thought, since we don't believe in a Goddess, we wouldn't see theft as a sin, so we'd be quite happy for her to pick up anything in Westernfort that took her fancy."

Now Lynn joined in. "Elson was a bit more complicated than that. She was so self-centered, she couldn't see that she was in any way to blame for the trouble she got into. Therefore, it had to be the fault of the Militia and the Sisterhood. She thought that if she got away from them, she could carry on like she always had, without having any problems."

"Either way, having her executed was unpleasant and not something I wish to repeat," Kim said firmly. "But you've put your finger on something. You couldn't spend five minutes with Elson without noticing the chip on her shoulder, whereas all these three seem well-adjusted."

"I'm happiest with the daughter, Jess," Ash said. "Though I'd be hard-pressed to explain why."

"Try."

Ash was silent for a while, collecting her thoughts. "It sounds odd, but it's because you can see that she's hiding something and she's unhappy about it. And my first remark doesn't apply to her. As the journey went on, I did get to know her better."

"Perhaps we should have Dani here," Mirle Lorenzo suggested. "She might have a better feel for someone her own age. You said they got on well."

Ash laughed. "I'm afraid they got on slightly too well for Dani's feelings to be relevant. Lack of privacy meant that nothing much happened between them on the trail, but she's invited Jess over this evening. Even as we speak, I'd guess that Dani is in the process of completely compromising her objectivity."

"Oh, that would explain it," Mirle said, grinning. "I called around on Dani today to arrange a debriefing meeting, and she was tidying her room."

"Dani was tidying her room!" Lynn exclaimed in astonishment.

Once the general amusement had faded, Ash asked, "Has there been any more information from Jules since I left?"

Mirle answered. "Just a quick note, apologizing profusely for landing us with them. Jules said she recruited the family shortly after they arrived in her area and only suspected later that they'd been less than honest with her. She can't swear they're horse thieves, but she has grave doubts. Soon after the family arrived, horses started to go missing. There was nothing in the way of proof, but Jules didn't want to send them here until she'd had a chance to get to know them better, but they were denounced as heretics and had to flee. The worst part is that Jules thinks they may have informed against themselves anonymously to force her hand." Mirle's face became grim. "If Jules comes to harm over this, I'll personally make sure they wish they'd never heard of Westernfort."

"Did Jules have any idea why they wanted to come here?"

Mirle shrugged. "From one or two clues, she suspects that the family have heard of our imprinted horses. Maybe they haven't got the first idea about life outside the Homelands and don't realize they won't be able to find buyers in the next valley."

Ash shook her head immediately. "Not this lot. Certainly, Cal Rowse is familiar with the wildlands. You could tell on the journey, just from the things she watched and the things she ignored. She knows what to look out for. She claims that she used to work as a fur trapper."

While Ash spoke, Chip Coppelli had been listening intently, with a slight frown on her face. Chip was captain of the Westernfort Rangers. She had an open, easygoing manner and a playful sense of humor that led many people to underestimate her on first meeting. Ash could have warned them that it was not a wise thing to do. Chip had been sitting beside the fire, toasting the soles of her feet. The news caught her attention. "Really? Well, if they turn out not to be thieves, that's a useful skill to have around here. And I can put her on the reserves list for the Rangers."

The frown on Kim's face had been getting deeper while the debate progressed. "Something doesn't add up. Despite what Jules wrote, I'm sure they're not petty thieves."

"So maybe they're completely aboveboard," Lynn said. "For all we know, Jules' next letter might apologize for worrying us and say that the real gang of horse thieves has been arrested in her area."

"But we'll have to wait until spring now to get that," Mirle added.

Chip let her head drop back and sighed. "Either they're thieves, or they're not. If things go missing around here, we'll know where to start looking. And if they try running off with some horses, I'm sure we'll have no trouble tracking them down. Then we can just dump them back on the border of the Homelands for the Militia to deal with. Now that the Sisterhood knows where we are, there's no other information they could pass on. So we wouldn't need to deal with them quite as decisively as we did with Elson."

Kim looked thoughtfully at Chip. "So your advice is to do nothing until they step out of line?"

"Yes. I don't see that we're running any risks."

"And how about you, Ash?" Kim turned her head as she spoke.

Ash drew a deep breath. She would have liked to have agreed with her captain, but nagging doubts churned inside her. "I don't know. And like I said about Jess, she's got a guilty conscience about something."

"Maybe lustful dreams of Dani," Chip suggested, smiling.

"I...I think it's more than that. But I could be wrong."

"I've had a thought," Lynn said. "I need help with the animals, and the family needs work. So why not assign Jess to me? It will give us plenty of opportunity to chat without her parents around and allow me to give you a second opinion on her."

Kim nodded. "That sounds like a good idea. Jess seems to be the one who's most likely to let something slip...if there is anything to slip. But I also want someone to keep an eye on the parents. That will be you." She pointed to Ash.

"I don't know if it's necessary. There isn't a single thing I could point—"

Kim cut her off. "You have a hunch that something's wrong. And I'd happily stake my life on one of your hunches."

Ash opened her mouth and closed it again. Then she smiled and gave a lazy salute. "Yes, ma'am. And what exactly do you want me to do?"

"Watch out for suspicious behavior. Keep on their trail without spooking them."

"I'm not sure if I'm any good at that."

"Of course you are. Just pretend that they're a pride of snow lions." Kim smiled grimly.

❖

Lynn's animal enclosure was situated half a kilometer out of town, on the slopes above the lake. Snow was falling steadily the next morning as Natasha tramped toward it along the track. The work was not what Natasha would have chosen, but refusing the assignment would have drawn attention to herself. She could hardly explain to Mirle Lorenzo that she thought imprinted animals were unholy abominations.

Barking was the only reply to Natasha's shout. She pushed open the barn door and slipped inside. It was warmer and less biting out of the wind. Once her eyes adapted to the dim light, she saw that the barn housed an assortment of animals, mainly cows, pigs, and sheep. A dog bounded over to sniff her. Natasha was not sure whether it was a guard or part of the experiments.

She looked at the creatures with distaste. The blessed Himoti had forbidden the imprinting of animals. What the heretics were doing in the barn was sacrilege. Natasha decided to take advantage of being alone to offer a quick prayer to Celaeno, asking forgiveness for assisting the blasphemous Imprinter in her crimes. Her pious endeavor was distracted by the dog butting its head against her hand in an appeal for attention, and before she had finished, she heard footsteps approaching.

"Good morning, Jess." Lynn entered the barn and was immediately pounced on by the dog, with its tail wagging.

"Good morning, Madame Imprint—" Natasha's formal greeting was interrupted.

"Forget the 'Madame' bit. Just call me Lynn."

Lynn sidestepped the dog's enthusiastic welcome and stood by the cows. "Good morning, girls." The cows spared her a contemptuous glance and went back to chewing. "Have you noticed how cows never leave you in any doubt that they consider you dull and not worth bothering with?" Lynn threw the thought over her shoulder.

"Yes, ma...er...Lynn," Natasha floundered. Horrified fascination gripped her. In the Homelands, Imprinters were revered as the chosen of the Goddess. Even as a Guard, Natasha had never before spoken with one. Yet Lynn had turned against Celaeno and willingly joined the heretics. *And I'm going to help kill her.* Natasha tried to reconcile her thoughts with the ordinary woman standing less than two meters away, talking to the cows.

Lynn turned around and faced Natasha. "Right. What have you been told about the work here?"

"Er..." Natasha paused to choose her words. "That you imprint animals, and you need me to help look after them."

"I guess that sums up the main points." Lynn grinned. "Up until now, these animals have been cared for by the general farmhands, but I want to have one person assigned to them exclusively, on the basis that there'll be less chance of messages becoming scrambled. But I'm afraid your work is not going to be very interesting. Have you looked after animals before?"

"Horses," Natasha answered truthfully. It had formed part of her training as a Guard.

"It's the same sort of thing. Your work will mainly involve sticking food in one end and shoveling away what comes out of the other, with a few variations."

Lynn went on to describe the diets of the different animals, show where the tools were kept, and explain exactly what needed to be done. Then she helped with the jobs requiring more than one pair of hands, showing no trace of the aloof arrogance expected from Imprinters. Once the tasks were over, they stopped to catch their breath. Natasha was hot from the exertion.

"I hear you visited Dani last night," Lynn said conversationally.

"I...er, yes." Natasha was caught off guard and felt herself blushing at the speculative look Lynn gave her. "I just had a mug of tea, and then I went home." Her face grew even hotter as she heard how defensive the words sounded.

"Oh," Lynn said. Then she grinned apologetically. "I'm sorry. I shouldn't pry, but Westernfort is nearly as bad as a temple sanctum for gossip."

Natasha swallowed and tried to sound casual. "I wouldn't have thought there was much to gossip about in the average sanctum."

"Don't you believe it. Most Sisters keep their vow of celibacy most of the time, but that just heightens the titillation value when one of them slips."

"But..." Natasha was not sure if she was being teased. What Lynn was saying was scandalous, but there was no reason for her to lie. The suggestion also brought to mind something that had been nagging at Natasha. The Chief Consultant had asserted that Lynn and Kim could not be lovers, since the loss of virginity would destroy an Imprinter's power. Lynn was still an Imprinter. Natasha had already seen enough children running around Westernfort to prove it. Therefore, either the Chief Consultant was wrong, or Lynn and Kim were not truly lovers.

Natasha recoiled. The question was not one that she could come right out and ask, but suddenly, it was very important for her to know whether the Chief Consultant was infallible, and she had an opening to approach the subject.

"In the temple, do Imprinters ever...slip?"

"Imprinters are virtually held prisoner in the sanctum. They don't get the chance to do anything much." Lynn looked thoughtful. "But from what I know of human nature, I'd lay money that some have managed it. They didn't go around boasting about it, though."

"Wouldn't it be noticed? I mean, doesn't it have any effect at all on the ability to imprint?"

"Doesn't for me." From Lynn's smile and tone, it was impossible to doubt that she was telling the truth. "I couldn't imprint while I was pregnant. But that was due to the extra complexity in identifying DNA sequences, rather than loss of ability. One of the first things you learn is to screen out your own DNA when you're in the imprinting trace so you don't accidentally splice it in as well. But for nine months, I had another set of genes there as well."

"You've got children!" Natasha could not help exclaiming.

Lynn looked a little surprised at the tone but then smiled. "Yes. Kim and I have five between us. And speaking of them, I'd better get back. Ardis is fond enough of her younger sisters, but she isn't the most reliable of babysitters." She became more businesslike. "You'll be okay on your own here?"

"Yes."

"Right. I'll drop by and see you again later today." Lynn smiled a goodbye.

Natasha stood and stared at the door for some time after the Imprinter had gone. Everything had seemed so straightforward back at the temple in Landfall. Now there were five children she would be making orphans, and to her utter dismay, Natasha realized that Lynn gave every appearance of being a nice person.

❖

After a few more days working with Lynn, Natasha was in despair. She envied the Guards in the companies sent to storm the walls. They had died for the Goddess, honestly and openly, without betraying anyone's trust. Now she prayed that she would be given a supporting role in the assassinations.

Late one afternoon, Lynn called in at the barn with her youngest child, Becky, a toddler of three. The sheep had been out in the open fields and were being brought in for the night. Lynn and her daughter waited by the gate, watching. One of the older shepherds had come to help and continue Natasha's training in the art of controlling sheepdogs. The lessons were fun, although Natasha would rather not have had an audience for her incompetence.

Natasha whistled what she hoped was the command for "Go left." The sheepdog, Tipsy, lay down. Natasha knew it was a safe bet that she, rather than Tipsy, had made the mistake. The sheep took advantage of Tipsy's obedience to make a bolt for a ditch. Natasha tried to work out the correct command to whistle. There were a number of signals the dogs understood, but none of them was "Do whatever you think best." Which, to Natasha's mind, was a big oversight, since Tipsy definitely had more idea of what to do than she did.

Becky gave a high-pitched giggle of excitement, jumping up and down. The elderly shepherd was no more restrained, bent double in laughter. But eventually, the gray-haired woman got her breath back and took pity on Natasha. After a few more helpful words of advice, the sheep were rounded up. A count revealed one missing.

"I'll take Tipsy and go find it," Natasha said.

"Becky and I will come too. In case you need help." Lynn's voice was gently teasing. Over the previous few days, Natasha's lack of experience in handling sheep had become very obvious.

At the word of command, Tipsy set off in a straight line up the hillside. Lynn and Natasha followed, swinging Becky along between them. The child squealed with laughter as she kicked up snow. Bobbles of ice stuck to the fringe on her fur-lined snowsuit.

"Are sheep always this awkward, or is it due to them being imprinted?" Natasha asked.

Lynn threw back her head and laughed. "Does having a soul make you self-willed?"

"I didn't mean I believed in..." Natasha broke off, wondering whether she had made a blunder and displayed her lack of knowledge of the heretics' doctrine.

Lynn seemed unaware of any contradictions. "It's just the way sheep are. Anyway, these adults are cloned. It's the lambs they're carrying that I've imprinted. The climate here is a bit more extreme than the Homelands. I'm trying to produce a hardier strain."

"What will happen to the lambs when they're born?" Natasha could not stop herself from asking.

"Are you worried someone will eat them?" Lynn responded quickly, but she was grinning. "You're not the only one here with reservations about imprinted animals. Gina was convinced that the equation of uniqueness with having a soul was utter rubbish. But it's one thing to know something rationally and another to act on it. The lambs will be kept for breeding. Their cloned offspring will be fair game for a stew, though. Which keeps everyone in Westernfort reasonably happy."

Natasha thought of the horses killed in the avalanche. "Dani didn't seem bothered in the slightest about eating imprinted animals."

"Yes...well, she wouldn't," Lynn said. "Cloning humans is the other side of the debate."

"Surely there aren't..." Natasha's words died as an appalling possibility occurred to her.

"We haven't cloned anyone in Westernfort yet. But it may come to it."

This did not answer Natasha's question. Dani had been born in the Homelands. But before Natasha could begin to frame the words, Lynn continued, "I won't last forever, and I doubt we'll be able to help another Imprinter escape from the temple. It's been the hardest dilemma of all. We gave a lot of thought to whether I should clone myself."

Tipsy had led them to a small copse and disappeared into the trees. They let go of Becky's hands, and the child scrambled forward beneath the branches, while the two adults forced their way forward more slowly through the tangle of twigs and knotted vines. Natasha was too confused to know what to say, but Lynn appeared not to notice and continued talking.

"Of course, there was no guarantee my clone would be an Imprinter, and it didn't seem logical to create one clone to avoid making any others. In the end, we reached a compromise. Did you know Gina was originally an Imprinter?"

"Er...no."

"She lost the ability due to a head injury, but it wouldn't have affected her DNA. So we decided Gina would be gene mother to Becky."

"Didn't Kim mind?" Natasha was feeling dazed.

Lynn shook her head. "No. She was fond of Gina, and we already had four children. We'd both carried two, and..."

Suddenly, from up ahead, Tipsy erupted into furious barking. Becky shrieked and then stopped. At the sound, Natasha leapt forward, hurling herself through the trees, not noticing the branches whipping her face. She broke into a clearing where a huge dead tree had fallen and created a small landslide. Lynn was half a step behind her.

Becky stood in the open, five meters away, frozen in fear. Tipsy was tearing back and forth around the edge of the clearing, snarling at the animal crouched at bay with the dead sheep at its feet. It took Natasha several stunned seconds to recognize the beast as a mountain cat. Not that she had ever seen one before, but she had heard them described. The wild predator was much larger than Tipsy, with a dappled brown coat and long saber teeth. The animal was angry and agitated. Its eyes darted between dog and child.

"Becky..." Lynn began.

"Stay still, Becky!" Natasha snapped the order. Any sudden movement, and the cat might pounce. Natasha formed her lips into a circle and whistled. Instantly, Tipsy stopped cavorting, dropped to the ground, then looked at Natasha, tongue lolling in a canine grin, happy now that there was someone to take charge of this new game. Natasha pulled out her knife and whistled again, calling the dog on while she also advanced slowly. Lynn needed no instruction and took up a position between them, forming a row.

The cat watched them get closer. A low, threatening rumble sounded in its throat. The beast's ribs were visible down its side, and its eyes were hazy. It was old, starving, and unpredictable. A young, fit cat would have run—would never have taken a sheep in the first place. Natasha wondered whether it had discovered that it could not eat the sheep and now thought the child a better prospect.

She whistled Tipsy on again. The dog shuffled forward on her belly. The cat snapped its teeth, half rose, and then retreated. Step by step, Natasha advanced, never taking her eyes off the cat. She passed the point where Becky was standing. The child tried to grab her leg. Natasha disentangled herself. She dared not take her eyes from the mountain cat. Then Lynn said, "It's okay, I've got her."

"Get her back to safety."

"Won't you—"

"Tipsy and I will cope with it."

Natasha heard the sounds of Lynn's cautious retreat. But what should she do next? If they all left the clearing, would the cat take it as a signal to attack? And she did not want to take the risk that Tipsy might bite the mountain cat. Wild animals were even more poisonous to domestic ones than the other way around. Maybe if they pushed the cat far enough, it would turn and run.

Natasha took more slow steps forward, using herself and Tipsy to drive it along the trunk of the fallen tree. The cat's agitation grew, and it was less willing to back away. Natasha lifted her foot again, but her toe caught under a branch. She looked down, her attention distracted for a second, and the cat pounced.

Guards were not trained in this sort of combat, but Natasha's instincts were good. She threw up her left arm to protect her throat. The cat's jaws locked onto it, teeth sinking through clothes and flesh. But Natasha's other hand was free and punched forward with her dagger. The cat fell back with a yowl of pain. Natasha shifted her weight into a snap kick under its jaw. The force shot the cat's head up, breaking its neck and somersaulting it backward to lie, unmoving, on the snow.

Tipsy gave a whine of disappointment that she had not been able to play as well, and Becky started crying.

"Jess! Are you all right?" Lynn hurried to her side.

"Yes. I'm...er..." Natasha looked down. Her sleeve was soaked in blood.

"Let me help."

Natasha insisted that they move away from the dead mountain cat first; Tipsy was altogether too interested in the body. They didn't stop until they reached the outer edge of the wood. Then Lynn took hold of Natasha's hand and closed her eyes. The healer's trance swept over her. Immediately, the burning in Natasha's arm faded and disappeared. The adrenaline-induced shaking went also. Lynn continued to exert the healer sense long after Natasha felt fully better, but at last, she opened her eyes and released Natasha's hand. Natasha knew that if she looked, the bite would be no more than a ring of clean scabs.

Becky's crying had subsided to an intermittent grizzle. Lynn picked up her daughter and hugged her close, burying her face in the child's neck. When she looked at Natasha again, there were tears in her eyes. "Thank you. I don't know what I'd have done without you there. I don't even have a knife on me."

"It was noth...er..." Natasha felt herself blushing. "I'm just surprised I remembered the right signals for Tipsy." She shrugged. "I guess my memory works better under pressure."

Lynn's eyes continued to hold hers. "I'm in your debt. If you ever need someone to speak up for you, I'm on your side."

Natasha dropped her gaze to the ground. It was a rather strange thing to say and, in the circumstances, sickeningly ironic.

❖

Lynn and Kim sat by the fire in their home. Kim held one of Lynn's hands in her own, gently rubbing a thumb over Lynn's knuckles. Lynn had gone through various stages of shock and was now feeling calm. She stared silently into the flames. Kim was also preoccupied with her thoughts. A potentially messy situation had become even more complicated. If the worst fears about the new family were confirmed, it would make an unpleasant decision more painful.

There was a knock on the door, and Chip Coppelli entered. "We've checked the woods as best we can for now. We'll go out again at first light tomorrow, but it looks like it was just one rogue animal." She stood hesitantly by the door.

"And what else?" Kim asked.

"In regard to...?" Chip queried.

"You're looking nervous."

"I'm frightened you're going to bawl me out for being careless with security."

Kim laughed, mainly in relief. "Would I do that?"

"Yes. About once every five years. I think it's due again."

Kim beckoned the captain over and pointed to a chair. Chip had been lieutenant when Kim was in charge of the Rangers. They were close friends of many years' standing, dating back to long before the 23rd Squadron had deserted.

"Was it an old animal?" Kim asked once Chip was settled.

"Yes. Too sick to hibernate, but it was huge. I wouldn't relish the thought of taking it on with just a dagger. Jess must have a kick like a mule. If she does turn out to be straight, I might try recruiting her for the Rangers."

Lynn had been frowning thoughtfully. Now she spoke. "Chip, I know this will sound odd, but do you mind if I check something— your DNA?"

"Er...no." Mystified, Chip held out her hand.

Lynn took hold of it and closed her eyes. For a while, there was silence in the room, apart from the crackling of the fire. When Lynn released Chip's hand, her expression was even more puzzled than before.

"So? Are you going to tell us anything?" Kim asked.

"Jess is a relative of Chip's. So either Cal or Rohanna must be as well."

"What?" Kim said.

"I don't know why I did it, but when I healed the bite on Jess' arm, I looked at her DNA." Lynn shrugged. "I wasn't in a fit state to think clearly. She'd just rescued Becky, and I wanted to know who she was. I haven't got a clue what I expected to find out, but the DNA was familiar. I've been trying to remember from where, and then you came in."

"If my family is involved, it's trouble," Chip said. "Do you have any idea how close Jess is, or on which side?"

"I'd guess at something like second cousin. If I found out which parent she relates through, I could be more precise. But there's no way I could tell which side of your family."

"And either side make unlikely relatives for a fugitive horse thief," Kim said.

Chip frowned. "I know what you mean. None of my family are petty criminals. They are top-ranked, major-league criminals."

"Is that any way to talk about two of the most respected families in Landfall?"

"Yes," Chip retorted. "The Coppellis are powermongers, and the Tangs are just plain stinking rich. They do what they like and then buy or blackmail the judges. I wouldn't be surprised to find any of my relatives involved in theft, but not small-scale theft. They aren't the sort of people to steal a woman's horse. They'd pay someone to forge evidence against her, have her imprisoned, and confiscate everything she owned."

"You escaped from them. Maybe one of Jess' grandmothers did the same," Kim suggested.

Chip looked thoughtful. "I remember talk about a great-aunt who fell in love with a farmer and ran off with her to the country."

Lynn shook her head. "I don't think that's it. Jess is city-born and bred. She's okay with horses, but before she got here, I'll bet the only time she was close to a pig or sheep was when it was lying on her plate."

"Oh, well. But as I said before, if my family is involved, it's trouble," Chip said grimly.

CHAPTER TWELVE—GAMES FOR THE GUARDS

The cemetery was on a hillside overlooking the town. Only the traditional wooden grave markers showed above the snow covering the ground. Natasha followed Dani along a trampled pathway between lines of crosses. Thick fleece-lined coats protected them from the cold. Frost rimmed the edge of Natasha's hood where her breath had frozen.

When Dani invited her along, Natasha had considered using the weather as an excuse not to go, but it would be strange for a new heretic to avoid paying her respects to the founder of the cult. Fortunately, her unease could be passed off as regret at not meeting the living woman. Dani also was subdued as she led the way to the spot where Gina was buried.

The grave was distinguished only by the newness of the wood. In death, Gina was not being granted any special status. Natasha stood beside Dani and gazed around. The scene was peaceful, as one would expect from a cemetery. Despite her mixed feelings about the grave they had come to visit, Natasha could not restrain a feeling of reverence in the presence of the dead. Whatever crimes these heretics had committed, they were now answering for them to Celaeno.

The cemetery was not large, barely a hundred graves, quite reasonable for somewhere the size of Westernfort after sixteen years. Natasha bit her lip. It represented half the number of Guards who were buried in a common grave below the wall. Really, she should be there, mourning the loss of comrades who had died bravely in the name of the Goddess.

"It's a shame you didn't get to meet her." Dani's voice broke into Natasha's thoughts.

"Yes. I'd been looking forward to..." *Killing her*. Natasha bit back the last two words.

"She was an amazing person."

Natasha made a noncommittal noise. Gina was the reason why Dani would spend eternity in hell. Natasha did not feel generous toward the woman.

"So much knowledge has gone with her—stuff the Sisters want to keep hidden. Gina used to be an Imprinter; then she had her accident. It cracked her skull, and she lost most of the healer sense. They wouldn't let her leave the temple, so they forced her to work in the library." Dani was rambling, unable to cope with the silence of the graveyard. "She spent over thirty years there, secretly reading the books about the Elder-Ones—the real ones that tell the truth, not that stupid *Book of the Elder-Ones* someone made up. Gina wrote down all the important stuff she'd found out, but she'd read so much, there wasn't enough time for it all...not when she was running the town as well. And there were so many little things she knew that would just pop into her head when something prompted her. Like..." Dani pointed to the head of the grave. "Do you know why people always put a cross where they bury someone?"

Natasha frowned. Every grave she had ever seen had been marked by a cross. It was traditional, but the design was too manifestly practical to require any explanation. "It's a marker post with a horizontal bar to write the person's name on."

Dani shook her head. "It's an old symbol of another goddess, who people used to worship on the original Earth. Gina found out all sorts of things like that. Of course, she wasn't supposed to read the books in the library. Nobody was supposed to read the books. She was just there to dust and sweep. And now she's gone, and..." Dani's voice was becoming less steady, with a hint of desperation. "Nobody else is going to get the chance to read anything in the temple library. The Chief Consultant ordered the doors sealed after Gina fled. Without Gina, there's no...no..."

Suddenly, Dani's self-control broke. Her lips twisted, and she covered her eyes with her hand. After the barest hesitation, Natasha put her arms around Dani's shaking shoulders and hugged her close. At last, Dani's sobs eased, and she turned her head to look back at the grave.

"I'm really going to miss her," Dani said in a weak voice. "When I came to Westernfort, I was fifteen, a bit too old to be called a child, but I was all on my own, and Gina was...not like a mother—more of a substitute granny to me. She used to refer to herself as an irritable old know-it-all, but she wasn't. She was lovely."

Natasha also stared at the grave. Gina had made up ridiculous stories about the contents of the temple library. She had infected others with her insane blasphemy, and she had taken advantage of a vulnerable girl and taught her to defy the Goddess. Gina must certainly pay for her sins, but it was impossible not to respond to the pain and loss in Dani's voice. Natasha was very grateful that it was no longer part of the mission to send the old heretic to the Goddess for judgment. She could not bear to be the one to hurt Dani so much.

❖

Throughout the Homelands, Midwinter's Day was celebrated by eating and drinking too much and generally causing as much mayhem as one fancied. Or could get away with. The heretics in Westernfort were no different, except that none of them would be going to the Sisters the next day to confess their sins and make a suitable payment as a sign of their contrition.

Natasha finished her work with the animals early and made her way to the tavern. She was becoming familiar with most of the young women her age. Two of the blacksmith's apprentices were squashed in by the door and greeted her when she arrived. Dani's friends, Madra and Jenny, hailed her from the far side of the room. The tavern was packed solid. It took five minutes for Natasha to get from the doorway to the bar and another five minutes to get served.

She had just caught the barkeeper's attention when a voice at her neck said, "If you get me a mug of the same as whatever you're drinking, I'll be unbelievably grateful."

Natasha turned her head to see Dani standing behind her. Dani's arm was the one currently embedded in her back. She bought two drinks, and they pushed their way out of the worst crush around the bar. Even then, there were so many people that they were pressed together, with scarcely enough room to lift the mugs to their mouths. Since she could not avoid the contact, Natasha decided to enjoy it, and Dani was not making any effort to create space between them either. The noise level in the tavern meant they had to shout into each other's ears to be heard. The faint touch of Dani's breath on her cheek was something else Natasha decided to enjoy.

Only once did a faint doubt come into Natasha's head: when she remembered Lynn's cryptic comment connecting Dani and cloning. Natasha studied the animated smile on Dani's face. Dani was watching Madra's and Jenny's antics on the other side of the tavern, but then she glanced back quickly. For a moment, their eyes held contact. Then Natasha dropped her head, but her doubts had dissolved. Dani had a soul. She would stake her life on it.

They were finishing their second drink when the music began outside. The sound emptied the tavern so rapidly Natasha nearly fell over. It was as though someone had pulled out the plug. The women from the tavern spilled into the main square—quite literally in some cases, due to the combination of snow and alcohol. The sky was dark—the short winter's day already ended—and flares lit the scene. Women were appearing from all directions, wrapped in cloaks, coats, and even blankets against the cold.

At one end of the main square, a band with drums and pipes stood in the light of a bonfire, and someone was singing clearly enough to be heard over the chaos. The wild activity that ensued could only be described as dancing in the loosest sense of the word. The slippery footing reduced it to the dancers hanging onto each other in a line that moved in one direction or another by general consensus. The music added to the feeling of a party, but fewer than half the women appeared to be paying any attention to the rhythm. Children ran around shrieking.

Natasha was not surprised to find that she ended up with her arm around Dani. She was just not sure whose doing it was. When they passed the bonfire, Natasha saw that the singer was Lynn.

"She's got a really good voice, hasn't she?" Dani volunteered her opinion.

"I know. She sings to the cows sometimes."

"Are they impressed?"

"It's hard to impress a cow with singing. You have to juggle as well." The conversation was getting silly.

The music continued for nearly an hour, with the lines shifting and reforming. Several filed off down side streets to reappear from another direction. Revelers would break off and lob snowballs whenever the lines drew close. The air was cold. Breath showed as white clouds in the light of the flares, and noses were red. Even before the music stopped, the numbers in the square began to dwindle as the oldest went indoors to continue their celebrations. When the drums finally fell silent, the remaining lines drifted apart as women collected scarves and cloaks discarded during the dancing.

Natasha and Dani were some of the last to let go of each other. They were close to the bonfire. Dani looked like she was about to speak when Lynn's voice was lifted once more in song.

> *The western mountains tower high,*
> *Their rivers deep and cold,*
> *And there dwells—*

Lynn got no farther. A mock scream rang out nearby, quickly followed by a snowball.

"Can I take it that Kim doesn't like the song?" Natasha asked, feigning seriousness.

Dani scrunched her nose. "I don't think she was too keen on it even before Lynn started amending the lyrics."

Natasha watched the two women indulging in a snowball fight like a couple of adolescents. Several of their children joined in. *I'm going to murder them.* The thought shot through Natasha's head, destroying all her enjoyment.

"Dani." The voice belonged to Shelly. The young Ranger trotted over. "We're carrying on the party at the new barracks. Do you want to come?" Shelly glanced in Natasha's direction. Her happy expression was childishly eager in the light of the bonfire. "You can come too."

There really was something of the puppy dog about Shelly. Disliking her was impossible. She was far too naively openhearted, but Natasha was no longer in the mood for a party and considered heading off alone. Before she could make up her mind, Dani agreed on behalf of them both and propelled Natasha after the gaggle of young women leaving the square. They walked along side by side in silence, while Shelly scampered on ahead. As the barrack block came into sight, Dani suddenly caught hold of Natasha's arm and pulled her aside into the cover of an alley.

"Will you give me a kiss for good luck on Midwinter's Day?" Dani asked.

The drink and the dancing and the need to recapture her good mood overwhelmed Natasha's better judgment. She intended no more than the lightest, sisterly kiss, but even as her lips brushed Dani's, she knew it was a mistake. Her arms slipped behind Dani's back and pulled her close. The softness of Dani's mouth molded against hers, growing in passion with each nuzzling movement. The first touch of Dani's tongue ripped through all Natasha's self-control. Their bodies pressed hard against each other.

"Hey! Are you two coming?" Shelly's voice was like a bucket of cold water. Natasha sprang away.

Dani drew a deep breath, and her lips pulled down at the corners. "Not quite, but I'm getting there." She peered around the edge of the alley at the figure silhouetted in the barracks doorway and then turned to Natasha. "Do you want to forget the party and come back to my place?"

"I...I'm sorry. I..." Natasha hung her head. She did not know what she wanted. Or, rather, the things she wanted were irreconcilable. She wanted Dani. She wanted to do her duty for Celaeno. She wanted never to have come to Westernfort.

At the confused misery on Natasha's face, Dani's expression shifted to a sad smile. "That's all right. I'll wait." Her voice held a soft sincerity. "I think you're worth waiting for." Then she tossed her head in self-parody and added, "Me...smooth-talking... no problems." But Natasha thought she could see under the glib façade.

They stepped out from the alley and ran into the barracks, trying to ignore Shelly's hurt expression. A large number of the younger Rangers and their friends were present, with beer, cider, and an assortment of food laid out at one end, although the prevalence of bread, cheese, and cold meats indicated that the young Rangers had not spent much time cooking. The atmosphere was excited, but Natasha could not reconcile herself to the laughing faces and soon made her excuse to go.

"This early?" Dani caught her at the door.

"Your clay will happily hang around until you're ready to wake up tomorrow. Lynn's animals aren't so understanding." Natasha smiled and tried to make her voice sound cheerful, but she failed, and she knew it.

Natasha got back to their room at almost exactly the same time as Cal and Rohanna. The two older Guards were concerned about something and whispering urgently, but Natasha could not summon the interest to find out what it was. She was reaching out to climb the ladder when Rohanna caught hold of her arm.

"We've just discovered something." Rohanna hissed as the three gathered together. "Gina Renamed was gene mother to Lynn's youngest child."

"I know," Natasha said.

"You knew? Why didn't you say?"

"It was just something Lynn mentioned. Why is it important?"

"Because Gina was originally an Imprinter as well, and so—"

Natasha cut her off. She was not in the mood to be patient. "Yes. Lynn said that as well. They hope the child of two Imprinters will be one as well."

Rohanna stared at her. "And you ask why it's important! The heretic numbers are growing here. Which is why Lynn's execution is our most critical goal. If we only succeed in removing her, we'll have struck a great blow for the Goddess, but it will count for nothing if they have another Imprinter. The child must be eliminated as well."

She's only a baby! Natasha bit back her horrified words and fought to keep the shock off her face. An emotional appeal would not move Rohanna. If Becky's life was to be saved, it would take the right approach, and Natasha knew she would have only one chance. She forced a slightly confused smile onto her lips. "But the child won't be an Imprinter, will she? Imprinters are chosen by Celaeno to receive the gift of Himoti. It's got nothing to do with genes."

The expressions on Cal's and Rohanna's faces froze as they juggled with the idea. Natasha tried to act calm. Overplaying her argument would be a mistake. At last, Cal nodded ruefully. However, Rohanna's frown deepened. "We can't take the risk."

"There's a risk believing what's in *The Book of the Elder-Ones*?" Natasha's tones reflected incredulity. "How can there be a risk? Celaeno will never choose this child to be an Imprinter."

Unexpectedly, Cal came in on Natasha's side. "She's got a point. Maybe we've been here too long. We're starting to think like the heretics."

Rohanna sighed and dropped her head. "Yes. You're right. We must hang on to our faith. The child does not matter." She put an arm around Natasha's shoulder and hugged her.

Natasha climbed the ladder and got into her bed, but she could not sleep. *We must hang on to our faith.* The words echoed in her head. Her sense of relief turned to dismay. Not that she regretted that Becky would live, but she realized that in the debate, she had used the name of Celaeno as a means to achieve her aim, without giving thought to the will of the Goddess, without belief, without faith.

Natasha slipped out of bed and knelt, eyes closed. Desperately, she began to pray.

❖

The blacksmith's forge was in the part of town nearest the main stables. Along one wall, the building opened onto a forecourt, where the bigger items for repair were stacked. Inside, the furnace roared. Even in mid-January, the workers were lightly clothed. The blacksmith herself was a short, square woman who appeared to be composed largely of shoulders. She looked around as Natasha entered the smithy.

"What do you want?" Despite the blunt words, it was a friendly greeting. The blacksmith was a good-natured woman.

"This has snapped." Natasha held up the broken hook in question. "Lynn wondered if you could fix it." She paused apologetically. "Quickly?"

The blacksmith wiped the sweat from her hands and examined the damage. "Ten minutes." She smiled. "Do you want to wait?"

Natasha nodded and backed away from the furnace. Although it was a freezing-cold day, one could have too much of a good thing. She wandered the length of the smithy until her eyes caught on a rack of swords. Rohanna had been working on preparations for the mission. Soon, they were going to need weapons. Natasha forced herself not to dwell on the use they would be put to.

The Rangers' swords were shorter than those used by the Guards. The weapons on the rack were stabbing blades, intended for use in dense forests and close combat. Natasha picked up one. It was heavier than she had expected, the center of balance two-thirds of the way down the blade. Natasha shifted it in her hand experimentally. It would be useful for hacking blows, but not the elegant thrust and parry of her training. Natasha tried a few more ambitious swings.

"You're waving that around like a Guard." Ash's voice rang out from behind. Natasha froze, unable to speak, as the Ranger sauntered up to her side. "And your grip is all wrong. It's much too wristy. Here, let me show you." Ash took the weapon from her hand and demonstrated the correct way to hold the short sword.

Natasha felt her heart thumping. She had been careless, and she had to recover her composure. A guilty expression would only make things worse. She tried to look innocently interested in the lesson.

"A Ranger's sword isn't for show; we leave the fancy twirly games for the Guards. When you draw a Ranger's sword, you should mean business," Ash said.

"I'm afraid I was treating it like a softball bat." Natasha tried to sound casual.

"And there I was, thinking it was the way you use a switch to herd cows." The blacksmith joined in from the other end of the smithy, laughing.

Natasha felt stupidly self-conscious. She did not know how to respond. If she joined in the laughter, it would sound forced; if she grinned, it would look sickly. She wanted to study Ash's face for signs of suspicion but was sure the Ranger would be watching her. She wanted to shift the conversation onto safer ground, but nothing came into her head.

"Here you go." The blacksmith doused the repaired ironwork in a tub and held it out.

"Thanks." Natasha's heartfelt gratitude was as much for the chance to escape.

"And what are you after, Ash?" The blacksmith moved on to her next customer.

Natasha restrained her urge to run. She left the smithy, concentrating on her knees, forcing them into a purposeful stride, keeping her head up and her shoulders square, and then wondered if she looked too much like a Guard on parade. It was ridiculous. She did not even know if she was being watched. At the far side of the yard, she risked a quick glance back. Ash was talking quietly to the blacksmith, and they both appeared to have forgotten her.

❖

Lynn and Kim lived with their children in a moderate-size house on the main square. Natasha had been told it was the oldest building in Westernfort, which still made it less than seventeen years old. It had become the town leader's residence and had been expanded and modified from its original design to fulfill both its official and domestic roles.

Natasha sat by the fire and looked around. The main room was ten meters long and nearly as wide, able to hold a full council meeting, although currently, it held only her, Lynn, and Becky. Several doors opened on either side to give access to bedrooms and other chambers. Somewhere was a furnace room for the under-floor heating. The fire was for cooking and possibly for the charm. The sight of dancing flames was relaxing.

A long table was pushed against one wall, still cluttered with plates and mugs from a meal. Cloaks and a sword belt hung on pegs by the door. Becky's toys were strewn across the floor. Natasha was very conscious that she was sitting as a guest in the home of two women she had sworn to kill. She pushed the thought away and tried to concentrate on what Lynn was saying about plans for the next month until Becky began to cry.

"I'm sorry. She needs to go to sleep. Do you mind waiting?" Lynn said.

"No, I'll just sit here and toast my feet in front of the fire."

"That's Chip's favorite trick."

The sideways look Lynn gave her, as she collected her daughter and left the room, seemed to hint at something behind the words, although Natasha had too much on her mind to give it thought. As soon as she was alone, she slipped out of her chair and tiptoed to a cupboard. From previous visits, she knew that one shelf held maps of the wildlands, prepared by the Rangers. It took seconds to find the one she wanted: an old map showing details of fords on rivers and mountain passes. The paper was stained and torn in parts, and not likely to be missed soon—she hoped. Natasha folded the worn map and pushed it inside her shirt. Long before Lynn returned, she was safely back in her chair.

Concentrating on details of animal feed and similar concerns was a strain. The map felt as though it had come to life and was creeping over her skin. Fortunately for Natasha, nothing too complicated cropped up, and soon, the instructions were over. She was preparing to depart when the outer door opened and fourteen-year-old Ardis stuck her head in.

"Hi, Mom. Has Tanya been looking for me?"

"No," Lynn replied.

"Oh, well, if she does, can you tell her I'm at Dee's?" Ardis' head disappeared before her mother could answer.

Lynn stared at the closed door. "Have you been introduced to our eldest daughter?" she asked Natasha.

"I've met her briefly."

"If you ever get to speak to her properly, could you let me know what she's like?" Lynn spoke with heavy irony.

"I think she's a fairly standard teenager," Natasha said, reaching for her coat.

Lynn smiled. "Maybe. I'm afraid I haven't much experience with what teenagers are like. I missed out on it myself." Her face became pensive. "I was twelve when I was tested in the temple and they found I had enough of the healer sense to be an Imprinter. I never saw my parents again. I missed them so much. I spent years dreaming of what it would be like to still live with them. It never occurred to me that if I had the option, I might have been spending all my time out with my friends. Ardis is starting to make me feel superfluous, but I suppose I can comfort myself that she'd miss me if I weren't here."

Natasha mumbled a reply and left the house. She had the dangerous temptation to run after Ardis and tell her to make the most of both her mothers while she had the chance. Natasha remembered her own adolescence. Of course, she would not have missed her own mother, but it was hardly a fair comparison. Lynn was not a vicious, self-centered alcoholic.

Natasha closed her eyes briefly. She must have faith in the Goddess. It might not seem fair to her, but she had to believe that Celaeno oversaw everything, and in the end, everyone would be treated as they deserved. *Not my will, but yours,* she repeated in her head.

Rohanna was waiting in their room when she returned. Natasha held out the stolen map and her dagger; then she stood back to watch while Rohanna opened their secret cache. The hidden compartment in the base of the box bed was a work of craftsmanship—all the more so since it had been constructed within the framework of what was already there. One of the slats had been loosened and then refitted with two internal catches. From the outside, there was no trace of the locks, and the plank felt as firm as its neighbors. To open it, two daggers had to be inserted at the correct points along the join. Already, several items were stored inside, and they still had more than a month to go before Cal expected the journey through the wilderness to be feasible.

"Will we copy the map and return it?" Natasha asked.

"No. If they notice that it's gone, they'll simply think it's been misplaced. If it makes an unexpected reappearance, they'll know something is up." Rohanna smiled. "You've done well."

Yes. I've stolen from someone who trusts me, Natasha wanted to say. *I've been a liar. Now I'm a thief. Soon, I'll be a murderer. And all I ever wanted to be was a soldier.*

CHAPTER THIRTEEN—AROUND THE KILN

The daylight was fading fast as Natasha walked up the hill toward the woods. The mountain peaks were reduced to dark, jagged shapes against the pale blue sky. Bare tree trunks stood in stark contrast to the white snow. The kiln had been built in a clearing a short way into the forest. As she spotted the brighter patch ahead, Natasha caught the first faint scent of wood smoke on the wind. A few more steps, and she stopped at the edge of the open space to study the scene.

The kiln was in the center of the clearing, an earth-covered dome slightly less tall than Natasha at its apex. A pit had been dug close by on either side, and twin columns of smoke were rising from them, with a third issuing from a hole in the middle of the kiln. Heat had melted most of the snow away, and what remained around the edges had been trampled into slush. A huge pile of chopped wood was stacked under the trees.

Two of Dani's friends were present. Madra stood by the woodpile with an ax in her hands, while her partner, Jenny, was peering into one of the fire pits. Both women were of middling height, with soft, plump outlines and identical raucous laughs. They shared farming rights on the east side of town. Natasha still had a tendency to get them confused. Dani was stalking back and forth around the kiln in a manner reminiscent of the sheepdogs.

"Are you frightened it'll make a bolt for the woods?" Natasha called.

Dani trotted over to her, smiling. "What?"

"Never mind." It was not worth explaining.

Dani half opened her mouth to protest, but then shrugged and said, "Lynn gave you tomorrow morning off?"

"Sort of. I had to put in some extra time today."

"You've done a double shift to get some time free and then volunteered for *this*?" Madra shouted in mock disbelief.

"Ignore her. It's fun." Dani grabbed Natasha's hand and pulled her forward. "I started the fires this morning, just a gentle drying, but you've arrived at the right time. We're about to get serious."

They reached the side of the kiln and Natasha looked down into the fire pits. They were, in fact, the two ends of a shallow trench, running under the curved walls of the kiln. The convection draft was gently drawing smoke along the tunnels. Natasha leaned against the side of the kiln and craned her neck to peer in through the circular hole at the top. Despite the smoke and rippling currents of heat, she could make out the shapes of pots and bowls carefully packed inside. The earthen side of the kiln was warm against her hands.

"Right," Dani said, patting Natasha on the back to get her attention. "The whole trick is to build the heat slowly. I need to be sure the pots dry out thoroughly before it gets too hot. Else, the expanding water vapor will make them explode, and I'll cry. So..." She smiled at her helpers. "Let's toss on a few extra logs and get stoking."

Control of the temperature was achieved by the size of the fires and their closeness to the entrances of the tunnels. Initially, the work consisted mainly of throwing on more wood. Dani darted from side to side, giving instructions and using a long-handled rake to adjust the position of the burning logs. Often, she stopped and stretched her hand over the central vent to judge the temperature inside.

After about an hour, there was one sharp retort from the kiln. Dani swore and froze.

"Was that a pot exploding?" Jenny asked.

Dani's agitated nod looked more like a nervous twitch.

"What do you want us to do?" Jenny asked.

Dani flapped her arms, swore again, and then gestured for them to continue.

Slowly, the fires were edged closer to the tunnel entrances, and the airflow through the kiln began to increase. The draft over the wood made it burn ever more furiously. By the time the fires stood under the walls of the kiln, the flames were roaring, the wood blazed white-hot, and the work had become frenetic. A luminescent red light shone from the center hole. They used rakes to push more wood into the fires and pull out the spent remains. The trench filled with gray ash and red embers. The heat above it was intense. Natasha had damp rags wrapped around her arms for protection when she bent low over the opening.

"How are you doing?" Dani asked during a brief lull in the activity.

"I think I've cooked my hands," Natasha replied.

"Oh...if I knew you were going to do that, I wouldn't have bothered bringing the kebabs."

"You've got food?"

Dani laughed. "Later. You haven't got time now."

Natasha wiped the sweat from her eyes and looked up. Laurel was directly overhead, midnight long past. She had no idea that the hours had been passing so quickly, but there was no opportunity to stand and stare. The fires now burned so hot that the wood seemed to crackle and disintegrate the second it landed. Sparks were flying from the center of the kiln, rising up into the dark sky, and dancing between the stars. Time passed in raking, stoking, and rushing around with armfuls of wood. But Dani was right; it was fun. Laugher and jokes flew among them.

The dull red glow from the inside of the kiln grew lighter and brighter. Dani climbed a nearby tree so she could look down into its heart and judge the color.

"Are we there?" Madra called up.

"Nearly."

"Just as well. The wood is going down."

Dani jumped to the ground. "One last push. Let's go for it."

The four set to work with renewed frenzy until at last, Dani called a halt, and they all collapsed around the fire at one end. Laurel had dropped to the treetops, and the night was nearly gone. Dani brought out the promised kebabs and positioned them over the trench. With the heat, they would be cooked in minutes.

Madra uncorked a flagon and looked at it affectionately. "Of course, this is the only reason I came here, you know." She took a deep swig and sighed with contentment.

The flagon made its rounds. Natasha took her share. Its contents were strong enough to cause a pleasant warmth inside. The food, when it was cooked, tasted wonderful. In the light from the fire, she could see the others' faces covered in soot. She guessed that her own looked the same.

"When do you get the pots out?" she asked.

"In a few days, after the kiln cools down."

"Is there much else to do at the moment?"

"A bit of tidying up. I can take care of it, if you want to go," Dani answered.

The conversation went on for a little longer, but now that the action was finished, tiredness was creeping over them, and the other two women declared their intention to seek their bed for a few hours' sleep. Dani let them go with words of thanks.

"You can go as well. I'll be all right," Dani said to Natasha, but her tone and manner did not give the impression that she wanted Natasha to leave.

"I'll stay a bit longer."

Dani smiled and made no further attempt to persuade her. The final few jobs did not take long, and they again settled in the warmth radiating from the sides of the kiln, sharing the last of the flagon. Natasha felt filthy, exhausted, and completely at peace with the world.

"So you've finally spent a dirty, sweaty night with me. It wasn't so bad, was it?" Dani's voice was teasing.

"I've had worse."

In the silence, Natasha could hear faint clinks from the cooling kiln and the rush of the breeze over the treetops. The stars glittered undimmed, although dawn was less than an hour away.

"You know I really want you." The teasing had left Dani's voice.

"I..."

"And I think you want me." Dani's voice was gentle. "It's okay. You're quite safe to talk. I'm too shattered to take advantage of you at the moment."

Natasha hung her head. Of course, Dani could see how she felt. Despite the tiredness, Natasha could feel her whole body responding to Dani's closeness, aching with a desire she had sworn she would not give in to. She would be the one taking advantage—advantage of Dani's ignorance of the truth. Dani hated all Guards with a passionate intensity. Once she learned what Natasha was, Dani would hate her as well—quite justifiably. Since accepting the mission, Natasha had lied and cheated and stolen. When the truth came out, would Dani recognize in her self-denial the one shred of honor Natasha had been able to cling to? Would Dani be relieved that she had not been tricked into taking her sworn enemy as a lover? Or would Dani feel regret that they had not shared what they could, in innocence on her part? Even with a Guard? There was no way Natasha could ask her. Not until it was too late.

"That woman you left behind must have been quite something," Dani said softly.

"Why do you hate Guards so much?" Between tiredness and drink, Natasha no longer cared about the wisdom of the question.

"Can I take that as a subtle change in subject?"

"I want to know."

There was no reply. Natasha turned her head and saw Dani staring over the treetops, her face impassive. But just when Natasha thought she was not going to get an answer, Dani looked back. "Because of my family."

"Were they killed by Guards?"

"Yes. You want to hear the whole story?"

"Not if you don't want to tell it."

Dani's gaze slipped to the ground beyond her feet. The muscles in her jaw twitched. Neither spoke until Dani at last sucked in a deep breath. "Oh...why not?" She drew up her legs and rested her chin on her knees, still staring at the ground. "It starts okay. My birth mother was a cloner; my gene mother was a potter. I didn't have enough of the healer sense to induce cloning, so..." She vaguely indicated the kiln behind her.

"I was eight before my parents had saved enough money for another payment of imprinting fees. Their finances can't have been good. I'm not sure why. I was too young to be involved in the money. All I can remember is being excited that I was finally going to have a sister.

"We lived in a small village. I went with my parents to the temple in the nearest town. I don't think I'd ever been outside the village before. I can vaguely remember the imprinting chapel and my gene mother lying on the altar. And us coming out, and being told my sister would be with us in nine months. And then we all went home. We used to live over my gene mother's shop. It was only a few nights after we got back that the place caught fire." Dani broke off, her face strained.

"You don't have to tell me if you'd rather not," Natasha said. She did not know where the story was going, but she felt rising alarm at Dani's evident distress.

"No. I've started now." Dani took a deep breath, gathering herself. "My gene mother got badly burned. My birth mother had enough of the healer gift to save her life, but not the life of my sister inside her. The miscarriage was days into the pregnancy. My parents lost everything in the fire. They could borrow enough to set them on their feet again, but it would take years to repay the debt and save for more imprinting fees, and they weren't young. There was no telling if they'd get another chance. So they decided to clone my gene mother."

Pain had been underlying Dani's voice; now it began to rip through. "They must have thought they could get away with it. They had the imprinting certificate. My sister would seem a little overdue, but not much, especially if my birth mother used the healer sense to induce an early labor. And my gene mother's face had been so disfigured in the fire, they probably thought no one would notice the resemblance. Of course, they didn't discuss it with me. I can just remember them being frightened and talking quietly. I thought they were worried because my gene mother had been so badly hurt.

"They borrowed money for a new shop, and we moved to Eastford. As a child, I didn't think anything of it, but obviously, they wanted to go where no one would remember what my gene mother had looked like."

Natasha had been listening with a shocked expression on her face. She could not help it. "Your sister—" She bit off her words.

Dani turned to face her, tears in her eyes. "Are you going to tell me my sister had no soul?"

Natasha could not speak.

"I'd challenge anyone to have taken my sister and three other girls the same age, stood them in a row, and said which one didn't have a soul. My gene mother made a set of clay farm animals. I can close my eyes and see my sister sitting on the floor in our home, the same age as Becky, pushing them around and giggling. I remember her trotting after me, calling my name. I remember having lessons on the potter's wheel and how she'd creep up behind me and tickle my ribs. Her name was Ellen."

Dani faced away again and looked out at the trees. After a while, she calmed down and went on. "My gene mother's face had been scarred so badly..." She shrugged. "They never told us how they came to suspect. I remember the morning they came for us. I was a few days short of fifteen. We'd finished breakfast, about to open the shop, and there was a noise outside. I was sitting beside Ellen. I looked up just as the Guards kicked the door in. They took us to the temple to be tested...all of us, me included.

"I was frightened and confused. I didn't have a clue what it was about. Of course, my parents knew, and I saw their faces and knew something terrible was going to happen. I was so surprised when an Imprinter in blue arrived. She touched us all in turn, and when she got to Ellen...that's when all hell let loose."

Dani broke off, distracted. "Is there any more drink left?" She shook the empty flagon.

Natasha could tell it was an excuse while Dani gathered herself to continue. She felt she ought to say or do something, but maybe letting Dani take her own time was the most support she could give.

Dani put the empty flagon down and wrapped her hands around the neck. Her eyes were unfocused, staring at scenes long past. "They held a trial in the temple. They declared my sister an abomination. They said she was an animal. She was only six. When she started crying, one of the Guards knocked her to the floor. They didn't want an animal disturbing their solemn temple procedures.

"Afterward, they took us outside into the main town square. I was dragged along...I'm not sure why. I hadn't been accused of anything, let alone found guilty. Perhaps they thought watching would be good for my soul...seeing that I had one."

Tears were now running down Dani's face. "The Guards slit Ellen's throat with a butcher knife. They actually sent to a butcher to make sure they got the genuine article. Ellen was calling, 'Mommy!' Then she screamed. Then she was quiet.

"They burned her body on a fire. My birth mother had broken the most sacred rule for a cloner, so they hanged her after they'd finished with my sister. And my gene mother had allowed her body to be defiled, so she was flogged unconscious, doused with water to revive her, and flogged again.

"I saw it all. Two Guards had hold of my shoulders, keeping me at the front of the crowd so I'd have a good view. And do you know what I saw that hurt the most?"

Natasha could not speak.

"The Guard who cut my sister's throat walked away laughing and swaggering, as if she'd done something funny. And all the time, the Sisters were singing hymns to the Goddess.

"When it was over, all the Sisters trotted back into the temple, and the Guards let me go. My birth mother's body was dragged off to a criminal's grave, my sister's ashes were thrown on the town midden heap, but they left me to deal with my gene mother.

"Somehow, I got her home on my own. I was so relieved to get through the door, I wasn't even upset when I saw that Guards had wrecked the shop. There wasn't anything to eat, no money... everything was smashed. I tried to get a healer, but the Guards threatened anyone who helped us. So I used what skill I had, but it wasn't enough.

"For ten days, I nursed her alone until she died as well, the day after my fifteenth birthday. I buried her beside my birth mother...at least they were together. My sister's ashes..." Dani shrugged and wiped her eyes.

"After I'd buried my mother, I wandered around the town. I had nowhere to go. I ended up standing in front of the temple. I snapped. I screamed that I hoped all the Sisters and all the Guards would burn in hell forever, that the Goddess wasn't worth pissing on, that Himoti was a fucking evil bitch...and so on. Every blasphemous thing I could think of. Then the Guards came after me, and I ran away. If they'd caught me, I guess I'd have joined the rest of my family, but there was a heretic in town who got to me before the Guards. She hid me for a while, and when things had calmed down, she sent me on to Westernfort.

"And that's the end of the story. And that's why I hate Guards." The pain had burned out of Dani's voice, leaving only a desolate loss.

Natasha leaned forward and rested her head in her hands. *At least it answers the question of whether she'd still want me if she knew I'm a Guard,* Natasha thought bitterly. There was no point saying that it had all been Dani's parents' fault. She was not sure she fully believed it herself. Certainly, Dani had been a completely innocent casualty in the affair. Yet the Guards had also been blameless. They had only been obeying orders, and there was no point telling Dani that the Guard who had laughed was probably doing it to mask her nerves.

"The Guards were just doing what the Sisters said," Natasha tried to say.

"No. The Guards *enjoyed* doing it. I saw them," Dani said firmly. "And if it weren't for the Guards, it wouldn't matter what the Sisters say. It was the Guards who used the knife on my sister. It was the Guards who put the noose around my birth mother's neck. It was the Guards who stopped a healer from coming to help my gene mother. And they laughed.

"One of these days, I'm going to kill three: one for my gene mother, one for my birth mother, and one for my sister. I was so frustrated when the Guards attacked Westernfort. Most of the time I was stuck with Lynn and the other healers. The few occasions I got to stand on the wall, the Guards all stayed in camp. I'm a lousy archer, but by all accounts, you couldn't miss them when they tried storming the gates."

Dani stood up, dusted herself down, and glared around the clearing. "Anyway, I think we're finished here. The fires are done. Let's get back."

They walked through the trees in silence. Natasha tried to think of something to say, and failed.

Dawn was breaking on the eastern horizon when they reached the outskirts of town. The shutters on windows were opening, and people were starting to emerge. Westernfort was waking to a new day. Natasha yawned, grateful for Lynn's generosity in expressing no more than a vague hope that Natasha might put in an appearance at the barn sometime that day.

During the walk, Dani had recovered at least a veneer of cheerfulness. She sighed. "Well, from past experience, you've got three choices. You can go home filthy and have your bed reek of smoke for days. You can go to the bathhouse and wash in ice-cold water. Or you can wait an hour until the fires are going and have a hot bath."

"What do you recommend?"

"I'm afraid smelly sheets win out every time."

Dani tried to smile, but Natasha could see that the attempt at humor was a weak cover. She wanted to put her arms around Dani and hug her, offering whatever comfort she could. *But she wouldn't want it from a Guard,* she told herself. The knowledge hurt.

They stood shuffling their feet and making offhand jokes, but their tiredness was growing. Natasha went back to her loft. *And what would I have done, had I been ordered to kill a child?* As sleep overtook her, Natasha was grateful that it was one question she would not have to answer.

CHAPTER FOURTEEN—THE WILL OF THE GODDESS

The first of March was an unseasonably warm day. Small puffy clouds dotted the sky. The light wind carried the scent of returning life. With her eyes closed, it was easy for Natasha to imagine that summer had arrived—as long as she was not standing under the drips from melting icicles. The snow had cleared from the main square; however, the ground was wet, so a waterproof sheet had been laid out in the middle. Virtually the entire population was gathered around the edge. Lynn was taking advantage of the weather to perform an imprinting in the open air.

As a Temple Guard, Natasha had often done duty in the imprinting chapels. She was curious to see how the heretics arranged things. There were no altar, no incense burners, and, of course, no Sisters singing hymns. Natasha's lips twitched. She for one would not miss the droning. But despite the improved setting, she was not intending to hang around for long. Doubtless, most of the audience would also drift away, so her departure would not attract attention. Natasha had witnessed enough imprintings to know that as a form of entertainment, it could appeal only to the most besotted prospective grandmothers.

In the temple, the mother-to-be lay on an altar with her partner kneeling by her side. The Imprinter would place her hands on them both and go into a trance for up to six hours. During this time, the attending Sisters would burn sticks of incense and sing monotonous hymns, and everyone else would reach a state of near-terminal boredom. Natasha had known that she was in the presence of life's most sacred mystery but had preferred doing sentry duty outside the gates, where she was watching people who moved.

Natasha looked around at the assembled women and wondered how soon she would be able to make an inconspicuous departure.

Anyway, she told herself, *no matter how long I end up waiting here, it can't be as tedious as the temple*. For one thing, she did not have to stand rigidly at attention, and second, Dani was beside her.

"Does Lynn often imprint in the square?" Natasha asked, leaning her head over.

"She always does. It's sort of become a tradition."

"Doesn't she get cold? I mean, it's okay now, but suppose it clouds over?"

"Oh, she'll be finished in under half an hour," Dani replied breezily.

"But..." Natasha stopped herself. She did not want to reveal just how familiar she was with the temple ceremony. Most women her age would have witnessed no more than two or three, but questions seethed in her mind. Imprinting never took less than two hours. Was Lynn really so exceptionally talented?

While Natasha had worked with her, Lynn had made various remarks about her life in the Homelands. She had spoken of the temple as a prison, the Sisters as jailers, and Imprinters as little better than slaves. Natasha had always been confused by this attitude. The temple existed to protect Imprinters from the impurity of the world so that their spirits might be freed to become conduits for the Goddess's gift of souls. The rules and rituals were designed to maximize an Imprinter's talent. Outside the holy walls of the temple, it should have been impossible for Lynn to imprint. At the very least, her ability should have been severely damaged. And it was not as though Lynn, with both a lover and children, was voluntarily keeping herself shielded from worldly contamination.

As she stood there, Natasha was struck by the thought that Lynn might have more insight into how to conduct imprinting than the Sisters did. But she did not have long to reflect on the heretical idea, because at that moment, there was a stir as Kim and Lynn appeared at the door of their house. Natasha watched Lynn walk into the center of the square alone and beckon the young couple over to join her. She talked to them quietly; then the three sat down and held hands in a circle. Natasha was stunned—even shocked. This was life's greatest mystery, and the heretics were treating it like a picnic. By every teaching of the Sisterhood, the informality was an insult to the Goddess. But...

Natasha raised her eyes to the blue sky. *The Book of the Elder-Ones* claimed that Celaeno, the physical manifestation of the Goddess, was quite literally hanging over their heads. If Celaeno disapproved, why did she not strike them down? Lynn was certainly not hiding from her sight.

Natasha looked back to the three women in the center of the square. She knew that unlike the Sisters, Lynn would accept no money for imprinting, sharing the Goddess's gift as freely as it had been given to her. Lynn herself might not express it in that way, but Natasha was suddenly quite sure that the Goddess would approve. She knew Lynn was not evil.

❖

Rohanna was sitting by the cooking fire in the common room when Natasha knelt at her side and whispered, "Can I talk to you?"

After only one quick look at Natasha's face, Rohanna stood and beckoned her along to their room. Fortunately, Cal did not follow. Natasha knew she was going to find the conversation difficult enough without Cal's presence. The ex-Ranger disapproved of Natasha's friendship with Dani and the amount of time she spent in the tavern. The relationship between them was still professional, but not as warm as it had once been. Rohanna was far more understanding, treating Natasha with something close to maternal indulgence.

"What is it?" Rohanna asked quietly once they were in their room.

Natasha swallowed. "Today. In the square. The imprinting..."

"You were outraged by the sacrilege?"

"No. That's just it. I wasn't. I think Lynn's misguided, but her heart's in the right place. She—"

Rohanna cut her off, but her voice was still gentle. "No. Her heart is not in the right place. The heart of an Imprinter should be with the Goddess who chose her."

Natasha struggled to find words. "Yes...but...I think Lynn's heart is with the Goddess, but she doesn't know it. She's got some wrong ideas, but she isn't evil. I know she isn't."

"How can a woman stand against the Goddess and not be evil?"

"If the Goddess is angry with her, surely Lynn wouldn't still be an Imprinter. And I wondered if...maybe the Chief Consultant was wrong, ordering us to kill Lynn. Perhaps she hasn't interpreted the will of the Goddess correctly. In fact, I'm sure she's made a mistake—"

Rohanna drew a sharp breath and placed her hand over Natasha's mouth to silence the disjointed mumbling. Her expression was hard to read—possibly shock, possibly anger. *I went too far,* Natasha thought, surprised by her own words. It was not quite what she had intended. A junior Guard had no right questioning the commands of the Chief Consultant. If she had said the same to a senior officer in Landfall, she would have been in line for a court-martial. Rohanna did not have that option open to her, although Natasha's supposed age was not so very old for a mother to take a belt to her.

Instead, Rohanna wrapped her arms around Natasha and hugged her tightly.

"It's hard. I know," Rohanna whispered. "But you must be strong for a little while longer." She pulled back so that their eyes met. "I've been impressed with you. It's easy to follow the will of the Goddess when you're surrounded by the faithful, but so much harder when you're in the midst of heretics. There are many experienced intelligence agents who wouldn't have withstood the ordeal so well. I know Cal criticizes you for associating with the other youngsters, but you have to. You must act like one of them, though it makes your task harder. Cal and I have been able to support each other, but you've been isolated. Yet your faith has not weakened. I can tell."

Gently, Rohanna stroked the hair back from Natasha's face. One corner of her mouth pulled up. "If I'd ever had a daughter, I'd have wanted her to be like you."

Natasha's eyes were filling. She was too choked to speak.

Rohanna went on. "I should have been more support to you. I should have shared my experience. Come...this is a trick I use. Close your eyes." As she did so, Natasha felt tears squeezing out. "You cannot go to the temple to pray, but you can rebuild the temple in your mind. Imagine you're in the temple at Landfall; imagine the peace, the stillness. Now stand before the main altar, and look at Himoti's sacred flame. If you calm your thoughts, you'll see it. Himoti's fire burns in the heart of every Guard. From it, you can draw the strength you need."

Natasha worked to bring the vision to her mind, and slowly, her confusion faded. She remembered the night she accepted the mission, kneeling before the altar, and the oath she had sworn. *I promise, Celaeno, I will destroy your enemies. My life is yours to do with as you will. Make me strong in your love that I may triumph for your sake, and if I turn aside from this task, may I be damned forever.*

"We are fighting for the glory of the Goddess. Will you fail?" Rohanna asked softly.

Natasha spoke with her eyes still closed. "No."

❖

Early the next morning, Kim was sitting with Mirle and a huge pile of paper: stock lists and forecasts. Spring was arriving, and they had to put the finishing touches on their plans for the coming year. The people at Ginasberg were going to need help if they were to be freed to work on their defenses. They could not build walls and plow fields at the same time. Fortunately, Westernfort had resources to spare; it was simply a question of making the best use of them.

"Perhaps I should visit Ginasberg and see the situation for myself," Kim said.

"That might be a good idea. You could—" Mirle was interrupted by the door opening.

From Lynn's expression, it was obvious that she was both confused and worried. Kim half stood in alarm. "What's happened?"

"Oh, it's..." Lynn waved her hands. Confusion was winning. The situation was clearly not an emergency requiring immediate action. She plonked herself down at the table, cupping her chin in her hand, while the lines in her forehead deepened. "There's been a slight accident...nothing serious. A cartload of brick slipped.

The only casualty was Cal Rowse, who sprained her ankle. I was nearby, so I did my bit as a healer, and took the opportunity to check her DNA."

"And is she related to Chip?" Kim asked.

"No." Lynn paused. "She's not related to Jess, either."

"What!" Kim exclaimed, startled. "But...she's her gene mother."

"No, she isn't."

The three women sat around the table, all looking equally baffled. At last, Mirle frowned and asked, "So what does it mean?"

Kim sighed. "It means that Jules was right all along. They're a gang of thieves."

"No. I'm sure that Jess isn't." Lynn spoke up.

"It's the only thing that makes sense. They've been so well behaved, I'd just about convinced myself that they're on the level. I was going to tell Ash she could stop watching them. But they're after something. I'd guess that Jess is a youngster they've taken on as a sort of apprentice. Plus, she helps give the appearance of a family, which always seems more respectable. Although the Goddess alone knows how they managed to recruit either one of the Tangs or the Coppellis."

Lynn shook her head. "There has to be another explanation."

"Such as?"

"How about...Jess' family is very rich. When she was a baby, Cal and Rohanna kidnapped her. They were going to demand a ransom, but Jess awoke all their maternal feelings, so they kept her instead. And they've never told her anything about it."

"It's not very likely. I think Chip would have heard if one of her cousins had been kidnapped. And it would still mean we have a pair of criminals on our hands." Kim combed her fingers back through her hair. "But at least it clears up one thing that's bothered me. I've never thought Cal looked old enough to be Jess' mother. I know she claims to be over forty, but in that case, she's wearing well."

"And Jess appears a shade on the old side for eighteen," Mirle added.

"I don't like it...putting it mildly," Kim said.

"What are you going to do?" Mirle's thoughts, as ever, had turned to the practical.

"I could have them arrested, tied up, and dumped back on the borders of the Homelands."

"On what grounds?" Lynn asked.

"They've lied. What else do I need?" Kim stood and paced the length of the room. "But I wish I knew what their game was. What are they hoping to steal?" She stopped and stared at the ceiling. "I'm going to get Ash to be a bit more assertive. Perhaps if we prod them, they'll run."

❖

The three Guards bid everyone in the common room good night and walked along the passage. The day had been a trial, and Cal was limping heavily. Natasha held the lamp high to light the way, and Rohanna made a show of fussing excessively. Cal would be all right. The wrench had been nasty, but Lynn was more than competent as a healer. In a day or so, Cal's ankle would be fully recovered.

Natasha led the way into the room and was about to hang the lamp on its hook before heading for the ladder when a sharp gesture from Rohanna stopped her dead. The intelligence agent was studying the room intently; her hands indicated that Cal and Natasha should not move.

"Someone's been here?" Cal mouthed.

Rohanna nodded. She began to step around the room carefully. "How's your ankle doing, my love?" she asked in loud, affectionate tones, but her eyes were on the steps of the ladder.

"A bit stiff, but it'll be okay." Cal went along with the charade.

"You've got to be more careful in the future." Rohanna moved on to inspect the chest where their official belongings were kept.

"Oh, don't fuss. I'll be fine."

Natasha watched the proceedings. She knew that Rohanna had left various markers around their room: faint chalk marks to show scuffs, and bristles held in hinges. It took five minutes for Rohanna to complete a thorough examination. Then she beckoned them into a huddle. "We've been searched," she whispered.

"You're sure?" Natasha asked.

"Oh, yes. It wasn't someone innocently wandering in here by mistake. They've been through everything..." Rohanna paused. "Except for the one place they should have looked." Her eyes traveled to the bed.

"They didn't find the stash?" Cal's tone was more statement than question.

"They checked the bed frame, but not well enough. It wasn't opened."

"What would they've been after?"

Rohanna smiled at Natasha's question. "Oh, this is where it all gets fun. We hope they think we're horse thieves. We couldn't have a horse hidden in here, so can we assume their doubts have moved on? And do they know we're aware of their suspicions?"

"You've lost me," Cal said.

Rohanna sighed. "Basically...you know you've been on the undercover game too long when you start enjoying the paranoia."

Cal held up her hands. "Okay. I'm not enjoying it. Just keep it simple. What do we do?"

Rohanna thought. "The weather's been mild these last few days. Do you think we'll be safe to head home?"

"I'd rather wait a few weeks. But then, I'd rather wait until midsummer." Cal pursed her lips. "With the Goddess on our side, we'll make it."

"Do not doubt that we have Celaeno's blessing on our mission," Rohanna said earnestly. "And this is how I read the situation. They've searched our room and found nothing, so we're in no immediate danger and don't need to do anything rash. But they're starting to ask awkward questions about us. We shouldn't drag things out further than necessary. Soon, the Goddess will give us our chance. We must be ready to take it."

Natasha bowed her head, aware of a confusing tangle of emotions. She did not want to go through with the mission, but since she had no option, it would be best to get it over with. She wished it were possible to step straight into the future; then she would have nothing to deal with except the guilt. And maybe Celaeno would smile on her. Perhaps in the temple at Landfall, she could recover her old certainties.

Natasha turned her head and looked at the bed frame. She wondered who had searched their room. If only they had discovered the hidden compartment. It would have made things so much simpler.

❖

Three days later, Natasha got back to the lodgings late. Many of the lambs had been born over the previous few days. Strictly speaking, however, it was not the extra demands of the lambing season that delayed her. Natasha was more fortunate than ordinary farmhands, who were out in the fields all day and most of the night at that time of year. All Lynn's animals were kept inside, and they were so carefully monitored that no unexpected problems arose. Natasha's workload had hardly increased at all. The reason for her late return was the pleasure she got from watching the young animals, safe in the knowledge that they would all grow to old age. She found it hard to tear herself away; she had even started to give them names. After all, they had souls.

Natasha grabbed a cold dinner from the leftovers in the common room. Some of the other inhabitants spoke to her while she ate. One passed on a message about a get-together in the tavern. She had almost finished her meal when she realized that Rohanna and Cal were not there. It was unusual for them not to be chatting by the fire.

She wolfed down the last mouthfuls and wandered along to the room they shared. As soon as she got through the door, Natasha knew that something important had happened. Rohanna beckoned her over.

"Celaeno has shown her will. She's given her enemies into our hands. I told you we didn't need to worry," Rohanna whispered triumphantly.

"What's happened?" Natasha asked.

"We've heard news. The day after tomorrow, Ramon is setting out to visit Ginasberg. The only other person going with her is Coppelli. It's five days' journey to Ginasberg, and they'll be gone nearly two weeks in all. Their first night's stop is at the outpost where Ramon met us on our way here. It's exactly what we need. The Goddess must have put the idea into their heads." Rohanna clenched her fist in triumph as she spoke.

"What are we going to do?"

"Two of us will leave for the outpost tomorrow after dark. It'll be a hard walk, but O'Neil said it was possible in a day. We're in better condition than when we arrived .We can walk all night and all day, and part of the next night as well. All that's necessary is to get there before they wake the following day. We want to ambush them while they sleep."

"As long as they don't post sentries," Cal interjected.

"They won't. There will be only two of them, and they'll be sure no Guards are about this early in the year, since they'll assume we'd need to travel from the Homelands." Rohanna smiled grimly. "Once we have executed them, we'll hide the bodies. Then we'll take their horses and head east. They'll only have enough supplies for five days, but that will include blankets, tent, a tinderbox, and things like that. We have enough food stashed to supply the rest of our needs."

"You said two of us will go. What about the other one?" Natasha said hesitantly.

"Yes. That's what we were discussing when you came in. One of us must stay behind for two reasons—apart from the fact that there won't be a horse for her. First, she'll need to cover for the absence of the others. We don't want the alarm raised too early. Second, she'll be the one to execute the degenerate Imprinter— ideally, at the same time as the other executions. I think we can safely predict that as soon as Lynn's body is found, someone will be sent to tell Ramon. We don't want her arriving at the outpost and spoiling the plan. We're counting on the confusion caused by messengers riding to Ginasberg and back to give the two who are heading east a better chance of escape."

Rohanna sighed. "The only unfortunate part is that the one who is left behind won't get the same chance. I don't want to tell a woman to kill herself, but she mustn't be taken prisoner. Inexplicable disappearances are what we want, creating as much confusion as possible. If they aren't certain what's happened, they'll try to cover every possibility, which will weaken the resources they can set to any one task. If they capture one of us, they'll learn that the other two are Guards and heading for Landfall. Every Ranger will be sent on their trail. And don't make the mistake of thinking you won't betray your comrades. There are ways of persuading a woman to talk, and by comparison, death isn't such a bad option."

Cal had been nodding while she listened. Now she spoke. "What we were trying to work out is...who stays?"

Rohanna looked sadly at Natasha. "Yes. That's the awkward question. Obviously, it can't be Cal. She's the only one who understands the wildlands. So I'm afraid it's down to you or me."

Natasha was surprised by how little the announcement bothered her. She shrugged. "When I volunteered for this mission, I didn't expect to return. I've always been willing to die for the Goddess."

"The same is true for us all," Rohanna said.

Cal bit her lip. "I'm reluctant to speak, since it's not my neck we're discussing, but Jess has the best access to the Imprinter."

"And I have the most experience at subterfuge, which might be crucial in covering for the missing pair." Rohanna pointed out.

Natasha looked between the two faces. *Neither is saying what she means,* she thought. *Cal prefers Rohanna's company to mine, and Rohanna is worried that I won't have the nerve to carry out the execution on my own.* She considered her own feelings. She did not want to be the one to kill Lynn. But at that moment, she realized that she did not want to go back to Landfall. She could not imagine ever again standing sentry duty outside the temple gates—a toy soldier in a pretty red uniform. She thought of the way her mind drifted during the long, boring hours; the recollections she dredged up; the scenes she relived—and then she thought of the new memories she would be taking back with her. *I can't do it; I'd rather die.*

Natasha opened her mouth, about to volunteer to stay, but Rohanna spoke first. "The Goddess will decide. We'll toss a coin. Heads, I stay. Tails, it's Jess."

Cal pulled a coin from her purse, flipped it in the air, and let it fall. It landed tails.

Chapter Fifteen—A Change of Plan

Night had fallen over the valley when the three conspirators climbed the hill to the east of town. The trail leading to the footpath known as the side gate showed as a muddy rut through the rough grass. Below them, the outline of the town was clear in the moonlight. Both Laurel and Hardie were nearly full, which was unfortunate. Darkness would have been preferred. But whatever the light, it would not be possible for Rohanna and Cal to leave by the main gates. They could not sneak away without being seen, and since both were blatantly dressed for a long journey, they would attract comment. Natasha, on the other hand, was wearing the clothes of a woman out for an evening stroll.

The three rounded the side of the hill, and the town was lost from sight. The path was a gentle climb beside a cascading stream. Before long, though, it would turn into a precipitous trail, better suited to goats than to women. This route was also guarded, but there would be only a single sentry. At one of the more treacherous parts, the path crossed a deep ravine. The Rangers had erected a drawbridge at the spot and built a fortified watch post.

Rohanna's plan to deal with the sentry was simple. The Ranger on duty would not expect trouble to come from within the valley. When they reached the post, Natasha would engage her in conversation, lure her to the side of the ravine, and then push her in. The sentry's body would be found the next day, of course. But with no sign of a struggle, people would assume that the woman had fallen by accident. An investigation was unlikely to uncover the true culprits in time to prevent them from completing their mission.

After a few minutes, the sentry post came into sight. The stone walls and raised drawbridge showed stark in the moonlight.

Rohanna and Cal dropped back into the shadows, leaving Natasha to saunter the rest of the way on her own. Again, she wondered whether it was really necessary for her to be involved. Either Cal or Rohanna could have slipped off her backpack and waterproof cape to avoid alerting the sentry. *Perhaps Rohanna hopes that if I kill a woman tonight, I'll find it easier to kill Lynn tomorrow,* Natasha thought. *And perhaps she's right.*

"Who goes there?" The sentry's voice rang out. Shelly was standing in the doorway of the watch post.

"It's me...Jess." Natasha walked the last few meters. Shelly looked at her with a beaming smile of welcome that made Natasha's heart sink. *Why couldn't it have been someone I don't know well?*

"What's up?"

"I just wanted a walk and came to have a chat."

Natasha strolled on to the brink of the ravine, staring out over the moonlit scene. After the bridge, the path crept around the flanks of a mountain, crossing a steep scree slope. Anyone leaving would be visible for a full half kilometer until the path dropped from sight over the brow of a ridge.

Shelly obligingly came to stand by Natasha's side. It was too easy. *Please, Celaeno, help me.* Even as the despairing thought went through Natasha's head, she saw the hollow on the other side of the ravine a few meters off the trail. A change of plan occurred to her. She turned to the woman at her side. "I want to ask you something." Natasha looked over her shoulder theatrically, as though she feared eavesdroppers. "Not here. Let's go over to the other side."

The excuse to cross the ravine was not particularly logical, but Shelly was not the sort of woman to notice a thing like that. They loosened the rope controlling the drawbridge, and once it was down, Natasha steered Shelly to the hollow she had spotted. They sat on convenient rocks, with Shelly's back to the trail. Now the plan required something to keep the young Ranger occupied for ten minutes, and Natasha knew the very thing.

"It's about Dani," she said. "I don't know what to do. You know she's been chasing me, but..."

Natasha had a vague agenda worked out to keep the conversation going, but she need not have bothered. Asking Shelly about Dani was like turning on a tap. She was just hitting full spate when Natasha saw Rohanna and Cal appear on the trail above the young Ranger's shoulder. *Now just don't turn around,* Natasha mentally commanded, for Shelly's sake rather than her own. They were still close enough to the edge of the ravine to implement Rohanna's plan, if necessary.

Rohanna looked down at them in the hollow and nodded approvingly. It would, of course, be the absence of an inconvenient body, not the avoidance of killing, that she liked. And it meant that they did not need to worry about the possibility that the sentry might survive the fall and live to tell the story. Natasha worked to keep her face neutral as her two comrades tiptoed over the wooden planks of the drawbridge and began creeping across the scree slope.

Shelly kept on enthusiastically. "...because, you see, Dani's a lot like me. She doesn't always admit what she feels, not even to herself. She holds it all back."

Natasha tried not to look skeptical, but she would not have recognized either of them from the description.

"I mean, I can see Dani isn't right for you, but me and her—we're, you know, an ideal mesh. She hides it well, but basically, I think Dani needs support. I've got to show her I'm the woman who can offer it."

Natasha pinched the sides of her mouth. It was not just nerves that made her want to giggle.

The minutes passed agonizingly while Rohanna and Cal completed their passage across the scree. At last, they stood on the crest of the distant ridge. Natasha saw them raise their hands in a salute, and then they were gone, but it took her another five minutes to conclude her conversation with Shelly.

"Yes, well, thanks. I've got to head back to town. But you've really helped me put my thoughts in order," Natasha managed to get in eventually.

Shelly's smile almost split her face in two. Probably no one had ever said that to her before. Taking advantage of her gullibility gave Natasha a stab of guilt, and even knowing that it had saved the intended victim's life did not help.

They went back over the bridge. Natasha helped Shelly pull it up and then bade her good night. She walked back toward Westernfort alone. In bleak detachment, her eyes traveled over the view: the stars, the mountains, the houses. A slight feeling of relief skittered around the edges of her mind. But the worst was still ahead.

❖

The small bedroom was both quiet and disquieting. The absence of the other two was a more painful strain than their presence had been. It was impossible for Natasha to apply herself to the task of making enough noise for three with any conviction. And the better part of an hour remained before it would be time to sleep. She wanted to get away but had to be there to answer the door in case someone knocked. Surely it must arouse curiosity that all of them were staying in their room.

Natasha was about to open and close the window shutters loudly when another idea came to her. She grabbed her jacket, laced on her boots, and headed for the common room. Obviously, the inquisitiveness of several residents had already been tweaked. As soon as she appeared, one middle-aged woman called, "Hi, Jess. Where are your parents?"

Natasha sauntered over, carefully adjusting her expression to one of indulgent amusement. "It's the anniversary of the day they first met. I've just helped them finish the bottle to celebrate, and I got the feeling they wanted to, um..." She paused for effect. "Commemorate the occasion in a traditional fashion. So I'm going to leave them to do it in private."

"They've been keeping that quiet."

"Yes." Natasha let her eyes deliberately travel in the direction of the room and back. "And hopefully, they'll continue to keep the noise down. But if not, just bang on the wall."

Natasha had pitched her voice loud enough for most of the women present to hear. Several laughed. Natasha grinned again and left, confident that enough people had caught her innuendo to be sure no one would try disturbing the supposed activity in the bedroom.

It was easier to breathe outside. Natasha would have liked to have spent the time before sleep simply walking off the nervous tension, but it was too cold for such behavior to be anything other than suspicious. No rain had fallen that day, but the paths between the houses were thick with mud, and the wind blew in icy gusts. The tavern was the obvious place to go, although drinking was definitely to be undertaken with caution, and she was not in the mood for happy chatter.

As she approached the main square, Natasha saw a light burning in the room at the back of Dani's shop. Since the kiln firing, she had tried to avoid being alone with Dani, but the chance for a final quiet talk looked like a blessing from the Goddess. Natasha could think of no better way to spend her last evening on earth.

She stuck her head around the entrance to the shop. "Hello... Dani?"

The rear door swung wide, and Dani appeared, silhouetted in the light from the fire. "Jess."

"I was on my way to the tavern, and I saw you were here. Can I come in? Or would you like to join me at..." Natasha stopped. Already, Dani had stepped back, waving her in. Natasha paused only to remove her mud-laden boots and strip off her jacket before trotting into the back room.

A fire was burning in the hearth. The room felt snug and warm, and was much the same as the first time Natasha had seen it, although rather less tidy. Dani made the effort to shove a box full of something under a table, using her foot, and cleared the bench in front of the fire.

"I wasn't expecting company." She apologized for the clutter.

"That's okay. I'm used to it. My mother's..." Natasha bit off her words. *My mother's place was always a mess*, she had been about to say. The chaos of her mother's house had always irritated her, whereas Dani's home seemed friendly and comfortable. The idea struck Natasha that many of her actions and attitudes had been inspired by the need to reject her mother. Now that her mother was no longer around, had she finally outgrown it? The thought lodged in her head, driving out any hope of putting a safe ending on the sentence.

Luckily, Dani was too agitated to notice. She swept up three half-empty mugs from the fireside. "Um...I could offer you tea...or maybe warm some wine?"

Natasha stood, staring into the flames. "Tea will be great."

"How are you doing?"

"Fine," Natasha replied, adding mentally, *Except that tomorrow, I'm going to murder Lynn and then kill myself.*

The burning logs mesmerized her, recalling the sight of Himoti's sacred flame burning in the temple the night she had accepted the mission. If she could go back and talk to herself, what would she say? What could she say? How could she even begin to explain things to the young soldier who had knelt before the shrine? Natasha was not the same person anymore. She had lost her certainties, her dreams, her innocence. And what had she gained in their place? *It's a bit late to start working out what I want to do with my life.*

Aloud, the rambling conversation of faltering question-and-answer continued while Dani covertly cleared the piles of rubbish. Natasha was half aware of the activity and half aware that her subdued manner was going to be noticed soon. She knew that she ought to be more alert but could not drag her thoughts into the present. Any attempt at acting her part had gone.

"Are you sure you're all right?" Dani put down the things she was holding and stepped to Natasha's side.

"Oh...yes." Natasha knew her words sounded too unconvincing to be considered a lie.

"What's wrong?" Dani caught hold of Natasha's arm and pulled her around so that they were facing.

Natasha looked into Dani's eyes and saw there a place where she could lose her thoughts, her pain, her soul. *I'm going to die tomorrow. What does it matter?* Natasha lifted her hands and placed them on either side of Dani's waist. Dani's expression was still caught in confusion, but then Natasha slipped her hands up Dani's back, pulling her close. Her lips claimed Dani's in a kiss.

At first, Dani was frozen in surprise, but she melted quickly, leaning against Natasha. Her arms wrapped around Natasha's back, clinging to her shoulders. For a while, they explored the softness of each other's mouths. Natasha gave her entire being over, letting raw desire obliterate all reason, all doubts. She ceased to think, but after a while, Dani's body stiffened, and she gently pushed them apart.

Her eyes searched Natasha's face. "Why do I suddenly feel this is a bad idea?"

Natasha's spirits crashed, but it was all she deserved. "Do you want me to leave?"

"I never said I was going to be sensible. I just..." Dani's words died, while her questioning eyes continued to stare at Natasha. Then she placed her hand on the back of Natasha's head and pulled Natasha's mouth hard against her own.

The surging passion of the kiss swept over Natasha, blotting out the past and the future. Tomorrow ceased to exist. She slid her hands down Dani's back and then lower, pressing their hips together. She felt Dani shaking and realized that her own legs were none too steady. She broke away. "I need to sit down."

Dani buried her face in Natasha's neck and murmured, "I can go one better than that."

Dani guided Natasha backward across the room until her knees hit the side of the bed and she collapsed on the quilt. Natasha had no complaints. She swiveled around so that her head was on the pillow. Immediately, Dani was lying beside her, holding her close, mouth traveling in a wandering kiss from Natasha's eyes to her ears and along her jaw. Natasha found herself nuzzling Dani's hand, using lips and tongue to study the shape of fingers and knuckles—hands strong and skillful from working the clay.

Abruptly, Dani half rose, climbing onto Natasha so that she was sitting astride Natasha's hips, pinning her against the mattress. Her eyes met Natasha's, holding her motionless on the bed with the intensity of the gaze. Dani's hand moved to the fastening at her own neck.

In silence, Natasha watched as the buttons were loosened one by one. She waited for both shirt and undershirt to be removed; then she lifted her hands to cup Dani's breasts. Dani's neck arched so that her face was toward the ceiling. A long, high whimper sounded from the back of her throat. Natasha braced an elbow on the bed and pushed herself up, curling, until her mouth could reach Dani's breasts; her lips opened around a nipple. Dani's arms wrapped around Natasha's shoulders, holding her in place, but their balance was unstable, and they both fell to the bed, clinging together.

Natasha had no memory of undressing, but their clothes were gone, and they both lay between the sheets, arms and legs entwined. Dani's fingers lightly ran over Natasha, teasing every nerve in her body in waves that rippled beneath her skin. Dani's eyes were closed, and her mouth was open. Harsh breaths rasped between her lips. "Jess. Oh, Jess."

The false name hit like a kick to Natasha's stomach, driving the air from her lungs. She covered Dani's mouth with her own to silence the sound, closing her eyes tightly to hold in the tears. The words leapt through her head: *Dani, I've lied to you since the day we met, but there is one honest service my tongue can do for you.*

Natasha's lips slipped into the smooth hollow of Dani's throat and then moved on to the hard ridge of Dani's collarbone before meeting the contrasting softness of Dani's breast. Natasha's chin moved over Dani's stomach. Her cheek brushed the curly triangle of hair. She shifted down farther and then stopped. Dani was lying on the bed, arms thrown wide, lost in passion. Natasha felt totally in control. She stroked her hand up between Dani's legs, watching the effect radiate through Dani's entire body. With a thumb, Natasha pulled back the hood and saw the small pearl hidden beneath. Deliberately, she lowered her mouth to the warm scent of musk and the clean metallic taste of a woman.

Natasha timed the strokes of her tongue to the rhythm of Dani's breathing. She watched the tremors shaking Dani's shoulders, legs, and arms. Dani's gasps became more violent, her stomach rose and fell, her whole torso working in the fight for air. And then Dani's voice broke into a cry, her back arched, and her hands stretched out, clenching convulsively into fists. Her body rose and fell in waves as though it were being shaken.

At last, Dani dropped back to the bed. Her hands reached in a feeble attempt to draw Natasha to her side. They lacked the strength to pull her up, but Natasha went willingly. Dani wrapped her hands around Natasha's back and buried her face in Natasha's breasts. To her surprise, Natasha realized that both of them were crying.

Natasha stroked Dani's shoulders, murmuring nonsense words. For a while, Dani did nothing apart from breathe, but she recovered more quickly than Natasha expected. Almost before Natasha knew what was happening, Dani pressed her back onto the sheets and bent over her, staring down into her eyes.

"I'll do the same for you, if you want, but I'd rather watch your face as you come," Dani said carefully, and then smiled. "For this first time."

"Whatever," Natasha gasped with difficulty. Dani could do anything she liked—just as long as she did something.

Dani's hand slid down Natasha's side to her thigh. "Open your legs."

Natasha obeyed. She wanted to open her soul and let Dani take every last fragment of her being. She wanted to give herself totally to Dani, holding nothing back. She wanted, just this once, to be totally true to her heart. Dani's fingers slipped inside her. The sensation ripped through Natasha's body, smashing any hope of self-control. Dani's hands moved with confidence, sweeping Natasha along, a helpless witness to what was happening to her. She was enslaved, and she did not care. The touch of Dani's fingers was the fixed point in a growing maelstrom of ecstasy. Her orgasm exploded inside her, blurring the boundaries of her body, an experience of release too intense to be called simple pleasure.

Natasha opened her eyes, gasping as her breath returned. The bedclothes had long since been kicked aside. The heat from the fire warmed her along one side, and Dani's body was hot on the other, while a draft stirred cold waves over the sweat on her stomach. The ceiling of the room shifted in the flickering red light. Natasha turned her head slightly to view Dani's face.

Dani's eyes swept the length of her body and back. "Very nice," she said, and smiled. "I knew you'd be worth waiting for."

Natasha still did not have sufficient control of her breathing to answer.

Dani bent her head and gently brushed her lips across Natasha's; then she looked across the room, frowning. "Now, where were we?" She snapped her fingers. "Yes, that was it. I'd offered you tea, and er...did you say you wanted some?"

Natasha could feel Dani laughing silently. The body beside her was shaking. "I...I think I...said yes," she said between gasps.

"Right. Well, how about I make us a drink? And then...maybe a second round?"

"Of tea?"

Dani rolled on top of Natasha and kissed the tip of her nose. "If that's all you want."

Dani slipped from the bed and went over to the fireplace, picking up the discarded kettle. Natasha turned onto her side and watched. The sight of Dani naked in the firelight was so beautiful that it brought tears to her eyes.

❖

Natasha awoke from a light doze. She was curled tightly around Dani's back. Some time had passed, and the fire had burned down, lighting the room with a gentle red glow. Natasha carefully shifted herself up onto one elbow. She looked down on Dani's face.

"Dani, are you awake?" Natasha asked quietly.

There was no response.

Natasha continued staring at the face on the pillow. She could not tell whether she was going to burst from happiness or cry from despair. *Please, Celaeno. Freeze time now. Let me spend all eternity at this moment,* Natasha prayed.

There was a sound as the logs in the fire shifted. The world continued on its way. Morning would come.

Natasha lifted her hand to brush the hair from Dani's forehead, but stopped. She could have screamed from the pain. The miserable situation was no more bearable for knowing that she had walked into it open-eyed. But if only she had known where her choices would take her, surely she could have made it work out better. The bitter thought repeated in her head: *I've left it a bit late to start working out what I want to do with my life.* But now she knew at least part of the answer for certain.

Natasha spoke in the softest of whispers, "Dani, I know you're asleep and can't hear me, but I want to tell you how much I love you. I know that by this time tomorrow, you aren't going to believe it. You're going to doubt everything I've ever said to you. But this is true...I love you with all my heart, and I always will."

Dani's eyes remained closed, but the corner of her mouth drew up in a slow smile. "I heard that," she said drowsily. "And I know what I'm supposed to say back. But you're going to have to wait. Maybe I'll tell you tomorrow."

Dani's lips relaxed as she drifted back to sleep. Natasha slipped down in the bed and wrapped her arm around Dani's waist. Tears squeezed from under her eyelids, but with effort, she stopped herself from sobbing and eventually fell into a deep sleep.

CHAPTER SIXTEEN—DAMNED FOREVER

"Dani!" Natasha jerked up in bed and stared around wildly. For a moment, she thought the pounding was her heart until she realized that someone was thumping urgently on the door. The bedclothes beside her stirred, and Dani's face emerged, looking just as confused as her own.

"What is it?"

"Are you ill?" The voice from the shop called.

"No...I..." Dani rolled out of bed and grabbed her shirt. "What time is it?"

"I know it's a bit early, but I need a large bowl, for breakfast."

Dani shook her head and then grinned down at Natasha. "I don't believe it," she said quietly, before raising her voice again. "I'll be there in a moment." She pulled on her pants and sidled out, leaving the door slightly ajar behind her.

Natasha rose and also dragged on her clothes. From the shop came the sounds of bartering. She considered waiting until Dani's customer left but decided against it. The gossips would have far worse to talk about come nightfall, and a slow, private farewell to Dani would be more than she could bear. She went into the shop to reclaim her boots and jacket.

"Oh, I didn't...er...good morning, Jess." The customer's face shifted from surprise to amusement.

Dani's eyes jumped between the woman and Natasha. "You're off? Umm...okay, I'll see you later." Her voice held both uncertainty and disappointment.

Natasha nodded and escaped. It was a miserable goodbye. *But it's probably for the best*, she told herself. *Anything more emotional, and I'd have cried.* Tears were not far away as it was.

Dawn had broken by the time she trotted across the main square, anxious to get to the animal barn quickly. Her attention was caught by a small gathering outside Kim and Lynn's house. She knew it was a mistake, but she paused to watch. Kim and Chip were standing there in riding gear, surrounded by their families. Natasha was close enough to hear Chip say goodbye to her partner, Katryn, and promise her daughter to be back in time for her birthday.

The day was particularly important for young Tanya Coppelli. She would be sixteen, and it was no secret that she was desperate to follow both her mothers into the Westernfort Rangers. Kim was carrying Becky. She lifted the toddler high into the air, swung her around, and sat her on Lynn's shoulders. The child's high-pitched laughter squealed through the morning hush. Kim bent her neck to kiss Lynn goodbye and then, with Chip beside her, walked across the open space, heading for the road to the main gates.

Natasha watched them go with something approaching horror. *Celaeno, is this really your will?* The words were shouted inside her head.

"Where are your parents, Jess? I thought they were supposed to be with me today." An aggravated voice from behind interrupted Natasha's thoughts.

She turned around. The speaker was one of the forewomen who oversaw general building work. Natasha forced herself to speak. "There must have been a mix-up somewhere. They've been sent to repair some sheep pens on the other side of the lake. They set off after breakfast."

Disproving the lie would not take much investigation, but it was very unlikely that anyone would put in the effort to do so. The forewoman looked peeved but not about to rush off and check. She snorted and stomped away.

Natasha looked back across the square. The small group was dispersing. Kim and Chip had vanished from sight. Natasha had to fight the urge to run after them. Every sickening doubt returned. *I wish I were dead.* She knew she would be before the day was out. It could not happen soon enough.

❖

"Where are Rohanna and Cal today?"

The forewoman stopped whatever she was doing at the bottom of the ditch and looked up, squinting against the midday sun in her face. Ash helpfully took a half step to the right so her shadow shielded the woman's eyes.

"Mirle sent them to work on some pens that need attention." The forewoman scowled in irritation.

"Did Mirle tell you that?"

"No. I had to find out for myself."

Every instinct in Ash screamed. She worked to keep her voice even. "So who told you?"

"Their daughter, Jess."

"Did she say exactly where they were?"

"The other side of the lake somewhere." The forewoman scrambled out of the ditch. "Why? Is anything wrong?"

"I hope not." Ash spoke mainly to herself. She looked at the confused expression of the other woman. "No. I shouldn't think so. I was just curious." She walked away, leaving a mystified forewoman behind. Not for the first time, Ash wished that Kim had given someone else the task of monitoring the family of thieves—someone with more experience in spying.

Ash was furious with herself. She had been lax. Three months of watching the family, and when they finally pulled something, she had not noticed until noon. She halted at the edge of the main square. Her gut reaction told her that looking for Mirle was a waste of effort. What should she do?

Ash chewed her lip. She did not have time to waste with more mistakes. Her next move had to be the right one; she had to avoid false trails. Which was easier said than done. *Just pretend they're a pride of snow lions.* Kim's words when she had given the assignment echoed in Ash's thoughts. Perhaps it was the best way to proceed. Snow lions she knew, and the place to pick up fresh trails was at the lair. Ash set off across the square.

At first glance, the room shared by the family looked the same as it had the last time Ash had seen it. On that occasion, she had searched the room, not in the hope of finding anything, intending only to let it be known that the room had been searched. It had been an easier and more intriguing job than she expected. She had spotted the fine bristle in the latch even before opening the door. That the family thought to monitor any intrusion into their quarters was an interesting fact in itself. For Ash's purposes at the time, it meant that she needed to go through their belongings only routinely to be sure that the family would get the message.

Alarming the family had been the sole aim of the search; she had hoped to push them into hasty action. But she had not expected anything quite so quick. If the thieves were going to try something dishonest, they would probably do it while Kim was away. It was the time Ash would have chosen in their place, and it would be wiser still to wait a day or two longer, letting things settle. So Ash had reasoned; otherwise, she would never have taken the break from surveillance. She had gone to bed early the previous evening, anticipating long hours of vigil in the nights ahead, and spent the morning in preparations. The mistake had been a bad one. And maybe the halfhearted search of the room had been another. Perhaps she should have been more thorough.

Ash went to the chest and knelt down, looking closely. This time, there was no hair caught under the lid; there was no chalk. Obviously, the thieves had ceased to be concerned about whether they were searched. Ash's eyes scanned the rest of the room. It was hard to put her finger on any one detail, but the analogy with snow lions stuck in her mind, and Ash knew with certainty what she was looking at: an abandoned lair. The dangerous occupants had moved on. Lifting the wooden lid confirmed her impression. The chest was not empty, but the missing items were significant.

Had the thieves gotten what they came for and fled? Something so trivial or obscure that its loss had not yet been noticed?

Ash sat on the chest and tried to pull all the threads together, desperate to see the pattern. She considered the report from Jules in the Homelands, the discrepancy between Jess' and Cal's DNA, the obvious and unexpected intelligence of the family, Cal's familiarity with the wildlands, Jess' guilt, Rohanna's evasiveness, the bristle in the lock, the premature flight and abandoned room.

Ash's forehead creased in a frown. It did not add up to anything sensible. Then a memory drifted through her mind from years ago, long before the 23rd Squadron had deserted. She had been on patrol and had stopped to watch a lone mountain cat stalk a herd of fenbucks. The cat had been dappled, its light brown fur almost invisible in the bracken. Its progress had looked random. Half an hour's maneuvering took it no closer to its goal until she saw that it was intent on stealth, putting camouflage and strategic position before a simple narrowing of distance. In the end, it had been the movement of the fenbucks that had brought them within striking range, and the mountain cat had burst from cover—a clever hunter, and a deadly one.

Ash stood up. She still could not tie together all the bits of information, but at least she recognized the pattern. Camouflage and position. She stopped in the common room by the side of an elderly resident, heating her lunch over the cooking fire.

"When did you last see any of Rohanna Korski's family?" Ash asked.

"They were here last night at dinner."

"And after that?"

"They went to their room. Rohanna and Cal stayed there, but young Jess went out." The woman's wrinkled forehead became more deeply creased. "What's this ab—"

Ash cut her off. "You haven't seen the older two since?"

"No, but—"

"How about Jess?"

"This morning. She called in on her way to work. She'd—"

Ash was already gone. She paused outside the doorway, considering her options. Going to check the other side of the lake would be a waste of time. If, by some chance, she had misread the signs, and the two thieves were working there, no problem existed. As leader in Kim's absence, Mirle should be told, but finding her might take time, and anyway, she would almost certainly want to start with the last of Ash's options, having a quiet word with Jess in the animal barn. Assuming that she was still there.

❖

Natasha doubled over as though she were in pain. She laid her forehead on her arms, which were resting on the low partition around the lambs' enclosure. "Please, Celaeno. I know this isn't your will. Give me a sign...strike me down with lightning.

Anything so I don't have to go through with this." The only answer to Natasha's prayer was a soft whine from Tipsy, who looked up at her with puzzled canine eyes.

Natasha pushed away from the partition and staggered, more than walked, to the pile of soiled straw she was supposed to be sweeping. She could not bear to look at the animals. She could not bear to look at the barn itself. It would be the scene of Lynn's death.

Natasha had worked out her plans for the murder. She needed to ensure that there was no chance of messengers carrying the news of Lynn's death reaching the outpost before Rohanna and Cal had dispatched their two victims. Yet neither should she delay and run the risk of being caught up by investigations into her parents' disappearance. She had decided to wait another hour before going to find Lynn and telling her that one of the animals was looking unwell. Lynn would come to see, giving Natasha the chance to kill her without being noticed. Then Natasha would hide the body and find somewhere secluded to kill herself. With any luck, neither of their deaths would attract notice until after nightfall, and as a final bonus, there was little chance that Lynn's children would be the ones to discover their mother's body.

Natasha groaned and closed her eyes. "Please, Celaeno, a sign. Show me your will," she whispered.

"Hi, Jess. How's it going?"

Natasha spun about. Lynn had entered the barn and was standing by the doorway. A rolled-up blanket lay over one shoulder. An easy grin was on the Imprinter's face. Natasha struggled to control her voice enough to answer. "Okay-ish. But I'm...a little behind with my work."

"Things on your mind?"

"Er...sort of." Natasha stood hunched by her broom. She felt physically ill. A sick headache was starting behind her eyes, and her stomach was gripped by cramps, but neither was an unequivocal sign of divine intervention.

"I thought as much." Lynn laughed. "I hear you visited Dani last night." She pointed an accusatory finger. "And don't tell me all you got was a mug of tea, because in that case, you were still drinking it this morning when Ella called in." When Natasha did not answer, Lynn laughed again and walked past her. "And you're obviously suffering from lack of sleep. So adding it all together, I've drawn some conclusions."

"Um...Well, I..." Natasha mumbled. Fortunately, an answer was not required. Lynn had moved on to the animals. She patted the flank of a cow.

"I've brought a horse blanket for Daisy. We'll see if it helps her." Lynn slipped the roll of cloth off her shoulder. As she did so, a sword belt fell to the ground. "Oh, damn. I was supposed to drop that in at the smithy as I went past. It belongs to Kim. A rivet has cracked." Lynn bent down to pick up the belt. A sword hilt protruded from the top of the scabbard. Lynn turned it over once in her hands and then held it out to Natasha. "I was already late with it. I'd promised the smith she'd have it by midmorning. Can you do me a favor and run it over to her? Go on. The exercise in the open air will do you good." Lynn grinned and deposited the belt plus scabbard into Natasha's unresisting hands. Then she turned back to the blanket and Daisy.

No, Celaeno! Natasha cried to herself in agony. *Oh, no, please. This can't be your sign!* But what could be clearer? Lynn herself had put the means of her death into the hands of her executioner. Natasha looked down at the weapon: a Ranger's short sword. The hilt was loose due to the cracked rivet, but it was more than adequate to kill an unarmed woman, especially if her back was turned.

The pulse pounded in Natasha's skull. She wanted to howl. Life should not be like this: foul, vicious, and unfair. But life would not be her problem much longer. And the sooner it was all over, the better. Natasha drew the sword.

At the rasp of metal, Lynn looked over her shoulder. "Jess?" she asked. Natasha said nothing and stepped forward. Lynn straightened to face her. "Jess, are you all right?"

Natasha swallowed the bile rising in her throat. The least she could give Lynn was the truth. "My name is not Jess. I am Corporal Natasha Ionadis of the 3rd Company of Temple Guards. I have been sent here, on the personal orders of the Chief Consultant, to carry out the sentence of death that has been passed on you for your blasphemy against the Goddess."

"You...what?" Lynn was too confused to be frightened.

Natasha's hand tightened on the hilt of the sword. She pulled back her arm to strike, and her eyes met those of the woman she was about to kill. Her oath to the Goddess impelled her onward, fighting against the knowledge that Lynn was not evil and did not deserve to die. She tried to draw a deep breath, but her chest was too tight. Then suddenly, the internal battle was over, and for the first time that day, a feeling of peace swept through Natasha. "And I can't do it," she said simply. She flipped the sword over and proffered the hilt in a formal gesture of surrender.

"You're a Gua..." Lynn's voice failed in the struggle to keep up.

Natasha nodded in answer. She felt light-headed, and the walls of the barn wobbled before her eyes.

"But...but...your parents?"

"Not my real parents. They're Guards as well, on the same mission."

"Where?" Bewildered, Lynn looked about as if she expected to see the pair standing in the barn.

"They're not here. They left the valley yesterday. They've gone on to the outpost to ambush Kim and Chip when they stay there tonight. I was to stay and cover for them. The three of us couldn't all go. I was left here to kill you, but..." Natasha's mind was no longer in control of her mouth. The words tumbled out beyond her control, but she did not get any farther. Lynn had taken a scant second to register the danger to Kim. She sprang toward the door and raced out of the barn.

Natasha was left alone, forlornly holding out the sword. Her sense of peace was vanishing, smashed aside by the knowledge of what she had just done. *I'm forsworn on my oath to the Goddess. I've betrayed my comrades in arms.*

Natasha's legs started to shake. The tremors rose through her. Her headache erupted again in pounding blows. The words of her oath repeated themselves on her lips: "If I turn aside from this task, may I be damned forever."

Natasha's gaze dropped to the sword in her hands, the blade pointing toward her heart. The second of her objectives was still outstanding. It had always formed the easier part of the plan. Perhaps she could manage to do this part right. Once she was dead, Celaeno could judge her actions. Natasha had no complaints, whichever way the verdict went. Uncertainty was the thing she could not bear. It would be nice to have the Goddess herself explain exactly what she had wanted. And why.

Natasha lifted her other hand to the hilt, wrapping her fingers around it firmly. The tip of the blade touched her chest. Her arms were trembling, their strength gone, but it would not take much. All she had to do was keep the sword in place while she fell forward. And falling would not be a problem. She was swaying on her feet.

Natasha looked at the ground, hunting for a clear spot. *I don't want to bang my knee as I fall.* The irony was too bitter to be humorous.

"If you want to do that, I won't try to stop you, but I'd regret your death." Ash's voice was soft and sad. Natasha turned her head. The veteran Ranger had slipped into the barn and was standing a few meters away. Ash continued to talk calmly. "I passed Lynn on the way here. She didn't hang about to chat. Still, I think I've got the general idea of things. I'll admit you're in a bit of a mess, but I wouldn't have thought you're the sort of woman to take the coward's way out. You'd be sparing the town council a tricky decision, and you might come to regret it, if the rescue doesn't get there in time and either Lynn or Katryn gets her hands on you. But all in all, I don't think you should do it."

Natasha gulped at the air. Her head was filling with wool, and her eyes would not focus. It was impossible to make any more decisions. She faced Ash and held out the sword. "I am Corporal Natasha Ionadis of the 3rd Company of Temple Guards, and I wish to surrender."

"I accept your surrender." Ash took the offered hilt. As soon as her hands were empty, Natasha staggered three steps to the nearest wall, braced herself against it, and threw up.

Ash waited until Natasha had finished; then she supported her for the short walk outside to a seat on the sawed-off trunk of a tree. Natasha sat hunched over. Her head was clearing, but she could not stop shaking. Ash stood close beside her, although her body language was more like that of a nurse than a Guard.

Natasha's eyes fixed on the town. Even at a distance, she could see the unusual level of activity, people gathering on the streets, attracted by the commotion. At last, she saw six women in Ranger uniforms race toward the entrance of the valley. At her side, Ash looked up. Natasha guessed that she was estimating the hour from the sun's position.

"Will they be in time?" Natasha asked, wondering what she wanted the answer to be.

"Maybe. They'll take spare horses for changing mounts, but they still won't get to the outpost before dark."

Then Natasha saw another woman running. Dani was hurtling up the track toward the barn. Natasha could not stand it. She wanted to hide, but she could not move. The pain must have shown on her face. Dani's footsteps increased in a final spurt. She skidded to a stop, sliding to her knees, and putting her arm around Natasha's shoulder. "Jess, are you all right?"

Natasha could neither move nor answer. The feel of Dani's arms around her was unbearable. It was everything she wanted— and everything she was about to lose. Her head sunk onto Dani's shoulder while she cursed herself for clinging to something she had no right to.

Dani pulled back and spoke again. "Are you hurt? I heard a Guard got into the valley and tried to kill Lynn in the barn. Were you there? Did you get injured?"

Natasha raised her head and met Dani's eyes, saw the love there, and knew that it was all about to go. She wetted her lips and said, "It was me."

"It...who?"

"The Guard. It was me. I'm a Guard."

"That's not funny." Dani's eyes moved to Ash as though she was seeking an explanation. Whatever she saw in the old Ranger's face must have warned her that something very awful was about to happen. Dani took her arm away and stood up.

Natasha's lips twisted in a grimace. "No, you're right. It's not funny. My name isn't Jess. I'm Corporal Natasha Ionadis of the Guards. I was sent here by the Chief Consultant to kill Lynn and Kim, but I couldn't do it." She looked up at Dani's frozen expression and forced herself to carry on. She had to speak.

"I've changed so much since I left Landfall, and you were part of the change. I've had to think about what I was doing, and I knew it was wrong. I was going to kill Lynn, but I couldn't. I've failed the Goddess, except I don't know if I have. I mean, I'm not sure what..." Natasha shook her head, fighting desperately to control her words. "I can't sort my own mind out. I don't know how I feel about anything except for you. Last night, what I said—I meant it. I truly love you..."

Tears were blurring Natasha's eyes. She did not see the hand coming. The slap knocked her head sideways, jarring her teeth. The side of her face burned. She looked up. Dani had pulled back her hand for another blow. Natasha made no attempt to defend herself, but Ash stepped forward, blocking Dani's arm.

"We don't mistreat prisoners. We leave that to the Guards," Ash said evenly.

For several heartbeats, nobody moved. Then Dani spun around and marched away, heading back to town. Natasha bowed her head and sobbed.

PART THREE

The Goddess
in Your Heart

Chapter Seventeen—Betrayal

B oth moons soared overhead, but their light was softened by a thin mist of high cloud. Snow that might have caught and amplified the milky glimmering had melted. The outpost was a hunched shape at the bottom of the hollow. Smoke from its chimney could be smelled but not seen, and the shadows beneath the trees and bushes were solid black.

Rohanna and Cal sat under the cover of an evergreen thicket, twenty meters from the door, resting after their long trek. They needed to be ready for the action ahead. In midafternoon, they had hidden while Kim and Chip overtook them on the main trail. By now, the heretics should have spent the better part of two hours at the outpost, easily enough time to tend to the horses and eat. No noise came from the building; probably, both occupants were asleep. But Rohanna restrained the urge to creep up and peer in through the crack in the window shutters. There was no need to take risks or rush things. With the grace of the Goddess, time was on their side.

Once again, Cal checked that her sword was loose in its scabbard. From the expression on the ex-Ranger's face, Rohanna surmised that the gesture was due neither to nervousness nor impatience; rather, Cal was rehearsing the forthcoming action in her mind. While walking, they had discussed at length the best method of dispatching the heretics. Luring them from the building and shooting them with bows was the more chancy option, although it held the advantage that there would be no bloodstains in the building to remove. In the end, the weak light forced the decision in favor of stabbing their victims while they slept.

Rohanna looked up thoughtfully at the wispy shroud in front of the moons. Heavier clouds were rolling in. The advancing line had reached the small orb of Laurel. Before long, the hollow would be utterly lightless. The wind was picking up, rustling the bushes. Suddenly, her ears caught a faint sound in the distance. She reached out to touch Cal's arm, but the ex-Ranger was clearly already aware of the noise and knew what it was. Within seconds, Rohanna had also recognized the pounding of hooves. The two Guards shrank farther back into the darkness of the undergrowth.

The hoofbeats grew louder until a group of mounted women burst over the rim of the hollow and charged up to the door of the outpost. One rider leapt out of her saddle, shouting, even before her horse had stopped. "Chip, Kim, are you there?" Rohanna identified the voice as that of Chip's partner, Katryn.

"What is it?" The door opened, and Kim Ramon stood silhouetted in dull amber firelight. Then the six riders and their spare horses clustered around the entrance, obscuring her from view of the Guards in the undergrowth.

"You're both all right?" Katryn's anxious voice sounded over the hubbub.

"Yes, we're fine. What's happened?"

"Jess Korski is a Guard. She was going to murder Lynn."

"She what?" Kim exploded. "Lynn isn't—"

Katryn cut in, "No, Lynn's fine. She wasn't hurt. Jess had a sword, but Lynn managed to escape."

"Get my horse," Kim ordered sharply. "I'll sort that—"

"No, wait." The horses shifted, and the two watchers caught a glimpse of Katryn with her hand on Kim's arm. "Everything's under control at Westernfort, but Rohanna and Cal are also Guards. They've come out here to murder you. They're probably somewhere close at hand even as we speak."

"We don't need to..." Kim's voice faded away, and she pinched the bridge of her nose between her thumb and forefinger. Then she raised her head and considered the sky. "You're sure Lynn is safe?"

"Yes," Katryn answered.

"And Jess?"

"She's a prisoner."

"Have Rohanna and Cal got horses?"

"We don't think so."

Kim nodded. "Okay. You're right. There's no point charging back in the dark and breaking a horse's leg. And we need to find the other two. Perhaps they'd like to join our little chat with Jess. I can't see it taking long to catch a pair of Guards in the wildlands. We can wait until first light tomorrow. It will be easier to see what we're doing then. Stable the horses, and get everyone inside. If Rohanna and Cal are close by, they'll have seen you arrive, but if not, they'll be in for a surprise when they try sneaking in here tonight, which will save us the trouble of hunting them down."

The Rangers were moving as soon as Kim finished speaking. Before long, the area around the outpost was empty and silent. The two Guards had not moved since the riders had appeared, but now they edged slowly back through the vegetation, keeping to the thickest shadows. They did not speak until they had left the hollow.

"So what now?" Cal asked.

Rohanna pursed her lips. "For starters, I think it would be a good idea if we make use of your Ranger training to get ourselves away from here and make sure we can't be tracked."

"And then?"

"And then, we stop and think."

❖

The cell beneath the Admin offices was not quite wide enough for Natasha to stretch her arms out straight and not quite long enough for her to lie flat. The straw-stuffed pallet she had been given took up well over half the floor space. The only light had come through a ten-centimeter gap under the door, which also let in an icy draft. The time was long after sunset, and the cell was in complete darkness. However, the draft was still there.

The absence of light did not bother Natasha. She had no wish to see her surroundings. After more than a day in the cell, she was totally familiar with every square centimeter of it, although she had not yet counted the bricks in the walls. She was saving that for when she got really bored. Mealtimes had formed the high points of her captivity, along with the brief interview from Mirle and Lieutenant Horte of the Rangers. They had not asked her much and told her even less. She guessed that they were waiting for news from the outpost, which they should have received by now.

Natasha pulled a blanket around her shoulders and huddled in a corner of the cell. She was desperate to know whether Rohanna and Cal had died from her betrayal and whether her warning had saved Kim and Chip. What she most wanted was for all four women to still be alive, although it would not be the easiest option on herself.

Kim Ramon would want information to help capture the two Guards. Natasha could tell her little enough, but it might make all the difference. If the hunters did not know about the stolen map and Cal's experience as a Ranger, they would assume that the Guards must return the same way as they came and would not waste time checking other routes to Landfall. If they did not know the importance Rohanna placed on the news about Ginasberg, they might assume that the Guards would stay around and make another attempt to carry out the executions. The more Rangers kept patrolling Westernfort, the fewer there would be for the pursuit.

Natasha remembered Rohanna's remarks concerning ways to make a woman talk and Shelly's story of the burns inflicted on her grandmother. She tried not to dwell on the thought. If she let herself become frightened, the battle would be lost before it started. She wanted to bow her head and pray to the Goddess for strength, but she did not think Celaeno would pay heed to one who had broken an oath sworn in the light of Himoti's eternal flame.

In the end, she prayed anyway. Rohanna and Cal were surely still in the grace of the Goddess, and it was their well-being she was pleading for. She could not bear to betray them again.

Footsteps interrupted her prayers. Raising her head, she saw a light beneath the door, getting steadily brighter. A key scraped in the lock, and the door swung open. Natasha got to her feet as two grim-faced Rangers entered the cell. One held a torch; the other, a loop of cord. From the noises in the corridor beyond, Natasha could tell that at least two more women were there.

"Turn around, and put your hands behind you," the Ranger with the cord ordered. The voice belonged to Ash. In the flickering light, Natasha had not recognized her.

Natasha obeyed, and her wrists were bound securely. With no other words, the four Rangers escorted her up the stairs to the ground floor and into a small room. The only furnishings visible were a table and chairs, which had been pushed against the far wall to clear the floor space. A shelf with ledgers hung at one side. The window shutters were closed and barred.

Two women were waiting in the room, leaning against the table: Kim Ramon and Chip Coppelli. The sight of them answered half of Natasha's questions, but there was no sign of either Rohanna or Cal.

One of the Rangers pushed her into the center of the floor. Natasha did not look back over her shoulder, but from the sounds of feet, the escort had taken up positions around the edges of the room behind her. The silence dragged on for a full thirty seconds. Then Kim pushed away from the table and stepped forward.

"Shall we start at the beginning? Perhaps you could introduce yourself properly," Kim said calmly.

Natasha focused on the wall. "I am Corporal Natasha Ionadis of the 3rd Company of Temple Guards."

"The 3rd Company? Not the Intelligence Corps?"

"I was assigned...temporarily before leaving Landfall, just for this mission, but..." Natasha floundered. She had never seen the transfer as being permanent, unlike her promotion to corporal. But both changes in her status had been made on the same day, and of course, both had been expected to last the rest of her life.

"Are you Intelligence Corps or not?" Kim snapped.

"Yes."

"And how about the women we knew as Rohanna Korski and Calinda Rowse?"

"Are they still alive?" Natasha asked eagerly.

Kim paused. "The game we're playing at the moment is you answer my questions, not the other way around."

"But are..." Natasha stopped. She was not going to get an answer, but surely if Rohanna and Cal were dead or captured, Kim would not be asking about them.

"Were Rohanna and Cal from the Intelligence Corps?"

Natasha clamped her jaw shut.

Kim took three slow steps across the room until she was standing so close that the open flap of her jacket brushed Natasha's arm. Natasha kept her gaze fixed on the wall, but she could feel Kim's eyes boring into her.

When Kim spoke, her voice was quiet, but there was a savage edge to it. "You came here as a spy, to murder me and Lynn. My lover. You drew a sword on her and threatened to kill her. I've never yet mistreated a prisoner, but at the moment, you're looking like a very good candidate to become the first one. You say you weren't in the Intelligence Corps for long. But did you ever get the chance to see the way interviews are conducted in the cells below the Corps headquarters?"

Natasha did not answer, but she felt her heart was pounding so hard that everyone in the room must be hearing it.

Kim went on. "The Intelligence Corps has some nasty interrogation techniques. Removing toenails with pliers; things like that. If you've ever witnessed one of these sessions, you'll know that sooner or later, you'll tell us what we want to know. It will be much nicer for everyone if you make it sooner."

Natasha turned her head and met Kim's stare. "Haven't I betrayed my comrades enough for you already?"

"No."

Kim's eyes seemed to be seeing straight through her. Natasha felt as if she were naked. At last, her head fell. "I don't want their deaths on my conscience."

"And you think you know something that might help us kill them?" Kim sighed and walked back to the table. "Okay. Let's talk it through. You're quite happy to admit you were transferred from the 3rd Company to the Intelligence Corps for this mission. It would be strange if the same hadn't happened to Rohanna and Cal. So your unwillingness to discuss their origins must be because of where they were before.

"With hindsight, Rohanna was obviously the team leader. I can't imagine the Intelligence Corps letting control of a mission like this out of their hands, so she must be one of their senior officers. Whereas Cal was from the Rangers. It was obvious to Sergeant O'Neil from the way she conducted herself on the journey here. You think if we don't know about Cal's background, we might underestimate her ability to elude us."

"If you already know, why bother asking me?"

Kim smiled without humor. "Because I want my guesses confirmed. Which you just did."

Natasha knew that her dismay showed on her face. Her eyes dropped to the floor as she stood, feeling stupid.

"Where were you going to meet up with the other two after murdering Lynn?" Kim's voice interrupted her self-reproach.

"I wasn't."

"You were going to try to get back to Landfall alone?" Kim asked sarcastically.

"No."

"So what were your plans?"

"I was going to kill myself."

"I think I prefer sullen silence to out-and-out lies."

Natasha's head shot up. "I don't..." *Lie.* The word died on her lips. She had lost the right to have her word believed.

"What were you planning to do after you murdered Lynn?"

"I was going to kill myself," Natasha repeated doggedly.

"Why?"

"So you couldn't capture me and force me to tell you anything."

Kim gave a bark of derisive laughter. "So you're telling me you've failed twice over?"

"Yes." Natasha hung her head, waiting for everyone else to laugh. It was a good enough joke.

"And you were quite happy when Rohanna ordered you to stay behind and kill yourself, while she and Cal escaped?"

"I've never been frightened to give my life for the Goddess."

"But Rohanna and Cal were?"

"No!" Natasha asserted angrily.

"That's a very touching faith you show in your comrades, given that they were planning on saving their own skins while abandoning you."

"They were as willing to die as me."

"You believed them when they said that?" Kim was scornful.

"We all volunteered for the mission."

"Volunteering for a dangerous mission is not quite the same as slitting your own throat."

"This mission was. When we volunteered, none of us expected to..." Natasha swallowed her words. She had said too much.

"None of you expected to go back?" Kim finished the sentence for her. "A suicide mission?"

Natasha swallowed but did not speak.

Kim smiled. "You know, it's really helpful the way you clam up when you think I'm about to find something out."

"You're wrong. It wasn't a sui..." Natasha's voice dried up.

Kim moved to stand directly in front of Natasha. "Okay. Look me in the eye and tell me that you all set out from Landfall with some hope of getting back to tell the tale."

Natasha tried to force the words out, but her throat and tongue would not obey her. The fact that Ash was standing there, witnessing the mess she was making of things, only made it worse. She could not help thinking of Ash as a friend, although the feeling was undoubtedly not reciprocated.

"So what made you change your plans?" Kim asked "And you must have changed your plans. Otherwise, you could have murdered us months ago. The only reason I can see for waiting until now was so those two could take our horses and head back to the Sisters."

Natasha bit her lip and hung her head.

"You're not going to say?" Kim said lightly. "Well, before we go and trouble the blacksmith for her pliers, perhaps I could try a bit more guessing. It must have been something you found out after leaving Landfall, and I can't see that you'd have discovered anything significant before you met with Sergeant O'Neil... possibly not until you got here. So what might it be? You would have learned that Gina died of natural causes, but I don't..." Kim paused, glancing over Natasha's shoulder. "Have you thought of something, Sergeant?"

Ash cleared her throat. "Ma'am, only that Rohanna has been asking an awful lot of questions about Ginasberg—where it was, and so on. And it's the only news I can think of that would be important enough for the Guards to delay killing you and Lynn."

"Oh, of course," Kim said. She reached out her hand and lifted Natasha's chin so that their eyes met again. "Much as the Chief Consultant would like to see Chip, Lynn, and me dead, Ginasberg is far more strategically important. Rohanna and Cal won't hang around for a second try at murdering us, but will go flat-out to get word back to Landfall. You want to give them the best head start you can. Even with Cal's experience, they've got an awfully long way to go through the wilderness on foot."

Natasha tried to keep her expression impassive, but she failed, and she knew it. Everyone in the room would be able to see the confirmation of Kim's words on her face. Natasha closed her eyes, but tears squeezed out under her lids. Kim had her completely outclassed in the game of question-and-answer and would keep on going until she had learned everything she wanted to know.

Natasha half wished Kim would get the blacksmith's pliers or a hot iron—something to leave a mark she could point to as proof that she had tried to keep faith with her comrades, proof that the information had been torn from her physically. But there was no need for Kim to resort to such measures. Natasha knew she was going to betray Rohanna and Cal again and again. And there was nothing she could do about it. The betrayal would be due to nothing more than her own incompetence.

❖

It was much later when Kim returned to her house. Midnight was not far off, but Lynn was waiting in the large central room of their home, dozing in a chair in front of the hearth. The fire had burned down low. One small candle was the only other light source in the room.

At the sound of the door closing, Lynn woke and looked up. "How did it go?"

Kim sighed and slumped down in a chair opposite. "Hard work, but don't worry; I didn't get rough with her."

"I never thought you would."

Kim pulled a wry pout. "I don't know. When Katryn brought us the news, I was ready to flay her alive. And if she'd laid a finger on you, right now they'd be scraping bits of her off the walls."

She looked at Lynn, slightly apologetically. "Sorry. I don't mean to sound..." Kim broke off, waving her hand vaguely.

Lynn got to her feet and went to sit on the arm of Kim's chair. She wrapped her arms around Kim's shoulders and hugged her tightly, burying her face in Kim's hair. After a few seconds, Lynn turned her head and stared into the fire. "If Katryn had been too late getting to you, I guess I wouldn't be feeling so charitable toward her myself."

"It was close. Chip and I had just dropped off to sleep, and they were only..." Kim groaned. "That's partly it. I'm fuming at myself. Rohanna and Cal were within spitting distance of us, and I let them escape. I was too confident that I could track down any Guard, but there had been enough clues that Cal was a Ranger. If I'd just ordered a quick search of the hollow, we'd have had them. In fact, we should have spotted them as the Chief Consultant's spies months ago. If only we hadn't been so focused on them as thieves. We were so busy wondering what they were going to steal that we never thought to look for any other explanation for all the discrepancies."

"So what do you do now?" Lynn asked.

"We try to stop them before they get back to Landfall with news about Ginasberg."

"Is that where they're heading?"

"So Je...Natasha says."

"Will we have to abandon Ginasberg if we don't catch them?"

Kim nodded "It couldn't withstand an attack, and it won't for another few years."

Lynn mulled over the implications for a while before asking, "What will you do with Natasha?"

"I can't let her go back with news about Ginasberg."

"You'll keep her prisoner here until Ginasberg is secure?"

Kim sighed. "We don't have the resources. Currently, she's in one of the storerooms under the Admin offices. It's not really secure. She could probably break out with a determined effort. We've got a jailer on duty outside, but it's only a short-term measure. Apart from anything else, Mirle wants the storeroom back to put things in."

"So what will you do?"

Rather than reply, Kim stared into the fire. Her stern expression spoke for her.

"You can't execute her," Lynn said quietly.

"I don't want to, but I don't see that I have a choice."

"She doesn't deserve it."

"Maybe not. But I won't risk the lives of everybody in Westernfort for the sake of one self-confessed assassin."

"The stakes aren't that high. I know we've put a lot of work into Ginasberg, but—"

"It's more a gamble with time, and we don't know how long we have. Strategically, we need a second settlement. The Chief Consultant isn't going to give up on us. Someday, she'll send a new, better-prepared force here. If we waste more years while we start from scratch at a new site, there's more chance that the attack will come before we're ready for it." Kim ran her hand through her hair. "Of course, if we don't catch the other two, they'll tell the Chief Consultant all about Ginasberg, so there'd be no harm in sending Natasha back as well. If we haven't found them in...say, three months, mid-June, we could let her go. We can probably keep her in the storeroom until then."

"I've got another idea."

"What?"

Lynn hesitated before going on. "Would you agree that Natasha is honorable? Trustworthy?"

"You mean for an attempted murderer?" Kim asked wryly.

"Kim." Lynn's tone was disapproving. She wanted a serious answer.

Kim took a deep breath and considered the question for a few seconds. "Yes. I'd probably throw in a few words like *naïve* and *idealistic* as well. And if you're trying to make me feel guilty at the thought of hanging her, you needn't bother. I already do."

"It's not that. I just want to know if you'd trust her word."

"Yes. She's no good at lying." Kim's expression became rueful. "When I think of the time we spent wondering what they were up to! In hindsight, I can see we let Rohanna do too much of the talking. I should simply have sat down with Natasha and asked a few direct questions. The Chief Consultant didn't pick the right woman for the job. Not that I'm complaining. Interrogating Natasha just now, there was no need to beat the information out of her. Her face gave everything away."

"You wouldn't have done it anyway," Lynn said confidently.

"I would if it were necessary to protect Westernfort, but I'm pleased I didn't need to. Natasha wanted to be loyal to her comrades, and I'd hate to be hard on any woman because of that." Kim paused and glanced at Lynn. "And if you're thinking that she could promise not to tell the Sisters about Ginasberg, it won't work. She still wants to be loyal to them."

"No. That wasn't my idea."

"Then where's all this going?"

"If she gave her word not to escape, would you release her on parole?"

"You're suggesting that I set a Guard free to wander around town? She came here to kill us, remember?"

"But she didn't. In fact, she saved your life by giving the warning. I'm sure you could trust her if she gave her word. You could always ask Ash's advice, if you want another opinion."

"And I'm sure I know what Ash would say. She's developed a bit of a maternal soft spot for Natasha." Kim sat back in the chair, frowning at the fire. But to Lynn's relief, she was giving the suggestion serious consideration. "I suppose we haven't got much to lose by trying. Without Cal, we'll have no trouble tracking her down if she breaks parole. And it would save the need to have someone permanently on jailer duty."

"Plus Mirle can have her storeroom back," Lynn added.

Kim's gaze shifted to Lynn. "So you're hoping that if the first three months go okay, we can extend Natasha's parole until Ginasberg is finished?" Kim shook her head. "I know one person who certainly won't agree to that: Natasha herself. She's so certain she's damned her soul, I feel sorry for her. If I explain it all to her, she'd feel I was offering her the chance to save her neck by yet another betrayal. At the moment, she's hooked on the idea of giving her life for the Goddess."

"But I doubt she's hooked on the idea of spending three months in an underground cell for the Goddess," Lynn pointed out. "Don't mention the possibility of long-term parole when you get her to agree to three months. You can even stress that when Rohanna and Cal are caught, she'll be executed along with them."

"It might still come to that," Kim interjected grimly.

"No, it won't. Because now that everyone knows who and what she is, we can all work on talking her into joining us here permanently."

"I don't think it's likely she'd do that."

"Oh, I'd say there's a very good chance. I'd even go as far as saying she's halfway there already. She's begun to think for herself, which is always a good start."

"You know her better than me," Kim conceded, although her expression was still skeptical. "Okay. I'm not saying yes right now to offering her parole, but I promise I'll think about it and talk it through with Chip and the others tomorrow." She sighed and ran a hand through her hair. "And it will take a bit of work to sell the idea to the rest of the town. I'd have to call a meeting to explain it to everyone."

"You're going to have to do that anyway, to stop the lurid rumors. From some of the stories going around, I'm surprised there isn't a lynch mob waiting outside the offices."

"I can guess. The first account I got from Katryn wasn't totally accurate."

"I don't think I was particularly coherent when I spoke to her. And I didn't want her to hang around until I'd gotten my head together."

Kim looked thoughtful. "Actually, the overblown rumors would help. By tomorrow morning, everyone will have had their fun with the gossip but won't want to appear gullible by acting as though they believed any of it. Some people will still object rather strongly."

"Dani, for one."

"Yes. I can see she might feel unhappy." Kim's tone was lightly ironic.

"You don't know all of it. They slept together the night before you left."

Kim's lips formed in a silent whistle. "In that case, I'm surprised Dani isn't outside the cell as a lynch mob of one."

"Hopefully, she won't cause too much trouble, though, and you shouldn't have many problems with everyone else. Natasha is actually very likeable."

"She's certainly won you and Ash over. I wanted Ash in on the interrogation, in case we had to play the 'nice and nasty' game. Ash wouldn't have needed to pretend for the nice part, and you could see she was tying herself in knots that I was going to start playing it nasty."

Lynn's head tilted back as her thoughts moved on. "Now that Ash doesn't have to watch the family, perhaps you can give her the job of talking Natasha into joining us. I think it's a challenge she'll enjoy."

Kim gave her partner a sideways look. "You're talking as if it's a foregone conclusion we'll offer Natasha parole."

Lynn dropped a kiss on Kim's forehead. "Of course it is. I know just how much you'll hate yourself for executing Natasha when she hasn't done anything to really deserve it. This is your best chance to avoid having to do it."

Kim laughed softly. "So we're counting on Ash's ability at religious conversions?"

"I'll be doing my bit as well with Natasha, when we're working together in the barn."

"No," Kim said sharply, jerking upright. "She's not going back to working with you."

"Why not?"

Kim shook her head. "I'll agree that she is generally safe to release on parole. But she came here to kill you, and she's still devoted to Celaeno. If the two of you are alone together, it will only take a split-second impulse to redeem herself with the Goddess, and you'll have a cracked skull. I don't want to give her a second chance to kill you."

"She won't. If she didn't stab me when I put a sword in her hands, she never will. And she may be pious, but she hasn't given away her conscience. If you could have been there and seen her face..." Lynn smiled and took Kim's hand. "Believe me, I was in no danger whatsoever."

CHAPTER EIGHTEEN—A BROKEN HEART

The crowd in the main square listened to Kim in something approaching silence, with no more than a scattering of muttered comments around the edge. Natasha also stood at the top of the broad steps to the council offices, a little way back and to one side. Her hands were still bound, and a Ranger stood at either shoulder, grasping her arms above the elbow. *Just in case anyone is unsure which one of us is the prisoner,* Natasha thought ironically. Even without the two minders, she had not the slightest chance of escaping.

Natasha did not look at the montage of faces staring up at her. Instead, she fixed her eyes on the roofs of the houses opposite. She was used to being stared at. She tried to recapture the vacant disdain of sentry duty at the temple gates, but she had never felt so exposed. She half wished that the vote would be to refuse her parole, so she could go back and hide in the cell.

She lifted her gaze still higher. A light wind was racing small clouds across the spring sky. The noon sun was bright without being hot. It sparkled on the snow-covered peaks. The air was moist and clean from the previous night's rain.

Natasha took a deep breath. She should make the most of it. The odds were that she would not have much longer to enjoy such things. The likelihood was not good that Rohanna and Cal, on foot, would evade all the mounted Westernfort Rangers. And Kim had been quite frank about what her comrades' failure would mean for her fate. Natasha had agreed to the offer of parole so she would not spend the final few days of her life in the tiny underground room.

Kim's speech was coming to an end. "I've discussed this with Captain Coppelli and the rest of the council. We're all willing to release Guard Corporal Ionadis on parole. The terms will run for three months from today. She'll swear not to leave Westernfort during this time or harm anyone here. If anyone finds her carrying a weapon, or if she's seen outside the town by night or beyond the farmlands by day, she may be killed on sight. Are there any questions?"

A voice on the left called out, "Do you think you can trust her?"

"No. I think she'll murder me in my bed. That's why I'm proposing to free her." Kim was at her most sarcastic. "Does anyone else have a question?"

Someone closer at hand asked, "So your name isn't Jess?"

The question was aimed at Natasha. She looked down and recognized the speaker as a woman from her lodgings. Natasha cleared her throat. "No."

"What do we call you, then?"

Before Natasha could reply, a suggested answer was shouted at the back of the crowd. "How about *that fucking bitch?*"

Natasha again fixed her eyes on the rooftops, struggling with the lump in her throat while she waited for the scattered laughter to fade. The voice had sounded like Dani's. When there was silence, she said, "My name is Natasha Ionadis. My friends call me Tash."

"I can't see anyone here needing to know that." It was the same voice, and it was definitely Dani.

Kim stepped forward. "Are there any more questions?"

A few were shouted out and quickly answered. Kim took the vote. Natasha chose not to watch and averted her gaze, but from the relative volume of rustling as arms raised, it was obvious that a large majority was in favor of releasing her on parole. Feeling a little numb, Natasha repeated the words of her oath loudly so that everyone in the square could hear, and Kim cut the rope around her wrists.

Natasha waited at the top of the steps for the assembly to disperse. She did not want to remain on show, but neither did she feel inclined to barge her way through the crowd in the square. Fortunately, most women were eager to return to their work or find somewhere more private to gossip. Within a few minutes, patches of ground had appeared between the groups, and she could make out individuals on the far side of the square.

Kim also stayed where she was. Her eyes were scanning the faces of the departing women, probably judging the mood of likely troublemakers, and she did not speak. Natasha tried to concentrate on massaging her wrists, though it was not really necessary. The bonds had not been tight. In the end, she could not stop herself from looking across the square to where the heckling shouts had come from. In the middle of an open space, as if wanting to be seen, was Dani, standing with Shelly. They were chatting happily, their arms wrapped around each other's waists, faces so close that their noses were almost touching. Natasha looked away just a little too late to avoid seeing them kiss.

❖

The barn was exactly the same as the last time Natasha had been there, except that someone had removed the pile of sweepings and a new litter of pigs was burrowing against their dam. Tipsy bounded over to greet her. Natasha knelt to rub between the dog's ears and looked around, confused. Somehow, she had been sure that the barn would look totally different, but it had been only two days. The changes were entirely within herself.

Natasha stood and wandered along to the low fence around the pigpen. The eight tiny piglets seemed even smaller by comparison with the bulk of their mother. The sight brought a grin to Natasha's face, although her mind was in a state of chaotic upheaval. The last time she had entered the barn, she had still been a loyal servant of Celaeno, a Guard on a mission, hand-picked by the Chief Consultant. Now she was a prisoner who had informed on her comrades and broken faith with Celaeno. She was an eternally damned traitor. It made no sense that she should be feeling more at peace with herself.

Natasha was so lost in thought that she was unaware of Lynn's arrival until the Imprinter joined her, leaning on the wall of the enclosure. Natasha leapt up, startled.

Lynn was completely unperturbed and continued watching the animals. "You know, I always find something reassuring about pigs. It's probably because my parents were pig farmers. Memories of my childhood and all that." Lynn leaned over the barrier and patted the flank of the sow.

It was the first time that they had met since the aborted assassination attempt. Natasha took a stumbling half step back and then stopped, feeling like a fool. She was not the one with the right to be nervous. Lynn stopped fussing over the pig and stood to face her. Neither spoke. Lynn's expression showed no hostility, but Natasha felt her own face flush crimson.

Lynn raised an eyebrow and asked, "Before we start work, is there anything you want to say?"

Natasha's eyes dropped to the ground; her cheeks were burning. Both "Sorry" and "I didn't really want to kill you" would sound pathetically banal. At last, she swallowed and burst out, "How can you still trust me?"

"What makes you think that I do?" Lynn laughed.

"Because you..." Natasha stopped and looked over her shoulder, suddenly wondering whether Lynn had brought an armed bodyguard with her, but they were alone in the barn.

Lynn tapped Natasha's arm, regaining her attention. "I was joking. I do trust you."

"Why?"

"Because after three months working together, I know the sort of person you are."

"But I lied to you. You don't know me at all. You didn't know I was a Guard," Natasha said, shaking her head.

"I said the *sort* of person, not the details of your life story."

"I tried to kill—"

Lynn interrupted quickly, "No, you didn't."

"I—" Natasha broke off in confusion.

"You made no attempt to use the sword. And you may have been playing a part, but you couldn't hide the fact that you're a decent young woman who would never do anything you knew to be wrong." Lynn smiled easily. "That's why you didn't try to kill me. You knew it would be wrong. And that's why I trust you."

"The Chief Consultant said..." Natasha's voice failed.

"That I was evil and deserved to die?"

"Yes. But you aren't."

"And neither are you. Which is an important lesson for you. The Chief Consultant can get things wrong."

Natasha slumped down, sitting on her heels with her back pressed against the wall of the pigpen. She bit her knuckles.

"Now you look as if you're in pain," Lynn said quietly.

"I am."

"Why?"

"Because I'm damned forever."

"So am I, if you listen to the Chief Consultant." Lynn shrugged. "It doesn't hurt that much."

"It's easy for you. You don't believe in the Goddess."

Lynn pursed her lips. "I don't believe in the Chief Consultant. The Goddess, I'm a bit more open-minded about."

"You think Celaeno was a ship built to fly between the stars," Natasha said defiantly.

"True," Lynn conceded. "Gina did get me to agree with her about that. But she couldn't prove that there isn't a real Goddess, and sometimes..." She paused and sighed. "I'd like to think there is one."

"Do you think your version of the Goddess would forgive me?"

"I doubt she'd find anything to forgive."

"It would be nice to think that." Natasha's voice held little hope.

"Well, I'm going to be doing my best to convince you. That's why I talked Kim into granting you parole."

Natasha stared up in surprise. "You? Why?"

At first, Lynn did not answer. Her eyes fixed on the far wall of the barn. Then she looked back. "Did Kim tell you what would happen if we catch Rohanna and Cal?"

"Yes. She made it clear."

"We're not against you personally, but we can't let news about Ginasberg get out."

Natasha gave a one-shouldered shrug. "That's all right. I understand. And I'm not afraid to die for—"

Lynn cut her off. "So I've heard. But fear doesn't come into it. You rescued Becky from the mountain cat, you gave the warning that saved Kim's life, and you didn't murder me. Though on the minus side, the smith was very late getting the sword for repair, even after I'd asked you to run it over to her." Despite her light tone, Lynn's expression was very serious. "Weighing it all up, I'm still on your side, and I couldn't bear to watch you dangling by your neck."

Natasha's gaze dropped to the straw in front of her knees. She could feel her eyes filling with tears, prompted by the unmistakable tenderness in Lynn's voice. Her mouth opened to speak a couple of times before she finally said, "Perhaps Rohanna and Cal won't get caught."

"I wouldn't count on it. Which is why I wanted the chance to talk you into agreeing to join us here in Westernfort."

"Become a heretic?" Natasha said incredulously.

"If you want to put it like that."

Natasha shook her head. "You won't talk me into renouncing the Goddess."

"My aim wasn't that ambitious. It'll be enough if I get you to agree that the Chief Consultant was wrong to tell you to murder people, and she has about as much understanding of the Goddess as Tipsy has of lace making."

Natasha wet her lips. "It's not that simple."

Lynn studied her face. "You've got close family back in Landfall? Some other reason why you can't stay here?"

"Oh, no. When I volunteered for the mission, I was told there was no hope of returning, and I'm not sure I want to go back anyway. But it doesn't mean I..." Natasha's words dwindled away.

"It sounds like I'm halfway home already. And I've got a full three months to convince you."

"Rohanna and Cal might be caught tomorrow."

"Makes no difference. You gave your word to keep the terms of your parole until the ninth of June. I'm going to insist that you're held until the very last day. Plus I'm going to have a lot of help in bringing you around. Do you know you're going to be very popular in Westernfort?"

"I'm...you're joking."

"No. At least you won't lack people to talk to." As Natasha continued to look skeptical, Lynn went on, "There are a lot of elderly heretics in Westernfort. Some of Gina's first recruits. They're passionately devoted to her teachings. You're the first potential convert they've been able to get their hands on for decades. I warn you, you're in for hours of theological discourse. They're probably brushing up their arguments even as we speak, and sorting out a suitable little award ceremony for the woman who succeeds in converting you."

"Oh." Natasha bit her lip, but a half smile formed at the corners. "I must admit, I was a bit worried about tonight. I've been told I can keep the room I shared with Rohanna and Cal. I was looking forward to getting the proper bed, but I was worried I'd be ostracized in the common room."

"You might end up wishing you were."

Natasha's face shifted through a succession of emotions and ended up as a grimace of pain. "Some people still won't want to have anything to do with me."

"Dani," Lynn suggested quietly.

Natasha nodded. "It's all I deserve. And I guess it looks like I've done Shelly a favor." She tried to smile bravely, but it did nothing to hide her grief.

Lynn looked at Natasha in sympathy before offering a hand to pull her up. "Come on; we've got work to do, and there's nothing like mucking out pigs to help heal a broken heart."

❖

Natasha was a little surprised to find that the heretics celebrated the festival of Landfall on March 23 as conventionally as anywhere in the Homelands. In fact, in this rural community, the traditional rites of spring made more sense than in the paved streets of Landfall. The plow carried through Westernfort was the genuine article, not a gilded imitation, decorated with spring flowers. As stockman for Lynn's experimental animals, Natasha played her part in the tallying of livestock, and she joined the procession to hear the calling out of the fields—a ritual designed to ensure that no herder could claim ignorance of which fields had been put aside to graze animals and which would be growing crops. The only thing Natasha missed was the Chief Consultant standing on the balcony over the Guards' parade ground and reading from *The Book of the Elder-Ones*. The traditional text for the day was the account of Himoti's first footfall on the world Celaeno had chosen for her daughters.

As evening fell, a bonfire was lit in the main square. A band began to play, and couples danced around the flames. Natasha watched them enviously. Guards were not supposed to indulge in such impious pastimes on a holy day. Or at any other time. Natasha could no longer use the need to maintain her disguise as an excuse to join in, but it was not only religious principles that kept her away from the revelry.

Natasha had discovered that Lynn was absolutely correct about the missionary zeal of the elderly heretics. Over the days, she had come to recognize the eager glint in their eyes as they homed in on her. Sometimes, she was able to elude them; sometimes not. Her current situation was a good example. Three old women had quite literally blockaded her into a doorway. The ambush had been a well-executed maneuver. One second, Natasha had been leaning against a wall; the next, she was hemmed in and being bombarded with explanations of the origin of the festival.

In what was probably an unintentional parody of the Chief Consultant, one of them was quoting the account of the first landfall from Peter McKay's diary—the book Gina claimed to have found hidden in the temple library; the source of her heretical doctrine. It made no sense to Natasha. She had no idea what an SA chamber was, or a retrojet, and she could not stop herself from flinching at the phrase *Celaeno's rear loading bay*.

Natasha did not want to elbow her way out. The three ancient women were too frail to risk knocking over, but they were taking no notice of her hints that she wished to leave. She looked past them to the boisterous group around the bonfire. The music and dancing were getting more lively. Natasha decided that as soon as she could escape, she would join in. After all, no one was going to report her to an officer. Then she saw Shelly and Dani dancing together in the center of the gathering and changed her mind.

"Excuse me for disturbing you." A fresh voice broke in. Tanya Coppelli had appeared behind the siege wall of old women. She met Natasha's eye. "Lynn wants a quick word with you. Are you free at the moment?"

"Yes. If...um..." Natasha looked expectantly at the heretic who had been talking. The crone broke off in midflow. She glared at Tanya in vexation but then tutted and shuffled aside.

As soon as she was out of the doorway and walking around the edge of the square, Natasha's face and shoulders sagged in an expression of relief.

Tanya laughed. "They were giving you an ear bashing?"

"And some more. I was tempted to agree with them just so they'd let me go." Natasha sighed and raked her fingers through her hair. "Where is Lynn?"

"I'll show you."

"Did she say what it was about?"

"No."

They walked a short way in silence. Then Tanya said, "I understand we're related."

"So Lynn tells me." Natasha turned her head to study her companion. Tanya's sixteenth birthday had been two days before, and now she wore the uniform of the Westernfort Rangers. Tanya combined Katryn's cool good looks with Chip's easy smile. In the contact they'd had, Natasha had found her outgoing and cheerful. She had a mischievous sense of humor, which Lynn claimed she had inherited from Chip. Apparently, in her youth, the firm Ranger captain had not been quite so mindful of the rules. As blood relatives, Natasha could not help thinking that both Tanya and Chip were vast improvements on her mother.

"Are the Tangs as rich and nasty as Mom says?" Tanya asked.

"They're rich, but I can't comment on them as people." At Tanya's confused expression, Natasha went on to explain the circumstances of her birth and childhood.

"So why did you join the Guards?" Tanya clearly thought it had been a big mistake on Natasha's part, but her tone was one of sympathy rather than criticism.

To prove I was better than my mother. Natasha bit back the words. "Um...it's hard to say."

Fortunately, Tanya changed the subject. "What's Landfall like?"

"Big and noisy."

They chatted easily. Tanya was curious about the city she had never seen. Natasha was halfway through a description of the marketplace when they reached the spot where Lynn was standing with Kim. Tanya left and trotted back to the bonfire.

"You wanted to see me?" Natasha asked

Lynn grinned. "I thought you needed rescuing. I could see you weren't going to get out alive, so I sent Tanya to liberate you."

"I...oh...thanks," Natasha mumbled. Over Lynn's head, she could see Kim's shoulders shaking with laughter.

"Now go off and enjoy yourself. And don't get caught again."

"I'll try my best."

Natasha smiled and looked around. Tanya had not gone far and was talking to a group of other young Rangers. Natasha considered going over to finish the conversation; Tanya had seemed genuinely interested in the stories of city life. But then Natasha saw that Shelly was also a member of the group, with Dani hanging on her arm. Natasha turned around sharply and headed off in the opposite direction.

The tavern seemed a safe destination. Anyone robust enough to brave the buffeting around the bar was fair game to be elbowed aside. Natasha bought herself a drink and joined a group of shepherds in a quiet corner. She could not quite match their enthusiasm for wool yields and pasture capacities, but at least they were not discussing rear loading bays.

The conversation had moved on to the more interesting topic of sheepdog training when the door opened and Shelly and Dani came in with a couple of others. Their eyes seemed to pass straight through the spot where Natasha was standing without seeing her. Was it coincidence that after getting their drinks, they ended up standing less than two meters away?

Natasha told herself that she was being overly sensitive. It was merely the largest free area of floor space. But whatever the reason, the strain was more than she could bear. She drained her drink quickly and left.

By now, true night had fallen, and the bonfire was burning higher than ever. Natasha strolled around the edge of the square, watching the dancing. At the corner of a street leading away, she came across Ash, sitting alone on a low wall in a patch of deep shadow.

"Do you mind if I join you?" Natasha asked.

"Of course not."

Natasha hesitated. Even if Ash had wanted solitude, she would not be so blunt as to answer yes, but her smile of welcome was genuine. Ash patted the wall. Natasha hopped up and accepted a swig from the flagon pressed into her hands.

"Are you enjoying yourself?" Ash asked.

"In parts."

Ash did not ask her to specify which parts, and they sat quietly, grinning at the antics of a group of less-sober revelers.

"I hear Lynn thinks you can be talked into joining us here," Ash said after a while.

"Yes."

"Do you think you could be talked into it?"

"I doubt it," Natasha said slowly. "And to tell the truth, I'm surprised people would be prepared to let me stay."

"Most folks see you as an innocent young thing who's been led astray by the wicked Chief Consultant."

"Do you see me like that?"

"Not entirely."

"Would you be pleased if I agreed to stay?"

"Of course I would." Ash spoke with unexpected passion. "But I'm terrified that you're going to be stupid and insist on Kim stretching your neck."

"But that's..." Natasha was taken aback by the vehemence.

"You've been betrayed, but you don't know it," Ash said forcefully. "You joined the Guards looking for honor and glory. It's what they promised you. Then they tried to turn you into a liar and a murderer, and they've made you think you're a failure for following your conscience. You're feeling cheated out of your self-respect, and you want it back. I can see you refusing to join us just so people can't say you abandoned your faith or you were frightened of dying."

"I..." To Natasha's surprise, tears blurred her vision. She could not think of a single thing about herself she felt proud of, and she had not realized that it hurt so much until Ash had spoken.

Ash patted her shoulder. "Take my advice. You're on parole until mid-June. Take every day to think it over. Work out for yourself what you ought to be doing with your life."

"I don't think two and a half months will be long enough. I'm doubting everything I was ever certain about. I don't know where to start." Natasha hung her head.

"Start with the uncertainties that hurt the most. What are the doubts you can't bear?"

Natasha thumped her chest. "I can feel the Goddess in my heart. I know she's there, and I can't bear to lose her."

"That's handy. If she's in your heart, you don't have to go back to Landfall to talk to her." Natasha glanced over sharply, thinking that Ash was joking, but the elderly Ranger's expression was sincere. "This Goddess in your heart. Did she want you to kill Lynn?"

Natasha frowned as she thought about the question. "No, but—"

"So why don't you listen to her?"

"Because she's only—"

"She's only the Goddess you can't bear to lose?" Ash suggested. "Your mistake is to think she's the same Goddess as the Chief Consultant's, but obviously, she isn't. You can drop one without dropping the other. Make sure you do it the right way around. Don't abandon the Goddess in your heart and die for the one in the Chief Consultant's books."

Natasha's frown turned slowly into an amused smile. "I know three little old ladies you could give lessons to on how to persuade Guards to reconsider their beliefs."

"I've talked you into staying?"

"You're getting there."

Natasha lifted her gaze to the sky. Neither moon had risen, and the stars were brilliant points of light. For the first time, she considered the idea that she might stay—not because she had no other options or because her life was worth so little that it did not matter what she did, but as a positive choice.

Her eyes dropped to the buildings on the other side of the road. Diagonally opposite was the entrance to a narrow alleyway. Two figures stood there, kissing passionately. Despite the darkness, Natasha had no trouble recognizing them. It was getting beyond a joke. Anyone would think that Shelly and Dani were deliberately following her around.

Natasha buried her head in hands. "I can't stay here."

Ash glanced to the other side of the road and then back to Natasha. "You could always think about going to Ginasberg." She pulled Natasha down from the wall and began walking with her.

"I don't know anyone there," Natasha said. Although, on second thought, she wondered whether a fresh start might be a good thing.

"You'd know me."

"You're going to Ginasberg?"

"Yes. That's what I was thinking about when you joined me." Ash looked rueful. "They want me to take charge of the Rangers there."

"I'd say it was about time you were promoted." Natasha had often thought it strange that someone of Ash's experience should still be a mere sergeant.

"So they tell me, but I've been turning it down for the last twenty-five years."

"You've turned down promotion?"

Ash did not reply immediately. "Over the years, I've led some women to their deaths—not many, but a few. What I've never been able to face is the idea of sitting safe behind a desk and sending women out to die. The journey here made me realize I'm getting old. The worst thing of all would be for women to die because I'm too stubborn to know when to quit. I've got the choice of taking promotion or leaving the Rangers altogether. So I guess the desk has finally caught up with me."

"I shouldn't think you'll be physically tied to it," Natasha teased.

Ash managed a grin. "At the time the 23rd deserted, I was coming toward the end of my regulation service time. Even if I'd re-enlisted, all I'd have gotten was an indoor job at Fort Krowe. I wasn't too happy at first about joining the heretics, but it's worked out well. I've always worshipped the Goddess in my way. But my way is out in the wide open world she's chosen for us, with her trees, mountains, and animals. At Westernfort, nobody was going to take me away from the wildlands until I was ready."

"Do you still believe in the Goddess?" Natasha could not help asking.

"Yes...in my heart." Ash smiled. "I'd have willingly followed Kim to far worse places than here, but as I said, I wasn't happy about it. It took me a couple of years to realize what I just told you. The Goddess in my heart wasn't the same as the one the Sisters talk about. Maybe when I die, I'll be up before Celaeno and she won't be pleased with everything I've done. I won't know until then. But I'm absolutely certain that the Sisters won't get her approval, either. Their books and temples are monuments to themselves, not the Goddess." She met Natasha's eyes. "Don't let them fool you."

Chapter Nineteen—A Broken Pot

The rain fell in sheets, as it had all day; an April downpour. Natasha stood at the door of the barn and considered the road leading into town. Puddles of water filled the ruts left by carts. The rest of the surface was mud. With a pained grimace, she raised her eyes to the dark clouds and took a deep breath. All her tasks with the animals were complete for the moment. Now would be a good time to do what she had to in Westernfort, but it was not merely the thought of getting wet that made her unwilling to leave the shelter of the barn.

Impatient with herself, Natasha snatched an oiled cape from a hook by the door, pulled it around her shoulders, and stepped out into the open. Her feet squelched and skidded in the mud. Walking quickly was impossible. By the time she reached the first of the houses, the rain had soaked through the cape, her shoulders were damp, and drips were running down her neck. Natasha cursed her own cowardice for not getting the ordeal over and done with immediately after breakfast. She could have saved herself the walk into town and back. Delaying had gained her nothing.

One of the common-room rules was that anyone who broke an item of collective property had to replace it. The rule was fair enough, and Natasha could not deny that the smashed pot was her fault, the result of not paying enough attention to what she was doing. She had to obtain a new pot before people began cooking the evening meal, and there was only one place in Westernfort where she could buy one.

As she crossed the square, two young girls ran toward her, squealing when a harder belt of rain pelted them. Natasha was tempted to offer the children a few extra coins if they would go into the shop and buy the pot for her, yet she let them race by. She could not describe her requirements accurately enough to be sure that they would get what she wanted. *And I couldn't let the story get out that I was frightened*, Natasha thought bitterly. A sound halfway between a groan and a sigh escaped her lips. *Even though it would be true.*

Natasha stopped in the shelter of an overhanging roof and looked down the street to the door of Dani's shop, rattling the coins in her purse. It was ridiculous. She would rather have walked into a snow lions' lair with a sign around her neck saying *Please eat me* and volunteered to give the lions a reading lesson. Natasha clenched her teeth and walked the last few meters.

"I'll be there in a minute," Dani called from the back room at the sound of the street door closing.

Natasha felt her stomach tighten into a sick knot. She looked around desperately, trying to examine the terra-cotta shapes filling the shelves. If she could find a suitable pot quickly, she could speed her departure, but she was unable to concentrate enough to make sense of what was before her eyes.

"Okay. What can I..." The voice died. Natasha turned around and saw Dani standing frozen in the rear doorway.

Dani's expressions shifted through a range of emotions, none of them welcoming. Natasha was the first to find her voice. "I need to buy a replacement for a broken pot."

"What makes you think I'd sell anything to you?" Dani said with contempt.

"It's your trade."

"I can choose my customers."

"But I can't choose my potter. You're the only one in town, though you..." Natasha bit back the rest. She did not want to sound surly. "If you insist, I can go back to the common room and explain that I tried to buy one, but you refused to sell it to me. I'm sure everyone will sympathize with your motives."

Dani turned her head and glared at the shelf beside her. She took several deep breaths; then she swallowed and took a step forward, turning so that her back was to Natasha. She pointed to her wares, a hand movement more reminiscent of swatting flies. "What sort of pot do you want?" Her tone could have cut through glass.

"It was a large roasting dish...with a lid."

"*All* roasting dishes have lids." Dani spoke as though she were reprimanding an idiot. She stamped across to a corner of the shop, reached under a low shelf, and pulled out four examples of varying dimensions. She arranged them in a line on the floor and then stepped back.

Natasha moved into the space Dani had vacated and knelt to examine the pots. None was exactly the right size. She was trying to build up the courage to ask whether anything else was available when Dani spoke again. "Are you enjoying this?"

Natasha glanced up. Dani was standing with her back against a wall and her arms crossed defensively in front of her.

"No," Natasha replied, truthfully.

"I thought it might be the sort of thing you found funny... like fucking someone who wouldn't have gotten within spitting distance of you if she'd known what you really were."

Natasha turned back to the pots, but her eyes refused to focus. "I'm sorry." She could not force her voice above a whisper.

"For what?" Dani challenged.

"I'm sorry I lied to you. I'm sorry I abused your trust. I'm sorry I slept with you. I'm sorry I hurt you."

"You think you hurt me?"

"If you can tell me I didn't, it would be a load off my conscience."

"You've got a conscience?" Dani mimicked astonishment.

"I didn't intend to..." Natasha's voice failed her.

"It all happened by accident?"

Natasha could not answer. She picked up something and pretended to inspect it, turning it over in her hands, but she was too upset even to work out whether it was a base or a lid.

Dani watched her in silence for a while. "Why did you wait until the last night?"

"Please. There's no point in—"

Dani cut her off, speaking with a forced, conversational tone. "Because I've come up with two theories, and I wondered if you could tell me which is right. One is that Rohanna and Cal were your superior officers, and you had to wait until they were out of the way before breaking your Guards' vow of celibacy. The other option is that the thought of killing Lynn the next day made you feel turned on. Apparently, some murderers get off on that kind of thing."

Something inside Natasha cracked open. Her chin shot up. "I did it because I was in love with you, and had been for months." *And still am*, she added silently. "*You* were chasing after *me*, but I knew you wouldn't have had anything to do with me if you'd known the truth, and I tried to respect that. It wasn't easy. In the end, I'm afraid, I wasn't strong enough. It wasn't the thought of killing Lynn that got to me. It was the fact that I was planning on killing myself the next day. I'm sorry. It was selfish of me, but I wanted to take the memory of you with me."

The flow of words dried up, and they stared at each other.

Natasha was the one to break eye contact. She grabbed the nearest pot and stood up. It was a little bigger than the one she had broken, but surely no one in the common room would mind.

Dani was still glaring at Natasha. Her expression was as venomous as her tone. "Kim shouldn't have wasted time with parole for you. She ought to have hanged you straight off. It would have been fun to watch."

"You've still got it to look forward to when they catch Rohanna and Cal. The weather is getting better. If it's a nice day when they hang me, perhaps you could take a picnic along and make a party of it," Natasha retorted. Then she held out the pot. "How much do I owe you for this?"

"I wouldn't dirty my hands by touching your money."

"But I—"

"You can have the pot."

"I don't want to take anything from you."

"More than you already have?" Dani's voice cracked. She averted her face. "Call it payment for the night's work you put in at the kiln. Just get out of my house."

Natasha drew a breath as though she were about to argue the point further, but then she turned and strode out of the shop.

The door swung closed behind her. Dani remained motionless, staring at the wooden slats. As her lower lip began to tremble, she caught it between her teeth and wrapped her arms tighter around herself. But she could do nothing to stop the tears that began to flow silently down her face. The first sob shook her body.

❖

Chip Coppelli groaned and sank down in her chair. "Do you remember me saying once that if Natasha turned out to be on the level, I wanted her for the Rangers?" Her tone was rhetorical. "Well, I definitely want Cal Rowse. We can keep her tied up. I just want her to give lessons to the squadrons."

"The patrol that came in today found no sign of them?" Mirle asked from the other side of the table. The other council members looked anxiously back to the Ranger captain, awaiting her answer.

"I'd have come running to tell you if they had." Chip scowled in frustration. "There were the footprints leading away from the outpost. We tracked them as far as the river, and then they might have taken wings and flown, for all the trail they've left."

"All things are possible with the grace of the Goddess," Lynn joined in with heavy irony. She tilted her head to one side. "Have you considered that they might have fallen in the river and been drowned and swept away?"

"It would be lovely if they had," Chip said in heartfelt tones. "And there's also the possibility that they were caught by snow lions. The map they took went as far north as the pass over the Blackstone range. Renie's patrol reported signs of a large pride around there. Late March would have been the dangerous time. If Rohanna and Cal went that way."

"It's the *if* part that's the problem." Kim spoke for the first time. "We're going to have to make some hard decisions soon. We need to know for certain whether news of Ginasberg has gotten back to the Chief Consultant."

"You're thinking about Natasha?" Mirle asked.

Kim shook her head. "Not yet. There's over a month left to go of her parole—"

"And she's going to want to stay here anyway," Lynn interrupted confidently. "Even if we told her she could go back to Landfall, I doubt she'd take us up on the offer."

"It's actually Ginasberg I'm concerned about," Kim said, frowning. "I don't want to commit a lot of effort to the defenses if we're going to have to abandon it, and I don't want to waste the summer if Rohanna and Cal's bones are already littering the wilderness." She turned to Chip. "I think it's time to stop trying to catch them. If they've been traveling east for these last two months, they'll be nearly back in the Homelands by now.

"Send a couple of women up to the Blackstones to see what they can find. The lions shouldn't have chewed much off them and probably spat out most of it. And if the lions did eat them up completely, they'd have died of iron poisoning. So a heap of lion carcasses would be another pointer. Also check out Lynn's suggestion about the river. I know she wasn't being totally serious, but it was a very dark night. The river isn't deep there, but with the melting snow, it would have been cold enough to give nasty cramps to anyone trying to cross. We're going to have to make a decision about Ginasberg before the end of May."

"Yes, ma'am," Chip said crisply.

Kim smiled at her friend and then looked down at the paper in front of her. "Okay. The next thing on the agenda."

Mirle picked a sheet of paper. "I've just received a new report from Jules. Things got a bit hot in her area, and she had to make a run for it. But she got to a safe house near Watersmeet. She wants to know what plans we have for her."

The meeting moved to a review of the Homelands agents.

❖

From the hills above Westernfort, the town looked peaceful in the soft light of early evening. Natasha strolled down the pathway with two older shepherds, the dogs scampering back and forth before them. She had been uncertain whether the high pastures counted as farmlands. However, Kim had clearly been amused when she went to ask whether working up there would break the terms of her parole. There were still twenty days of the period left to go. Everyone seemed to take it for granted that when the time was up, she would ask to remain in Westernfort. Natasha suspected that they were right, but she was still not completely happy with the thought.

The path swung around a last belt of woodland and joined a larger road. Tipsy and another dog went bounding into the undergrowth and had to be called back. They came a little unwillingly at first—Tipsy clearly thought there was something worth investigating—but then they raced on ahead. The edge of the town was less than a kilometer away. Downhill from the road was a level riverside meadow where a group of young women played football, making the most of the warm May evening.

"Hey, Tash!" At the cry, Natasha looked over and spotted Tanya among the players. "We're playing Rangers against the rest. We've got the numbers even, but we're wiping the floor with them." Her words raised some indignant retorts. Tanya went on, undeterred. "Why don't you join their side and try to make a game of it?"

"I've got to take Tipsy back to the barn and give her some supper," Natasha called back.

One of the shepherds spoke up. "Nah. You go and sort those Rangers out. We'll take care of Tipsy for you."

"You're sure?"

"Yes. Go on." The shepherd waved her away.

"Thanks." Natasha jogged onto the meadow. Too late, she saw Shelly and Dani among the players. Neither looked pleased at her arrival, but they made no comment, and the game resumed.

Before long, Natasha had realized why the Rangers were having the best of it. Even in a friendly game, several were using blatantly intimidatory tactics, tackling the weaker opponents hard. Natasha smiled grimly. One did not survive long in the marketplace at Landfall without learning how to deal with things like that. The second time she had possession of the ball, she had a chance to put her experience into effect. One of the Rangers came charging toward her, clearly expecting Natasha to back off, but instead, it was the Ranger who ended up on the ground after being shouldered aside.

The next Ranger in her way was Shelly, who was easily outmaneuvered and left flat-footed. Natasha passed the ball on, grinning at the muttering from the women behind her.

After another ten minutes of play, her team was definitely seeing Natasha as an asset. The ball was coming her way more often, and the Rangers were treating her with respect. All four times she and Shelly had contended for the ball, Natasha had been the one left in possession. Natasha tried not to look smug, but she was starting to enjoy herself. Shelly's expression could best be described as a thundercloud.

Play flowed up and down the meadow. Natasha intercepted the ball at midfield. She took it a few meters forward and then chipped it over the heads of some advancing Rangers to one of her teammates. Natasha raced up the field, keeping level with the ball as it was passed from woman to woman. It ended up with Dani, who sent a high, floating shot across the goal line. Natasha connected with the ball and pounded it in for a goal.

Dani's and Natasha's eyes met. Both women were exultant, both shouting in triumph. They held the contact for a second before Dani's face blanked over and she turned away. Natasha was surrounded by the rest of her teammates, who were patting her back and congratulating her. Natasha's heart was pounding. She did not know whether it was due to exertion, the thrill of scoring, or the fact that for the first time in months, Dani had looked at her with something other than hatred.

The game continued. The next time Natasha had the ball, she advanced a third of the way up the field and then passed it to someone who had found a good clear patch. Natasha slowed a little to catch her breath. Suddenly, her legs were kicked from under her. She hit the ground hard, driving the air from her lungs and leaving her curled on the grass, hugging her shins in agony. When her head finally cleared, she was aware of an argument going on above her.

"That wasn't just a late tackle."

"I'm sorry. I didn't see she'd passed the ball."

"Even then, you can't chop at people's legs like that."

"I said I was sorry." The pain was fading. This time, Natasha recognized Shelly's voice.

Tanya knelt by Natasha's side. "Tash, are you all right?"

Natasha rolled onto her back. "I will be." She opened her eyes. Tanya's face was closest, looking concerned. Beyond her was a ring of others. Shelly looked sullenly defensive. A couple looked angry. Several looked embarrassed. They all knew that it had nothing to do with the game of football.

Natasha managed to sit up. Her shins were not too bad, but her left knee was throbbing. With help from Tanya and others, she got to her feet, but she could not put her full weight on the leg.

"You'd best get into town and have a healer look at it," Tanya suggested.

"I think I'll be okay."

"Even so."

There was not going to be any more play. The huddle around Natasha started to disperse. Dani was the first to leave the meadow, followed by Shelly. Most stayed to accompany Natasha and offer assistance as she hobbled along. Nothing was said to Natasha on the subject of the poorly disguised assault, but she caught a few remarks from the rear of the group directed against Shelly. Some included Dani in their criticism.

The thought occurred to Natasha that the heretics were siding with an ex-Guard against one of their own people. She clenched her teeth. It was a painful way to learn that she was accepted in Westernfort.

And that she thought of herself as an ex-Guard.

❖

From the cover of the trees, two women watched the group of footballers depart.

"Treacherous little bitch." Cal spat out the words.

"Well, it answers some questions," Rohanna said in more measured tones.

"She's broken her oath to the Goddess and joined the heretics."

"I'm afraid you're right. I had hoped..." Rohanna broke off and sighed. "I knew her faith was weakening and she'd failed in her assignment, but I'd hoped she had remained true."

"She'll answer to Celaeno."

"As must we all, and I know I'm not blameless. I should have been the one to remain here and deal with the Imprinter."

"And leave me with her?" Cal sounded incredulous. She put her hand on Rohanna's arm. "I'd rather be in the shit with a comrade I trust than taking it easy with a lousy traitor. I know it's

Celaeno who'll judge her, but I'd like to be the one who sends her to the Halls of Judgment."

"Her soul will be forfeit," Rohanna agreed sadly.

"You sound sorry."

"I am. She could have been a worthy Guard. I was her leader, and it must be partly my fault she went astray. I failed her."

Cal shook her head. "Don't blame yourself. She's the one who turned her back on the Goddess."

The footballers were gone from sight. The two Guards retreated farther into the undergrowth and then began to climb the hillside, still keeping to dense cover. After a while, Cal said, "I'm amazed they trust her, after she betrayed us."

"The heretics can be gullible, in their way. I suppose there must be a few doubts in the minds of some of them, yet it..." Rohanna's voice dropped, and her face became thoughtful.

"You've thought of something?"

"Just an idea, but with the grace of the Goddess, it might work. It will mean waiting and keeping close to the town, which has its risks."

Cal's face became grim. "Well just make sure we keep away from dogs in the future. I thought we were done for when they came bounding over our way."

"Have faith. The Goddess will protect us."

"So what's your plan?"

"You said you wanted to be the one to send her soul to Celaeno. You will get your wish."

CHAPTER TWENTY—DOUBTS

The carving of the sheep was starting to take shape. Natasha whittled away cheerfully, a small pile of wood chips forming by her feet. It was not going to be a work of art, but she was sure Becky would like it. Already, with a bit of imagination, one could see what the model was going to be, and the better part of a month was left before the child's birthday, giving her plenty of time to finish it.

Natasha sat on a three-legged milking stool just inside the wide-open doors of the barn. Bright afternoon sunshine streamed in over her shoulder. She spared a quick glance around the interior. All the animals were out in the fields, and there was nothing for her to do until the cows were brought in for milking in half an hour. Natasha's lips formed a broad grin, and she returned to her carving.

An old drinking song from her days in the Militia came to mind. Natasha pursed her lips and whistled the tune to herself. Somehow, shaving flakes off the rough wooden block was very satisfying. She could easily get carried away and end up making a toothpick, especially since the long knife was on the clumsy side. But it was all right for forming the rough outline, and the blacksmith had offered to lend her a small file for the finishing touches.

Her whistling was not loud, but it was enough to cover the sound of stealthily approaching footsteps and the dull whisper of a sword being loosened in its scabbard. The first Natasha knew of her visitor was when a shadow fell across her. She looked up and saw Shelly standing just outside the door.

"Hi," Natasha said.

Shelly did not answer. The sun was at the Ranger's back, making it difficult to judge her expression, but her posture was tense. Natasha wondered if she had come to apologize for the incident at football the day before.

"Did you want something?"

Natasha lifted one hand to shade her eyes. Screened from the worst of the glare, she could see Shelly staring at her other hand, lying in her lap with the knife and model sheep. The Ranger looked unwell—an impression enhanced by the croak in her voice when she snapped, "What are you doing?"

"It's an addition to Becky's toy farm. Her birthday is—" Natasha's words were cut off.

"You've got a dagger." Shelly made it sound like an accusation.

"It's only the knife we use around the barn."

"Your parole. The terms say you mustn't carry a weapon."

Natasha stared at Shelly, caught between irritation and confusion. "It's only the old knife we use around the barn." Natasha repeated, emphasizing each word.

"Kim said if you were caught with a weapon, you could be killed on sight."

"Don't be stu..." Natasha's voice died at the sight of Shelly's hand moving to the hilt of her sword. "Shelly!" she shouted in disbelief, at the same time tossing both knife and carving aside and holding up her empty hands.

The gesture of surrender had no effect. Shelly drew her sword and glared at Natasha. "I'm allowed." The childish sulky tone would have been funny if not for the circumstances.

"You can't—"

Even as Natasha started to rise, the sword came slicing toward her. She threw herself back, and the blade bit into the wooden door frame, missing her by centimeters. Natasha hit the ground in a roll and came up holding the milking stool out like a shield. Shelly advanced, following her into the barn.

"Shelly! What's up with you?" Natasha yelled, but got no response.

Shelly's face was set in a tight scowl. Her eyes glinted under puckered eyebrows. Her movements were stiff, as though every muscle in her body was taut. She jabbed out twice with the sword. They were heavy, vicious lunges, but poorly timed, and both were deflected by the stool.

"Shelly, stop being stupid. We can go to Kim if you want, tell her I had a knife." Natasha could hear the panic in her own voice.

She might as well not have spoken. Shelly continued to press ahead, forcing her back down the wide central aisle between the pens. Another thrust of the sword struck the stool. Then Shelly brought the blade down in an overhead swipe that took a chunk out of the seat. The assault contained no element of subtlety, as if the violence of the strokes was an end in itself rather than an attempt to shed blood. Shelly moved with all the grace of a puppet. Her sword lashed out in a series of wild hacks. Each was far too poorly aimed to pose much direct threat, but on the eighth hit, Natasha felt one of the legs of the stool start to loosen.

Natasha's eyes darted left and right. Nothing suitable for use as a weapon against the sword was at hand, and once the stool was gone, even the clumsy attack would be impossible to withstand. Through the barn door, Natasha could see the distant town. Shelly stood between her and the way out, but even if the route had been clear, Natasha would not have fancied her chances. A healer had tended to her knee after the football game. So far that day, the injury had given Natasha no problems, but her leg was not up to a race.

Yet another blow smashed against the stool. Natasha heard the faint creak of splintering wood. She was going to have to chance her luck. She took two quick steps backward to make room and feigned first to one side and then the other, as if hoping to wrong-foot her attacker and make a break for the door. Shelly responded immediately, moving quickly to block off the escape.

But that was not Natasha's plan. Shelly was off balance, expecting her quarry to rush forward, and she was just a little too slow to respond when Natasha hurled the stool underarm, like a bowler aiming at pins.

The seat cracked on Shelly's knee. One of the legs caught on the heel of her boot, and another was under her foot as it came down. Shelly staggered, arms flailing. Natasha leapt forward. Her fist thumped hard into Shelly's ribs. A second punch sent the Ranger spinning. Natasha completed her offensive by catching Shelly's shoulder and flinging her, face down, onto the floor. Before Shelly could regain her breath, Natasha had her pinned to the ground by a knee in the back, with one arm twisted up behind her. The sword was torn from her hand and tossed to the far side of the barn.

"What the fuck do you think you're playing at?" Natasha's fear evaporated in anger.

Shelly's cheek was pressed into the straw covering the floor. She clenched her teeth, breathing harshly. For a moment, her face held an expression angry enough to match Natasha's, and then it crumpled, like a lost toddler's. Tears squeezed out of Shelly's closed eyes, and her shoulders shook with sobs.

"What's this all about?" Natasha shouted.

"Dani."

Natasha pulled back slightly. Did Dani hate her so much that she would try to talk Shelly into murdering her? "Dani told you to do this?" She asked for confirmation, but Shelly shook her head as far as was possible with her face pressed into the ground. Natasha looked at her defeated opponent in confusion. Her anger faded. "If I let you up, do you promise not to try to kill me again?"

"Yes," Shelly whispered, nodding.

Natasha let go of Shelly's arm and shifted away. Shelly rolled over and pulled herself up so that she was sitting with her back against one of the animal enclosures. Tears were still running down her face, although her sobbing had subsided.

Natasha remained kneeling on the floor. "What's this about?" she repeated her question.

"It's Dani. I'm jealous," Shelly mumbled.

"I'd have thought I had more reason to go for you on that score."

Shelly shook her head. "She doesn't want me." Her lower lip began to shake, and she caught it between her teeth.

Natasha bowed her head. The outcome was predictable, if she had thought it through. From what Dani had said before, it was obvious that a relationship with Shelly was unlikely to last. Dani had fallen into the first pair of arms to come along, in the shock of finding out that she had been seduced by a Guard. But now that the initial distress was over, Dani had dropped Shelly. Shelly was feeling badly used and was looking for someone else to take it out on. Natasha could not help feeling a degree of sympathy—with the motive, if not with the expression it took.

She raised her head and looked at Shelly. "Why go for me?"

"I thought...if you weren't around, she might..." Shelly's mumbling ground to a halt.

"Why should I make a difference?"

"Because you're the one she's crazy about."

"Are you nuts?"

Shelly met Natasha's astonished gaze. "No. I'm serious. You're the one she wants."

"Then she's doing a first-class job of hiding it." Natasha's voice was full of skepticism. "Look, just because Dani has dumped you, it doesn't mean—"

Shelly interrupted. "She hasn't dumped me."

"You think she's going to?"

Shelly's face twisted in pain before she hung her head. "I've got some pride, and I'm not stupid. She's just using me to get at you. She's all over me whenever you're around, and the rest of the time, I might as well not be there."

"That isn't the..." Natasha's words trailed off.

Shelly went on in a dead voice. "That first night when you were locked up...I went around to see Dani. She was really upset. I just meant to comfort her, but she was..." Shelly shrugged. "She virtually dragged me into bed. I admit I didn't take much dragging. I knew it was because she was cut up over you, but I thought it was my chance. I thought I could show her how I felt and make it work." Shelly's head dropped into her hands. "At first, I was just too happy to notice, and perhaps she was so desperate to distance herself from you that she put some effort into it. But she hasn't gotten over you, and I don't think she ever will. I used to think if I had Dani as a lover I'd have everything I wanted, but it's a sham."

Shelly raised her head and looked directly at Natasha. "You probably never see it, but I do. Sometimes, we're sitting in the tavern, and you walk in. Even if I don't see you, I know it's you from Dani's face. For a fraction of a second, her face lights up before she remembers she's supposed to hate you. I'd give anything to have her face light up like that for me."

"I'm not sure that's what it means," Natasha said carefully.

"Oh, you can be sure. I'm sorry about going for you just now. I came up here to see you. I'm not certain what I was planning, and when I saw the knife, I thought..." She broke off. "It was stupid of me. If you weren't here, Dani would lose her only reason to notice my existence." Shelly's tears had stopped, and her expression was back under control. She took a deep breath and continued. "But like I said, I've got some pride. If Dani wants to get at you, she should have it out to your face and not use me. I'm not going to let her carry on with the game. You asked if she'd dumped me..." Shelly shook her head. "No, but I'm going to dump her."

Natasha looked at Shelly, unable to think of anything to say.

"It's taken me a long time to build up to it. I love her; I always will. It's going to be too hard to hang around here, seeing her every day, but I could go to Ginasberg and make a new start. What do you think?" Shelly looked at Natasha anxiously.

"I think..." Natasha floundered for a moment. "It might be a good idea. I'm considering it myself for exactly the same reason. I don't think you're right about Dani's feelings for me." She grinned wryly at Shelly. "And Ginasberg does seem the right sort of distance to nurse a broken heart. Once my parole expires, I might join you there. We can commiserate with each other."

Shelly shook her head. "You shouldn't give up so easily. If I was you, I'd go talk to her—force her to say what she really feels. Tell her that if a woman has something to say to another, she should say it and not play games."

Natasha was about to speak, but she was interrupted by the sound of lowing from the field beside the barn. She rose to her feet. "That's the cows. They're due for milking, and you've wrecked my milking stool."

"Sorry." Shelly also stood, looking shamefaced.

"I'll cope without it today, but I'm not sure how I'll explain the damage."

"If I get you a replacement, will you keep quiet about all this?"

"I won't lie if anyone asks me directly, but..." Natasha smiled and shrugged.

"Oh, of course. But I think I know where I can lay my hands on one by this evening. And it would be embarrassing if the story got out. I mean, I had a sword, and you had a milking stool, and you won."

Natasha laughed. "I won't tell anyone, if I can avoid it." She started to walk toward the doorway, followed by Shelly, who stopped briefly to reclaim her sword. They separated at the gate to the field. The six cows were clustered on the other side.

Shelly took a few steps along the road to Westernfort and then turned back. "You know, for a Guard, you're not so bad."

❖

The two Rangers rode slowly along the banks of the river, as they had for the previous eight days. Now they were far to the southwest of Westernfort, and the terrain was changing. The range of mountains had fallen away, and a wide plain stretched before them to the horizon. The river had broadened and slowed, meandering in sweeping sinuous curves, and the land on either side was swampy, forcing the Rangers to keep farther from the banks than they wanted. At last, one of them, a corporal, reined in her horse and stood in her stirrups. Sunlight glinted off the water as far as the horizon. There was either a lake or, more likely, a marsh ahead.

The corporal called out, "I don't think there's any point going much farther. If the bodies were washed into that, we'll never find them."

The other Ranger looked at the area where her comrade was pointing. "And there's no telling whether any bodies are here to find." She raised one eyebrow. "Do we head back now?"

"We'll go another kilometer or so and get closer to the water. Where the river slows as it flows into the swamp is the sort of place it would dump anything it was carrying. But if we can't find anything around there, we might as well turn back."

The soft ground obliged the women to leave their horses behind. They continued on foot through the long reeds for ten minutes until something caught the eye of one Ranger. She shouted to her comrade and carefully advanced to the river's edge, with her feet sinking in mud.

"What is it?" the corporal asked, staying back.

The Ranger by the water held up the rotted remains of a bundle of straw, twisted like a thick rope and about half a meter in length. An attempt had been made to pull it apart and scatter it, but now that they were alerted, they both could see other sections strewn between the reeds. The piece in the Ranger's hand was the largest. Despite its condition, neither Ranger had any difficulty recognizing what it had once been.

"They made a round raft from straw and a tarpaulin and floated downriver," the Ranger said, looking at the evidence in her hands.

"No wonder we haven't seen any sign of them to the east."

"Where do you think they've gone?"

The corporal shook her head. "I don't know. But it's going to be our job to find out."

The two Rangers headed away from the river and collected their horses. Night was falling when they found the next trace of their quarry: the blackened stones of a campfire. The corporal examined the site and looked toward the mountains in the distance. She stood for a while, chewing her lip, and then said, "We might as well stop here tonight. We don't want to miss anything in the dark. But first light tomorrow, we'll press on, and we're going to have a hard ride."

"You sound worried." The Ranger's tone made it a question.

"I am."

"Why?"

"I've got a nasty feeling I know where they're headed. They're circling back to Westernfort. They might think they've got some unfinished business back there."

"You think they'll make another attempt on Lynn and Kim?"

"Yes."

The Ranger started to build the fire and then stopped. "Natasha said they'd be going back to the Homelands."

"Maybe she lied."

"If she's still one of them..."

The corporal's voice was grim. "Then she'll come to regret it. We haven't time to waste. We need to get back to Westernfort as quickly as possible, and then perhaps Kim and the captain would like to ask Natasha a few more questions."

❖

Natasha dumped the food into the pig trough and stepped back from the stampede of piglets, but her eyes and attention were not focused on her work, and she collided with the gatepost on the way out.

Lynn was watching her from the doorway of the barn. "Have you got something on your mind?"

"Pardon?" Natasha jumped slightly when she was spoken to.

"I asked if you had something on your mind, and obviously, you do. So I guess my next question concerns whether it's any of my business."

"Um, it's...er..."

Lynn laughed. "It's all right. I was teasing. If it's what I suspect, then it isn't."

"Isn't what?"

"Isn't any of my business."

"Oh." Natasha frowned and then looked more sharply at Lynn. "What do you suspect?"

"Well...rumor has it that yesterday afternoon, Shelly came up here to talk to you. And then, last night, she and Dani had a major bust-up, where your name was shouted a few times. I did warn you about gossip in Westernfort." Lynn's expression was apologetic. "My guess is that the two events are linked with whatever you're thinking about."

Natasha leaned back against a rail and let her eyes drift over the fields before her. She opened her mouth to speak; then she shrugged and started again. "You're right. Shelly did say something that's got me thinking." Her expression was somewhere between a smile and a frown. "She reckons Dani is still in love with me and has just been using her as a..." Natasha's voice died as the frown won out. "I know Shelly isn't the best judge of character, but she seemed really certain."

"And if Dani is still in love with you, would you be interested?" Lynn asked softly.

"I'd walk from here to Landfall, barefoot on broken glass, if it would help me get her back. But I've only got Shelly's say-so, and if I go talk to Dani, I might upset her. I've treated her badly enough already." Natasha raised her eyes to Lynn. "What do you think I should do?"

Lynn groaned. "I guess that question is what I deserve for sticking my nose in." She bit her lip. "And the answer is, I don't know. After what happened to her family, it's going to take a lot for Dani to look kindly on a Guard—even an ex-Guard. Maybe she can't stop herself from being in love with you, but it doesn't mean she'll be willing to forgive you. And you've given her quite a lot to forgive."

"I know. I wish I could..." Natasha closed her eyes and sighed.

Lynn patted her arm. "You asked for my advice. OK, here it is, though I can't promise it's any good. I think you should go and talk to Dani. You might just upset both her and yourself, but it isn't like either of you is cheerful to start with, so you can't ruin anything. Until you've resolved things, I can see that Tipsy and I are going to have a hard time." She looked at Natasha. "Do you realize that you dumped Tipsy's dinner in with the stuff for the pigs?"

"I..." Natasha glanced guiltily between Lynn and the sheepdog. The expression in Tipsy's liquid eyes seemed to convey feelings of both hurt and rejection.

"You'd better get something else for her to eat. Then go get your own lunch, and see if you can concentrate a bit better this afternoon."

Just the faintest hint of criticism underlay Lynn's tone, but Natasha felt herself blushing as she rushed off to get more food for Tipsy. She knew she had been careless all morning and dreaded to think what other mistakes she might have made. She stopped and looked toward the town. The only way she was going to be able to keep her mind on her work was if she could clear her doubts about Dani, and soonest was probably best. Before her nerve went.

Once Tipsy had her nose in the bowl, Natasha left the barn and jogged down the road to Westernfort. By the time she reached Dani's shop, she had almost worked out what she wanted to say. The trick would be avoiding sounding either arrogant or groveling. Not that she would refuse to grovel if there was any sign that it would help. She had braced herself to enter the potter's shop when she saw the note pinned to the door, saying that Dani was up at the kiln.

Natasha swore silently and looked at the sun. Her lunch break was not long enough for her to get to the kiln and back. On the other hand, there was not much point returning to the barn with her head in its current state, and maybe a meeting by the kiln might not be a bad idea. Raised voices were quite likely. The news would make the rounds of Westernfort as it was. She would rather that the gossips did not have a word-for-word account of everything that was said.

CHAPTER TWENTY-ONE—SOMETHING TO SAY

The clearing around the kiln looked very different now that summer was on the way. Natasha stood at the end of the path and peered around. Dense undergrowth filled the space under the trees, making an encircling wall of green. Small yellow flowers were scattered across the grass. The kiln itself looked like a boiled egg with its top broken open. She heard the sound of chopping before she spotted Dani at the edge of the clearing, almost hidden behind a pile of heavy logs.

All of Natasha's resolve ebbed away. She resisted the urge to sneak off again quietly but was unable to make herself step forward and speak. Dani swung the ax as though she wanted not merely to split the logs, but also to bury the blade in the ground underneath them, throwing her whole weight into the action. Possibly she caught sight of Natasha out of the corner of her eye, because she stopped abruptly and glanced over her shoulder. Despite Shelly's assertion, Natasha did not see the slightest flicker of anything other than anger on Dani's face when she straightened and turned to face her.

"I'd ask what you think you're doing here, but I can guess." Dani spat out the words.

"I wanted to talk to you."

"Oh, I'm sure you do, since you've been talking to Shelly. I heard all about it last night...a complete load of bullshit. If you listened to a word she said, you're a bigger fool than she is."

"I didn't believe everything Shelly said without question. That's why I came here—to find out what you'd say."

"You came here thinking I was going to fall into your arms." Dani's voice was raw with anger.

"No. I don't expect anything. But I thought the two of us should talk."

"That's all? Just talk?" Dani sneered. "I know exactly what you want. But I'd rather slit my throat than crawl into bed with you again. I don't know where Shelly got her delusions, but she was wrong from start to finish."

At Dani's furious glare, Natasha's gaze dropped to her feet. The conversation was not following any of her planned scripts. The best thing all around might be to turn and leave, but then one last thought surfaced in her mind. Natasha looked up. "No, Shelly was dead right about one thing."

"Really?" Dani's voice was viciously sarcastic.

"If a woman has something to say to another, she should say it and not play games."

Dani advanced until she was only a few steps away. The ax was still in her hands. She hefted it menacingly. "And you think I've got something to say to you?"

"You're the only one who knows that. But I know I've got something I ought to say to you." Natasha paused. "I love you."

Dani's hands tightened around the shaft of the ax. She took a half step back and then yelled in fury, "How have you got the fucking nerve to say that?"

"Because it's true." Natasha kept her voice calm. "I'm sorry if it offends you. I know it must. But it's the truth. I've lied to you so much in the past, it's the least I owe you now—to tell you honestly how I feel. I love you with all my heart and soul."

"And from all that crap you swallowed from Shelly, you think I'm going to squeal with delight, throw my arms around you, and say I love you too?"

"No. I think I've lost any chance of that, which is all I deserve." Natasha could feel tears starting to sting her eyes. "You've got every right to hate me."

"Generous of you to concede that."

"Why shouldn't you hate me? I hate myself for the way I've treated you. I care about you more than I've ever cared about anyone in my life. If there's one woman in the world who I'd like to think well of me, it's you. And I haven't given you grounds to think of me with anything other than contempt. It's all I deserve. I love you, and you hate the sight of me." Tears were starting to roll down Natasha's face.

Dani was unmoved. "Do you know how pathetic you look?"

"Probably as pathetic as I feel."

"Am I supposed to pity you? You can have all the pity your friends in the Guards showed to my sister and mothers."

"I don't expect your pity."

"No. But I know what you did come here expecting. You talk about love. Shall I tell you what love means to me? I loved my mothers, and I loved my sister. You thought you could wander up here, give me a smile, and I'd forget all about them. You can't have the first frigging idea what love is, if you were counting on me feeling anything for you other than disgust."

"I wasn't counting on it."

"So why did you come here?"

"Because I couldn't stop myself from hoping against the odds." Natasha tried to wipe her eyes. She could not bring herself to speak. Her legs were shaking, and her feet felt as if they were glued to the ground. It was the only thing stopping her from fleeing back through the woods.

Dani was watching her, looking as if she were about to be sick. She half turned away; then she swung back and started shouting again. "How could you even dream I'd soil my family's memory? Do you think you're that good? Do you really imagine that anyone would want you? I can't even respect you for the few virtues Guards are supposed to have. You've lied. You've cheated. You've abandoned your faith. You've betrayed your comrades. You might pretend you followed your conscience when you didn't kill Lynn, but I'll bet it was just that you lacked the guts. Did you have many friends back in Landfall? I'd find it hard to believe. Presumably your mother liked you, but she must have been the only one."

"Dani, I'm sorry." Natasha managed to force the words out through her clenched teeth.

"Sorry for being such a fucking awful excuse for a woman?"

"If there's anything I can do to make..."

"To make me feel better about you?" Dani finished the sentence. She stormed across the clearing and hurled the ax down, embedding it in the side of a log, and walked back until she was close enough to shout into Natasha's face. "Yes. There is something you could do that I would really appreciate. Get yourself a rope, select a tree, and hang yourself." Dani barged past Natasha and marched off along the path through the woods. Her footsteps became quicker as they faded away.

Once she was alone, Natasha managed to force her legs to move. She stumbled across the clearing and slumped against the side of the kiln. Her eyes slipped around the painfully familiar scene. The memory of the night she had spent there taunted her. She had been happy then, and Dani had been her friend. Was there anything she could have done to have kept things that way? Natasha buried her face in her hands. But she knew that the situation had been impossible since the day she had volunteered for the mission.

The time was well past the hour when she should have been back at the barn. Perhaps she could find a job to take her mind off the pain. Natasha shook her head at the thought. Dani's last suggestion was the only one that would stop her from hurting, and she was frightened by how tempting the idea was.

She drew a deep breath, wiped her eyes, and stared bleakly at the path back toward Westernfort, trying to summon the enthusiasm to force her legs to walk. After another deep breath, she pushed away from the kiln. But before she had gone four steps, she was brought to a halt by a stern voice from the trees behind her.

"Stand still, and put your hands in the air."

Natasha gasped. Of course, she had broken the terms of her parole. The forest was not part of the farmlands. She complied with the order; the excuses could be saved for Kim. The soft sound of footsteps approached from the rear. Then one of her hands was grabbed and pulled behind her back. Natasha made no attempt to resist as a rope was tied around her wrist. The knot was secure, but not so tight as to hurt. In fact, it felt as if the bonds were cushioned with something soft. Her other hand was treated in the same fashion. Then her captors stepped around and stood in front of her. To her horror, Natasha found herself staring at Rohanna and Cal. Both were armed, and both were looking hostile.

Cal's eyes traveled deliberately to the path Dani had taken and then came back to Natasha. "What a shame, after you sold us out for her." In a sudden move, she reversed the sword in her hand

and punched the hilt hard into Natasha's stomach. Natasha doubled over. Cal pulled back her arm for a second blow, but Rohanna grabbed her hand.

"Stop that. Remember, we don't want her marked."

"I thought a few little bruises could be put down to mischance."

"Cal." Rohanna's tone made it a warning.

"All right."

Rohanna caught hold of the back of Natasha's shirt and pulled her upright. Natasha was still fighting for breath and hardly aware of what was happening as she was dragged from the clearing and into the forest. By the time she was able to pay attention to her surroundings, the clearing was lost far behind among the trees. Cal was in the lead, following the stony path of a dried-up river bed. Once she saw that Natasha was able to walk unaided, Rohanna released her hold and pushed Natasha forward to go in the middle, while she took a position at the rear. Only birdsong and the breeze through the branches broke the silence as the three women climbed the hillside, heading away from town.

❖

It was over an hour later when they reached the campsite the Guards had picked, high on the walls of the valley. Through a break in the trees, Natasha could see the town of Westernfort several kilometers away. The camp was at the bottom of a narrow gully, overhung by dense forest. The piles of blankets and backpacks were further hidden under a mass of large-leafed shrubs. Someone could have passed within five meters of the spot and not noticed any trace of the women or their gear.

Natasha was directed to sit. Then Rohanna bound her legs from ankle to knee, using large wads of raw sheep's wool as padding under the cord. When the last knot was secure, she looked at Natasha. "Is that nice and comfy? I'd hate it if you got rope burns." Her ironic tone made it clear that her motivation had nothing to do with Natasha's well-being.

"There'd be no risk at all if you didn't tie me."

"It's so we'll know where you are when our backs are turned. Don't worry. I'll untie your legs before we leave. We've got no intention of carrying you."

A short way off, Cal was sitting on a rock and staring at Natasha. Her expression was one of utter revulsion. "You don't know how lucky you are that our plan involves keeping your stinking skin in one piece, because I'd really enjoy the chance to demonstrate just how I feel about you." While she spoke, Cal's fingers clenched as though she were controlling them only with effort. Her voice rose. "When we heard you'd been captured, we thought you'd tried to do your duty and had failed through bad luck. We had visions of you being locked up, tortured, and killed. Then we get here and find you playing football. When I think of the good tears the two of us wasted over you..." Words were no longer enough. Cal sprang to her feet and crouched over Natasha. Both her hands were balled into fists.

Rohanna put out her arm as a barrier and gently pushed Cal away. "It's all right. We can safely leave vengeance to the Goddess."

For a moment, it looked as if Cal would not be able to stop herself from striking Natasha; her fist lifted up. Then she spun away and slumped back on her seat on the rock.

Rohanna returned her attention to Natasha. "Actually, we should have guessed that you had not simply suffered bad luck. Celaeno had been working for us. She'd delivered her enemies into our hands. With the Goddess so clearly blessing our venture, we could only have failed through treachery. It won't happen this time. Once again, the Goddess has provided the help we need to perform her work. The leaders of the heretics will be destroyed, and you'll pay for your faithlessness." She raised her hand to stroke Natasha's cheek. Despite her ominous words, the gesture was sorrowful, even tender. "Were you aware that it was divine will that lured you into the woods? I'd thought taking you prisoner would be difficult, but with the Goddess on our side, it was so easy. We'd barely completed our plans when we found you standing alone, waiting to be captured. And the last words of the potter...an omen if ever I've heard one."

"What are your plans?" Natasha asked.

"We're going to kill you." Cal snapped out the answer.

"There has to be more to it." Of that, Natasha was certain. Otherwise, why was there concern about not injuring her?

"Oh, yes," Rohanna answered her. "We're going to execute Ramon and her degenerate Imprinter. Although unfortunately, we'll have to let Coppelli go."

"And you're hoping I'm going to play some part in the plan?"

"No. Your death is." Rohanna settled back on her heels and continued speaking. "When we failed to execute the heretics, I wondered whether I'd been wrong in trying to send back news about Ginasberg. After all, the Chief Consultant had given us a very specific duty to perform. I thought perhaps I'd been guilty of overambition. So Cal and I decided to devote ourselves solely to our appointed task. It hasn't been easy living in the wilderness, hiding our tracks, climbing over a mountain to get back into the valley unnoticed. You can see we're not looking our best." Rohanna held up her arms to illustrate her words. She had lost weight, and her clothes were ragged. A long graze marked one side of her face.

Natasha glanced at her ex-comrades and then looked down. *Why was I so sure Rohanna and Cal would return to Landfall?* Natasha berated herself silently. The answer occurred to her in the next instant. *Because I tried to put myself in their place, and I'd have grabbed any excuse to avoid murdering Lynn.*

Rohanna went on speaking. "Then we got back here and found you alive and at liberty. And I realized that the fault was in you, not me. You're the one who tried to thwart the will of the Goddess. But you cannot. No mortal can. In the end, everything can only serve to glorify her. Your sins provide the opening that will allow us to complete the mission in full. Tonight, we'll enter Westernfort. They're so sure this valley is impregnable, they don't post sentries in the town. We'll go to Ramon's house and carry out the two sentences of death. Then we'll hang you from the rafters of their house and make sure that it looks like suicide. Do you see how it will work? Everyone will assume you were so distraught at the potter's rejection, you had another change of heart and returned to the Goddess. You fulfilled your mission out of anger or remorse and then killed yourself. They won't be looking for anyone else, which will give Cal and me our chance to return to Landfall."

Rohanna stared directly into Natasha's eyes. "Aren't you afraid of Celaeno's anger? Can't you see that you bought your life with your betrayal, at the price of your immortal soul? Your life is now forfeit, but your soul may yet be saved. Repent of your sins. Let the love of the Goddess into your heart. From the way you've fallen into our hands, I know Celaeno is blessing our mission. Think. Would you be sitting here as a prisoner if Celaeno herself had not intervened?"

Natasha met Rohanna's gaze. For a moment, the absolute certainty she saw there overwhelmed her. It was impossible to question that Rohanna was right and the Goddess was demonstrating her will. Then the spell broke. Rohanna's certainty was nothing, apart from the blind refusal to doubt. Despite the situation, Natasha almost laughed. For the first time since meeting Ash and Dani in the abandoned homestead, there were no contradictions tearing her apart. If she was going to die, at least she could do it at peace with herself. She shook her head. "I'm sitting here prisoner because you've had some good luck."

"You deny the hand of the Goddess?"

"You wouldn't know the hand of the Goddess if she slapped you around the face...especially if she slapped you around the face. You're so convinced that Celaeno is on your side, you're incapable of seeing any evidence to the contrary. You've decided what the Goddess wants, and nothing that happens can change your mind. Every tiny coincidence that supports your belief, you seize on as proof, and you ignore everything else. You think the Goddess intervened to help you capture me? I can think of a thousand ways the Goddess could have intervened that would have been more helpful to you. In fact, if she wants Lynn dead, why doesn't she strike her down with lightning?"

"I would not presume to try to understand the working of her will. I only trust in her bounty. You cannot expect the working of the Goddess to be comprehensible to human reason." Rohanna's voice was austere.

"But you've already told me why the Goddess sent me to the kiln and explained the part it plays in her overall design. Can't you see that you're always certain you understand the working of the Goddess only when you can put a slant on things that agree with your preconceptions?"

"We have the guidance of *The Book of the Elder-Ones*."

"By your own admission, the Goddess doesn't follow human logic. Perhaps she gave us *The Book of the Elder-Ones* as a test, to see if we can reject unthinking obedience and follow the conscience and common sense that she gave us."

"I see you've damned your soul and rejected your creator," Rohanna said angrily.

"I don't think so. I went to the kiln on a whim—the result of a trivial string of events. You say it was the working of the Goddess..." Natasha shrugged. "I can't say I felt divinely inspired. But when I was about to kill Lynn, I knew, in the very core of my being, that it would be an evil act. My soul was in revolt at what I was preparing to do. If ever I have felt the touch of the Goddess in my heart and my mind, it was then." She looked back into the startled eyes of Rohanna. "But of course, you *know* that can't have been the case, because you *know* the Goddess wants Lynn dead, and there is nothing Celaeno herself could do to persuade you otherwise. Ask yourself—"

Natasha was allowed to go no further. Rohanna snatched another wad of wool with one hand while she prized Natasha's jaws open with the other. The wool was rammed into Natasha's mouth and fixed in place with a strip of cloth as a gag. Then Rohanna stood and glared down at her. "At least that will keep our ears free from your heretical rambling."

Natasha looked up, confused by her own reactions. Once, she had felt admiration and even affection for Rohanna. She had been proud to be a member of her team. Now she could not begin to recapture the emotion. She could feel only horror at what Rohanna and Cal were proposing to do, exasperation at their inability to question, and shame that she had once been like them.

Cal had already taken one of the backpacks and pulled out various items, including a length of rope, presumably in preparation for the night's work. Rohanna treated Natasha to one last, bitter look before joining her comrade. "If I were you, I'd spend the time remaining in preparing yourself to stand before Celaeno and answer for your sins." Her eyes glanced toward the sun, estimating its position, and then back. "I'd say you have about eight hours left."

Chapter Twenty-two—Confrontation

Dani stomped out of her shop and slammed the door. She was feeling generally angry: angry at Natasha for her gall, angry at Shelly for her idiocy, angry at her customers for dithering, angry at the clay for not behaving on the wheel, and angry at herself for leaving the ax behind at the kiln. She had only just remembered it. The sun was dropping toward the mountains, and dusk was less than an hour away. The weather was showing no sign of rain, but the ax was valuable and should not be left out overnight to rust in the dew.

With any luck, Natasha would not still be at the kiln. Dani never wanted to see her again. In fact, she wanted never to have seen her at all. She wished that Natasha would be blasted off the face of the world. *I hate her. I despise her. I hate her.* Dani mentally chanted the mantra in time to her footsteps as she marched along, head down and shoulders hunched. She paid no attention to the other people on the road until one tapped her arm.

"Oh, Dani. Tell Natasha I sorted out the animals. Just this once, as a favor." Dani raised her head and saw Lynn grinning at her.

"Why should I be seeing her?" Dani snapped.

Lynn's smile faded. "Didn't she...I thought she was going to talk to you."

"Yes. But that was ages ago."

"Hasn't she been with..." Lynn stopped. "I'm sorry. When she didn't show up this afternoon, I assumed..." Again, Lynn's voice trailed away.

Dani added someone else to the list of people she was angry with. She could imagine what Lynn had assumed. "No, she hasn't spent the afternoon with me—in or out of bed. I told her to go hang herself."

"Right." Lynn's voice held both surprise and regret. "Well, hopefully, she hasn't."

"I didn't mean her to take me literally."

"I'll tell her that when I find her."

"I don't—" Dani broke off in uncertainty as Lynn gave her a long, hard look.

"When did you last see her?" Lynn asked eventually.

"About lunchtime. I was up at the kiln."

"Do you have any idea where she went?"

"No, I left her there." Dani's eyes dropped to her feet. She could feel a blush rising on her cheeks. Something in Lynn's expression was making her very uncomfortable.

"I'll go check her room." Lynn hesitated and then added in a lower voice, "It was my fault that she went to speak to you. I'm sorry if you found the conversation unpleasant." She turned and walked away.

Dani watched until Lynn was out of sight before resuming her trek. Her anger was shifting into a jumble of emotions not so easy to name. By the time she reached the kiln, a fair chunk of guilt was making itself known. She picked up the ax and stared at the spot where Natasha had stood. "I don't care. I hate her." Dani spoke aloud to the empty clearing, but even she could hear the lack of conviction in her own voice. She looked around at the trees, dreading the sight of a figure dangling from one. However, nothing was close by and the deepening twilight made it impossible to see far into the woods.

"She wouldn't." Dani whispered the words. Then she drew a sharp breath and shouted, "Damn her!" Her face twisted in pain. She marched back through the forest, trying to recapture her earlier anger as a defense against the growing anxiety. It did not work.

The sun was setting by the time she reached the outlying buildings of Westernfort. The light was sufficient to see outside, but the room at the back of her shop was fading into gloom. Dani propped the ax in a corner, lit one candle, and sat staring at the flame. It took all her willpower not to go in search of Lynn and ask whether Natasha had been found. *She's probably moping in her room or in the tavern, getting drunk,* Dani tried to convince herself. Surely it was ridiculous to worry just because Natasha had not returned to her work at the barn.

Dani closed her eyes. She called on old memories: her sister playing, her mothers sitting together by the hearth, their home, and their deaths. She tried to picture Natasha in a Guard's uniform, waving a bloody butcher knife and laughing. The images would not fit together. Dani tried again, working on the details of Natasha's face.

Suddenly, the vision came to life, beyond Dani's power to control. All other thoughts were swept away by the memory of the last time Natasha had stood in the room. Dani could not stop herself from recalling the firmness of Natasha's arms around her and the softness of Natasha's lips—the touch and the taste and the scent of her. Dani whimpered and buried her face in her hands.

The sound of the street door opening pulled her back to the present. "Dani?" a voice called out.

"Yes. I'm here. Come in." Dani gathered herself, pinching the bridge of her nose.

Ash entered the room. "Oh, good. I was worried you'd be asleep."

Dani looked around, surprised by how dark it had become. The candle had burnt low. "Er, no...I was...um..." A cold knot formed in her stomach. "Is this about Natasha?"

"Yes."

"Have you found her?"

"No." Ash's voice was grim. "It seems that you were the last person to see her, so I've come to ask you a few questions."

"Oh...yes." Dani tried to keep her voice calm.

"Lynn says you spoke to her at your kiln."

Dani nodded. "Yes. It was just after midday."

"Did she say anything by way of a clue as to where she might be now?"

"Well...it's not so much what she said...more what I said."

"Which was?"

"I told her to go hang herself."

"You had an argument," Ash said dryly.

"Yes. I was angry and got carried away, but I didn't really mean for her to kill herself."

"You seriously think she might have?"

"No. At least, I didn't at the time...not until Lynn said she was missing. But Natasha was quite upset...I said a few other things I wish I hadn't. But no, I don't think she would...probably." Dani's disordered mumbling ground to a halt, and her eyes fixed on the floor.

"And there's nothing else you can tell me?"

"No."

"OK. It's too dark to do anything now, but I'll go up to the kiln at first light tomorrow and see if I can pick up her trail. Let me know if you think of anything else." Ash turned toward the door.

Dani blurted out, "Isn't there..."

"What?"

"You know something else, don't you?"

"Why do you ask?" Ash sounded genuinely confused.

"You're taking this very seriously. She's a grown adult. And running off after an argument...it doesn't normally warrant a full search so quickly."

"Of course there's more to it," Ash said curtly. "It's after dark, and she's not in town. She's broken the terms of her parole, which could have grave consequences. Not the least is that she can be killed on sight by anyone with a grudge against Guards."

Ash made the last part of her pronouncement with a sharp edge, but Dani was too stunned to be cut by it. The conditions of Natasha's parole had not occurred to her before. "Will she be in serious trouble?"

"That will be for Kim to decide."

"It's my fault. I shouldn't have said what I said to her."

"Natasha gave her word not to be outside town after nightfall. There was no proviso about people being nice to her."

"I didn't want..." Dani could not finish. She did not know what she wanted.

Ash spoke in a softer tone. "As long as she gives herself up without a fight, I can't see Kim being too hard on her. Natasha may have lost her option to stay in Westernfort, but it looks as though Rohanna and Cal have gotten away. So at worst, I'd guess she'll be locked up until she can be sent back to the Homelands."

"I suppose that might be for the best anyway." Dani hung her head. "But if need be, I don't mind admitting my part. I wouldn't want Kim to be unfair...even to a Guard."

"And Kim wouldn't want to be unfair either. I'm sure she'll be very glad to hear what you have to say after Natasha is found."

"Just as long as she isn't dead."

Ash pursed her lips. "Well, if it's any comfort, no one has reported any rope going missing." She gave a nod of farewell and left.

Dani lit a second candle and sat watching it burn down. The time when she should have gone to bed was well past, but she knew she would be unable to sleep. Maybe if she waited until she was tired enough, she would drop off as soon as her head hit the pillow. When she finally stripped off her clothes and slipped between the sheets, however, her thoughts were still in turmoil, and sleep would not come.

After a frustrating hour of tossing around, Dani swung her feet out of bed and went to pour herself a drink of water from the urn. The night had grown chilly. She wrapped a blanket around her shoulders and wandered into the shop. The row of buildings opposite were the only thing visible through the unshuttered window. While sipping the water, she stared out bleakly. The moonlit street was bleached of all color and deserted. It looked harsh and joyless in monochrome and matched her mood.

Dani drained her mug and left the window. She stood in the doorway to the back room. Her bedclothes were disheveled. She tried to muster the enthusiasm to straighten them, but no matter what state they were in, Dani knew that she was not about to sleep.

The silence was broken by the sound of footsteps in the street. Dani twisted around just in time to see three figures flit past her window. The brief glimpse was not enough for her to identify them all, but she was sure that the middle one had been Natasha. Dani rushed to the window and pressed her face against the glass, trying to peer up the street, but the angle was too acute, and she could not catch sight of the women who had passed by. She leapt to the door. Again, she was too slow, and the street was now empty.

Dani closed the door and leaned back against the wooden slats. Her certainty that Natasha had been one of the women was fading. In fact, she was starting to wonder whether she had completely imagined all three. Dani bit her lip. If her first impression was right, presumably the Rangers had caught Natasha and were escorting her to see Kim. Or maybe not. Dani trotted through to the room at the back and reached for her clothes. She might as well go and find out, because there was no way she was going to get any sleep until she knew the answer.

❖

Natasha did not struggle as she was taken through the streets of Westernfort. The effort was better saved until she had a reasonable chance of catching someone's attention. Her hands were tied securely behind her back, and the wool gag in her mouth prevented her from making any sound loud enough to wake people inside the solid stone houses. But surely she would get an opportunity soon. She just had to be alert and ready.

At the edge of the main square, Rohanna gave the signal to halt and peered around the corner. Nobody was in sight. She beckoned them forward again. The door of the house where Lynn and Kim lived was unbarred. What need was there to lock any door in Westernfort? Cal pushed it open and slipped through.

This is my chance, Natasha thought. The door was open, and her captors were separated. If she could start a scuffle, the noise might be enough to wake someone and raise the alarm. Her muscles tensed, but Rohanna was one move ahead of her. Before Natasha could act, Rohanna caught hold of her bound wrists and wrenched them upward.

Only the gag stopped Natasha from screaming. Her shoulders felt as if they had been dislocated. By the time her mind had cleared enough to think, she was in the middle of the main room of the house. Rohanna still had her hands pulled up high behind her, which had the effect of compelling her to stand on tiptoe and bend double while forcing half her weight onto her strained shoulder joints. From this awkward position, she peered around frantically.

Brilliant moonlight flooded in through two windows, overwhelming the dull red glow from the dying embers in the fireplace. The room seemed even bigger than Natasha remembered, easily twelve meters long. The sparse furniture was pushed back against the walls. The only thing close enough to kick was Rohanna's legs, and since they were slightly in front of her, she could not hit them hard enough to achieve anything worthwhile.

Cal stood to one side with a rope in her hands, looking up at a heavy suspended candle holder. She nodded in satisfaction and then stepped over to collect a chair that she could use as a ladder. Beyond her, in the corner of the room farthest from the entrance, was the door to the bedroom Kim and Lynn shared. Natasha's face twisted in despair. Her ex-comrades knew which room it was; she had drawn them a map of the house months ago.

Natasha's eyes darted around the room. Two meters away, a large earthenware jug was balanced on a round stool that someone had used as a makeshift table. Natasha clenched her teeth. If she launched herself to one side, with luck, the sudden movement would tear her free of Rohanna's grasp and send her into the stool. Her shoulders would possibly be wrenched out of their sockets, but this was not a major issue under the circumstances. Natasha was bracing herself for the dive when the door behind her opened again.

"What's going..." The two words were enough for her to identify Dani's voice.

Rohanna was the first to recover. She whipped out a dagger and leapt toward the door. Dani shrank away and ended up in a corner. The instant her hands were released, Natasha also made her move. The dive sent her into the stool with enough force to knock it flying. The jug smashed on the floor. At the same time, a draft slammed the door shut. The twin sounds shattered the silence of the night. For a second, no one moved.

"Who's there?" Kim's voice from the next room was synchronous with the rasp as Cal drew her sword.

"Forget these two. We'll get the ones we came for." Rohanna snapped out the order.

Cal nodded, but before either Guard could move, the door at the back was pulled open and Kim appeared, clad only in a loose thigh-length shirt. Cal was a couple of meters away. She tightened her grip on her sword and took a step forward.

Natasha had rolled onto her knees. Despair and anger battled at the sight before her. Kim would stand no chance, unarmed and outnumbered. The bound hands impaired Natasha's balance and limited her options, but they did not stop her from powering herself up and forward like a sprinter coming off the mark. Cal's attention was fixed on Kim, and she was too slow to respond to the charge. Natasha was still rising as she made impact.

The top of Natasha's head slammed into Cal's stomach and sent her crashing into the wall behind. The Guard gasped and crumpled to the floor. Natasha ended up sprawled on top of her. Hastily, Natasha pulled herself up, added a blow with her knee to Cal's jaw, and then twisted around to view the events unfolding in the room.

Kim was staring desperately at where her sword belt hung on a peg beside the door. However, Rohanna was between it and her. Dani was the nearest, and she had recovered from the frozen paralysis of surprise, yet there seemed to be no hope that she could pass the weapon to Kim in time.

In swift strides, Rohanna advanced up the room, sword in one hand and a dagger in the other. Kim had also moved forward, balancing lightly on her feet, preparing to sidestep, but Rohanna was clearly aware of her intentions and was covering the angles. Then Natasha straightened herself and very deliberately stood in Rohanna's way.

The pair of them stared eye to eye, motionless. Rohanna could not go around Natasha without leaving Kim a clear path to the door, and Natasha had no intention of stepping aside. The confrontation had only one possible outcome.

❖

Natasha's attack on Cal was the spur that got Dani thinking and moving again. She followed the direction of Kim's eyes and saw the sword belt hanging nearby. Dani scrambled over and grabbed it off the peg. A tug at the hilt pulled the sword free of the scabbard. Briefly, she considered the sharp edge, but she knew she did not have the skill to use it. She bent and skated the weapon across the tiled floor to Kim. When she looked up, she was just in time to see Rohanna draw back her arm and thrust her sword deep into Natasha's gut.

Dani wanted to scream, but her throat felt blocked. She watched Natasha crumple to the floor and Rohanna step over her body. Then Kim snatched up her sword and leapt forward to meet the Guard. The sound of metal on metal rang out as blades clashed. Dani began to edge around the room toward where Natasha lay. A nearby door opened, and the face of Kim's fourteen-year-old daughter appeared around it. The voices of younger children were raised in the background.

"Ardis, get back in the room, and keep your sisters there!" Dani barked. Her voice must have held sufficient authority, as Ardis obeyed instantly.

Dani turned back to the battle. Her knowledge of sword fighting was hazy, but it seemed that Kim was getting the better of it despite having only a sword against the two weapons her opponent wielded. Natasha was not moving. The combatants maneuvered around her, although Rohanna, in dodging an attack, tripped on an outflung leg and stumbled. Kim seized on the blunder, and Rohanna was forced to retreat farther down the room.

Kim swung her sword up a little too high, leaving her front open—an obvious mistake, or so it looked to Dani. Rohanna drove her sword at Kim's exposed body, but nothing was there; Kim had started to swing around even before Rohanna moved. The trap was perfectly executed on Kim's part, stretching her opponent too far forward and leaving her with neither sword nor dagger in position to defend.

Kim's blade sliced down—a short, chopping blow hitting at the point where neck met shoulder. Rohanna stumbled back, and Kim struck again—a final, fatal thrust.

"Oh!" A gasp of relief came from the rear of the room.

Dani's head jerked toward the sound. Lynn was standing in the doorway of her bedroom. Dani did not know how long she had been there. The Imprinter took one hesitant step forward, and then another, her attention fixed on Kim.

Suddenly, Dani saw movement out of the corner of her eye. Before she could shout a warning, Cal launched herself off the ground and grabbed Lynn from behind, wrapping an arm around her throat.

"At least one enemy of the Goddess will die!" Cal howled. Her short sword was held pointing upward, close in front of her victim. The elbow at Lynn's neck moved, forcing her chin up and exposing the underside of her jaw to a stab from the sword—one that would go straight up through her brain.

The attack was swift. Dani took a half step forward, but neither she nor Kim was close enough to have any hope of intervening. Dani watched in horror as Cal's hand clenched on the pommel, the precursor to the upward thrust of the sword. She could hear Kim charging across the room in a futile race. Lynn herself seemed to be too surprised to struggle.

Cal's arm twitched. The sword point started its drive—and then stopped dead, as though it had hit a brick. Cal also froze. Without any sign of injury, the Guard slowly toppled over and crashed to the floor.

"No!" Lynn screamed the denial.

"What happened?" Kim sounded as stunned as Dani felt.

Lynn did not reply.

"Lynn! What happened?"

"I killed her." Lynn buried her face in her hands. "I killed her."

Kim moved forward, reaching out. "How?"

Dani's attention shifted. She did not know what had happened to Cal; neither did she care. Natasha was lying on the floor where she had fallen. Dani skidded to the ground beside her, heedless of the liquid that soaked through the knees of her pants until she realized that it was blood.

The gag in Natasha's mouth prevented Dani from checking for breath. She looked around frantically. Rohanna's dagger lay a meter away in a patch of moonlight. Dani grabbed it and sliced through the rag and then the cord around Natasha's wrists. A faint rattle sounded at the back of Natasha's throat, and her fingers clenched spasmodically. Her eyes were open, but it was doubtful that she was truly conscious.

Dani looked up. Lynn was wrapped in Kim's arms, crying. Her words were incoherent. Kim was murmuring to her.

"Lynn." Dani's voice broke over the quiet sounds. "Lynn. Natasha's alive. You've got to help her."

Lynn looked in her direction but showed no sign of seeing anything. Her eyes slipped around the room, not fixing on anything. Her expression was horrified and utterly desolate. She made no move to come to Natasha's aid.

"Kim! Make her help!" Dani pleaded, bewildered by Lynn's inaction.

Kim, at least, seemed to understand the situation. Gently, she urged her stumbling lover to Natasha's side. Lynn looked vacantly at the body on the floor while tears rolled down her face.

"Please, do something!" Dani cried out. "I don't have enough of the healer sense to deal with this."

"No." Lynn stared at her own hands and shook her head. "I can't...I can't. I killed her with it. I'll never—"

"Lynn!" Dani cut her off. "Please. Help her."

Lynn slumped to her knees on the other side of Natasha. Her eyes met Dani's, but without recognition. "The healer sense...Cal was touching me...I just...I..." Lynn's voice faded and then rose again. "It's supposed to heal, not kill. I abused—"

Dani had no time for the rambling. "Don't let Natasha die." She began sobbing. "Please."

Nobody moved. Even the jerking of Natasha's fingers stilled. "Please."

Then, slowly, Lynn's face lost its blankness. Her eyes and jaw hardened. She looked down at Natasha as if she was really seeing what she was looking at, and then raised her face to Dani's once more. Dani could feel the tears spilling from her eyes, but Lynn's were dry now. Again, Lynn's gaze lost its focus, but this time in the purposeful trance of the healer sense. Wordlessly, Lynn stretched out her hand and placed it on Natasha's forehead.

CHAPTER TWENTY-THREE—VISITORS

Natasha opened her eyes. The ceiling above her shifted around for a few seconds before dropping into focus. Reflected sunlight glowed on speckled white plaster. A wooden candle holder hung in the center of the room. The sight of it brought back a rush of memories and rising confusion. The ceiling looked far more mundane than anything she had imagined for Celaeno's Halls of Judgment. Pillars of light and infinite fields of stars would be more in keeping.

Someone was holding her hand. She turned her head. Lynn was sitting on a stool beside her bed. Two other narrow bunks were made up with fresh bedding, although they were currently unoccupied. The tiled floor was clean scrubbed and glinted in the sunlight. The walls were plain white plaster, like the ceiling.

"How are you feeling?" Lynn asked.

"I'm alive."

Lynn smiled. "Is that a question or an answer?"

Natasha tried to sit up and felt a stinging tightness in her stomach. Lynn put her free hand on Natasha's shoulder. "You should lie still. I've had you sedated for the last three days, to speed up the healing process. You're doing well, so I've let you wake up, but you must try not to move too much."

Natasha nodded. At last, she recognized her surroundings as one of the sickrooms in the infirmary. "What happened?"

"How much do you remember?"

"Rohanna and Cal took me to your house. They were going to kill you. Then Dani came in. I did my best to stop Cal, but Kim didn't have a sword, and Rohanna was going for her. So I...tried to help, and she stabbed me. That's about it."

"That's pretty good. People sometimes lose their memories of the last few minutes leading up to a major injury."

"So what happened after?"

"Dani took advantage of the delay you caused and tossed Kim her sword. Kim fought Rohanna and..." Lynn hesitated.

"Kim killed her?"

"Yes."

Natasha squeezed her eyes closed. Emotions ripped through her. Rohanna had been wrong. Rohanna had let her certainties drown out the voice of her conscience. Rohanna had been going to kill her. But once, Natasha had loved her like a mother.

Lynn's hand tightened on her shoulder and then released. "I'm sorry. I know you...despite everything, I know you were close."

Natasha nodded. "And Cal? Did Kim kill her too?"

"No." Lynn paused. "I did."

The surprise snapped Natasha's eyes open. "But how?" Cal was a veteran fighter. Surely Lynn would have had no chance against her.

Now it was Lynn's turn to look distressed. "I followed Kim into the room. I watched her fighting. I was so frightened for her, I didn't pay attention to anything else. Cal recovered from the knock you gave her and grabbed hold of me. She was going to kill me. I panicked and hit out at her."

"With what?"

"The healer sense." Lynn's eyes fixed blindly on her hand holding Natasha's. "Cal had me by the throat. There was skin-to-skin contact, and that's all it takes. I'm so used to stepping into someone else's body—adjusting the heart rhythm, mending tissue, setting bones. When Cal grabbed me, I dived into her, and..." A tear rolled down her face. "It's just as well that no one has asked for a report on the cause of death. There'd be about twenty things to choose from."

Natasha stared at the weeping Imprinter. "You had no option. Cal was going to murder you."

"That's what Kim says. She's been talking me through it...she has the experience." Lynn wiped her eyes. "Sometimes, when I saw her agonizing over old battles, I'd wondered what it must be like to kill a woman. I guess when I've thought about it, I've imagined times like when the Guards were camped outside the valley. Back then, I was occupied with the wounded. I didn't get to send as much as a filthy look over the wall. But if the Guards had gotten inside, I wouldn't have sat wailing while they butchered everyone. I imagined grabbing a sword from the smithy, or something like that...not that I'd have posed a threat to anybody with one. But the healer sense...I'd never thought how easy it would be to kill with it. And even if I had thought it, I'd never have done it...not on purpose, regardless of the danger."

"Even if you'd done it on purpose, it was the only option you had."

"Except now I feel as if I've corrupted something holy. I've been with the heretics for seventeen years, and I was never a devout believer, even when the Sisters were smothering me with theology in the temple. But I guess somewhere deep inside, I still thought of my ability as the Goddess's gift of life."

Of course, Natasha thought, the healer sense could be used as a weapon—a very deadly weapon. And Lynn was not alone in never before considering the possibility. Nothing in the Sisters' teachings even hinted at the idea. But was that deliberate? Had someone decided that they did not want to risk putting the idea into people's heads, in case the Imprinters might realize that they did not have to meekly accept all the restrictions put upon them? Or was it just doctrinal blinkering? *The Book of the Elder-Ones* explained the religious significance of the healer sense, and the Sisters could not think of it in any other way.

Natasha's frown cleared as she remembered what Ash had said to her. The Goddess in the Chief Consultant's books was not the one she believed in. Or cared about.

"Cal was in the wrong, not you. Back in the barn, when I was going to kill you, the reason why I didn't was that I knew you stood in the grace of the Goddess—more than Cal or Rohanna or the Chief Consultant ever would. It was true then, and it still is."

Lynn squeezed her hand. "Thank you. But you didn't kill me because you're not a murderer."

"Neither are you."

"Maybe it's when things reach a crisis point, that's when you find out what you really are. You didn't kill, and I did."

"No. We both did the right thing for the situations we were in. Anyway, it's not the same. It wasn't my life in danger when I drew the sword on you in the barn."

"But it was when you stood in Rohanna's way." A faint smile returned to Lynn's face. "Kim says it was the most suicidally brave thing she's ever seen."

"I'll settle for simply suicidal."

"Why did you do it?"

"Partly it was because, before Cal and Rohanna took me down into the town, we'd been talking, and I realized that it wasn't just that I had doubts. I was totally opposed to them and what they stood for. I knew what they were planning was evil, and I wanted to demonstrate my opposition." Natasha's mouth twitched up at the corner. "And partly, I was feeling very guilty."

"About what?"

"Because I was the one who'd said Rohanna and Cal would head back to Landfall. If it hadn't been for me, Captain Coppelli might have caught them, and then you wouldn't have been in danger at all."

"It still sounds pretty brave to me, standing up to an armed woman with your hands tied behind your back."

"Not just any armed woman. It was someone I knew very well. In an odd way, a stranger would have been far more threatening."

"Did you think that Rohanna wouldn't kill you?"

"Oh, no. Quite the opposite. I was very sure that she would. The biggest surprise was when she hesitated two seconds before doing it. From what you said, without the delay, she might not have been killed herself." Natasha stared at the blankets as memories of Rohanna teased her. "I wish there could have been another way to work things out."

"You can't blame yourself."

"No, but...we were comrades. More than comrades. She was acting the part of my mother, and I don't think it was entirely an act. I think she felt genuine affection for me, or had once. I know I felt..." Natasha shrugged awkwardly.

"She was going to kill you, even without the fight. She was going to hang you."

"And she would probably have hesitated two seconds before doing that as well. Two seconds may not sound like much, but it's more time than my real mother ever had for me."

Lynn leaned over and kissed Natasha on the forehead. "Then your mother is a fool. And you deserve better."

Natasha dropped her eyes. It was a maternal gesture, one that she remembered Rohanna making on many occasions. *If I could chose my mother?* The words shot through her head. Tears threatened. To head them off, she pushed her thoughts onward. "If I can't move around much today, what can I do to keep away boredom?"

Lynn smiled. "One of the reasons I've let you wake up is to get all the people off my back who want to visit you. If you don't mind, you're in for a day of visitors."

"Who?" A sudden hope routed thoughts of her ex-comrades.

"Ash insisted on being first on the list. Kim wants to see you, but she's been dragged off to inspect the side gate path and won't be back until late. Shelly has been asking at least five times a day. Also, Tanya, Madra, and Jenny..." Lynn continued down the list. Dani was not on it.

"Oh." Natasha forced a smile, not that she minded seeing any of them, but the burst of excitement faded. Of course, Dani would not want to see her, would not care whether she was hurt or not. But it did not mean that she felt the same. "Um...Dani was in your house that night. She didn't get injured at all, did she?"

"No. You were the only one."

"Oh." Natasha licked her lips nervously. "Do you know what she was doing there?"

"She was awake and saw you being taken through the town, but didn't recognize Rohanna and Cal. She thought they were Rangers who'd arrested you for breaking parole, and she went to see what was happening."

She wanted to gloat. Or maybe she was frightened that Kim would have me hanged on the spot, and didn't want to miss out. For the second time in two minutes, Natasha choked back tears.

"Would you like to see Dani?" Lynn asked softly.

Natasha shook her head. "No, not really...not if she doesn't want to see me."

Lynn stood up, squeezed her hand again and let go. "OK. Then we'll start with somebody who definitely wants to see you. In fact, I'm amazed that Ash isn't banging on the door, asking when she can come in."

As predicted, the elderly Ranger was waiting impatiently outside. Ash strolled into the room without needing an invitation. Her face held a broad smile. "Hey. So how's the hero doing?"

Lynn slipped away.

❖

The spinning wheel slowed gradually and finally came to a halt. The jug in the center was perfectly formed, with a long, graceful neck. Dani stared at it dispassionately. With one clay-encrusted finger, she pushed the wheel round, examining the jug from all sides. It was the first decent pot she had thrown for days. She lifted her fist and smashed it down on the soft clay.

Dani continued to stare in the direction of the wrecked lump on the wheel, but her thoughts were far away, her eyes no longer focused. Clay was so easy to mold. Why could her emotions not be the same? Dani toyed with the image of taking her own heart and slapping it on the potter's wheel. She could form it into the shape she wanted. *Then I could carve my mothers' names into it and fire it, so it would never change.* Dani rested her head in her hands, heedless of the clay that clung to her face. *But do I really want that?*

When the clay began to dry, it tickled her nose and forehead. Dani poured a bowl of water from the urn and washed the major part of it off. Did she know what she wanted? She stared at the clouds of terra-cotta in the water. Or was it just that she could not bear to admit what she wanted? Shelly thought that she knew.

Dani closed her eyes. The smoldering anger had gone, replaced by guilt. She had no right to be angry at Shelly; rather, it went the other way around. She had used Shelly. Deep inside, she had known it all along. Up until the end, Shelly had been a willing tool, but that did not make it right.

The sound of someone entering the shop interrupted her brooding. Dani turned and saw Lynn standing in the open doorway.

"Can I come in?"

Dani gestured vaguely in the direction of the bench, dithered back and forth, and then dropped onto her stool by the wheel.

"How are you?" Lynn's tone made the question more than a simple greeting.

"Fine."

"You're sure?"

"Of course. Why shouldn't I be?"

Lynn sat and considered her for a while before continuing. "I thought you might like to know that Natasha is now able to see visitors."

"That's nice for her," Dani said listlessly.

"You wouldn't consider calling on her yourself?"

"I don't pay get-well visits to Guards."

"Ex-Guard."

Dani shrugged as though the point were not worth contending, but she could not meet Lynn's gaze.

Lynn continued, "I was talking to Ash this morning about the conversation you had with her the evening Natasha went missing. She told me you were upset. You regretted arguing with Natasha."

"I didn't want her death on my conscience."

"I remember hearing you say you'd happily kill any Guard, by any method whatsoever."

"So?"

"Either you've softened your attitude, or you don't see Natasha as a Guard. And either way, you could consider dropping by to visit her."

"I know where you're heading, and I'd have thought you had more sense." Dani tried to put passion into her voice, but even she could hear the weakness. "After what happened to my family...how could anyone imagine I could ever—" She broke off. "I loved my sister, I loved my mothers, and Natasha is just..." Again, she could not complete her sentence. "I don't want anything to do with her. I don't want to be in the same room as her. I just wish she was... somewhere else."

"You don't have to pretend to hate her just to prove you loved your family."

"What makes you think I'm pretending?"

"The way you reacted when Natasha was stabbed."

Dani opened her mouth but could not speak. The image of Natasha, lying on the floor, in the dark spreading pool, was the one she had fought to keep out of her head. Now it claimed her. She could see Natasha's fingers jerking spasmodically as her lifeblood seeped away.

Lynn spoke again. "I had another reason for coming to talk to you. I wanted to thank you."

"For what?" Dani's head jerked up.

"For that night, in our house, when I killed Cal. You were there. You saw the state I was in. I completely lost my grip, and Natasha was lying wounded, needing my help. She'd just saved Kim's life... mine as well. She'd taken Cal out of the fight temporarily and held off Rohanna long enough for you to pass Kim her sword. If she'd died because of her actions, that would have been bad enough, but if she'd died because I couldn't pull my head together in time, I'd never have forgiven myself. Without you, I'd have stood there wailing like a pathetic idiot until it was too late. I was off in a flap. The only thing that got through to me was the emotion in your voice." Lynn looked directly at Dani. "And that emotion wasn't hatred."

Dani swallowed and stared at the ruined pot on the wheel. After a few seconds of silence, Lynn got to her feet. She patted Dani once on the shoulder and walked to the door. Dani did not move, but at the sound of Lynn's hand on the latch, she said, "With Natasha, I...I've not been very pleasant to her. Do you think she'd want to see me?"

"I wouldn't like to answer for her. But I know an easy way of finding out."

❖

Shelly sat beside Natasha's bed, chatting happily. "Now that we know news about Ginasberg won't be getting to the Chief Consultant, building work will be going at full speed. A party is setting out from here in three days' time, and I'm going to be in it. Lieutenant O'Neil said my advice and help would be really useful, since I'm a veteran from the fighting five years ago."

Natasha had been helped into a sitting position, supported by a large pillow on either side. She smiled at the enthusiasm. "Hopefully, Lynn will let me up in the near future. Look for me as soon as I'm fit to travel."

"You shouldn't give up on Dani. You know what I said."

"Yes, but last time I tried talking to her, it didn't go too well. Ginasberg sounds safer."

"You're being too hasty."

Natasha grinned. "You're right. Kim hasn't yet confirmed that I won't be sent back to Landfall, or hanged."

"Oh, of course you won't." Irony was lost on Shelly. "Nobody is going to accuse you of breaking parole. All the girls back in the barracks are saying that you ought to get an award, except we've never gone in for things like that here. And Abby made us laugh when she said that any Westernfort Ranger could take out a Guard with one hand tied behind her back, but you'd outdone us...like, because you had both hands tied."

"But I lost." Natasha pointed out.

"Not really, 'cause you're still alive, and Cal and Rohanna aren't."

Natasha bit her lip. Explaining her conflicting emotions to Shelly would be impossible, but she had to say something. "Their deaths were a loss as well. There was a lot about them to admire. They were ready to give their lives for what they thought was right. It's just that what they thought was right, wasn't. I hope the Goddess looks on them kindly."

"I bet they wouldn't have said the same about you."

"Maybe not Cal. But I'm sure Rohanna would have felt a few twinges of regret. We'd spent six months living together as a family." Natasha stopped and frowned. "It's just occurred to me that I'll never know what either of their real names were."

Shelly looked startled. "Weren't they Rohanna and Calinda?"

"No more than mine was Jess."

"Then it's a good thing they were buried in the common grave with the other Guards. Otherwise, the wrong names would have been put on the grave markers."

Natasha could not help herself from smiling. "You have a wonderful talent for focusing on the practical side of things."

"Yes. That's what I've been told before." Shelly looked pleased. "And what you said about admiring Cal...she was practical as well. Do you know how they managed to avoid us and get back into the valley? Two Rangers came in yesterday who'd been on their trail. Cal made a raft and floated downriver; then they swept around to the west. And she didn't need a map or anything. Actually, the two Rangers were angry at you. They thought you'd deliberately lied about your comrades racing back to the Homelands. But don't worry. We set them straight."

"I'm pretty angry at myself. I was so sure they'd do anything to get the news about Ginasberg back to the Sisters that I forgot the Chief Consultant herself had said killing Lynn was our most important priority."

Shelly looked doubtful. "I'm not sure if I'd forget hearing someone say something like that."

The earnest lack of humor in the young Ranger's voice threatened to destroy Natasha's composure, and she had already discovered that laughing was a painful strain on her stomach. With effort, she controlled herself, and the conversation turned to other subjects. After a while, Shelly made her goodbyes and went, promising to visit again each day until she left for Ginasberg.

❖

Natasha settled back. The window was slightly ajar, letting in both a gentle draft of warm afternoon air and the sounds of activity in the town: hammering from a carpenter's workshop and the softer clack of a weaver's loom. Traders called their wares. Friends walked by, chatting. And children's voices chanted a skipping rhyme that she remembered from her own childhood in the streets of Landfall.

This is my home now. The thought was disconcerting. Not that she regretted it, but the change in her life was irrevocable now. *I'll never see my mother again or stand sentry outside the temple.* She would not want to do either, even if the chance were offered, but they defined so much of how she had seen herself. *And what am I going to do with the rest of my life?*

She could continue working with Lynn and her animals, but that would put her far too close to Dani for the comfort of either of them. *I wonder if Ash wants someone to stand sentry outside the gates of Ginasberg?* The thought put a smile on her lips. Listening to the unhurried rhythms of Westernfort, Natasha drifted away in a light doze.

The sound of the door woke her some time later. Natasha opened her eyes.

"I see you're alone," Lynn said.

"Oh...yes. Shelly went a while back."

"Are you up to the excitement of another visitor?"

"Just so long as they're not as funny as Shelly."

Lynn grinned at her. "Okay, but remember, you aren't better yet. Don't get carried away. I don't want you to do anything silly and undo all the effort I've put into healing you."

Natasha matched the grin, although she did not know what sort of unwise activity Lynn had in mind. Sitting up and talking was all she felt capable of. Lynn slipped out, holding the door open for the person outside. Natasha waited expectantly. This visitor was clearly not as impatient as Ash.

Then, after a lengthy delay, Dani edged in and stood, looking nervous. They stared at each other. Natasha felt her stomach flip.

"I'll go away if you want."

"No...please. Come in."

Dani shuffled to the stool. Her movements were so clumsy that she almost knocked it over before managing to sit down. She swallowed visibly. "How are you feeling?"

"I'm fine."

"I just wanted to...see how you are. Lynn said you were... um..."

After her initial flare of joy, anger kicked in. Natasha clenched her teeth. Dani's eyes were fixed on the side of the bed. She was showing no sign of wanting to be there. Obviously, Lynn had bullied her into paying a visit.

"You don't have to stay. You've seen that I'm okay. You can go now."

Dani's head jerked up. "That's what you want?"

"It's obviously what you want."

"No. No, I don't. At least not until I've said...I wanted to..." Dani drew a deep breath. "Not before I've said that I'm sorry for what I said, up at the kiln. I didn't mean it."

Astonishment literally rocked Natasha back in the bed. The jolt caused her wound to give a momentary stab of pain, which was, in its way, reassuring. She knew that she was not dreaming. Her thoughts vanished in chaos. She could not have put together a coherent response even if she could have controlled her jaw enough to deliver it.

Dani went on. "I was lying to myself. I was hoping if I just kept on saying things loudly enough, I could make myself feel what I thought I ought to feel. And I never stopped to think whether it was what I wanted to feel. I've been a complete bitch. And now you probably hate me. That's all I deserve, but I..." Dani's voice choked off.

Natasha grabbed her hand. "I don't hate you. I couldn't."

"I've given you every reason to."

"Not as much as I gave you."

For the first time, Dani's eyes met hers. "You mean I haven't blown it?"

"No. And I'm the one who should be saying sorry."

Dani's gaze dropped to Natasha's hand. She turned it over and examined it as if she held something strange and valuable. Then she lifted it and pressed the knuckles against her lips. Her eyes returned to Natasha's. "You already have. It's my turn."

"I...I...er...it..." Natasha could not speak. Her insides had melted, and she had forgotten how to breathe.

Dani continued. "Coming here to see you, what I most wanted to say...I mean...I know I've missed a couple of opportunities in the past when you've said it, but what I really want to say is...I love you too."

❧❧

About the Author

Jane Fletcher was born in Greenwich, London in 1956. She now lives alone in the south-west of England after the sudden, untimely death of her partner.

Her love of fantasy began at the age of seven when she encountered Greek mythology. This was compounded by a childhood spent clambering over every example of ancient masonry she could find (medieval castles, megalithic monuments, Roman villas). It was her resolute ambition to become an archaeologist when she grew up, so it was something of a surprise when she became a software engineer instead.

Jane started writing when her partner refused to listen to yet another lengthy account of 'a really good idea for a story' and insisted that she write it down. After many years of revision, the result, *Lorimal's Chalice*, was published. This book was short-listed for the Gaylactic Spectrum award in 2003.

Lorimal's Chalice will be re-released as Book One and Book Two of The Lyremouth Chronicles in the coming year (*Book One: The Exile and The Sorcerer, Book Two: The Traitor and The Chalice*) along with the *all new* Book Three in the series: *The Empress and The Acolyte*.

Jane is also the author of The Celaeno Series. All three books in this series will be available from Bold Strokes Books in 2005 (*The Walls of Westernfort, Rangers at Roadsend*, and *The Temple at Landfall*).

Jane can be contacted at <u>js.fletcher@btinternet.com</u>

Other Books Available From
Bold Strokes Books

Distant Shores, Silent Thunder by Radclyffe. Ex-lovers, would-be lovers, and old rivals find their paths unwillingly entwined when Doctors KT O'Bannon and Tory King—and the women who love them—are forced to examine the boundaries of love, friendship, and the ties that transcend time. (1-933110-08-2)

Hunter's Pursuit by Kim Baldwin. A raging blizzard, a remote mountain hideaway, and more than one killer-for-hire set a scene for disaster—or desire—when reluctant assassin Katarzyna Demetrious rescues a stranger and unwittingly exposes her heart. (1-933110-09-0)

The Walls of Westernfort by Jane Fletcher. All Temple Guard Natasha Ionadis wants is to serve the Goddess, and she volunteers eagerly for a dangerous mission to infiltrate a band of rebels. But once away from the temple, the issues are no longer so simple, especially in light of her attraction to one of the rebels. Is it too late to work out what she really wants from life? (1-933110-24-4)

Change Of Pace: *Erotic Interludes* by Radclyffe. Twenty-five hot-wired encounters guaranteed to spark more than just your imagination. Erotica as you've always dreamed of it. (1-933110-07-4)

Fated Love by Radclyffe. Amidst the chaos and drama of a busy emergency room, two women must contend not only with the fragile nature of life, but also with the mysteries of the heart and the irresistible forces of fate. (1-933110-05-8)

Justice in the Shadows by Radclyffe. In a shadow world of secrets, lies, and hidden agendas, Detective Sergeant Rebecca Frye and her lover, Dr. Catherine Rawlings, join forces once again in the elusive search for justice. (1-933110-03-1)

shadowland by Radclyffe. In a world on the far edge of desire, two women are drawn together by power, passion, and dark pleasures. An erotic romance. (1-933110-11-2)

Love's Masquerade by Radclyffe. Plunged into the often indistinguishable realms of fiction, fantasy, and hidden desires, Auden Frost discovers a shifting landscape that will force her to question everything she has believed to be true about herself and the nature of love. (1-933110-14-7)

Beyond the Breakwater by Radclyffe. One Provincetown summer three women learn the true meaning of love, friendship, and family. Second in the Provincetown Tales. (1-933110-06-6)

Tomorrow's Promise by Radclyffe. One timeless summer, two very different women discover the power of passion to heal and the promise of hope that only love can bestow. (1-933110-12-0)

Love's Tender Warriors by Radclyffe. Two women who have accepted loneliness as a way of life learn that love is worth fighting for and a battle they cannot afford to lose. (1-933110-02-3)

Love's Melody Lost by Radclyffe. A secretive artist with a haunted past and a young woman escaping a life that proved to be a lie find their destinies entwined. (1-933110-00-7)

Safe Harbor by Radclyffe. A mysterious newcomer, a reclusive doctor, and a troubled gay teenager learn about love, friendship, and trust during one tumultuous summer in Provincetown. First in the Provincetown Tales. (1-933110-13-9)

Above All, Honor by Radclyffe. The first in the Honor series introduces single-minded Secret Service Agent Cameron Roberts and the woman she is sworn to protect—Blair Powell, the daughter of the president of the United States. First in the Honor series. (1-933110-04-X)

Love & Honor by Radclyffe. The president's daughter and her security chief are faced with difficult choices as they battle a tangled web of Washington intrigue for...love and honor. Third in the Honor series. (1-933110-10-4)

Honor Guards by Radclyffe. In a journey that begins on the streets of Paris's Left Bank and culminates in a wild flight for their lives, the president's daughter and those who are sworn to protect her wage a desperate struggle for survival. Fourth in the Honor series. (1-933110-01-5)